GONE ASTRAY

Michelle Davies has been writing professionally for twenty years as a journalist on magazines, including on the production desk at *Elle*, and as Features Editor of *Heat*. Her last staff position before going freelance was Editor-at-Large at *Grazia* magazine and she currently writes for a number of women's magazines and newspaper supplements. Michelle has previously reviewed crime fiction for the *Sunday Express*'s Books section. She lives in London and juggles writing crime fiction with her freelance journalism and motherhood. *Gone Astray* is her first novel.

GONE ASTRAY

Michelle Davies

MACMILLAN

First published 2016 by Macmillan
an imprint of Pan Macmillan
20 New Wharf Road, London N1 9RR
Associated companies throughout the world
www.panmacmillan.com

ISBN 978-1-4472-8420-8

1 3 5 7 9 8 6 4 2

A CIP catalogue record for this book is available from the British Library.

Typeset by Ellipsis Digital Limited, Glasgow
Printed and bound by CPI Group (UK) Ltd, Croydon, CR0 4YY

Visit **www.panmacmillan.com** to read more about all our books
and to buy them. You will also find features, author interviews and
news of any author events, and you can sign up for e-newsletters
so that you're always first to hear about our new releases.

To Rory and Sophie, my sunshine

1

Tuesday

Lesley Kinnock dumped the six shopping bags just inside the front door and lunged at the alarm keypad on the wall to her left, finger poised to punch in the code that would silence its shrill cry. Halfway through inputting the number she realized with a start the alarm was already switched off. She tapped the digital display as it blinked intermittently at her, baffled as to why it wasn't set as it should be. The system was supposed to be infallible, able to outsmart power failures and the most adept of intruders, which was why they'd paid so much to have it installed in the first place. In a house as big and as rambling as theirs was, there were too many corners a person could hide around, too many nooks to steal themselves within. Without the invisible protection of motion sensors and CCTV, she'd never relax.

Punching the code in again made no difference and her anxiety was raised a notch. What if someone *had* managed to bypass it? Her husband Mack insisted any burglar worthy of his profession would find it easier to break into a prison than they would their fortressed home, but what if he was wrong? What if someone was prowling around at that very moment?

Lesley peered cautiously into the entrance hall. Brightly lit by the daylight flooding through the opaque glass panels either side of the front door, she could see, to her relief, the space was empty. But while her body unclenched, her imagination had other ideas, drawing her attention to the five doors leading off the hall and whispering to her that behind one of them was someone just waiting to be disturbed.

Hardly daring to breathe, she fumbled in her bag for her mobile phone. As she pulled it out, the screen lit up to reveal a picture of her daughter, Rosie. It took less than a second for her brain to make the connection and, as it did, a wave of relief crashed over her. Of course! That was why the alarm was switched off – Rosie was at home today too. In her panic she had completely forgotten.

'Rosie?' she shouted shakily, her anxiety abating far slower than it had taken hold. 'Are you upstairs?'

There was no answer from the floor above. Wincing, Lesley picked up the bags weighed down with groceries and heaved them across the entrance hall, her flip-flops slapping noisily against the parquet floor. The thin plastic handles of the bags cut into her palms like cheese wire, but she kept her grip until she reached the kitchen and could set them down on the floor next to the fridge, a huge, double-door, American-style appliance that could hold more than a month's worth of food.

'Rosie?' she called out again.

As she flexed her sore and trembling hands, she realized

the house was far too quiet for Rosie to be anywhere indoors and she must still be in the garden. At fifteen, her and Mack's only child viewed peace and quiet with the same disdain people reserved for traffic wardens and footballers with inflated salaries, and Lesley had grown so accustomed to music thumping through the ceiling and the TV blaring out from the lounge that the lack of noise jarred as much as the usual cacophony.

She kicked off her flip-flops, sending them skidding across the kitchen floor, knowing Mack wouldn't be impressed if he saw them sullying the natural slate tiles. He nagged her to chuck them away, complaining they looked cheap and she could afford better, but what was the point of her dressing up when he was away and she had no job to go to, no friends to see? The rest of her outfit also reflected the apathy that was her default setting of late: a knee-length denim skirt more than five years old that gaped at the waist because it was too big for her now, paired with a navy T-shirt faded from being washed too often. Her face was devoid of what little make-up she usually wore and her fine blonde hair was scraped off her face into a messy ponytail because she hadn't bothered to wash it since Saturday, the day Mack had left for his latest golfing trip.

The tiles felt chilly beneath the sweat-slicked soles of her feet but she welcomed the sensation. It was a hot day and the shopping had taken longer than she planned, but at least it was done now. In one of the carrier bags was a bottle of South African Chenin Blanc she planned to open that evening while catching up on the soaps. With Mack away she could watch them in peace without his sarcastic commentary running in the background. So what if Albert Square was nothing like real life? As she often retaliated, this new life of theirs wasn't that far removed from fiction either.

She wouldn't tell him about her reaction to finding the alarm switched off, she decided, in case he thought she was just being silly again. He accepted her neuroses regarding how secure the house was, but only up to a point; today's incident would most likely provoke more eye-rolls and sighs than sympathy.

A glance at the clock on the range cooker told her it was 1.13 p.m. If Rosie hadn't eaten yet – and the tidy state of the kitchen suggested she hadn't – they could have lunch together on the terrace. It was one of those rare, cloudless days in late May when it was so balmy it felt more like high summer. Having a break might take Rosie's mind off her next exam for an hour or so and draw her out of the shell she'd retreated into as her GCSE revision consumed her.

Glancing over, Lesley saw the back door was shut but she reckoned her daughter was probably still out in the garden. When she'd left to go shopping just before 10 a.m., Rosie was already sprawled on a blanket on the lawn, reading through a textbook. Her next GCSE exam was two days away on Thursday, and it was science, the subject she struggled most with and had done least pre-paration for. The school she went to permitted pupils to revise at home on certain days around their exams, but Lesley had doubts about the effectiveness of the policy as Rosie could be easily distracted. But it was the kind of 'progressive education' the private, all-girls school had built its reputation on and why it ranked as one of the best in the south of England.

The school, like their house, was in the village of Haxton in Buckinghamshire, a county to the west of London known for being home to the Prime Minister's country residence, Chequers, Pinewood Film Studios, a moribund furniture industry and a belt of homes owned by once-famous television stars of the seventies and eighties. With a population of 8,318, Haxton was one of the smaller villages in the area, but what it lacked in size it made up for in affluence. Homes there rarely sold for less than a million and every year it featured in the *Telegraph*'s top-ten most desirable places to live in Britain. It was worlds away from Mansell, the town five miles down the road where the Kinnocks had lived before their £15-million win on the EuroMillions lottery had upgraded their existence to include gated communities and schools that cost £4,000 a term.

Lesley headed over to the back door but gave the solid oak island counter in the middle of the room a wide berth as she went past, as though it had more right to be there than she did. It was too big, too imposing, and in the fourteen months they'd lived at Angel's Reach – the name given to their house long before they bought it and which she would change in a heartbeat if only Mack would let her – had come to represent everything she loathed about their new wealth. It was all about show.

The presence of the island counter also embarrassed her, reminding her as it did of the first time they viewed the house and she'd asked the estate agent to explain what it was for, because she'd never set foot in a kitchen that had one before. The young woman, all glossy hair and glossed lips, had looked at Lesley more with pity than surprise.

'You want to know what the point of it is?'

More than a year on, Lesley's cheeks still grew hot at the memory.

'There are all these worktops already,' she had eventually replied, stumbling over her words. 'I just don't see why we'd need this great big thing in the middle of the room as well.'

Then, just to complete her mortification, Mack had burst out laughing, grabbed her by the hands and swung her in a circle, boyish excitement melting a decade off his forty-six-year-old face.

'Oh love, does it matter what it's for?' he crowed. 'With what we've got in the bank we can buy a thousand of the bloody things and keep them in a field if we want!'

The estate agent had echoed his laughter – no doubt cheered by the belief she was about to make a sale. But Lesley couldn't bring herself to join in and squirmed self-consciously as Mack danced her around the kitchen, her movements as jerky as a marionette's. In the end she was so desperate to leave she'd let him make an offer of the full asking price on the spot, even though it was the first house they'd looked at and she wasn't convinced it was worth the money. Still wasn't.

The flagstone terrace running along the back of the house was bathed in sunshine and Lesley raised her hand to shield her eyes against the brightness. White spots fluttered across her vision like tiny butterflies and she blinked hard to vanquish them.

'Rosie, I'm back. Are you hungry?'

When there was no answer she walked to the edge of the terrace and scanned the lawn, an immaculate carpet of jewel-green turf that stretched forward for 200 feet and was half as wide across. A red and green tartan picnic blanket was laid out on the grass, but her daughter wasn't on it. All Lesley could see was a textbook and Rosie's headphones coiled beside it like a thin white snake.

Her insides balled instantly into a knot, a familiar, corporeal reaction to not seeing her child when she expected to. Frowning against the sun, Lesley scanned the lawn again. Where the hell was she? Then common sense gave her a nudge: if the back door was shut, then Rosie had to be inside. She'll be upstairs and didn't hear you the first time you called out.

As the knot in her stomach loosened, Lesley went back through the kitchen, into the entrance hall and took the stairs two at a time. The door to Rosie's bedroom was ajar. She hesitated for a moment, knowing how Rosie felt about her poking around her room, but something caught her eye that propelled her inside. There was a bright yellow Selfridges box open on the bed, empty apart from some scrunched-up yellow-and-white-patterned tissue paper. Next to the box was a delivery note with the previous day's date and a receipt. Lesley snatched the receipt up. It was for a pair of ballet pump-style shoes in gunmetal grey with silver, crescent-shaped toecaps.

'You are bloody well kidding me,' she snorted.

Lesley couldn't see the shoes anywhere in the room

7

but recognized them from the receipt's description. A fortnight previously, Rosie had begged her to order them online but Lesley refused, saying the £320 price tag was far too extravagant for herself, let alone a fifteen-year-old. Despite Rosie whining that all her friends had a pair, Lesley stuck to her guns and assumed that was the end of it. Clutching the receipt, anger displaced her anxiety for a moment. Rosie must've persuaded Mack to buy the shoes instead and either thought Lesley wouldn't notice or didn't care if she did.

Annoyed at being undermined again, she barged into Rosie's en suite bathroom without knocking. It was empty, but the shower had recently been used judging by the droplets of water still clinging determinedly to the glass door. She could also detect the rich, sweet, coconut scent of Rosie's shampoo. The aroma, along with the sight of her daughter's hairbrush left on top of the sink unit, long dark hairs trapped in its metal bristles, prompted a fresh wave of anxiety and the knot in her stomach squeezed tighter.

Anger forgotten, she ran to the top of the stairs.

'ROSIE!' she screamed as loudly as her voice would allow. Then she waited, ears straining for the slightest sound. Nothing. The house remained cloaked in silence.

Her heart beat wildly as fear overwhelmed her. Rosie knew better than to go out without letting her know first. She bolted back downstairs, pulse racing. In the kitchen she checked the marble-topped units but there was no note from Rosie saying where she'd gone on any of them. On the island counter she found a small pile of letters that must have been delivered while she was out.

Lesley tore through the envelopes in case a message from Rosie had got muddled up with them. Usually she steered clear of any post they received, scared of what she might find. While bills held no fear for her these days, it was a new kind of demand that gave her sleepless nights: begging letters from strangers wanting a slice of their fortune. Mack usually dealt with them so she didn't have to read the threats and the pleas from people she didn't know and didn't want to.

There was no note from Rosie in the pile, so she dropped the letters back onto the counter and checked the corkboard on the wall next to the fridge, in case Rosie had pinned a note over the photos, cards and slips of paper listing the phone numbers of her school, their GP, dentist, the golf club. The corkboard stuck out like a sore thumb against all the marble, but it was the one concession she'd wrestled out of Mack when she argued the kitchen would be too sterile if they stuck to his plan of keeping every utensil and container out of sight, and every wall bare, so as not to spoil the sleek lines of its design. It was the same corkboard from their old kitchen in Mansell and gave Lesley a sense of home in a house she otherwise hated.

There was no message awaiting her attention. Her eyes strayed to the centre of the board, to a photograph of Rosie hugging Mickey Mouse, taken when she was nine and they'd scraped together enough money to go to Disney World in Florida. Rosie's hair was shorter then, cut into a neat bob that fell just below her ears, and had yet to darken to the brunette it was now. It was one of Lesley's favourite pictures, which was why it had pride of place in the centre, with everything else orbiting it like planets around the sun. As nine-year-old Rosie beamed out at her, she began to shake. She had to be somewhere. She wouldn't just go off . . .

Then it hit her. Kathryn. Rosie's best friend, who lived next door and was in the same year at her school. What was the betting she had the day off too? Rosie had probably gone round to see her and lost track of the time.

Buoyed by the certainty that's where Rosie was, Lesley fetched her phone from her bag, which was on the floor next to the shopping. She'd call Rosie first and if she didn't pick up, she'd try Kathryn next. She pressed her thumb down on the 'R' key, which was programmed to speed-dial her daughter's number.

Walking back out onto the terrace, she lifted her face to greet the sun as she waited for Rosie to pick up, luxuriating in the warmth on her skin. It took a few moments before she became aware of the faint echo of a phone ringing. Puzzled, she followed the noise down the terrace steps and onto the lawn. Reaching the picnic blanket, she saw Rosie's iPhone lying on top of it, the word 'Mum' and a picture of Lesley illuminated as it rang. She hung up, trembling.

Rosie never went anywhere without her phone, the thing was practically glued to her hand. She'd never leave it behind unless forced to. Lesley looked wildly up and down the garden.

'ROSIE!'

There was a rustle in the line of fir trees that stood sentry along the bottom of the garden.

'Rosie, is that you?'

As she took off towards the trees, the grass suddenly felt sticky beneath her bare feet. She stopped, surprised, and looked down. There was a dark, damp patch on the grass, like something had been spilled. She reached down and grazed the blades of grass with her fingers and, as she drew her hand back, she let out a strangled cry. The tips of her fingers were stained red and when she lifted them to her nose and inhaled, she could detect a strong metallic scent, like the smell of pennies.

Or blood.

2

On the stage at the front of the hall, a girl of around ten was wailing the words to 'Over the Rainbow', skinny knees exposed in a blue gingham dress and cheeks daubed with clown-like circles of blusher. As the girl hit a high note, a woman on the front row whooped loudly and clapped.

'I thought this was assembly, not a football match. Or maybe she thinks it's *The X Factor.*'

Four rows back, Maggie Neville laughed louder than she intended to as her sister Lou whispered in her ear. An older-looking man sitting directly in front cast a dirty look over his shoulder, to which Lou's eight-month-old daughter Mae, cradled on her mum's lap, responded by bursting into noisy wails. No amount of soothing noises or rocking would placate her.

'Give her to me,' whispered Maggie as people turned to look. 'I'll take her outside for a bit.'

'Thanks,' Lou replied in an undertone, handing Mae to her sister with a grateful smile. 'Scotty should be on in about ten minutes.'

Scotty was Lou's middle child and his class was

performing 'Any Dream Will Do' from *Joseph*. For a little school, Rushbrooke Primary liked to aim high with its assemblies and today's celebration of musicals was no exception.

Cradling her niece to her chest, Maggie pushed her way along the row towards the side of the hall, where the exit was. A man swore as she trod on his foot.

Outside in the playground she sat down on a bench so low it could only have been designed with children in mind and Mae's wails quickly subsided to a whimper. It was just after 2.30 p.m. and the sun pulsed strongly in the afternoon sky. Maggie wished she'd worn a skirt instead of the wool-mix trousers that were part of her usual work attire and were making her overheat. Her laundry basket was overflowing as usual that morning and the trousers and tomato-red T-shirt she had on were the only clean clothes she could find.

From across the playground Maggie could hear the low hum of traffic barrelling along the M40, the motorway that carved through the Chiltern Hills to the north of Mansell town centre. One carriageway took drivers all the way to Oxford, the other to London.

'Mrs Green, are you ... Oh, I'm sorry, seeing you with the baby there I thought you were Scotty's mum.'

Maggie identified the young woman approaching her as Donna, the teaching assistant from Scotty's class.

'No, I'm his aunt.'

'I should've realized you weren't Mrs Green, seeing as your hair is so different,' she said with a laugh.

Maggie self-consciously brushed her long fringe out of her eyes. Lou owed her auburn tint to Clairol Nice'N

Easy but her own hair was still the same dark honey blonde of her youth, still the same shoulder-length style. Boring, according to Lou, but Maggie liked that it wasn't fussy. In between work and helping out with the kids, she didn't have the time or inclination for anything more elaborate.

'Scotty always talks about you,' said Donna, whose own hair was cropped short and dyed peroxide blonde. Maggie could see she had a tattoo of a seahorse on the inside of her wrist. 'He loves having a police officer for an auntie.'

Maggie flashed her a tight smile. The last thing she wanted on her day off was to be drawn into a conversation about her work as a detective constable with Mansell Force CID. Experience taught her that when meeting a police officer in a social setting, people either saw it as an opportunity to rant about the lack of beat officers or criminals being let off with lenient sentences, or to ask crass questions like, 'Do you ever use your handcuffs in bed?' which she never knew quite how to answer without appearing completely humourless.

But Donna only wanted to talk about Scotty.

'He was so excited you could come today,' she chattered on. 'Normally we have our assemblies in the morning but this one's been quite the production. If we'd done it earlier we'd have been late starting lessons.'

'I'm glad I could make it,' said Maggie, meaning it.

Swinging a day's personal leave at short notice wasn't easy but when she found out Scotty had a line to sing by himself, she didn't want to miss it. Afterwards they were collecting Jude, Lou's eldest, from football practice, then going to Pizza Hut for their tea.

Donna leaned forward to tickle Mae's cheek and Maggie caught a whiff of cheese and onion crisps on her breath. Her own stomach growled to remind her that all she'd eaten since breakfast was a Dairylea triangle, squeezed straight into her mouth from its foil wrapper. She'd been too busy helping Lou finish Scotty's costume to manage anything else.

'Between you and me,' said Donna conspiratorially, 'if I have to hear the songs one more time I'll scream. Still, the kids do love putting on a show and you must be proud Scotty has a line to sing all by himself. He's such a kind, sweet-natured boy,' she added, as though Maggie might be clueless about her own nephew's character. 'He's a credit to your sister. It can't be easy for her, coping on her own. We did wonder if his stepdad might come today but I guess after everything . . .'

She trailed off as Maggie eyed her suspiciously. Did Donna really know the circumstances of Lou's break-up with Rob or was she fishing for gossip to pass around the staffroom? Not prepared to test either theory, Maggie rose to her feet, hitching Mae, by now gurgling happily, onto her hip.

'I'd better get back inside,' she said politely.

The hall felt even stuffier after the fresh air of the playground. A sullen-looking boy wearing boxes sprayed with silver paint and matching tights had joined the girl in gingham on stage and was singing through gritted teeth. Maggie pushed back along the row, this time managing to avoid standing on any feet. As she eased into her seat, Lou, red-faced and flustered, turned on her.

'Your phone keeps ringing and I can't work out how to turn the sodding thing off,' she whispered, handing Maggie her mobile in exchange for Mae.

'Shit, sorry.'

Checking the screen, she was surprised to see she'd missed three calls from Detective Inspector Tony Gant. It was, what, two months since they'd last spoken?

'I need to make a quick call. It's work.'

'But you'll miss Scotty,' Lou replied sharply.

The man in front turned round and glared again. Lou stuck her middle finger up at him.

But Maggie was already out of her seat, bag slung over her shoulder. 'I won't. I'll be one minute.' There were loud tuts as she went back along the line.

Maggie paced up and down the playground as she waited for her call to be answered, her empty stomach cramping with nerves. DI Tony Gant was the Family Liaison Coordinator for her force and she was among a hundred or so officers he'd recruited from the ranks to train as a specialist family liaison officer for Major Crime cases. Or she had been until Gant received a complaint about her conduct during her last case and she was suspended from his roster. Four months on, Maggie still wasn't cleared to return to FL duty and her last evaluation with the Force Welfare Department had been a fortnight ago. As she stalked the playground she feared Gant was trying to reach her because her assessor, Wendy, had found cause to make her suspension permanent.

'DI Gant,' a male voice barked.

'It's DC Neville, sir. Sorry I missed your calls.'

'Hello, Maggie. How have you been?'

Unprepared for small talk, she could only stammer the briefest of replies. 'Not bad. You, sir?'

'Fine, fine. Have you got your notebook to hand?'

Maggie said yes as she delved in her bag to find it.

'I need you for a case. Missing teenager.'

She sank down onto the same bench she and Mae had sat on earlier. 'Really?'

'Don't sound so surprised. Four months is plenty of time to have learned your lesson and I can't afford to have decent FLOs sidelined indefinitely. Luckily for you, Wendy agrees and has signed you off just in time for DCI Umpire to personally request you.'

Maggie was glad to be already sitting down. Stunned, she asked Gant to repeat himself and he chuckled as he did.

'Yes, it turns out you're forgiven. Right,' he said sharply, as if there was nothing else to discuss on the matter, 'the girl's disappearance is being treated as a critical incident because blood found at the scene suggests she didn't go willingly. Hence why Major Crime are running it. Umpire's the Force Senior Investigating Officer on this one and he wants you as lead FLO to her parents.'

'But what about his complaint?' she asked.

'Withdrawn.'

The word hung in the air like a bubble that might pop at any second. Then relief flooded through her.

Family liaison was something she did a few times a

year, a specialist sideline to her day job as a detective constable. Although she was stationed in Mansell with Force CID, as a Major Crime FLO she could be deployed anywhere within the force's jurisdiction, for however long the case took. Some old-timers dismissed family liaison for bringing little more to an investigation than tea and sympathy and historically they could have successfully argued the point, until a series of high-profile cases – including the 1989 Marchioness boat disaster on the River Thames and the murder of London teenager Stephen Lawrence in 1993 – highlighted how vital the role was and how officers required specific training for it. A national strategy was put in place after those cases, following the light-bulb realization that if the public saw FLOs as being the face of the police, the role had to be taken more seriously.

As Maggie saw it, an FLO was the conduit between the investigating team and the family – broadly defined as partners, parents, siblings, children, grandparents, guardians and those with a close relationship to the victim, such as best friends – and her job was to conduct the flow of information between them. She had to make sure the family understood what was going on – if the victim was dead, that included explaining the sometimes baffling coroner's process – while uncovering every pertinent detail of the victim's daily life to feed back to her colleagues. By asking the right questions, she could elicit information from the family that was vital to the case – or even catch them out if they were the guilty party. It wasn't just about sitting on someone's sofa enquiring how many sugars they took.

Why DCI Umpire's sudden change of heart, though, she mulled? He was the SIO on her last case and the one who got her suspended. A dozen more questions whizzed around her head but, knowing it wasn't the time to ask them, she mentally filed them for later.

'Tell me about the girl,' she said, pen poised.

'Name is Rosalind Kinnock, Rosie for short. Fifteen. Last seen at approximately ten a.m. at the family home in Haxton village.' Gant's voice sounded mechanical in a way that suggested he was reading from notes. 'Her mum left her there revising when she went shopping and when she got back just after one p.m., there was no sign of her except for some blood on the back lawn. Assumption is it's hers.'

Maggie scribbled fast to keep up. 'The mum's name?'

'Lesley. Dad's called Mack. He's in Scotland on a golf trip, yet to be informed.'

'How come?'

'Isn't answering his phone apparently. Patrol officers are with Mrs Kinnock now but DCI Umpire wants you to take over. He thinks she'll be happy dealing with you because the family lived on the Corley until a year ago.'

The Corley was a housing estate on the east side of Mansell and was where Maggie had lived for the first twelve years of her life. She flicked back through her notes.

'Their surname's Kinnock? It rings a bell.'

'They're the couple who won the EuroMillions last year. Got fifteen million and spent a chunk of their winnings on a huge pile on the outskirts of Haxton.'

'Of course – Lesley and Mack Kinnock. They were in the papers for weeks. Is their daughter going missing anything to do with the money?'

A shriek suddenly rang through the open windows of the school hall, followed by shouting. Maggie frowned at the disturbance, but stayed put.

'Too early to say. DCI Umpire will tell you more when you get there. He's at the house with forensics.' He gave her the address. 'Do everything by the book this time, Maggie,' he cautioned. 'I can't reinstate you a second time.'

The thought sent a chill through her.

'I know, and thank you, sir. It won't be a problem.'

'I should hope not. I've assigned DC Belmar Small from Trenton to work with you on this. It's only his second case but he's good, very intuitive. He's already on his way to Haxton.'

Maggie wasn't familiar with DC Small but was used to being paired with officers she didn't know. Gant liked his FLOs to work in twos because dealing with distraught and grieving families, often for weeks on end, could be emotionally draining for them, too, and sometimes they needed propping up by a colleague who could empathize with how they were feeling. For the same reason Gant rotated his roster so his Major Crime FLOs were never deployed more than three times a year.

'Once the media finds out Rosie is the daughter of EuroMillions winners there's going to be a shit storm,' he said.

Maggie knew what he was getting at. It was a lament-able rule of thumb that if a missing child – even one as old as fifteen – wasn't found within twenty-four hours, the chance of them turning up safe diminished with every passing hour. The Kinnocks' big money win would elevate them onto the same high-profile platform as celebrities and politicians, and the media and public pressure to find Rosie would be immense.

'I'll forward a picture of her to your phone,' Gant added, 'then I'll let DCI Umpire know you're on your way. Check in with me later.'

As she hung up, Maggie wondered what the reaction would be back at the station to her suspension being lifted. Gant would need to clear her joining the case with her own DCI, but she knew he wouldn't object, even though her FLO duty sometimes took her away from his command for long stretches. He knew how important being an FLO was to Maggie and had backed her application to complete the training.

The sound of raised voices floated through the open windows. Thirty seconds later her phone pinged to signal a text had arrived. Attached was a headshot of Rosie Kinnock. She had straight, dark brown hair that fell past her shoulders and while she wasn't conventionally pretty she had beautiful almond-shaped green eyes, a lovely wide smile and an unruly splash of freckles across the bridge of her nose. She looked younger than her age.

Maggie got to her feet and hurried inside. To her surprise, the lights in the hall had been turned up and people were chatting loudly in their seats. Some teachers were standing on the stage; one was holding a mop. She pushed back along the row.

'What's going on?'

'The Tin Man just threw up on Dorothy,' Lou said, grinning. 'They're clearing up, then Scotty's class is on.' She clocked Maggie's tense expression. 'What's up?'

'Umpire wants me to be FLO on a case.'

Lou's eyes widened with surprise. 'No way! What about his complaint?'

'Dropped, apparently. A teenage girl is missing in Haxton and it looks suspicious. He wants me to be FLO to her parents.'

'In what way suspicious?'

'I'm not sure,' Maggie fudged, knowing she mustn't divulge the discovery of the blood to her sister or anyone else. 'I'll find out more when I get there.' She glanced down at her T-shirt. 'I'll have to nip home and get changed.'

'Well, it's great he's asked for you, but I bloody well hope he apologizes for what he's put you through these past months.'

Maggie shrugged. 'I don't care if he doesn't. I'm just pleased to be reinstated.' She glanced at the stage. The teacher with the mop sloshed more water onto the surface. 'How long until it starts again?'

Lou squeezed her shoulder. 'It's okay, you go if you have to. It sounds serious.'

'But I can't miss Scotty singing,' Maggie fretted.

She knew she couldn't keep Umpire waiting but Scotty would be upset if she missed his big moment. He'd been so nervous that morning as she and Lou fitted his costume on him, which they'd made by Lou cutting up a few different-coloured shirts she picked up in a charity shop into strips and Maggie sewing them together to make a sort of coat.

'It's okay,' said Lou gently. 'I'll explain to Scotty you had to go. He'll understand.'

'Are you sure?'

'Yes. Now go. That girl's poor parents must be going spare.'

Maggie gave her sister a hug and kissed Mae on her downy head.

'Thanks, sis. I'll make it up to you and the kids.'

Lou smiled. 'I know you will. You always do.'

Maggie weaved back along the row, reaching the door just as Scotty's class filed onto the stage. Even from the back she could see her nephew was nervous from the way he was biting his bottom lip. She felt a pang of regret but as she glanced over her shoulder she saw Lou flicking her hand in her direction and mouthing the word, 'Go.'

As Maggie let the door swing shut, Scotty and his classmates began to sing.

3

'You're making a right mess of that. Here, give it to me and I'll throw it away.'

Lesley raised her head and blinked slowly, as though she'd just opened her eyes after a long sleep. A woman stood directly in front of her. Sarah Stockton. Her neighbour. Holding her left hand out expectantly. Lesley shook her head, confused.

'Come on, hand it over,' said Sarah, waggling her fingers. There were gold and diamond rings on each one.

'Hand what?'

'The tissue. Give it to me and I'll get you another.'

Lesley looked down and was surprised to see the tissue she'd been holding was shredded into small, worm-like pieces and littered like confetti on her lap. She couldn't remember doing it. She scooped the pieces into her hand and tipped them into Sarah's outstretched palm. Lifting her hands revealed the blood from the garden that she'd smeared on her skirt when she'd wiped her fingers on it in a panic. The sight made her stomach clench sharply and she began to tremble again.

Sarah flitted across the living room and deposited the

tissue into a waste-paper basket by the door. She wore a black velour tracksuit that strained across her ample hips and her short dark hair was backcombed so it sat on top of her head like a soufflé; as she scuttled back across the room Lesley was reminded of a fly circling a lampshade.

'There you go,' Sarah trilled as she handed over a fresh tissue. 'Mop your tears with that.'

Lesley buried her nose in the tissue and closed her eyes in the hope that not seeing Sarah would shut out the sound of her too. She couldn't cope with her being there and wanted her to leave. She wanted them all to go away.

The house was full of police officers and had been for the last three hours. Some were in uniform, a few in suits and the rest in white papery jumpsuits that crackled as they walked, who swarmed over the back garden like a colony of albino ants. The officers politely gave Lesley their names as they entered the house – including the one in charge, who had quizzed her relentlessly about where she thought Rosie might be – but she couldn't for the life of her remember a single one.

The first officers had arrived within twenty minutes, just as the emergency operator said they would. The woman also suggested she ask Sarah to come round and sit with her when Lesley admitted there was no one else nearby she could ask. Her parents were in Cornwall, retired to a four-bedroom cottage overlooking the sea at Crantock Bay which she and Mack had bought for them. But even if they were nearby, Lesley still wouldn't ask them to come. Her mum's ability to recognize her diminished with every visit and the last time she went she thought Lesley was a friend she hadn't seen since school. She might not understand Rosie was missing. Mack's parents and older brother were even further away, in Falkirk in Scotland. That left friends, but the wide social circle they were once part of in Mansell had shrunk to just one: Trudy, who lived two doors down from their old house on the Corley. But right now she was on a cruise around the Med, a thank-you present for sticking up for them when other friends cut them off because Mack wouldn't write them blank cheques. Trudy was the only friend who had never asked for a penny.

So the job of staying with her until the police arrived fell to Sarah, her next-door neighbour on Burr Way and someone she only knew a little. She couldn't fault Sarah's reaction to her request for help though – she had taken charge by calling Mack and leaving a message to ring straight back when he didn't answer his phone, then ordered her daughter Kathryn to call every friend the girls shared to see if any had heard from Rosie. All the while, Lesley sat sobbing quietly on the four-seater purple suede sofa in the lounge.

It was like the panic that made her race around the house looking for Rosie had paralysed her limbs and all she wanted to do was to curl up in a ball and not think about what might be happening to her little girl. Because every time she did, terror bubbled up inside her and her mind was flooded with horrible images of Rosie hurt and scared and crying for help.

'Are you sure you don't want one of these?'

Sarah raised a glass filled with dark amber liquid in Lesley's direction, her second helping from their drinks cabinet. It was for the shock, she said, but Lesley knew better. Sarah, who didn't work and whose husband was an in-house lawyer for a multinational bank, liked a drink and usually started early – the drama of Rosie going missing was just the excuse she needed to top up what she'd already imbibed that day. The extent of her drinking was most evident up close, revealed by the broken capillaries mapping her cheeks, the reddened nose even the thickest layer of foundation couldn't quite cover, and the fleshy jowls that quivered as she spoke.

'No, thank you,' said Lesley, twisting the new tissue between her fingers. 'What do you think they're doing out there?'

'In the garden? Looking for clues, presumably.'

Lesley was overcome by a wave of nausea.

'I can't bear this, I really can't,' she said, her voice rising. 'Why won't anyone tell me anything?'

'The chap in charge said two family liaison officers would be here soon to help you,' said Sarah. She spoke in a clipped accent that was typical of Haxton's residents and made Lesley have to remind herself that Mansell was only five miles away and not in a foreign country.

'I wish they'd get a move on though,' Sarah added.

Lesley seized on the comment.

'I'll be fine waiting on my own if there's somewhere else you need to be.'

'Oh, don't be silly. I couldn't possibly leave you now. No, I'll wait until Mack gets home at least.'

'What time is it now?' said Lesley despairingly.

'Four thirty. What flight is he catching?'

'There's one that gets into Gatwick at nine. So he should be home just after ten.'

She was dreading seeing him. He'd flown to Scotland with three men he knew from Haxton Golf Club, none of whom she considered a real friend and all of whom she doubted would have travelled all that way if Mack wasn't picking up their tabs as well as his own. He must've been playing a hole when Sarah first called – Lesley pictured him standing on the fairway at St Andrews in the garish new sweater and trousers he'd bought specially for the trip – and had only rung back an hour ago. On hearing about the blood on the lawn, he'd shouted at Lesley, saying it was all her fault for leaving Rosie at home alone, then slammed the phone down. After ten minutes, during which time she cried herself hoarse, he rang back and apologized for yelling at her but did not rescind his accusation of blame. Instead, he said he'd booked himself on the first available flight back and expected Rosie would be home long before he was, although the tone of his voice did not match the confidence of his words.

Lesley rubbed her eyes as they filled with fresh tears. She never knew it was possible to cry so much. Every mention of Rosie's name, every thought and memory that filled her head, heralded a fresh wave. She was debating whether a drink like Sarah's might actually help after all when a knock on the lounge door made her jump. Sarah scuttled over to answer it, her face set in a frown. She opened the door but only by a crack, so Lesley couldn't see whoever was on the other side. A woman spoke. She sounded young.

'I'm Detective Constable Maggie Neville and this is Detective Constable Belmar Small. We're the family liaison officers here to assist Mrs Kinnock.'

Sarah yanked the door wide open.

'Please come through, she's in here.'

Lesley's pulse quickened as the two officers stepped into the room and she struggled to stand up. Her legs were like jelly.

'Is there any news?' she blurted out. 'Have you found her?'

The woman was tall, at least five foot eight, dressed in a fitted, light grey trouser suit with a white shirt underneath. She had dark blonde hair that fell to her shoulders and looked concerned as she came over to Lesley. Her colleague, a strikingly handsome black man with a shaved head and wearing a dark pinstripe suit, stayed by the door. Sarah looked torn between the two but eventually trailed the female officer across the room. As she reached them, Lesley saw the woman flinch and guessed she'd just caught a whiff of Sarah's fragrance. Sickly sweet, like bubblegum, it was so cloying it slammed into the back of your throat and made you gag. Perfect for masking the smell of booze.

The officer took a step back. 'Sorry, you are?'

'Sarah Stockton. I live next door. I'm the friend Lesley called when she realized Rosie was missing.'

Lesley caught the swell of pride in her voice and wondered if she realized how inappropriate she sounded. Her only consolation was that she might leave now these two officers had arrived. As though she'd read Lesley's thoughts, the female one smiled at Sarah.

29

'Mrs Kinnock is lucky you live nearby and were able to wait with her. But I do need to speak to her on my own for a minute, so can you please excuse us? You've been a huge help so far, Mrs Stockton.'

Sarah soaked up the compliment. 'Of course, I'll leave you to it,' she said, smiling.

The male officer took his cue.

'Mrs Stockton, why don't we find somewhere quiet to have a chat too? I have some questions you might be able to answer.'

What kind of questions? Lesley thought, a new burst of fear flooding through her. What could Sarah possibly have to say about them?

'I'd be delighted, officer,' said her neighbour, giving him a lascivious smile that made Lesley cringe. But as they left the room she felt her body relax and her limbs loosen. She turned to the woman.

'Is there really no news yet?'

'Not yet, I'm afraid. Shall we sit down?'

Lesley complied and the two women perched on the edge of the purple sofa. Close up, she could see the officer was attractive to look at, with wide, open features; friendly, approachable. Her eyes were unusual though – blue-green irises ringed with light brown.

'DC Small and I are here to help and support you as the search for Rosie continues,' she said.

Lesley blinked back tears. 'Will you find her?'

'We're doing everything we can. My colleagues are searching the vicinity and our Forensic Investigation Unit is examining your back garden. They're the ones in the white jumpsuits, in case that hasn't been explained to you. We're also questioning your neighbours to see if they saw anything. Hopefully we'll find some witnesses who saw or heard Rosie before she went.'

'Is it her blood?' Lesley asked, twisting the new tissue into a knot.

'I don't know. Forensics will have to carry out some tests before they can say for certain. Has someone taken a DNA sample from you?'

'Yes, with a swab,' said Lesley, shuddering at the recollection. It was one of the most surreal moments of her life, standing in her kitchen with her mouth wide open while someone she didn't know wiped up her saliva with an oversized cotton bud. 'It's been nearly four hours now. What do you think has happened to her?'

If the officer was fazed by the question she didn't show it, but her words were slow and deliberate as she answered.

'There are a number of possibilities. The blood may be Rosie's or it might turn out to be someone else's. Maybe someone else was injured and she's gone off to get help and lost track of the time. Is she the kind of girl who would do that?'

Lesley nodded. 'If someone was in trouble, she'd help them.'

'The other scenario we need to consider is that Rosie didn't go off willingly.'

Lesley shook her head as fresh tears spilled down her cheeks. 'I can't bear it. Why would anyone do that? Why would anyone want to hurt her?'

'That's what we need to find out, if it does turn out to

be the case. Can you think of anyone who might want to harm Rosie?'

'No. We don't really know anyone around here and the few people we do, like Sarah's family, are nice. I can't imagine anyone wanting to hurt her.'

The officer looked pensive for a moment.

'The senior officer in charge of the investigation, what we call the SIO, is Detective Chief Inspector Umpire . . .'

'I met him earlier.'

'Well, he'll want to talk to you again at some point, but in the meantime what would really help is if you and I had another look at Rosie's room. I know you and the officers who arrived first have already done that, but looking again might make you notice or remember something you missed the first time.'

'Like what?'

The officer got to her feet and, with some effort, Lesley followed suit.

'Be aware of anything that looks out of the ordinary, anything out of place or missing. I know you've already looked once, but sometimes we don't always see what's right under our nose all along.'

4

On the upstairs landing Maggie saw Lesley hesitate. There were eight doors ahead of them, along two hallways that branched out on either side of the landing.

'Which one's Rosie's room?' she asked.

Lesley gestured to the corridor on the right. 'Down there, at the end.'

Maggie walked ahead.

'May I go in?'

'Of course, um . . .' Lesley blushed. 'Sorry, what did you say your name was?'

'I'm Detective Constable Maggie Neville, but just call me Maggie.'

'I'm sorry, it's just with everything . . .'

'It's okay, you've had a lot to take in. When's your husband due back?'

'Just after ten p.m.' Lesley wrung her hands fretfully, balling the tissue between them. 'I think he's angry with me that Rosie went missing while I was out. But I've left her alone before and he's never minded.'

'I'm sure he doesn't blame you,' said Maggie. 'It probably just seemed that way because he was worried.'

'No, he was very cross.'

'In my experience in a situation like this men tend to vent more when they feel helpless. Your husband's stuck up in Scotland waiting for his flight when I imagine all he wants is to be with you and help look for Rosie.'

Lesley looked away.

Maggie went into the bedroom first. It felt stiflingly hot inside as the sun beat against the closed window. Against the wall opposite the door was a king-size bed with a pewter frame, through the rails of which were strung star-shaped fairy lights. The duvet, pale blue and patterned with navy stars, was partially covered by a pile of clothes and there was a yellow shoebox next to them.

'Is there anything in here that immediately looks out of place?' she asked Lesley.

'Not that I can see,' she replied unconvincingly.

Maggie wanted to keep the conversation as relaxed as possible. This initial meeting between her and Lesley was not meant to be a formal witness interview but rather a gathering of facts about Rosie – what was referred to in family liaison training as creating a 'victimology'. She walked across to the desk in the far corner. Next to it was a bookcase crammed with titles. A few were school reference books, but Rosie also had every Harry Potter edition, the *Hunger Games* trilogy and some by an author called Sarra Manning, including one called *Diary of a Crush: French Kiss*. Maggie pulled it out, read the blurb on the back then replaced it.

'Does Rosie keep a diary?'

'Not that I'm aware of. She had one when she was

much younger, that had a lock on it, but I haven't seen it for years.'

'I suppose we could ask her friends if they know. They've all been contacted, haven't they?'

'Rosie's best friend, Kathryn, rang them for me after I first reported her missing. She lives next door; that was her mum, Sarah, you met downstairs. Kathryn spoke to the girls they go to school with but none of them have heard from Rosie all day.'

'Where's Kathryn now?'

'She's gone to see the ones who didn't pick up when she called, just in case Rosie's with them. I gave their names to the other officers.'

'What about boyfriends? Is Rosie seeing anyone?'

Lesley shook her head. 'No, my husband's very strict about boys. He thinks Rosie's still too young to have a boyfriend, but I think even when she's twenty-five he's going to think she's too young.'

Maggie peered at the wall above the desk. Stuck to it was a haphazard collage of photographs, ticket stubs, postcards, stickers and school timetables.

'Are these Rosie's friends?'

She pointed to a photograph of Rosie and three similarly aged girls smiling for the camera. Squeezed together in a huddle, the girls' temples were pressed so close together not even a piece of paper could separate them.

'Those are some of her old friends from Mansell.'

'Old?'

'She doesn't speak to them any more.'

'How come?'

Lesley bit her lip as though she was weighing up what to say.

'You know about our win?'

Maggie nodded. There couldn't have been many people in Mansell who didn't know about the Kinnocks' £15-million jackpot win.

'Rosie's never really talked about it, but I get the feeling that once we moved here, she and her friends felt they no longer had anything in common and the contact between them dried up. It's such a shame as they used to be inseparable. She's known Cassie and Emma,' Lesley pointed to the two closest to Rosie in the photo, 'since nursery. The other girl is Amy, who she met at primary school.'

'Rosie must still care about them if their picture's here.'

'I suppose so,' said Lesley sadly.

'Winning all that money must've taken some getting used to. How has Rosie dealt with it?'

Lesley gave a wry smile. 'She loves it. We weren't badly off before, but now she can do things other girls her age only dream of.'

'Like that?' Maggie pointed to a picture of Rosie and another girl with long, dark hair standing between the members of the pop group One Direction. The girls' smiles split their faces.

'That was taken at a radio station's Christmas concert. It was a charity event. Mack bought the most expensive VIP tickets so Rosie could meet the band afterwards.' Lesley's voice cracked. 'She was so excited I was worried she might faint when they said hello.'

36

'I was the same about Take That when I was that age.' Maggie smiled. 'I was never lucky enough to meet them though.'

She wasn't really a fan of Take That. She preferred listening to Motown soul, the music her parents listened to when she and Lou were little. No way could Gary Barlow hold a candle to Otis Redding. But sharing a few innocuous details, embellished or not, was how she got families to think of her as a person and not just a police officer. Someone they could open up to. She was always careful not to stray into areas too personal to avoid unhealthy attachments – she was there to be their FLO, not their best friend. At some point she would need to outline to the Kinnocks exactly what they could expect of her and Belmar, mark the line in the sand so to speak, but for now that could wait.

'You'll be amazed what money can buy,' said Lesley in a hollow voice as they stared at the picture.

'Who's the girl with her?'

'That's Kathryn.'

'Did she tell you when she last saw Rosie?'

'They spoke last night before bed and made vague plans to revise together today but it didn't happen. She said Rosie never called her about going round.'

'Do they often get the day off school to revise?'

'Today was the third time. They're doing their GCSEs and the school they go to thinks they'll get more revision done out of the classroom but I'm not convinced.'

'Is Rosie stressed about her exams at all?'

'She's been worried about a couple of subjects but not

enough to run away or do something silly, if that's what you're thinking. Rosie wouldn't do anything like that.'

That's what most parents say, thought Maggie, yet often they're the last to know if something is really troubling their child.

She looked around the room again.

'Where's her wardrobe? I'd like you to have a look through her clothes – sorry . . . hang on. Let me just get this.'

Her phone was ringing. She frowned as she checked who was calling, then silenced the call.

'Wasn't that important?' said Lesley anxiously.

'No, just my sister. It can wait. Shall we check Rosie's clothes now, in case any are missing?' She looked around again for a wardrobe but couldn't see one.

Lesley pointed to a white panelled door to the right of the bed.

'They're in there. It's more of a dressing room really. That one –' she nodded to an identical door on the other side of the bed – 'leads to her bathroom. I can guess what you're thinking, how extravagant for a fifteen-year-old girl to have either.' Her voice developed an edge. 'But it's the way the house is built. The biggest bedrooms are all the same.'

'I was thinking I'd have loved a room like this when I was Rosie's age,' said Maggie, smiling. 'It would've been nice to have some privacy from my sister. We always shared.'

'Is she older or younger?'

'Older, by two years.'

'I think Rosie would have quite liked a sibling.'

There was obvious melancholy in the way Lesley said it but Maggie didn't want to get off track by delving into why the Kinnocks never had a second child when the clock was ticking to find the one they did have.

'It would be great if you could describe to me what Rosie's like,' she said instead.

Lesley thought for a moment. 'She's a live wire, always on the go. I honestly don't know where she gets her energy. Um . . . well, she's bright and loves being creative – she does really well in art and English at school. I guess she can be quite shy though, especially with people she doesn't know. She's young for her age, probably because she's a summer baby. Her birthday is at the end of August and she's always the baby of her class.' Her voice cracked again. 'She's *my* baby still.'

Maggie gave her a moment to cry.

'I know this is really hard for you, but this is all really helpful, Mrs Kinnock. It's good for us to know exactly what Rosie's like. If anything, it sounds like you've managed to dodge the awful teenage years so far.'

'I wouldn't say that,' Lesley stammered. 'Rosie can be moody and argumentative when she wants to be.'

'With you?'

Lesley flushed bright red and balled the tissue between her hands again.

Realizing she'd struck a nerve, Maggie willed Lesley to be honest with her. 'I'm not judging you or Rosie, no one is. But if we're to find her, Mrs Kinnock, you have to tell me if there have been any rows between you recently and what sparked them. If she's upset about something, we need to know. It might be crucial to the investigation.'

Lesley's face crumpled.

'Sometimes I think she hates me,' she cried. 'She gets so cross whenever I ask her anything or try to talk to her. You've asked me to look at her things to see if anything's missing, but how would I know? She doesn't like me coming in her bedroom and we have two women who come every Friday to take care of the washing so I don't even know where she keeps her socks. She shuts me out and it sometimes feels like I know nothing about my daughter's life.'

'Did the two of you row this morning?' asked Maggie softly.

'No. We barely spoke. I suggested she revise outside, she said yes. That was pretty much the extent of our conversation. You're better off asking my husband about her bedroom. Rosie's far closer to him. I'm just the one who gets in their way.'

5

The gym was crowded and there was a queue to use the running machines. He used the wait to admire himself in the mirrored walls, flexing his feet so the muscles in his legs rippled beneath his lightly tanned skin. His physique was more sinuous than burly, more Michelangelo's David than Farnese Atlas. If he bulked up too much he looked ridiculous, like his head was too small for his body. It was how he'd been before the accident. Five foot ten of solid brawn. Now he was lucky to be in any kind of shape, the livid scar running the length of his spine both an ugly and constant reminder of that.

There was one person ahead of him in the queue. He jiggled on the spot, his body humming with a nervous energy only a run would subdue. This was the last part of his workout, a 5-km sprint on the treadmill. He couldn't skip it. His body would hate him for it if he did.

The jiggling stepped up as his mind rewound to earlier. He couldn't believe how easy it had been. It was as though fate had suddenly conspired to make everything he'd been wishing for this past year fall straight into his lap. He couldn't have planned it better if he'd tried, he thought with a grin. The execution was sloppy but at least what he did afterwards had been meticulous. Once he'd taken care of everything, his last act had been to set fire to his clothes, the girl's T-shirt and both their underwear in the old steel burner in his own back garden. The only evidence, reduced to ashes.

He had a brief moment of panic when he saw smoke rising from next-door's garden at the same time. The clement weather must have cajoled his retired neighbours outside for a late lunch: along with the smell of meat being cremated, he heard the sound of glasses being clinked and cutlery scraping against plates. It was ten minutes before he relaxed, finally confident they were too preoccupied with eating to pay any attention to the ghostly grey plume rising from his side of the fence. Besides, they knew he worked irregular hours, so him being at home during the day was not cause for alarm. Once the fire had burned itself out, he decided to stick to his routine of going to the gym for a workout. If he didn't, people might question it.

He edged closer to the mirrored wall and stared intently at his face, half expecting to see a stranger looking back. He looked the same but no longer felt like himself. Today he had crossed a line. After today he would never again be the person he was when he got up that morning.

From the corner of his eye he caught sight of the reflection of a woman using one of the exercise bikes across the room. She was watching him intently. Middle-aged, light brown hair cut short, in pink Lycra shorts and matching vest. Her legs pumped furiously on the pedals as sweat trickled down between her breasts from the hollow of her throat. They locked eyes and she smiled as if they knew each other. But she wasn't someone he remembered seeing at the gym before and guessed she was among the new intake that usually signed up at this time of year when it occurred to them summer was just around the corner and their bodies were in no fit shape to be unveiled on any beach. She'd come for a few weeks then her membership card would gather dust along with the shiny new trainers on her feet.

His eyes strayed to her left hand. Platinum wedding band studded with diamonds and an impressive diamond solitaire engagement ring. Sizeable diamond clusters also punctured her earlobes. Worth a few quid.

She slowed her pace as she continued to stare at him. He almost smirked. She couldn't honestly think he was interested in her? He was at least a decade younger than her and better-looking than any other man there. But there was no misinterpreting the look she gave him as she swung her leg over the crossbar and wiped her sweaty hands over her hips and down her thighs. She wanted him, married or not.

While experience had taught him it wasn't wise to get involved with someone at his workplace, why shouldn't he take advantage? She wasn't bad-looking for her age, somewhere around the mid-forties. It was always the horny middle-aged women desperate for attention who came on to him. The younger clients went after the hot personal trainers and weren't interested in someone like him with a job they thought sounded boring. 'Sports injury osteopath? What's that when it's at home?'

A quick fuck, that's all it would be, and he could do with the release. Multiple steroids combined to shrivel your balls if you weren't careful, that's what he'd been warned, but learning to stack his correctly had had the opposite effect on his sexual appetite. His balls were like bloody great melons.

Treadmill forgotten, he crossed the gym and introduced himself.

Nice name, she said.

You're beautiful, he lied.

There's a storeroom next to the changing rooms and I've got the key, he murmured.

Lead the way, she smiled.

6

Maggie was relieved when Lesley didn't make a fuss about going back downstairs. Insisting she continue to search Rosie's bedroom when she was upset about not knowing where her daughter kept anything would be cruel. They'd just have to wait until the dad got home, see if he had a better idea if anything was missing. In the meantime she needed to let DCI Umpire know that Lesley and Rosie were prone to rowing, in case it had some bearing on her disappearance.

They found Belmar and Sarah Stockton in the dining room, sitting together at one end of a long, highly polished wooden table that could comfortably seat another twelve people. Her new colleague was sitting casually back in his chair, elbow propped on the table, but Maggie could see his notebook was open in front of him and the page full of notes.

A look of understanding passed between her and Belmar when she said the search of Rosie's bedroom hadn't thrown up anything, but that Mr Kinnock should have a look too. Good, thought Maggie. It might be only his second case as an FLO but it appeared as though

Belmar already understood the visual shorthand FLOs needed to employ when it wasn't possible or wise to talk freely in front of a family. He clearly got that there was an issue with Rosie's bedroom but was smart enough not to ask with Lesley and Sarah present.

'Anything to report down here?' she asked him.

'Nothing that can't wait,' he said, glancing at Sarah, which Maggie took to mean there was something but he'd tell her later when they were alone.

'I'll speak to DCI Umpire now. He must be outside,' said Maggie. 'Can you wait here with Mrs Kinnock?'

Before he could answer, Lesley butted in.

'You can cut through to the garden from here . . . oh.' She stared across the room at the French doors. 'Someone's pulled the curtains.'

Belmar half raised his hand. As he did, the sleeve of his suit and shirt cuff drew back to reveal a stainless-steel Citizen watch encircling his wrist. Taking in the expensive-looking pinstripe suit and the shiny black shoes that narrowed to a point and were fastened by the thinnest of laces, Maggie concluded Belmar was probably the best-dressed police officer she'd ever worked with.

'I closed them,' he said. 'The sun's getting lower and the light was blinding us.'

Maggie suspected he was lying and knew why. He'd shut the curtains to block out the sight of the forensic team combing the back garden to find any fathomable reason as to why Rosie Kinnock's blood appeared to have been spilled across it. It seemed a bit pointless to her now, as Lesley already knew who was in her garden and why.

'Leave them shut,' Lesley nodded. 'Too much sun gives me a headache.'

As Maggie closed the dining-room door behind her, the prospect of facing Umpire made her weak with unease. When she'd arrived at Angel's Reach, the patrol officer in charge of the security log that kept track of everyone coming in and out of the crime scene said he was in the back garden. She should have gone straight out to see him, but Belmar was waiting by the front door to meet her and when he told her he'd already spoken to Umpire and been briefed about what Mrs Kinnock had said so far – mainly a rundown of her and Rosie's movements before she went shopping – Maggie said their priority should be to introduce themselves as the family liaison. If her new partner was surprised she didn't want to speak to the SIO herself, he didn't show it.

She hadn't seen the DCI for four months, not since the day the Megan Fowler case was wrapped up and he'd found out what she'd done. The look of disgust Umpire had given her as he walked away that day still haunted her.

Withdrawing his complaint was baffling enough – she'd read the wording of it and he had made it clear in no uncertain terms that he wanted her punished – but she was even more unsettled he'd requested her for FL duty the moment her suspension was lifted, when they hadn't even had a conversation about it. There were plenty of other FLOs on Gant's roster he could've chosen.

Maggie stopped in the middle of the hall to steel herself, using the pause to take in her surroundings. The parquet floor beneath her feet shone like the surface of an ice rink and she could see herself clearly reflected in it. The walls below the dado rail were papered with burgundy and dusky pink stripes, while above it the wallpaper was cream and patterned with large roses in the same pink. The only furniture in the entire space was a dark wood console table flush against the wall next to the dining-room door and it was bare except for a cordless phone in its stand and a framed photograph of the Kinnocks in which Lesley was almost unrecognizable. She'd lost a lot of weight since it was taken. Maggie decided that as impressive as the hall was, it still looked more like the reception area of a country hotel than a family home.

Knowing she couldn't put off seeing Umpire any longer, she ducked through the doorway into the kitchen. At the same time someone coming in the opposite direction ploughed into her, sending her flying. Maggie rubbed her shoulder where it collided with the door frame.

A short, dark-haired man with a florid face and wearing a crumpled dark grey suit grinned at her. It was DC Steve Berry, also from Mansell Force CID and the only colleague she considered a friend outside of work.

'Sorry, Mags, I didn't see you there.'

She frowned. 'What are you doing here? I thought you weren't back at work until next week.'

'So did I but Umpire's been given free rein to use who he wants from Mansell and he called me in.'

Maggie wasn't surprised the DCI wanted him on the case. Despite his air of dishevelment, Steve was one of their force's leading CCTV processing specialists and known for his microscopic attention to detail.

'What was Isla's reaction?'

'She went ballistic. I had to stop her getting on the phone to Umpire.'

'How's Bobby doing?'

Steve's wife Isla had given birth to their first child a week ago, a boy they had named Bobby, and Steve was meant to be halfway through his paternity leave. At the mention of the baby, his frown melted away.

'He's a little smasher. Here, quick, let me show you this before someone catches us.'

Steve flashed his phone at Maggie. The screensaver was of a sleeping baby wearing a white knitted hat. She smiled.

'He's gorgeous, and so tiny! I look at Lou's kids now and can't believe they were ever that small, even Mae and she's only eight months.'

'I was scared to hold him at first. Thought I might break him. But they're sturdy little things, aren't they? By the way, thanks for getting Isla all that Body Shop stuff. It was really nice of you to think of her when everyone else bought for Bobby.'

'You're welcome,' said Maggie, pleased her present was appreciated.

'You forgot my present though,' he teased. 'Where was my cigar?'

'You don't need to add smoking to the vices you've already got,' she said, looking pointedly at his shirt straining across his gut. 'When did you last go to the gym?'

'It's baby weight,' he deadpanned.

Maggie rolled her eyes. 'Much as I'd love to stay and lecture you, I need to find the DCI.'

Steve gave her a searching look.

'I was surprised to hear you were on this case.'

'You weren't the only one,' she said wryly.

'You okay? Ballboy was a right bastard to you last time. He shouldn't have gone off at you like that in front of everyone.'

Ballboy was the nickname bestowed upon Umpire by the ranks. It wasn't a sobriquet Maggie ever used.

'It'll be fine. I can handle him.' She stuck her hands in her trouser pockets so Steve couldn't see they were shaking.

'Yeah, I'm sure you can. Well, wish me luck . . .'

'Where are you off to?'

'To speak to the security firm that has the contract for Burr Way and the surrounding roads. Umpire wants me to go through all the CCTV from the street and all the houses. I'll have to get the owners' permission first though.' He sighed and shook his head. 'To think I could be at home cuddling my newborn son . . . See you later, Maggie.' He squeezed her arm affectionately then trundled off.

Umpire was the first person she noticed as she stepped outside. At six foot three, he wasn't hard to miss. Nor had he changed at all in the months since she'd last seen him. His short, strawberry blond hair was still doing a good job of disguising the creeping grey and, while broad-shouldered, his frame maintained a natural leanness. He wasn't smiling, which wasn't unusual, but when he did he was good-looking in a craggy, weather-beaten kind of way. Maggie didn't know his exact age but guessed he was around forty and he was married with two pre-teen children. She knew a few female officers who'd admitted to fancying him but she never would. She had a rule that anyone in a relationship was out of bounds even to daydream about.

He was standing on the terrace with Mal Matheson, the Chief Crime Scene Examiner and head of the force's Forensic Investigation Unit. Matheson noticed Maggie first and gave her a warm smile as she walked towards them, which she gratefully returned. She liked Matheson, everyone did. He didn't grandstand, pushed the labs hard for a quick turnaround and never turned down a request for a favour unless it was impossible. What was left of his silver hair was cropped millimetres short, which made him look far more intimidating than he was, but the only thing his colleagues feared was the fact he was two years from retirement and no replacement would match up.

'Hello, Maggie, good to see you,' he said. 'Have you been inside with the mother? How's she bearing up?'

Before answering, Maggie glanced quickly at Umpire, expecting him to say something about not checking in with him first, but he made no comment. Whatever his reaction was to seeing her after all this time, he wasn't showing it. His expression was inscrutable.

'She's okay,' she answered Matheson. 'Very distressed but trying to hold it together.'

Mindful of keeping her voice steady, she turned to address the DCI.

'Sir, Mrs Kinnock and I went through Rosie's bedroom again but Mrs Kinnock wasn't able to identify if any belongings are missing. I think we might have more luck when Mr Kinnock is here.'

'Why's that?'

And there they were: his first words to her. No recrimination, no aggression. Not even a hint of sarcasm. Maggie felt her confidence rise. Maybe it *would* be fine.

'Rosie doesn't like her mum going in her bedroom, so Mrs Kinnock isn't sure where anything is kept and can't tell if there's anything missing. It sounds like their relationship can be fraught at times. Mrs Kinnock says their conversation this morning was minimal.'

'I asked her earlier if she thought Rosie might've run away but she said no,' said Umpire.

'Even if she ran away of her own accord, that doesn't explain the blood on the lawn,' said Matheson. 'What we've found suggests a fairly significant loss and if it's not hers someone else was hurt here this morning.'

'How soon until we know if it's hers?' Maggie asked Matheson.

'It'll be a few hours until we can say for sure, but it's definitely human: the peroxidase test came up positive. There's a spatter line too, down towards those firs.'

Maggie saw a line of markers on the grass indicating where the blood was. The trail led to a row of fir trees at the bottom of the garden.

'Behind them is a fence approximately two metres high,' Matheson added. 'There's blood smeared across the top and down both sides. Rosie – if it is her blood – must've gone over it.'

'She only five foot one,' said Umpire. 'Could she have climbed it on her own, with an injury?'

'More likely dragged over.' Matheson grimaced. 'We're checking the panels for fibres and DNA. On the other side of the fence there's a pathway separating the houses on this side from the back gardens of the ones in the next street. One end of the path comes out by the security gate at the start of Burr Way, the other leads to a meadow. So far we've only found a couple of drops of blood on the pathway, which makes me wonder if the wound had been staunched by that point, but we're still looking.' He walked down the steps from the terrace and dug the plastic-covered toecap of his boot into the lawn. 'Our biggest obstacle is the hardness of the ground. Thanks to this dry spell, moisture is being quickly absorbed. It's not too bad with the patch by the blanket, because that's quite large, but it's harder finding smaller drops.'

Maggie didn't imagine they'd have much luck with eyewitnesses either. The Kinnocks' garden was far too secluded to be overlooked. The bushes bordering either side of the lawn were so dense she couldn't tell what was behind them, fence or wall. Between the tops of the firs, where the branches narrowed to a point, she could make out the slate-tiled roof of a house on the other side of the pathway. But it was too far away for whoever lived there to have heard a thing, let alone seen what happened.

'Any other signs of a struggle?' she asked.

'Not immediately,' said Matheson. 'The mother says the rug was laid out neatly when she came out.'

'There's no CCTV footage of Rosie going missing either,' said Umpire. 'The alarm system either went down or was switched off just after ten thirty a.m., including the cameras set up to monitor out here. I've not seen it yet, but apparently the last recorded footage of Rosie shows her going inside the house from the garden and she's alone.'

Matheson checked his watch as he returned to where they stood. 'It's five forty-five p.m., which means we've got three hours or so at most before the light fades.'

'Keep going for as long as you can, Mal,' said Umpire. He turned to Maggie. 'I need to speak to Mrs Kinnock again.'

'Yes, sir. She's got a neighbour with her, but I can get rid of her and then she's yours.'

'Ten minutes?'

Maggie nodded, painfully aware of how forced the exchange was. There was once a time when she would have asked the DCI how he was, when he'd have certainly asked the same of her. They had always been comfortable in one another's company and she'd liked it when they talked about topics other than work because he could be funny and interesting. Now it was like a layer of frost had settled over them.

'Has the neighbour had anything interesting to say?'

'DC Belmar spoke to her but he didn't have a chance to brief me before I came out here.'

'Make sure he feeds anything of note back to me and

fills out his log. That goes for you too, Neville. I want every word recorded.'

She knew immediately what he was getting at and so did Matheson, judging by the way he muttered something about checking the markers and peeled away from them.

Every family liaison officer was required to log their conversations with the victims' relatives and any friends who came by the house during an investigation. The idea was to make the record as verbatim as possible, so no detail was missed and the FLO could easily check back to see if there were lingering questions the family wanted answering. Maggie liked to make notes as she went along, whenever she had a minute to spare, but other FLOs she knew sat down at the end of the day to record theirs.

It was Maggie's log that had indirectly sparked Umpire's complaint against her during the investigation into the murder of eight-year-old Mansell schoolgirl Megan Fowler. For reasons she still stood by, Maggie chose not to record a particular conversation she had with Megan's mother. It had no bearing on the outcome of the case, but Umpire deemed the omission serious enough to report her to DI Gant for breaching FL guidelines.

As Matheson hurried down the garden away from them, she waited for Umpire to continue. But his mouth was set in a line and she could see he wanted an acknowledgement of his order, not a discussion, however much she itched to have one.

'Yes, sir,' she said resignedly.

'Good. I'm glad we understand each other. Let's keep it that way,' he said, and strode off in Matheson's wake.

Two forensic techs standing on the terrace eyed Maggie as she went past and one made a comment under his breath to the other that she assumed was about her and the exchange they'd just witnessed. Speculation about her inclusion on the case must be rife, she thought. The question they must all be asking – the one *she* was asking – was why Umpire was giving her another chance. She wondered if they agreed with what she'd done, though. Would they have done the same thing in her shoes? She'd love to know but dared not ask. Her fragile relationship with Umpire would not survive her gossiping about the Megan Fowler case with the rest of the team.

She was heading across the entrance hall when the sight of two teenage girls hovering by the front door with their backs to the room stopped her in her tracks. One had muted red hair braided into a French plait, the other had long, dark hair that hung below her shoulders. It couldn't be . . .

'Rosie?'

The sound of Maggie's loafers skidding across the parquet floor as she dashed forward must've startled them and their eyes widened like frightened rabbits' as they swung round to face her.

The brunette wasn't Rosie. Her hair was the same shade, and the same length, but her features were more angular, with high cheekbones and a sharp chin. The most recent picture of Rosie, the one DI Gant had text-ed, showed her face to be softer and rounder. Reaching her side, Maggie realized the brunette was the girl pictured with Rosie and One Direction in the photograph above her desk in her room.

'Are you Kathryn?' Maggie asked.

Nodding, Kathryn Stockton dissolved into tears.

'It's all my fault she's missing. I should've stayed, I should never have left her this morning!'

'Don't cry,' implored the redhead, rubbing Kathryn's arm. She looked terrified and her skin was so pale Maggie could see tiny blue veins fanning out like a spider's web beneath its surface.

'Are you a friend of Rosie's too?' she asked.

The redhead nodded. 'I'm Lily.'

'Lily what?'

'Flynn.'

'Do you live on Burr Way too?'

'No, my house is across the village.'

'How do you know Rosie? From school?'

'No, I go to Mansell High, the girls' grammar school.'

'Lily knows Rosie through me,' said Kathryn, still weeping.

'When did you last speak to her, Lily?'

'Yesterday evening. We FaceTimed for a bit before I went to bed. She was fine then.'

'What about you?' said Maggie gently to her friend.

Kathryn was too overcome to answer. She was crying so hard that trails of phlegm ran from her nose to her lips.

'Let's go in here,' said Maggie, steering the girls into the lounge and sitting them down on the purple sofa Lesley had earlier occupied. As she waited for Kathryn

57

to calm down, Maggie sat down opposite and explained who she and Belmar were. Both girls confirmed they were sixteen, which meant an appropriate adult wasn't needed to sit in, but Maggie still asked if they wanted one. Both said no.

'Kathryn, you said outside it was your fault Rosie's missing. What did you mean?' She kept her voice low and soft.

'We had a big row. I came round earlier to see if she wanted to go riding and she was in the garden. She said no, she needed to revise. I told her she was being stupid,' she said, bookending the sentence with sobs.

'Why did you think she was being that?'

Kathryn wiped her nose on the sleeve of her long-sleeved white T-shirt, which she wore with cream jodhpurs and silver trainers bearing a 'Superga' logo. Her large brown eyes were heavily made up with thick mascara and eyeliner and there were slicks of rose-pink blusher accentuating her sharp cheekbones. The kind of make-up Maggie was only allowed to wear on special occasions when she was that age. By contrast, Lily's face was scrubbed clean. She was dressed in jeans, an emerald green hooded top that zipped up the front and white Converse plimsolls.

'I know it sounds stupid, but I got really angry with her and I – I said some things I shouldn't have,' said Kathryn.

'Like what?'

'I called her a stupid bitch and said she was being a baby. I was just really angry. I also said if she didn't come riding with me I'd make her sorry.'

Maggie looked directly at Kathryn so she could see her expression clearly. She wanted her to see there was no judgement in it. She didn't care what she'd said to Rosie, just why.

'I'm sure she knew you didn't mean it,' she said, holding Kathryn's gaze. 'Even good friends row sometimes.' She glanced at Lily, who was even paler now as she listened. 'It does sound like you were very angry with her though.'

'I didn't mean what I said,' Kathryn cried. 'I was annoyed because she wouldn't listen to me and I was worried about her being at home on her own. I thought if she came riding then I could keep an eye on her. I went on and on until she told me to go away, so I did. But I shouldn't have left,' she wailed, breaking down again. 'I should've stayed until her mum came home.'

An alarm bell rang loudly in Maggie's ears.

'Why were you so worried about her being here alone?' she said carefully. Out of the corner of her eye she saw Lily fidget nervously in her seat.

'I can't say,' Kathryn mumbled.

'Is the reason something her mum and dad know about?'

Kathryn shook her head, her big brown eyes filled with fear. Lily also looked scared.

'No way. They'd go mad if they knew.'

Maggie remembered Lesley's comment about Mack being strict with Rosie and debated the best way to frame her next question. She wanted to know why Kathryn was worried, but had to ask in a way that didn't sound as though she was interrogating the poor girl. This wasn't a formal interview.

'Is it something to do with a boy, perhaps? Is there someone she likes?'

'She's never had a boyfriend – well, not while she's been living here.'

'No one she fancies at school?'

Kathryn shook her head. 'We go to an all-girls school.'

'Outside school then?'

Lily finally spoke up. Her voice was reed-thin. 'Rosie doesn't go out. Her dad doesn't like it. He's only just started letting her have sleepovers.'

'So why didn't you want to leave her alone, Kathryn?'

Kathryn wiped her eyes on her sleeve, leaving smears of mascara fanned towards her temples. She stared at the ceiling.

'You need to tell me why,' urged Maggie. 'You were so worried about her that you didn't want to leave her alone and now she's missing. I can see you feel like you have to protect her but you're not helping Rosie if you don't tell us the truth. It may make all the difference to finding her and we can't afford to waste time.'

Tears began to roll down Lily's face. 'Just tell her.'

After what felt like an age, Kathryn nodded. 'But do her parents have to find out?'

'Why don't you let me be the judge of that?'

'Please, you can't say anything,' Kathryn moaned. 'Rosie will kill us if they find out.'

Lily let out a sob and buried her face in her hands. Her shoulders shook as she cried.

'Stop it, Lily, you're not helping,' said Kathryn crossly.

Maggie watched them carefully. There was usually one girl within a friendship group who was the leader and something told her it was Kathryn in this one. She sat back, happy to wait until one of them was willing to speak up. DI Gant said one of the reasons she excelled at being an FLO, why she had sailed through the training and why he liked using her, was that she had infinite patience. Maggie could sit quietly for hours if that was what it took to get an answer from someone. The groundwork was laid in her childhood, growing up in Lou's wake and always having to wait to go second.

'I want to tell you but Rosie doesn't want her mum and dad to know, does she, Lily?' When Lily didn't react, Kathryn said more firmly, 'Isn't that right?'

Lily nodded dolefully.

Maggie leaned forward and rested her elbows on her knees. 'Look, I can't promise her parents won't find out. It might be too important for them not to know. But what I can promise is that I'll make sure Rosie knows neither of you wanted to tell me but I made you.'

Kathryn seemed satisfied with that but Lily kept her eyes fixed on the floor.

'I shouldn't have left her because when she's on her own she hurts herself,' said Kathryn.

Maggie's pulse quickened. 'How?'

'The blood in the back garden? We know it's Rosie's and we know how it ended up there.' She took a deep, dramatic breath. 'Rosie cuts herself.'

Unburdened of the secret, Kathryn slumped back on the sofa and put her forearm over her eyes. Lily didn't move. Maggie watched them for a few moments, trying to decide if Kathryn was being straight with her, wondering if there was anything they'd have to gain from lying.

'Are you saying Rosie is a self-harmer?'

Kathryn lowered her arm slowly. Her eyelashes had clumped together in little spikes.

'Yes. Rosie cuts herself until she bleeds. And she does it all the time.'

Maggie thought about the patch of blood on the lawn and the splatter line down towards the firs. Could Rosie have accidentally cut herself too deeply this time? It was possible. But why, she questioned herself, would she then climb over the fence at the bottom of the garden? Why not go back into the house to get help? Either way, Umpire needed to know about this.

'Thank you for being honest with me. I know it's hard because you don't want to feel like you're telling tales but I think what you've told me is really helpful. I'll just need your contact details now, in case we need to speak to you again.'

Lily reacted with horror. 'But I only ever hang out with Rosie after school, I don't know anything! Why will I have to be questioned again?'

'It's okay,' said Maggie soothingly. 'It's nothing to be anxious about. We'll just need you to give a statement about what you've told me. You can have your mum and dad sit in on the interview if you want.'

'Will you do it?' asked Lily anxiously.

'I don't know. It'll be up to the officer in charge.'

Family liaison officers were known to take formal statements during a case – the role did not preclude them from being part of the investigative team. The only issue was how involved Umpire wanted her to be. Maggie took the girls' details to pass on to him, including phone numbers for their parents.

'You're better off speaking to my mum. My dad's in New York,' said Kathryn sullenly. 'He works away a lot.'

'Actually, your mum's still here, with my colleague DC Small. Do you want me to get her?'

Kathryn shrugged. 'If you want.'

Maggie returned two minutes later with Sarah, who shot across the room to her daughter's side.

'What have you been saying?' she snapped.

For a second Maggie thought she was talking to her and was annoyed at her for questioning the girls. Then she saw that her anger was directed at Kathryn. The teenager shrank back in her seat.

'I didn't say anything, Mum. She was just asking us about how well we know Rosie.'

Sarah folded her arms across her chest and glared at her daughter. 'If you're causing trouble again—'

'She's not,' Maggie interjected. 'She's been really helpful.'

Sarah ignored her and gestured at Kathryn to stand up. 'Come on, it's time we left the police to it. That goes for you too, Lily. Isn't your grandmother expecting you?'

'They might need to be interviewed again at some point.' Maggie handed Sarah her business card. 'If you have any questions, please give me a call. I'm here to help Rosie's friends as well as her family.'

'Thank you,' said Sarah grudgingly.

As they went to leave, Lily turned to Maggie. 'Rosie's

really lovely,' she said timidly. 'She's never horrible to anyone and she doesn't deserve this.'

It was only after they left that Maggie thought about what Lily had said. If she and Kathryn were convinced the blood loss was caused by her self-harming, what exactly did Rosie not deserve?

7

Lesley struggled to catch her breath as she paced around the dining room. With Sarah gone at Maggie's behest, it felt like the walls were closing in on her and the air was being sucked out of the room. She tried to take deep breaths but her chest constricted as though crushed by the weight of her fear and when she spoke all she could manage was a ragged gasp.

'Why hasn't Maggie come back? Why is she taking so long?' she asked Belmar, who stood by the French doors as if he was guarding them.

'I'm sure she'll be back soon.'

'That's what you said a minute ago.'

Belmar didn't answer but glanced at the door leading to the hall. He's doing it again, Lesley thought. Every time she asked him what was going on, he looked to the door. Was something happening out there, was that why he kept checking?

'Is there something you're not telling me?' she croaked as panic forced the breath from her lungs again. 'Is that why Maggie hasn't come back yet? Can you please find out where she is?'

'I think I should stay here until she gets back.'

Lesley had never struck another person in her life but Belmar's refusal to act made her want to slap his face so hard she had to clench her fists to stop herself. As she did, an intense heat surged through her body and she swayed on the spot.

'Oh—'

'Are you okay, Mrs Kinnock?'

'I think I'm going to faint.'

Belmar darted forward and grabbed her arm. 'Come and sit down.'

'Please find out what's going on,' she said as he lowered her into a chair.

'If you're not well I should stay—'

'Please,' she implored him again. 'I'm going mad not knowing.'

He caved. 'Okay, but can you stay put until I get back?'

Too weary to argue, she nodded.

As he left the room, Lesley slumped over and put her face in her hands. Her skin felt clammy because it was warm inside the house and she was so exhausted she imagined she could fall asleep just sitting there like that. But her mind wouldn't let her rest and she began to cry again as it confronted her with image after image of Rosie looking terrified and calling for help that wouldn't come. The idea of someone causing suffering to her child was more than she could bear. For months she'd worried about the attention Rosie received because of their win and that something like this might happen. She should've listened to her instinct and been there to protect her. That was her job as her mum, the only job that mattered, and she'd failed her.

There was a knock on the door. Belmar entered first, clutching a glass of water. Behind him followed Maggie with a tall, striking man in a black suit who she'd spoken to earlier. He introduced himself again as Detective Chief Inspector Will Umpire, the officer in charge.

He took a seat at the dining-room table next to hers. Maggie and Belmar also sat.

'I want to thank you for your cooperation so far,' he began. 'I know it can't be easy—'

Lesley held her hand up to stop him. She didn't want to hear any more platitudes or apologies. Already she was sick of them skirting around what needed to be said.

'Just tell me what's going on. Is it Rosie's blood?'

Umpire echoed what Maggie had said about more tests needing to be carried out. Lesley nodded but she wasn't actually listening. The question about the blood wasn't the one she really wanted to ask. It was a prelude while she summoned the courage to articulate the question that had been swirling around her head like a maelstrom for the past few hours. The question no parent ever wanted to ask. But she had to, needed to. This man was in charge of finding Rosie and she had to know what he was thinking.

'Mr Umpire, do you think Rosie's dead?'

The room went still and Lesley became aware of two sounds – a pulse pumping wildly in her ears and someone shouting outside, although she couldn't make out exactly what through the double-glazing. She saw Umpire exchange a brief glance with Maggie before he cleared his throat to speak.

'At this stage I have no reason to believe she is.'

'But what if the blood does turn out to be hers?'

'We can assume she's been injured in some way. But while that's serious, it doesn't necessarily mean we should be looking for a body yet.'

'I think I'm going to be sick,' Lesley moaned.

Belmar passed her the glass of water but the tiny sip she took made her feel even more nauseous. She set it down on the table with a shaky hand.

Maggie leaned across the table. 'Lesley, if the blood does turn out to be Rosie's there may be another explanation for how it got there. Have you ever noticed any unusual marks on her skin, any cuts or grazes?'

Lesley frowned. 'Marks?'

'Yes, like her skin's been cut.'

Lesley felt her own blood drain from her face.

'You think someone's been cutting Rosie?'

'Not exactly—'

Maggie had no time to elaborate, as there was another shout outside, this time louder and clearer. A male voice shouted for DCI Umpire.

The four of them shot to their feet but Lesley was closest to the French doors and reached them first to yank the curtains open.

'Oh God, no. No, no, no . . .'

A man in a white jumpsuit with cropped silver hair was standing on the terrace holding a large, clear plastic bag. He looked furious. Beside him was a very young-looking officer in uniform who was puce and panting, as though he'd just run from somewhere.

Lesley heard Maggie behind her.

'Mrs Kinnock, please come away from the window.'

But it was too late. She had already seen it.

Inside the bag was a miniskirt. Made from a synthetic silver fabric, it was covered in a layer of tulle embellished with dozens of silver sequin stars – and blood.

It was one of Rosie's skirts.

Lesley smashed her fists against the glass. A deep, guttural moan like an injured animal might make filled the room. The noise grew louder and louder until she realized it was coming from her. She hit the window again but her body was weak from shock and the noise barely resonated. Then she felt hands grip her shoulders and pull her away. Lesley heard the urgency in Maggie's voice.

'Please come away from the window.'

Her body went slack as she allowed Maggie to lead her across the room. She felt numb, like she'd been given a general anaesthetic and woken up before it'd had time to wear off. Lesley tried to open her mouth to speak, but her throat had also seized up. She couldn't seem to make anything function.

'For God's sake, shut the curtains,' Umpire snapped. Belmar yanked them closed.

'I'm very sorry, Mrs Kinnock,' said the DCI with obvious contrition. 'You shouldn't have seen that.'

'The blood—' she rasped.

'Is it Rosie's skirt?' asked Maggie.

'Yes, but I don't understand how you've found it covered

in blood,' she stammered. 'She wasn't wearing it when I went out this morning. She had her shorts on, a navy pair.'

'Is the skirt a particular favourite of hers?' said Belmar.

'Yes, I guess.'

'Is there any reason why she might be a bit secretive about wearing it?' he pressed. 'You know, changing into it when she knows you aren't around?'

'Let's give her a minute,' Maggie cautioned, and she made her sit down in a chair.

It was a few moments before Lesley was able to answer Belmar's question. She roughly wiped her wet cheeks with her palms.

'I bought it for her about a month ago. Mack doesn't know she has it. He wouldn't like her wearing something so short. It wasn't expensive,' she felt obliged to point out. 'It's from Topshop.'

'So she only wears it when he's not around?' said Maggie.

'I suppose so,' said Lesley warily. She didn't like the way the conversation was going. It felt like they were ganging up on her. 'But I can't see her changing into it just to revise in.'

'When would she normally wear it?' said Maggie.

'Well, it's for going out.'

Maggie shot her an odd look.

'You told me earlier that Rosie wasn't allowed out with her friends in the evenings. Your husband's strict about that kind of thing, isn't he? If she doesn't go out and it's not for just wearing around the house, what occasion did you buy it for?'

Lesley bit her lip. She'd said too much.

8

He didn't bother to shower or even change out of his shorts and singlet before heading home. Perversely, he wanted people to smell the sex on him. Would they be scared if they knew what he was capable of? They should be.

His encounter with the woman at the gym had been perfunctory but satisfying. She hadn't taken too kindly to his handling of her and got upset when he'd pushed her face-forward over a stack of boxes filled with leaflets advertising the gym and fucked her from behind. What was she expecting, he laughed afterwards when she slapped him across the face and complained he'd hurt her. Foreplay? They were in a store cupboard at a municipal gym, not a suite at the Ritz. Close to tears, she slapped him again. He walked out then, leaving her alone to struggle back into her pink Lycra.

Women like her were all the same, he justified. Rich and arrogant, she'd batted her eyelashes at him, made it clear she was up for some fun then took offence when it was on his terms, not hers. She wouldn't tell anyone what had happened, though, of that he was certain. She wouldn't risk her husband finding out, whoever the idiot was. He also doubted he'd see her at the gym again.

It was gone three when he got home. On a whim he'd taken a detour, just to make sure he hadn't left anything incriminating behind linking him to the girl, but the police were everywhere and he couldn't get near the place. He'd try again tomorrow.

Unlocking his front door and pushing it open, the first thing he saw was the overnight bag he'd packed and left at the bottom of the stairs, ready for his departure. His passport was lying on top so he wouldn't forget it. He wouldn't need either of them now, nor did he have any use for the freshly laundered shirt, suit and tie on the coat hanger dangling from the door frame between the hall and the kitchen. He grabbed the hanger and tossed the whole lot onto the floor in a crumpled heap.

In the kitchen, he ran the cold tap for a minute before filling a pint glass with water. As he glugged it down, he peered through the kitchen window to make sure the burner that still cradled the ashes of his and the girl's garments was in the garden where he'd left it. He knew there was no reason why it wouldn't be, but months of taking steroids had heightened his sense of paranoia as well as his sex drive and he was no longer trustful of anything or anyone.

Draining the glass, he set it down on the side and went back into the hall. His phone was in a side pocket of his gym bag. He'd already worked out in his head what he was going to say and within seconds he'd typed and sent the text:

Had 2 cancel trip. Boss sending me to Basingstoke 2mw 4 client mtg.
Let's talk 2nite.

He spent the next ten minutes in a state of agitation, worried she'd call straight back to demand a fuller explanation when he needed more time to get his story straight. There was no client meeting – no boss, even – but she didn't know that. She thought he was an accountant, that he lived in south London and his name was Simon. All lies, carefully constructed to reel her in.

After twenty minutes he began to relax and took himself upstairs for a shower. She was probably at their meeting point already and unable to talk for fear of being overheard. He imagined she'd be going nuts at the change of plan, but he knew exactly how to placate her. The only concern he had was that she'd want to try a different approach now. He just had to bide his time until the events of that morning caught up with them.

He came downstairs wrapped in only a towel, idly fingering the fresh scratch that marked the right side of his chest just above his heart. It wasn't deep but it was sore – for someone so slight the girl had been surprisingly tough to overcome. She'd clawed at him like a cornered tomcat until he'd managed to render her unconscious.

He padded barefoot across the living-room floorboards and sat down on the edge of the sofa. His laptop was on the coffee table, opened on Twitter. He refreshed the page and was mollified to see no mention of the girl's disappearance on his feed yet, which he'd purposely curated to include the local newspaper, the *Mansell Echo*, the police and a few townspeople who seemed to know everything that went on before anyone else. When the story broke, he wanted to be ready.

That meant making contact with the parents. His previous messages had clearly been far too vague for them to bother responding to, so this time he would make his intention clear. Simple. To the point. If he was quick, he could make the last post of the day and it should arrive first thing.

How, he wondered, would they get the money to him? He couldn't just ask them to transfer it to his bank account and give them the sort code. But the idea of so much cash being left somewhere for him to pick up seemed equally risky. He decided not to issue any directions for payment until he'd googled what people did in a situation like his. It was all new to him.

He scrawled his note on a piece of paper torn from a spiral notebook, careful to disguise his usually neat handwriting. In the middle drawer of the kitchen dresser he found the crayons he'd used to address his more recent letters to the Kinnocks. They were the ones he'd written anonymously and had filled with expletives and threats after the parents failed to acknowledge any of the polite letters he'd sent with his details, asking them to get in touch. He fumbled open the packet – a souvenir from a previous relationship with a woman who had a son – and selected the red crayon. Yes, that would look nice. Keeping his hand steady, he wrote out the Kinnocks' address in plain capital letters. Sitting back, he admired his handiwork. Perfect.

On the coffee table next to his laptop were three more

mobile phones, which he'd bought when he'd stepped up his surveillance on the girl and her parents. Like his usual phone, they were all pay-as-you-go, all untraceable.

He picked up the Samsung first. There were only two numbers stored in the contacts and he dialled the first one while simultaneously opening his Gmail account on his laptop. He clicked through the automated options until a woman's voice came on the line.

'You've reached customer service. I'm Ruth. How can I help today?'

'I need to cancel my flight.'

'Do you have a reference number, sir?'

He rattled it off from the email open in front of him. He could hear Ruth tap-tapping on a keyboard.

'That flight's for eleven p.m. this evening, sir.'

'I know. I can't go now because of work. I'd like my money back.'

Ruth spoke briskly. 'Your ticket is non-refundable, sir. However, if you want to change the date of your flight, I can do that for a fee.'

'No, I want my money back now.'

'I'm sorry, sir, but we are a non-refundable airline. Our terms are very clear on our website.'

'I don't give a fuck how clear they are, I want my money back.'

Ruth paused. 'I'm sorry, sir, but that is the airline's policy. Are you sure you wouldn't like me to re-book the flight on another day?'

'What the fuck for?' he snarled. 'I don't need to go up there now.'

'Then I'm afraid there's nothing I can do.'

He clenched his fists to his temples. He needed to think but the white noise whooshing in his ears was making it impossible.

'I can't afford to lose that fucking kind of money,' he said. 'With all the stupid extras you charge it's nearly two hundred fucking quid.'

There was no reply from Ruth but he could hear the chatter of other operators in the background, so he knew she hadn't cut him off.

'Seriously, what the fuck am I meant to do?'

'If you want, I can put you through to our complaints department, but they will tell you the same thing, I'm afraid,' said Ruth.

Incensed, he called her a fucking bitch and slammed the phone down. He was about to dial the other number stored in the Samsung's contacts when he suddenly noticed it was nearly 4 p.m. His next jab was overdue.

Returning to the hallway, he extracted a small vial of clear liquid from the front pocket of his gym bag. There was a description on the label written in a language he couldn't read, Arabic or something, but he had been assured it was Deca, the steroid he relied on to ease joint stiffness. From his bag he also retrieved a black leather oblong box, the kind an expensive pen or necklace might come in. Flipping it open, he pulled a syringe out of its velvet bed and attached a new needle popped from a blister packet. Deftly, he filled the syringe with liquid from the vial, unwrapped the towel from his waist and let it drop to the floor, then injected himself on the right side of his groin. He didn't even have to look where he was doing it, barely noticed the sting as the needle pricked his flesh, and the whole process was over in thirty seconds. He put the used needle in the bin under the kitchen sink and returned the syringe to its velvet bed, snapping the box shut.

Still naked, he went back into the living room and picked up the Samsung mobile to make his second call. The woman who answered sounded much nicer than Ruth. Her voice was soft and melodic and soothing.

'I need to cancel my reservation,' he said.

'Of course, sir. Do you have your booking reference?'

'Sorry, not to hand.' He gave her the fake name he'd booked under, Simon Morgan. 'I'm afraid work is keeping me down south now.'

'You were due to arrive tonight?' she queried.

'Yes, but not until after midnight. I was meant to stay until Saturday, but, as I said, exceptional circumstances have forced me to change my plans.' He grinned to himself. Exceptional indeed.

'I'm afraid our cancellation policy—'

'It's okay. I understand it's short notice.' He didn't know if it was her lovely Scottish accent or the steroids that had calmed him down, but he didn't want to row with her.

'I've cancelled that for you, sir, and sent you an email confirmation.'

'Thank you.'

'That's quite all right, sir. I hope you'll be able to visit us in St Andrews another time instead.'

9

Maggie caught Umpire's eye and he nodded. Taking it as a sign he was happy for her to continue, she advanced towards Lesley, who was by now visibly shaking, and crouched down by her chair.

'We don't mean to upset you by asking about Rosie's skirt,' she said gently. 'We just need to establish why it's been found like it has.'

Lesley recoiled from her. 'Please stop asking me questions. I don't know why Rosie's skirt was outside and I don't know where she is!'

Maggie looked quizzically at Umpire. He shook his head resignedly.

'Let's leave it for now,' he said.

'I don't feel well,' Lesley mumbled.

'Do you want to have a lie-down? We can come and get you if there's any news,' said Belmar. In an aside to his colleagues he explained that Lesley had complained of feeling faint. Umpire agreed she should get some rest.

'We can call a doctor if you want,' Maggie offered.

'No, that's not necessary,' said Lesley. 'I'll just lie down for a bit.'

The three of them watched as she shuffled out of the room and closed the door behind her.

'Well, clearly she's not telling us everything,' said Umpire, raking his long fingers through his hair. 'Press her again on the skirt when she gets up. I want to know when it was bought and exactly when Rosie's worn it before, and who she was with when she did. And I think we do need to ask her dad about it. He may not know about the skirt but he might have an idea where she's been sneaking off to to wear it.'

Belmar cleared his throat. He looked nervous and fiddled with his cuff as he spoke.

'Sir, about Mr Kinnock. It doesn't look like he's been staying where he said he was in Scotland.'

Umpire frowned. 'Meaning?'

'Mrs Kinnock asked her neighbour Sarah Stockton to call his hotel in Scotland because he wasn't answering his mobile. Mrs Stockton did call, but she says the hotel told her Mr Kinnock had checked out on Sunday morning after only staying for one night. Yet Mrs Kinnock said he was meant to be there until the following Saturday morning, before flying home.'

'What's the hotel called?'

Belmar checked his notes. 'The Old Course Hotel. It's the closest to St Andrews golf course and the most exclusive, five stars.'

'The neighbour's sure that's what the hotel said? He's definitely in Scotland because I'm sending someone to Heathrow to meet his flight from Edinburgh and I've had confirmation of when it's due to land.'

'She was adamant, sir,' said Belmar.

The DCI looked pensive for a moment and Maggie knew better than to interrupt him when he was thinking.

'I'll have someone call the hotel and double-check what Mrs Stockton is saying. Maybe she's confused,' he said after a pause. 'But if Mr Kinnock did stay somewhere else for the past two nights, we need to find out where, and why. Your job in the meantime is to find out more about the family dynamic, the parents' relationship, etc. You know the drill.'

'Mrs Kinnock said to me upstairs that her husband and Rosie are very close and she feels like she just gets in their way,' said Maggie.

'The neighbour was also quite helpful on that score,' Belmar chimed in. 'She said the parents appear to live quite separate lives. Dad's always away on golf trips – or so he says – and the mum stays at home. She doesn't go out much, apart from the odd shopping trip, and they don't have many visitors. It sounds like Mrs Kinnock lives quite an isolated life.'

'Mrs Kinnock also said Rosie's cut herself off from the friends she knew living in Mansell. Maybe she's done the same,' said Maggie.

'Ask her about it when she surfaces. If they don't have many visitors, that narrows down the people who come into regular contact with Rosie, which might help in the long run. When the dad arrives, ask him about the friends who went with him to Scotland. But don't mention his hotel stay until we've checked it out. Not a word.'

'We should ask about his trip though,' Maggie shot back. 'It might seem odd if we don't.'

Umpire frowned so deeply his blue eyes almost vanished beneath his thick brows. For a moment she feared he was going to reprimand her for challenging him.

'Okay,' he conceded. 'Keep it general though.'

Maggie gave him a quick smile in response. When he returned it with one of his own, her stomach clenched. A fleeting flashback to how it used to be between them.

'I need to get back to the station to brief the rest of the team. Anything else before I go?' he asked.

'We were interrupted before I could ask Lesley about Rosie self-harming,' said Maggie. 'Do you still want me to raise it with her?'

'Yes, I do.'

'The thing is, sir, if Rosie persistently self-harms like Kathryn says she does, there would most likely be some scarring that her parents would notice when she was wearing shorts, like she was this morning.'

'Maybe she doesn't cut her legs. Maybe it's just her arms,' said Umpire, folding his own across his chest. His stance suggested he didn't welcome a debate, but Maggie ploughed on nervously.

'Wasn't she also wearing a sleeveless T-shirt when her mum last saw her? Sir, I researched self-harming for an abuse case last year and the areas self-harmers tend to target are wrists, the insides of forearms and thighs and sometimes the chest.'

'So Rosie's not a typical harmer.'

'But the whole point of self-harming is not to draw attention to what you're doing. Sufferers cut themselves in secret and hide the scars as a way of retaining control. If Rosie really is self-harming I'd expect her to cover up more to hide the fact she was doing it.'

'So you think her friends are lying?' said Umpire.

'It crossed my mind but I don't think so. Maybe Rosie does self-harm but not as much as Kathryn implied or as recently.'

'She could've started again this morning, cut herself in the wrong place and bled out,' suggested Belmar.

'I thought that too, but why go over the back fence?' said Maggie. 'You'd go into the house and call for help, wouldn't you?'

'DC Neville's right,' said Umpire. 'We've checked with the hospital, walk-in clinics and GPs in the area and no girl matching her description has turned up injured at any of them.'

'Unless she doesn't want to be helped,' said Belmar.

Silence fell over them. Had Rosie cut herself then slunk away to hide like an injured animal, thought Maggie? Had the fear of what her dad might say stopped her from seeking help? She scanned Umpire's face for any sign that he was thinking the same, but his features were set like granite, his eyes focused on the horizon beyond the French doors, and a full minute passed before he spoke.

'Accidentally or not, if she cut herself and is bleeding at the rate the blood on the lawn suggests she is, she'll need urgent medical assistance and we need to step up the search. Keep me updated.'

He swept abruptly from the room, leaving a tense Maggie and Belmar standing in his wake.

'So the rumours about Ballboy are all true,' said Belmar, mock-wiping his brow as he slumped into a chair. 'Everyone said he was a scary bastard.'

'What you just saw was not him being scary, believe me.'

'Yeah, I heard about what happened on your last case together, about him blowing up at you.'

She smarted. Well, of course he knew, everyone knew.

'It must be weird working with him again.'

'No, not really.' She hoped she sounded more blasé than she felt.

'So you two, you know, did it go on for long?' said Belmar, his dark brown eyes dancing with mischief.

'Did what go on for long?'

'You and him. You have . . . you know . . . haven't you?'

Her mouth gaped open. It was a few seconds before she could speak.

'You think me and him were . . . For fuck's sake, who the hell told you that?'

On seeing her reaction, Belmar began to furiously back-pedal. He rose from his chair. 'Oh shit, I'm sorry. I shouldn't have said anything. It was just something someone mentioned in passing. I didn't say I believed it.'

'Why would anyone even think it?' she said, aghast. 'I mean, does everyone think that?'

'I don't know about that. The person I talked to just said that you and Umpire had this big bust-up at the end of your last case and it was because you were sleeping together.'

'You have got to be kidding me,' Maggie retorted. 'The reason he went ballistic was because I dropped him in the shit with the victim's family. It had nothing to do with anything else. I mean, for fuck's sake, he's married.'

'No he's not.'

'What?' she said, stunned.

'Word is his wife left him a few months ago.'

As she joined the dots Belmar was verbally drawing for her, Maggie felt sick to her stomach. 'Do people think his wife left because of me?' she said hoarsely. Was that what the forensics techs were whispering about after she and Umpire spoke on the terrace?

Her new colleague didn't say anything. She could tell by his expression that he wished he'd never opened his mouth. Moving closer, Maggie stabbed her finger in the air towards him. Her cheeks burned.

'Let's get something straight. I would never have an affair with someone already in a relationship. *Never.* So you make sure you tell that to whoever said I did. Got that?'

Trembling with rage, she stalked out of the dining room and into the kitchen. Belmar followed her.

'Listen, I'm sorry. I was bang out of order saying it.'

'Yes, you were,' she snapped.

To busy herself – and so he couldn't see how upset she was – she began unloading the bags of shopping Lesley had left on the floor. Everything was warm from where it had been left out all afternoon. Belmar shuffled anxiously from foot to foot behind her.

'My wife's always on at me not to listen to gossip. Says I'm worse than a teenage girl. But I can see why people put you and Umpire together. You're attractive, single, and he's the senior officer everyone fancies.'

Maggie rounded on him again. 'How do you know I'm single?'

He looked even more embarrassed. 'Well, that's what I heard.'

She rolled her eyes. 'What else have you heard about me?'

'That you're really good at your job,' he said eagerly. 'Dedicated.'

'And?'

'Um . . . that you're close to your sister and her kids?'

She nodded, mollified a fraction. 'That's true, I am.'

'And wasn't it something to do with your sister, why you put yourself forward for family liaison training?'

Maggie went very still, the pack of sliced ham in her hand hovering halfway between the bag she'd taken it from and the fridge shelf.

'A road traffic accident, wasn't it?'

Belmar had done his research. As he raised his eyebrows in expectation of her answer, Maggie noticed for the first time how straight his hairline was. His hairdresser must have used a spirit level to shave his fringe.

She took a deep breath. There was no harm in telling him the background to her becoming an FLO. As the Kinnocks consumed their focus over the coming days, this was likely to be the most in-depth conversation they'd have. But she wouldn't tell him every detail. God, no. Even Lou didn't know the whole story – and nor would she ever tell her.

'Yes, it was. My sister's fiancé was run over and killed on a zebra crossing when they were expecting their first baby.'

'Shit, that's awful.'

'Yeah, it was. I was eighteen and due to start uni in

Leeds, but instead I stayed in Mansell to help her when Jude, that's their son, was born. She couldn't have coped with him on her own. I got the idea to join the police from a traffic officer called Lorraine who helped us through those awful first few weeks. She was fantastic.'

'So you became an FLO because you wanted to help families like yours?'

Maggie gave him a wry smile. 'Isn't that why most of us volunteer? DI Gant once told me he likes recruiting officers who've had experience of losing someone in tragic or violent circumstances because they tend to be more empathetic.' She caught the look that briefly clouded Belmar's face. 'So what's your story?'

'I had an uncle who was stabbed in a store robbery. Not here, but in St Vincent where I grew up. My parents moved to the UK about six months after it happened, when I was seven. There was an investigation but they never caught who did it. After that I decided I wanted to be a police officer when I grew up.'

'Is your wife one too?'

'Nah, she's in HR. Works in Milton Keynes.'

'Have you been married long?'

'Ten years this December. We got married on a beach in St Vincent on New Year's Eve. Saved us having to pay for our own fireworks.' He grinned.

'Kids?'

'No way. I'm only thirty-three. I don't feel ready.'

'I'm not sure anyone ever does . . .'

Maggie's phone going off ended the conversation. It was Umpire. Just hearing his voice made her blush. Was he aware of the false rumours being spread about them? She felt even more mortified at the thought.

He was still in his car on the way back to Mansell but he had news for them.

'The neighbour was right. Mack spent Saturday night in the hotel then checked out. But here's the weird thing: he was only booked for one night from the start, so it wasn't on a whim that he suddenly decided to leave.'

'So his movements are unaccounted for from the time he left the hotel on Sunday morning to now?'

'Yes. At the same time Rosie went missing, her dad was AWOL too.'

10

It was dark outside when Lesley woke up and for a split second she enjoyed the delicious ignorance of not remembering why she was in bed. Then it hit her with the force of a wrecking ball, jerking her upright.

Rosie was missing.

Clutching her chest as though her heart might give out, she turned to the other side of the bed where Mack normally slept. Beyond his pillow, on his bedside table, there was a digital alarm clock that told her there was still an hour to go before he was due back and she angrily kicked out at her absent husband for not being there when she needed him. It was a futile gesture, she knew, as her foot didn't make it even halfway across the expanse of mattress. Their bed was eight feet across and seven feet long, dimensions otherwise known as Caesar size. She hadn't known such a bed even existed until Mack decided they should buy the biggest one they could for their new master suite at Angel's Reach and found a specialist company selling the frames and mattresses on the Internet. His excitement had been palpable as he'd clicked up the sliding scale of sizes from Single to

Queen, Double, King, Super King, Emperor and Caesar. He didn't court her opinion, nor did she offer it, even though what she really wanted to say was, 'No, let's stick to a double like we've got now.' His mind was already made up.

'Think how much better we'll sleep when we're not rolling into each other,' he said.

She wanted to tell him that his warm limbs brushing against hers in the middle of the night was one of her favourite sensations, and that she liked knowing he was so close. But the words stuck in her throat and she left the room as he began filling in his credit card details on the order page.

The Caesar's sheets and duvet were 1,000-thread Egyptian cotton and specially made too, but Lesley found no pleasure in climbing between them every night. The only way she could get to sleep was to hug her knees to her chest by way of comfort while Mack snored contentedly, splayed on his back beside her. To him, the Caesar was further validation of his new status: the big bed for the big winner. He seemed to forget it was she who'd bought the EuroMillions ticket, an impulse buy from a petrol station when she'd filled her car up on her way to work, slid onto the counter at the last minute with a copy of *Essentials* magazine and a packet of sugar-free Polo mints. It was only because she'd seen a couple of other people in the line holding their filled-out slips that she'd even thought about buying one.

One Lucky Dip, that's all she did. A fluke. Their local paper, the *Mansell Echo*, ran a story a couple of months later saying people were queuing at the same petrol station every week to buy their tickets in the hope that the Kinnocks' luck would rub off on them. She liked to fantasize about what the reaction would be if she turned up to warn them how winning the jackpot would be the beginning of their troubles, not the end. None of them would believe her.

She rolled off the bed and went over to the window. Stars peppered the inky black sky like uncut diamonds rolled out on a jeweller's velvet tray and a glowing half-moon hung between them. She felt guilty for falling asleep but exhaustion had overcome her. The nap hadn't helped though; she felt as wrung out as she had before.

Their master bedroom was at the front of the house and, looking down, Lesley saw the floodlit driveway was choked with vehicles: two police patrol cars, a dark blue van with Forensic Investigation Unit printed on the side, the white Range Rover Evoque Mack had insisted she buy and two more cars she didn't recognize. Mack's Aston Martin Rapide and Bentley Continental GT were tucked away in the garage.

She gazed up at the sky as the minutes ticked by. Her mind felt blurred around the edges, like it was cushioned by bubble wrap, and she found it soothing to simply stand and stare into nothing. Better that than go down-stairs and be confronted by reality.

But soon the memory of the man in the white jump-suit holding up Rosie's blood-soaked skirt in a plastic bag elbowed its way to the forefront of her mind and took root. It refused to budge no matter how hard she tried not to think about it and a little voice inside her head began an accompanying narrative, needling her to go downstairs and find out what else the police had found. She didn't want to listen to what it had to say but it kept on, like a tape recorder on a loop. *What if they've found Rosie's body? What if they've found Rosie's body? What if they've found Rosie's body?*

The voice ceased its chatter when she reached the kitchen. Maggie and Belmar were on stools pulled up to the island counter and immediately they slid off them as she walked in, looking like two naughty children who'd been caught doing something they shouldn't.

'Mrs Kinnock, are you—'

She didn't let Maggie finish.

'Have you found her? Is there any news?' she asked. Her heart pounded with fear, but Belmar shook his head.

'No. We would've woken you if there was,' he said. 'It seemed better to let you rest.'

'Mrs Kinnock—' Maggie began.

Lesley held up a hand to interrupt her.

'You can call me Lesley,' she said wearily.

'We're so sorry you saw the evidence bag like that, Lesley. That should never have happened.'

Lesley ignored the apology. Her usual response to someone saying sorry was to act like she was the one in the wrong and say something that made him or her feel better. Mack always said she let people off the hook too easily and put others' feelings before her own. But that was who she was yesterday. Today she couldn't care less if they were upset. Let them be.

'Have you found anything else?'

'No, just the skirt so far,' said Belmar. 'But we'll keep

looking even when it's dark. We can set up lights to help us see if necessary.'

'There's a massive search underway beyond the meadow too,' Maggie jumped in. 'DCI Umpire is using every resource available and we won't stop until we find Rosie, I promise you.'

Lesley nodded, too fearful to speak in case she broke down again. She went to a cupboard and took out a tumbler. She was about to open the fridge when she stopped and looked down at the tiled floor. 'The shopping . . . I never put it away.'

'I unpacked it earlier, while you were upstairs,' said Maggie. 'I don't know if I've put it away in the right places but I thought the fresh stuff might spoil if it stayed out any longer. I hope that was okay.'

She nodded silent thanks as she opened the fridge, took out a carton of orange juice and poured a measure. The slate tiles beneath her bare feet felt even colder than earlier but it wasn't them making her shiver uncontrollably. That was the panic gnawing away at her.

'Do either of you want some?' she said, holding up the carton shakily.

'Not for me, thanks,' said Belmar. 'I'm heading off in a minute.'

'But I can stay,' said Maggie hurriedly.

Lesley looked at her blankly.

'Some people like their family liaison to stay with them overnight on a case like this, while they wait for news, but others prefer to be left alone. It's up to you, but I'm happy to stay,' said Maggie.

Unsure how to respond, Lesley asked what the time was.

'Just before ten.'

'Mack should be home soon.'

'He's about ten minutes away. One of our colleagues collected him from Heathrow and is driving him here.'

Lesley was suddenly alert with fear. She wasn't ready to face her husband: she didn't feel mentally strong enough to deal with his anger and his recriminations. And she certainly didn't want to tell him about the skirt. It was enough that he blamed her for Rosie going missing: he'd never forgive her when he found out her clothes had come to be soaked in blood, like the garden.

Maggie must have sensed her panic.

'Our colleague's informed your husband about the recovery of Rosie's skirt,' she said. 'We thought it was best that he was told straight away.'

'Oh, okay. Thank you.'

She desperately wanted to ask if they knew how he'd taken the news but stopped herself. She'd find out soon enough.

'Does Mr Kinnock play a lot of golf?' said Belmar casually.

'A bit. Now he's got more time on his hands,' she said, taking a sip of orange juice. She was grateful for the change of topic: anything to stop her thinking about Mack's reaction to Rosie's skirt being found.

'The course at Haxton is meant to be really nice.'

'Do you play?' Lesley asked him.

'Never tried. Football's my thing. I play in a five-a-side league at weekends. My wife's not a fan though, says it takes up too much of my time. The good thing about golf is you can join in too.'

Lesley pulled a face. 'I don't really like it.'

'So you never go with Mack on his golf trips?'

'I went on the first one because there was a spa at the hotel we were staying at, but I haven't gone since.'

'I think I read somewhere that the Old Course Hotel has got a lovely spa,' said Maggie. 'Does Mr Kinnock go away often?'

There was something unsettling about the way they were questioning her.

'Why are you so interested in Mack playing golf?' she asked.

'If he goes away a lot, I was wondering how Rosie feels about it. You said they were very close, so she must miss him.'

'It's not every week, it's once every six weeks, and only for a few days at a time,' Lesley snapped. 'Mack's not an absent father. He probably spends more time with Rosie than most dads do with their kids because he's here when she gets home from school every day.'

Maggie and Belmar clammed up after she said that and the three of them waited in silence for the next ten minutes until the front door opened and Mack's deep Scottish burr rang through the house. Tensing up, Lesley couldn't bring herself to look towards the kitchen doorway as her husband came crashing through it.

'Lesley?'

The crack in Mack's voice as he spoke her name made her spin round. Lesley gasped in shock. His face was pallid and drawn and his thick brown hair, the exact same shade as Rosie's before grey swept through it, stuck out at wild angles as though he'd been tugging at it. Behind his black-framed glasses she could see that his green eyes, also the same colour as Rosie's, were blood-shot and puffy from crying.

'Oh, Mack . . .'

He dropped the hand luggage he was carrying onto the floor with a clatter and they held each other tightly, tears running down their faces, oblivious to their audience.

'I'm so sorry,' she sobbed. 'I should've stayed at home and done the shopping online like you said—'

Mack cupped her face with his hands. Lesley's eyes roamed over his face, drinking in the features as familiar to her as her own.

'Listen to me,' he said firmly. 'None of this is your fault, sweetheart. I shouldn't have said that to you on the phone. It was an awful, unforgiveable thing to say.' He pulled her close again.

'I just want her home,' she said, burying her face in his chest. 'Why would someone hurt our baby?'

Mack tenderly kissed the top of her head.

'I don't know, sweetheart. I just don't know.'

11

The call came later than he expected, just after 11 p.m. He'd almost forgotten about her as he spent the rest of the afternoon and evening consumed by thoughts of what he must do next. He mustn't allow complacency to creep in, to assume the outcome would fall into place simply because he wanted it to. The odds had been stacked in his favour so far – the girl was taken care of, the post box was serendipitously being emptied when he arrived to post his letter, so he knew for sure it had been collected for delivery the next day – but it didn't mean they would stay that way.

He almost didn't recognize her voice at first, although the number that came up indicated it was her calling. Her voice was barely a whisper and there was a lot of background noise in the hotel bar that made it even more difficult to hear. Eventually, after twice telling her to speak up, he got the gist.

She wasn't asking for an apology for cancelling on her: she was asking if he'd seen the news.

'No, why?'

'Something terrible has happened.'

He feigned ignorance. 'What's happened? Are you okay?'

'It's not me. It's—' She let out a sob.

'You're scaring me,' he lied as he reclined on his sofa with his feet up, nursing a Diet Coke.

'You need to turn on the news,' she said.

'Hang on.' He pretended to switch channels, but his television was already tuned to the BBC's rolling news bulletin. The details were sketchy so far but the story was creeping further up the running order as the minutes ticked by and it was on the ticker at the bottom of the screen.

'Oh my God,' he breathed. 'I don't believe it.'

'What are we going to do?'

He pretended to stumble over his words before delivering his perfectly rehearsed answer. 'But it's nothing to do with us. You're in Scotland and I'm in London.' She thought he lived in a flat in Clapham South, just off the common, and that the accountancy firm he worked for was based in Euston.

'But what if Mack tells the police about us meeting up? They might think we're involved.'

'You, you mean.'

'What?'

'Well, I've not spoken to him. He doesn't even know I exist.'

'Are you trying to drop me in it?' Her voice grew louder as anger took hold. 'We're in this together. You said you'd help me.'

He took a mental step back. 'Of course we are, but we haven't actually done anything wrong. If this was tomorrow and I was at the hotel with you, it might be a different story. But it's not, so we don't need to worry. He's hardly going to say anything considering what's been going on between you two.'

The first time he saw Mack Kinnock with her he could've kissed the ground. Instantly he knew she was his trump card, the key to getting what was rightfully his. It was at the end of April, in Starbucks just off the station concourse at King's Cross in central London. He'd been trailing Mack as usual one Saturday afternoon when, to his surprise, he'd headed to Haxton station to catch a train into the city. Figuring Mack was off on another spending spree with *his* money, he followed him to Marylebone, then on the Bakerloo Line one stop to Baker Street, before changing on to the Metropolitan Line to travel the three stops to King's Cross. The kiss with which Mack had greeted her left him in no doubt as to the nature of their relationship. After all those months of waiting and watching it was like *he* had hit the jack-pot.

The atmosphere didn't stay genial for long though, and after an hour's heated discussion Mack stormed off and left her crying into her latte, at which point he'd swooped in, the benevolent stranger reading a newspaper at the next table, to offer her a tissue and a friendly shoulder to cry on. She was too upset to tell him to leave her alone and after some gentle cajoling he whisked her to a nearby pub and plied her with white wine until the whole sorry saga came tumbling out.

'But I want him to say something,' she hissed down

the phone as he took another leisurely sip of his drink. 'His wife needs to know.'

'This isn't the time. You need to sit tight until they find their daughter.'

'*We* need to sit tight,' she corrected.

'That's what I meant. My point is, now is not the time for people to find out about you and Mack. People won't understand. I also think,' he pretended to hesitate, 'you and I should lay off contacting each other for a bit. We know we've done nothing wrong, but the police might not see it like that.'

'I know. It's just that we were so close to getting the money.'

'You'll still get it. He can't back out, whatever happens.'

Another lie. She wouldn't get a penny – it was all his for the taking now and this was the last conversation they'd ever have.

Her voice quavered. 'What do you think has happened to her?'

'Run away, probably. You said yourself what Mack was like. Look, I think we should hang up now. I feel just awful.'

'Me too,' she said, letting out another sob.

He put down the phone and laughed.

12

Wednesday

The woman on the doorstep lived four houses down from Angel's Reach. When Maggie first answered the door to her, she thought she was there to offer her support to the Kinnocks. It took less than a minute for her to realize her motive for coming round was purely selfish. Overnight, a crowd of reporters had gathered on the other side of the security gate leading into Burr Way and the neighbour, who announced herself as Mrs Roberts, blamed Mack and Lesley for the intrusion. On discovering Maggie was a police officer, she launched into a tirade.

'Can't you get rid of the press? They're causing a nuisance.'

'They're not breaking any law by being there,' said Maggie. 'The side of the road they're on is a public one.'

The press office had issued a statement at 7 p.m. the previous evening announcing a teenage girl was missing in Haxton. It hadn't taken long for the media to find out Rosie Kinnock was the daughter of EuroMillions winners, largely helped by her school friends tweeting and Facebooking appeals for her to get in touch. Less than an hour later, 'Rosie' and 'EuroMillions' were top trending on Twitter.

'They're also on the other side of the security gate,' Maggie pointed out. 'They can't get anywhere near any of the houses.'

'That is beside the point,' said Mrs Roberts haughtily. 'There are vans parked on the grass verge and anyone trying to get in and out of the street is being harassed. I have someone coming to see me today for an appointment and I don't want him bothered. You have to move them on.'

If Mrs Roberts wasn't so unpleasant Maggie might've been impressed at how impeccably turned out she was at seven thirty in the morning, when she herself hadn't managed to even brush her hair yet. Judging by the creases lining her face, Mrs Roberts had to be in her early seventies. Her white-blonde hair was slicked back into a neat bun and her make-up artfully applied to give the impression she wore none. Slim in frame, she wore a floral blouse tucked into peach-coloured trousers and cream court shoes with a rounded toe. On her left wrist, just visible beneath the cuff of her blouse, was a bandage support.

'I'm sorry,' Maggie repeated, 'but as I said, it's a public right of way. We can't stop them being there.'

'But the noise they make as they film is intolerable.'

Mrs Roberts had already let slip that her house was further away from the security gate than Angel's Reach so there was no way she'd hear the reporters doing their pieces to camera. Maggie thought about pointing that out, but the look on Mrs Roberts's face told her it wouldn't be appreciated.

'I understand it's a difficult situation,' she said quickly, with as much politeness as she could muster. She really didn't have time to stand on the doorstep arguing: every minute wasted was one less spent looking for Rosie. 'However, the press coverage may well prove invaluable in finding Rosie quickly. There are two uniformed officers stationed at the gate to make sure residents still have easy access.'

'I'm sure the silly girl's just run off somewhere and all this nonsense is a waste of everyone's time, mine and yours included.'

Maggie's eyes narrowed. 'What makes you say that? Do you know Rosie?'

'Heavens, no,' Mrs Roberts sniffed, as though to suggest so was an insult. 'I have nothing to do with her or her parents. They keep to themselves, as do I.'

I'm not surprised they do if you're the sort of person they have to live near, thought Maggie sourly.

'Why do you think she's run off then?' she asked.

The reply came with a sneer. 'She's fifteen years old, for heaven's sake. She's probably doing it for attention and now we're the ones suffering.'

While the selfishness of some people rarely shocked Maggie – people wanting something that wasn't theirs was at the root of most crimes, after all – this woman was something else. Time to end the conversation.

'Rosie's been missing for almost twenty-four hours now and her parents are frantic with worry,' she said. 'I know they'll appreciate the support of their neighbours at this difficult time so I'll tell them you popped round.'

Maggie shut the door before the woman could react.

Returning briskly to the kitchen, she wondered if the rest of the neighbours were as stuck-up and self-serving as Mrs Roberts was. It would certainly explain why their door-to-door inquiries had drawn a blank. Umpire had revealed as much when he called her half an hour ago to update her on the investigation so far. FLOs weren't expected to attend every single incident room briefing because their place was with the victims' relatives, but it was vital they were kept in the loop and any important developments passed on immediately.

Umpire said the last known sighting of Rosie was still at 10.33 a.m., just before the CCTV cameras installed in the Kinnocks' back garden were switched off.

'Does Rosie know how to deactivate the system?' Maggie had asked.

'Yes. Her dad showed her what to do in the unlikely event she ever needed to reset it.'

'So the cameras were switched off before Rosie got changed out of her shorts into her party skirt and then went missing?'

'It looks that way,' said Umpire.

He said he'd be over later, after briefing the rest of the team at the Major Crime incident room he'd commandeered at Mansell police station. There was a station in Haxton but it was run on a part-time basis by volunteers and only dealt with minor matters such as processing documents for traffic offences. It had neither the capacity nor the technological set-up required to run a Major Crime investigation.

The ease with which Umpire spoke to her on the phone made Maggie relax about what Belmar had told her the previous evening. If Umpire had been aware of what was being said about them his voice would've betrayed him with the same awkwardness he showed when certain female officers flirted with him. Instead, they seemed to be edging back to how they were before the Megan Fowler case changed everything.

That case had been tough on everyone involved. Megan was only eight – the same age Maggie's nephew Scotty was now – when she was strangled and her body dumped behind some garages near her home on the west side of Mansell. Some killers take trophies from their crimes and Megan's had, for some inexplicable reason, hacked off her long blonde hair. It was a detail Umpire wanted to withhold from public consumption: he wanted to use the evidence to wheedle out anyone who claimed to have knowledge of the murder by establishing if they knew about Megan's hair being cut.

But that included not telling Megan's parents. Umpire said he didn't trust them not to divulge the detail, especially as they were making regular statements to the press about catching her killer. So, to maintain secrecy, he decided to delay them viewing Megan's body so they wouldn't see what the killer had done to her.

As their FLO, Maggie disagreed vehemently with the tactic: Paula and Jamie Fowler needed to see their little girl as soon as possible so they could begin the grieving process. She pleaded with him, suggesting they cover up what was left of Megan's hair with a shroud so the parents couldn't tell the rest was gone, or swear them to secrecy. But still he wouldn't budge.

As the days dragged on, Maggie was horrified to see Megan's mum Paula being driven to the cusp of a breakdown as her imagination conjured up scenarios of what the killer had done to Megan that were far worse than the reality. Again and again Maggie tried to convince Umpire to tell the parents why they couldn't see Megan but he still refused. He couldn't risk the killer evading arrest. After a long night wrestling with her conscience, Maggie cracked and told Paula the truth. To let her continue to suffer was a cruelty she simply was no longer prepared to inflict.

Once the news had sunk in, Paula agreed to keep it a secret even from Jamie. She understood the enormity of what Maggie had done and what she was risking to ease her pain.

Umpire remained unaware Paula knew until two days later, after he'd arrested Megan's killer, a twenty-one-year-old man with learning difficulties who lived in the next street and had attacked the little girl because she was rude to him. He cut off her hair because he erroneously thought it would stop him getting caught.

Maggie hoped that with the arrest made, that would be the end of it. But when Umpire turned up at the house to tell the Fowlers they had someone in custody, a distraught Paula let rip and accused him of playing God with her family's feelings.

Umpire's anger towards Maggie erupted like a volcano. Not only did she remember every word he said to her, but other little details also stayed with her: the swollen vein in his temple that pulsed as he swore at her on the pavement outside the Fowlers' house; the sensation of cold sweat trickling down her back as she absorbed his fury; the taste of the five cigarettes she'd chain-smoked afterwards to calm down.

The memory of that confrontation made her shiver now as she stood in the Kinnocks' warm kitchen. At some point she must find the courage to ask him why he had withdrawn his complaint, but for now she was going to enjoy the ceasefire.

She checked the time on her watch, a chunky silver Seiko designed for a male wrist and a Christmas present given reluctantly two years ago by her parents, who didn't understand why she didn't want a 'nice ladies' style' like the one Lou picked out. Maggie tried to explain she liked the weight of the Seiko against her wrist, the way it made her feel anchored, but her parents remained baffled.

It was 7.40 a.m. and she was expecting Belmar to arrive by eight. She poured herself another coffee from the pot she'd brewed and checked her phone. She'd sent Lou a text earlier to see how she and the kids were, but imagined her sister was too busy getting them ready for school to reply. She'd try to call her later. She was dying to know how Scotty's performance had gone.

Although patrol officers were stationed outside Angel's Reach and by the security gate, Maggie was the only police presence inside the house. A handful of Matheson's techs were re-examining the back lawn but the search was now being concentrated beyond its boundaries, to the meadow where Rosie's skirt had been found shoved into a bush and into Haxton village itself.

She added milk to her coffee. The Kinnocks hadn't surfaced yet but she doubted they were asleep. The worry would have kept them awake for most of the night. Just before midnight they had received the news that Matheson's lab tests had confirmed the blood on the lawn was Rosie's and it was a match with the blood on the skirt. Mack and Lesley took themselves off to their bedroom after that, rather than keeping vigil downstairs. Maggie knew not to judge – every family was different and there was no right or wrong way to behave in their situation. Some families liked to stay up all night discussing endlessly what was going on, as though voicing their fears somehow diluted them. Others, like the Kinnocks, preferred to keep their counsel.

Maggie had slept on the purple sofa in the lounge. She'd been loath to make herself at home in one of the guest bedrooms without checking first and she would not disturb the Kinnocks for something she regarded as trivial. She'd spent enough nights crashed out on Lou's sofa to know she could still function the next day on a few snatched hours and had found a throw in the laundry room next to the kitchen to keep herself warm.

She'd lain awake for an hour before falling asleep though, replaying the moment Lesley saw Rosie's skirt. She was angry with herself that she hadn't reached the French doors first and even more so with the eager probationer whose bright idea it was to bring the skirt to Matheson rather than call him to the meadow where it was found so it could be secured as a secondary crime scene. Umpire was furious it had been removed from its hiding place and potential forensic evidence destroyed. The probationer was already off the case and back on traffic duty.

Maggie returned the milk to the fridge. It was the biggest one she'd ever seen and must've cost thousands, yet its contents were at odds with the flash exterior: the shopping she'd unpacked for Lesley yesterday was mostly Tesco own-brand and the only luxury item, if you could call it that, was a Finest range ready meal of salmon en croute. Maggie imagined that if she had unlimited funds, she'd buy the best of everything: steak, lobster, champagne, you name it. All that money and Lesley still bought Tesco Everyday Value streaky bacon.

'Is there any news?'

She jumped in fright and turned to find Mack standing right behind her. He looked exhausted and the clothes he wore were the same ones he'd had on yesterday. She hadn't heard him enter the kitchen and, glancing down, saw why: his feet were bare and wouldn't have made a sound on the slate tiles.

'I'm afraid not,' she said apologetically. 'But DCI Umpire is coming over to talk to you and your wife shortly.'

Mack stared at Maggie like he had no idea what to say. Mindful of Umpire's warning that she must not mention the police were aware he'd only stayed one night at the Old Course Hotel, she kept the conversation light.

'Shall I explain what it is we do as your family liaison? We didn't really have a chance to go through it yesterday.'

'Go on then,' said Mack, his Scots accent lending his voice an abruptness Maggie cautioned herself not to take personally.

She recited the statement she gave every family at the start of an investigation, give or take a word.

'DC Small and I are here to offer you and your wife practical support such as helping you understand what stage the inquiry is at and providing all possible information where we can. There may be some things we aren't able to share if they could jeopardize criminal proceedings but we'll let you know if that's the case and why.' *Unless my DCI refuses to let me*, she silently added. 'What we can't help you with – what I'm afraid neither of us is trained to provide – is counselling. But there are organizations such as Victim Support who can do that and we can contact them for you.'

It was a distinction she hated making. She disagreed passionately with the no-counselling rule for FLOs, put in place to protect them from becoming emotionally overburdened. No, she wasn't a trained counsellor, but she had ears, didn't she? Most of the time that was all the families wanted – someone to listen to them. How could she be with them day in and day out and then excuse herself when they wanted to talk about how they were feeling? She'd happily listen to whatever they wanted to unload on her. But however dismissive she was of the rule, Maggie felt she had no choice but to stick to it.

'I can call them now if you want,' she said.

Mack shook his head. 'That won't be necessary.'

They all say that at the beginning, she thought. *We don't need any help. We can cope.* That's because they're praying it'll all be over in a few hours. But what if those hours stretch into days or even weeks? What then?

'Well, it's something for you to consider,' she said. 'I should also let you know that myself and Belmar will be making a note of conversations we have with you and your wife.'

Mack frowned. 'Why?'

'It's nothing to be alarmed about, Mr Kinnock. Logging our conversations makes it easier for us to check if there's anything you need us to do, such as finding out certain information, or if you want to go over anything you've already raised.'

She didn't add the aside that always popped into her head at this point in her speech, which was that logging all conversations also gave them the opportunity to review any discrepancies in the family's statements and flag up any suspicious comments or behaviour to the SIO.

'I do have one question,' he said. 'About the skirt you found.'

'Yes, about that . . .' She cringed. 'I'm very sorry—'

'No, that's not what I meant. Are you certain it's Rosie's?'

Taken aback, she said yes, they were. 'Your wife confirmed it.'

'I know, but she's very upset and could be mistaken. I've never seen it before and it's not the kind of thing Rosie wears. I certainly wouldn't let her wear something so short.'

'Mr Kinnock—' Maggie began, but he interrupted her, clearly agitated.

'That skirt does not belong to Rosie.'

Maggie could hear the desperation in his voice and faltered. Of course he didn't want it to be Rosie's. None of them wanted it to be Rosie's.

'Even if it does prove to be someone else's,' she said carefully, 'as we told you last night, the lab tests have confirmed the blood on the skirt is your daughter's. DCI Umpire will be able to explain more when he arrives.'

Mack squeezed his eyes shut behind his glasses and rubbed his temples with his fingertips. When he opened his eyes again they were filled with despair. But instead of breaking down, as he looked as though he was on the verge of doing, he pulled his shoulders back and exhaled.

'Okay. I'm going to take a shower now.'

He left the kitchen as quietly as he'd entered.

13

Belmar arrived twenty minutes late and full of apologies, bowling into the kitchen carrying a pile of letters and a takeaway coffee cup. He looked as if he'd had a far better night's sleep than she had and she was pleased. It wouldn't help the Kinnocks or the investigation if they were both tired.

'Sorry I'm late, I got waylaid on the way in,' he said.

'By the press? I hope you didn't say anything.'

'I'm not an idiot,' said Belmar, smoothing down his tie, which was royal purple and the exact same colour as the shirt he also wore beneath his charcoal grey suit. He looked impeccable again and Maggie idly wondered if he was the type to iron his socks. She could only imagine what he must think of her Next suits and practical but mannish black loafers that hadn't been polished since the day she bought them eighteen months ago.

'It was two of the security guards who work for the company that has the contract for this street,' he added. 'They wanted to offer their services.'

'To do what?'

'Join the search. They're pretty cut up about what's happened.'

'I'll bet. A girl going missing in full view of their supposedly sophisticated security system is hardly a great advert.'

'Ah, that's where you're wrong,' said Belmar, wagging his finger at her. 'If Matheson's right and Rosie went over the back fence, there are no cameras there that could've recorded it. The guards told me there's a dispute over who should foot the bill. The council owns the pathway and the residents reckon it should pay for CCTV rather than them. But the council says it's not a priority, so at the moment the area's not covered while the decision's being appealed.'

'Umpire won't be pleased when he hears that. So did they see anything?'

'No. The firm is contracted to carry out three patrols a day – one at ten a.m., one at three p.m. and again at ten p.m. The first was done as usual and the guard didn't see anything out of the ordinary, but by the time the second was due our lot were already on the scene.'

'Someone's interviewed all the guards, I take it?'

'I think the team's got it covered.' Belmar smiled benevolently. 'They have done this kind of thing before, you know.'

The dig annoyed her. 'I'm asking because I'm still a detective, as are you.'

'Maggie, I was teasing.'

'It's not funny,' she snapped.

The inference that being an FLO somehow made her

less of a detective was the one thing that bothered her about the role. The two weren't mutually exclusive. The way she saw it, being an FLO meant helping to solve a case from the inside out. You had to be a good detective to know what information provided by the family was worth following up.

'Can you get Mack to go through Rosie's room again to see if there's anything missing? I had a look with him last night but I'm not sure how thorough he was. He mostly sat on the bed and cried.'

'Sure,' said Belmar. He dropped the bundle of mail he was holding onto the island counter. 'I bumped into the postman on the way in too.'

The envelopes fanned across the counter. Maggie peered at one half hidden beneath the others.

'Is that crayon?'

Belmar used his elbow to carefully push the other envelopes out of the way. The one that was left was white, standard size and marked for Lesley's attention, with both her name and address written in crude capitals with red crayon. Maggie peered at the postmark. It was yesterday's date and the stamp said 'Mansell'.

'You don't think . . . ?' Belmar faltered.

'I'll get them,' said Maggie, sliding off her stool.

She took the stairs two at a time and knocked loudly on the Kinnocks' bedroom door. Mack was still pulling a T-shirt over his head as he yanked it open. Lesley hovered anxiously behind him in a cerise towelling dressing gown.

'What's happened?' he demanded to know.

'A letter has arrived for you that I'm concerned about.

114

I'd like you to come downstairs to open it. Whoever sent it wrote your address in red crayon to make it look like a child's handwriting.'

Mack grimaced. 'It'll just be someone after money. We've had a few of them like that. I'll throw it away like the rest.'

'You've had others written in crayon or others in general?'

'Both. After our win we had every scrounger in Britain asking for a handout. I've lost count of the number of begging letters we've received. Hundreds. Usually just pleading for cash, but sometimes you get threats.'

'Do you ever report any?'

'We don't take them seriously.'

'People think they can just stop you in the street and you'll hand wads of cash over to them,' Lesley piped up over her husband's shoulder. 'It's why I wish we'd never gone public about our win.'

It was only fleeting but Maggie caught the warning look Mack shot his wife, who flushed red. Waiving their right to anonymity was clearly an unresolved point of conflict.

'Even if you have received others, I'd still like you to open this one,' she said.

'Fine.'

They trooped downstairs to the kitchen. Belmar had already fetched a pair of protective gloves from his car and the four of them stood in front of the island counter, upon which the envelope lay.

'The letter is addressed to you, Lesley. Do you want

to open it?' he said, holding the gloves in her direction. Mack intercepted them.

'No, I'll do it,' he said, snapping them on. The sound made Lesley flinch. Her eyes were underlined by thick purple streaks, the hallmarks of a sleepless night.

Mack stared at the front of the envelope.

'Yep, this is like the other crayoned ones.'

'What did the previous notes say?' asked Maggie.

'The person wanted money for something but I can't think what. I remember there was a lot of guff about how we didn't really deserve our win,' said Mack. 'They harped on about the money being technically theirs. Nasty name-calling and stuff. It's not theirs, before you ask. We had the only winning ticket for that draw.'

'Were the notes signed?' said Maggie.

Mack stared at her, unsmiling. 'Would you write an abusive letter to someone you didn't know and put your name to it?'

'Have you kept them?'

'What would be the point? No, we throw them all away every week when the recycling comes. I don't even bother to read them now.'

Gloves on, he ripped the envelope open and pulled out the piece of lined paper folded up inside. The top edge was shredded, like it had been ripped out of a spiral-bound notebook. As he read the note, the blood drained from his face. Lesley, reading over his shoulder, let out a cry and clamped her hand over her mouth.

'What does it say?' asked Belmar urgently.

Mack held up the piece of paper for him and Maggie to read. The note was written in block capitals.

GONE ASTRAY

DEAR MRS KINNOCK

I'M SORRY FOR YOUR LOSS. IT MUST'VE COME AS A SHOCK TO SEE ALL THAT BLOOD. THOSE SEQUINS WILL BE MURDER TO CLEAN!

IF YOU WANT TO KNOW ABOUT YOUR DAUGHTER, IT WILL COST YOU £250,000. YOU'VE GOT 48 HOURS TO GET MY MONEY READY. I'LL BE IN TOUCH TO LET YOU KNOW WHERE YOU CAN SEND IT.

IN THE MEANTIME, DON'T GO SPENDING WHAT'S MINE . . . !

14

There was a guest bathroom just off the entrance hall. Lesley left the door wide open as she pitched forward and heaved into the toilet bowl. She hadn't eaten since yesterday morning and her abdominal muscles cramped viciously as they tried to expel the tiny amount of bile left in the pit of her stomach. She heard Mack say her name as he approached from behind but she frantically batted him away. She didn't want anyone anywhere near her. He didn't argue and closed the door as he left.

As she slumped against the toilet, grief ripped through her like an electric shock. Whoever wrote the note knew the design of Rosie's skirt and knew about the blood. What had they done to her?

The idea of her child suffering God knows what at the hands of a stranger made Lesley retch over and over until her body had nothing left to give. Eventually she sat up and dragged the back of her hand across her mouth to wipe it clean. Her skin felt like it was on fire so she lowered the toilet lid and rested her forehead against its cool surface, shivering involuntarily as her skin made contact. Then she wished, not for the first time, that she'd never bought the EuroMillions ticket.

Winning such a vast amount of money had changed everything and what she could never tell Mack, what he would find impossible to comprehend, was that she had been far happier before, living in Mansell in the decidedly average semi-detached house they'd scrimped to buy before they had Rosie. She missed her old job working part-time as an admin clerk for an optician chain in the high street and pined for their old friends, the couples with children Rosie's age that she and Mack would go out for a drink with on a Saturday night. It wasn't the most exciting life, nothing to boast about, but she cherished its simplicity.

Minutes slipped by until a knock on the door broke through her reverie.

'Lesley, it's me, Maggie. DCI Umpire is here. He'd like to talk to you. Do you feel up to it?'

She wanted to scream that, no, she didn't. She wanted them all to go away and leave her alone, even Mack.

Especially Mack.

She'd tried to convince him that allowing their names to be publicized as EuroMillions winners was a mistake and would make them targets of unwanted attention, but he cared too much about letting people know how rich he'd become. Before, he'd had a solid career as a town planner and was behind some of the better-received developments in Mansell, including the new shopping centre. But he earned nothing like the six-figure salaries his old uni friends took home as lawyers, architects and, in one instance, head of a media company. Knowing they were more successful meant the chip on his shoulder, honed in childhood thanks to his parents favouring his older brother, had sharpened with age. Winning the lottery was Mack's chance to shine at last.

'Lesley?' Maggie repeated, her voice full of concern.

'Do I have to talk to him now?' she said wearily.

'The sooner you answer his questions, the quicker he can return to the search.'

The insinuation that her being difficult might delay him finding Rosie landed like a punch and she clambered to her feet. Outside the door, Maggie was waiting with her hands tucked into her trouser pockets and she flashed a kindly smile that almost made Lesley break down again.

'You okay?'

She nodded, not trusting herself to speak.

'DCI Umpire will be as quick as he can with his questions. He knows how difficult this is for you and Mack.'

Umpire, Mack and Belmar were waiting in the dining room. Someone had already set down a glass of water on the table for her. Lesley glanced towards the French doors and was relieved to see the curtains had been left open; she didn't want to spend the whole time worrying about what new horror might lurk behind them. The brightness outside suggested another sunny day to follow and the dining room was already warming up. Lesley felt her armpits dampen as she took a seat beside her husband.

'Mrs Kinnock, I was just telling your husband that I'll be taking the note away for forensic analysis,' said DCI Umpire. 'If we're lucky we'll get something from it.'

The thought of more waiting filled her with despair. 'How long will that take?' she fretted.

'Hopefully only a couple of hours,' said Umpire. 'The letter is postmarked Mansell and must've been sent yesterday afternoon to make the last post. That does give us something to go on. You told my officers that whoever wrote the previous notes in crayon seemed convinced your win is rightfully theirs and now this letter demands you hand over a quarter of a million. Does anyone have a legitimate claim to the money? Have you been in dispute with anyone about the amount you won?'

She and Mack shook their heads.

'We had the only winning ticket for that draw across the whole of Europe,' said Lesley. 'You can check.'

'I don't suppose you can remember when the first crayon note was sent?'

'Not really. We started getting letters after the *Mansell Echo* ran an article about us moving here,' said Mack. 'The bloody paper printed a picture of the house they'd nicked off the estate agent's website and even though they didn't publish the name, they said it was on Burr Way. Then someone put it on Twitter and after that we got deluged by people asking us for money.'

'You had no idea the paper was going to print the story?'

'No. We didn't complain though because we'd been in the *Echo* a few times already, when they interviewed us after the win,' said Mack. 'I don't think they realized what they were doing.'

Lesley had to bite her lip to stop herself retorting that the real reason Mack didn't complain was because he wanted everyone to see how flash the house was. But she didn't, because she didn't want the police to see how angry she was with him for sacrificing their privacy for the chance to show off to his peers.

'Was it just the local paper that ran the picture?'

'At first, but once it was on Twitter, a national newspaper ran it and it was all over the Internet.'

'But you can't pinpoint the exact time the first crayon letter arrived?'

'No, sorry.'

'It's fine, Mr Kinnock,' said Umpire. 'I'll get someone to dig out the original article and we'll also get on to the lottery provider Camelot to see if anyone has disputed your jackpot.'

Mack's hands balled into fists as they rested on his thighs.

'We won the money fair and square. I bet the bastard who sent us that card is just pissed off they didn't. Pissed off enough to make us suffer.'

'By attacking Rosie?' said Lesley, horrified.

'Money can be divisive and brings out the worst in some people, while jealousy also makes people behave irrationally,' said Umpire.

'Abducting a child is not irrational, it's sick,' wailed Lesley. 'You have to find her! The thought that someone's—' She couldn't finish.

'There is something else I want you to consider as we check every line of inquiry,' said Umpire. 'DC Neville, do you want to explain?'

Maggie looked surprised but quickly recovered her composure.

'Yesterday I began to ask you about whether you'd seen any scars on Rosie, do you remember?'

'Yes, before we saw the skirt.'

'Well, some of Rosie's friends have said they think she self-harms by cutting herself and that may account for the blood.'

'No fucking way,' Mack erupted. 'She does no such thing.'

'With respect, Mr Kinnock, parents don't always know that's what their child is doing. But,' said Maggie quickly, as Mack swore again, 'I'm pretty certain you would've at least noticed some grazing or scars on her arms or legs or even her torso.'

'No, we haven't seen anything,' he snapped.

'He's right,' said Lesley. 'Earlier on I was thinking about how much it would've hurt her if she was dragged through the trees at the bottom of the garden because her skin is very sensitive and the branches would've cut it to ribbons. I've never seen a scratch on her that's been self-inflicted.'

'She might try to hide the scars, though.'

'No, absolutely not. Yesterday morning we ate break-fast together and she was still in the vest and shorts she wears to bed. There wasn't a mark on her.'

'Why do you suppose her friends think she does self-harm?' asked Umpire.

'Who cares? She doesn't cut herself and that's the end of it,' said Mack.

Maggie let the subject drop and Umpire took over.

'The other thing I need to discuss with you before I head back to the station is holding a press conference,' he said. 'We've had no witnesses come forward so far in the immediate vicinity, but a wider appeal might help. I'd like you both to take part.'

Lesley exchanged a worried look with her husband. 'You mean go on telly to talk about Rosie?'

'Yes. Let people see how much you want her home and the effect her being missing is having on you.'

'You want us to cry on TV?' Mack bridled.

'If that's what it takes to find her, then yes,' said Umpire matter-of-factly. His face was impassive but his eyes showed sympathy.

'What if I can't answer their questions?' said Lesley.

'Because you might be too upset? Then leave the talking to Mack. I'm not going to lie and pretend it won't be difficult – press conferences are emotional for every family in your situation. But if you try to stay focused on the fact that what you're doing could help Rosie you'll get through it. DC Neville and DC Small will be there to support you and talk through the process beforehand.'

Lesley looked at Maggie. 'Will it help?'

'TV appeals do jog people's memories,' Maggie replied. 'They can also prompt people to call in and report the names of people they think are behaving sus-piciously and might somehow be involved.' She fixed Lesley with her unusual eyes. 'I wouldn't encourage you to take part if I didn't think some good might come of it.'

'Okay, we'll do it,' said Mack, answering for the pair of them. 'When do you want it to happen?'

'This afternoon. Rosie's disappearance is already head-line news and all over social media – if we can get your appeal out sooner rather than later we'll keep the momentum going. We also need some more photographs of Rosie, as many as you can provide. We have the most recent picture of her that you gave us yesterday but it's always good to provide the media with a selection, including a couple of baby shots. And one of her in her current school uniform would be good to remind every-one how young she is.'

'Okay, we'll look some out,' said Mack.

Umpire said he would see them at the station for the press conference and left. Mack went upstairs to his office with Belmar to look for any other letters and Lesley went next door to the lounge with Maggie. Feel-ing restless and jumpy, she picked up the remote control and turned on the wall-mounted TV, flicking through the channels until she reached Sky News. A male reporter stationed by the security gate at the top of Burr Way was updating the viewers on what was known so far, which wasn't much. Rosie was still missing, he said, and although it was believed an item of her clothing had been found, the police had yet to confirm it. A press conference was expected to take place later in the day with Rosie's parents. Lesley hit the mute button.

'DCI Umpire doesn't waste time, does he? What if we'd said no to taking part?'

'The press conference would go ahead whatever you decided. It's really important we get the media on side to help find Rosie. We want them working with us, not against us.'

'Meaning what?'

'Sometimes the papers can be tough on victims' families if they think there's something suspicious about them or they have another agenda. I'm not saying that will happen to you and Mack, but because of your Euro-Millions win there's heightened interest and the press want to speak to you. If we can channel their interest into supportive appeals on your behalf, we'll get the public on side too.'

'So we have to pander to the press to find Rosie?'

Maggie shrugged apologetically. 'Unfortunately it's often how these things work these days.'

'If that's what it takes to bring Rosie home, I'll do it,' said Lesley firmly. 'Whatever they want from us.'

Her attention was diverted from the television to a folded-up throw left on the arm of the sofa.

'Where did that come from?'

'Sorry, I left it there. I borrowed it last night and forgot to put it back.'

'Oh, did you sleep down here?'

'Yes. I didn't want to disturb you upstairs.'

Lesley gave a short, mirthless laugh. 'Disturb us? You've seen the size of this house, haven't you? It's like a hotel. I'll get one of the spare bedrooms organized for you—'

She stopped mid-sentence, the words frozen on her lips like icicles. If Maggie needed to stay the night again, it would be because Rosie still wasn't home. She shuddered at the thought. Then something on the TV caught her eye and she gasped.

'Is that Kathryn?'

It was Kathryn and her mum, Sarah, their faces filling

the screen in close-up. Lesley turned the volume up just as an unseen reporter off-camera asked Kathryn how well she knew Rosie.

'She's my best friend,' she said, barely audible. 'I just want her to come home. Whoever's done this to her needs to tell us where she is.'

'Have the police told you they suspect she's been abducted, then?' said the reporter's disembodied voice.

Kathryn looked to her mother.

'Because of my daughter's close relationship with Rosie, we are in constant dialogue with the police,' said Sarah, smarming at the camera as she gripped Kathryn's hand. She had a pair of sunglasses perched on top of her hair like a headband.

Lesley was confused. 'Is that right? Are you telling them what's going on?'

'Not me,' said Maggie firmly.

The two of them watched as Kathryn repeated her plea for Rosie to come home. The teenager was dry-eyed but sounded distraught. Lesley ached to see her suffering.

'I must call her later, or go round to see her. She must be so worried about Rosie.'

'Are you and Mrs Stockton close, or is it just the girls?' Maggie asked.

Lesley tried to be tactful. 'Just them. Sarah and I had lunch a couple of times after Rosie and Kathryn first became friendly but, well, I suppose we're very different. She has her interests and they're not ones I share . . .'

She was cut short by Maggie's phone ringing. The officer's face brightened as she checked the caller ID.

'I have to take this,' she said. 'I won't be long.'

As Maggie shut the door behind her, Lesley returned her attention to the TV screen. Kathryn and Sarah had disappeared from view and a perky blonde was now delivering the weather report for the rest of the day.

Rain was coming.

15

Maggie took the call outside on the drive. The rear garden was out of bounds, sealed off by blue and white police tape that fluttered like bunting in the breeze that was picking up.

'It's me,' said Lou. Her voice was flat, exhausted.

'Hey, sis. I'm so sorry I had to leave you at the school yesterday. Did the rest of the concert go okay? How was Scotty's solo?'

Lou was in no mood to give a review and the graciousness she'd shown yesterday at Maggie's departure appeared to have deserted her.

'I'm ringing because you owe me twenty quid. I had to get a taxi home because you buggered off with the car.'

Maggie knew a taxi from the school to Lou's house would've cost less than half that but guilt stopped her from pointing it out.

'I'll give you the cash and I'll reimburse you for the pizza too.'

'We didn't have any. We didn't go.'

'Why not? The boys were looking forward to it.'

'I didn't have enough cash on me.'

'Couldn't you have used your card?'

'Stop interrogating me like I'm one of your suspects,' Lou snapped.

Maggie mentally counted to ten. When Lou was being this tetchy nothing she said would placate her. The best thing she could do was let her sister stew it out of her system.

'Fine. I'll try to drop the cash off later,' she said.

'When later? This afternoon? Tonight? I need it.'

'I get that, Lou, but I can't just leave when I want. I'm meant to stay with the family.'

She regretted the words the moment they left her lips. It was like dropping a lit match into a box of fireworks.

'What about your family?' Lou erupted. 'Shouldn't we come first?'

'You were fine for me to leave yesterday.'

'That was before.'

'Before what?' said Maggie, her own mood starting to sour. It was like arguing with a teenager.

'Before I ended up skint because I had to pay for the taxi home.'

'That's not fair, Lou. You could've asked someone for a lift. I do as much as I can for you and the kids but I have to work and this is my job.'

Maggie heard an intake of breath down the line, followed by a long, drawn-out sigh.

'I'm sorry, I shouldn't have shouted,' said Lou. 'It's just that with Rob gone you know I can't afford to treat the kids much and it pisses me off.'

Maggie hated hearing her sister sound so down. Since walking out, Rob had made only a handful of mainten- ance payments towards Mae's keep, leaving Lou struggling to provide for her and the boys. Maggie tried to help by transferring £300 into her sister's account every payday to go towards her bills and Lou also received a small amount from Jude's grandparents every month, but nothing from Scotty's absent dad or his family. Maggie and Lou's parents, Graeme and Jeanette, lived on the south coast near Portsmouth, and while they occasion- ally helped out financially, they otherwise showed little interest in their grandchildren. Maggie had long sus- pected it might have something to do with the fact Jude and Scotty were mixed race, although they'd both hotly denied it the one time she was brave enough to ask. But Graeme Neville in particular always bristled when his grandsons' parentage was raised and there were no photo- graphs of either boy anywhere in their seaside home.

'Look, I'm meant to be back in Mansell for a press conference with the parents this afternoon so I'll see if I can pop round after with the money,' she said. 'If you're really skint I can give you a bit more this month.'

She didn't begrudge a single penny she gave Lou. It was payback of a debt that had nothing to do with money and everything to do with the way her sister's life had turned out. Three children by three different men and not one of her relationships lasting beyond a couple of years – and it was all Maggie's fault. Because what she'd told Belmar yesterday was only half of the story. Lou's fiancé Jerome had died while she was pregnant and it was what pushed Maggie into joining the police. But what she didn't reveal was that his death had been entirely preventable – and she alone could've stopped it.

16

His hands were clammy even before he touched the young, firm flesh exposed before him. The room was poorly ventilated, the window unable to be opened beyond a crack. A small desk fan in the corner cranked loudly as it oscillated back and forth but it wasn't enough to chill the sweaty impact of another warm day. Moisture pooled in the small of his back as he got to work. It made his scar itch.

His first client of the day was a favourite. Charlie, a seventeen-year-old who'd been coming to see him for nearly three months for treatment for a frozen shoulder. Charlie was captain of his public school's rugby team and one of his teachers, another client, had recommended he book an appointment. He liked Charlie because he was fun to talk to, and through his connections had landed him another wealthy private client.

'Have you been in much pain this week?' he asked, using his fingertips to gently manipulate the boy's naked shoulder. The muscle was stiff and immobile beneath the skin and felt as hard as concrete.

Charlie winced. 'It's been really bad. It keeps me

awake. The painkillers don't seem to make any difference.'

'The last corticosteroid injection didn't help?'

The boy shook his head.

'I don't want to keep giving them as they can damage your shoulder in the long run. Plus you mustn't get reliant on steroids to manage the pain,' he said, the irony not lost on him.

'I just want to get back to normal,' Charlie moaned as he carefully rotated his shoulder and arm.

He washed his hands in the small sink in the corner of the treatment room, which was a few doors down from the store cupboard where he'd fucked the woman the day before and not much bigger. He put up with it because the council-contracted gym was only his base two days a week. The other three days he worked with private clients, treating them in their homes. As he dried his hands on a paper towel, he gave Charlie the worst-case scenario.

'It could take between six months to a year for your shoulder to be back to what it was. If the pain isn't improving with the injections, I'll need to refer you for an operation.'

Charlie's face fell. He had babyish features, incongruous with his powerful sportsman's physique. The lad was six foot two and managed to make him – a perfectly acceptable five foot ten – feel stunted.

'So I still can't do any training?'

He gave him an amused look. 'Charlie, you can't even lift your arm above shoulder height. So, no, training is out of the question right now. Enjoy the break. Spend more time with that pretty girlfriend of yours.'

Charlie looked like he was about to burst into tears.

'She dumped me yesterday.'

He stood still for a second as he absorbed the news. This was not good. He tried to plaster on a sympathetic smile.

'That's a shame. She seemed like a nice girl.' He'd met her when she came with Charlie to an appointment. Hadn't said much, just sat in the corner engrossed in her phone. Very pretty girl. Beautiful hair.

'She is, and that's what makes it worse. I can't believe she's done it, I thought we were fine.'

He wasn't surprised Charlie was opening up to him and nor did he mind. They talked about girls a lot, and especially sex. He liked hearing about what Charlie and his friends got up to. He had been a late developer, didn't lose his virginity until he was twenty-one, but Charlie had been having sex since he was thirteen. The girlfriend who had just dumped him was the sixth girl he'd slept with, and that didn't include the casual encounters he'd also racked up: blowjobs after school from girls he only knew to say hello to; trading explicit Snapchat pictures and having Skype sex while his parents were downstairs watching telly. Stuff he never in a million years imagined doing when he was Charlie's age.

The teenager sighed as he struggled back into his polo shirt.

'I'll give her a couple of days then see if I can change her mind.'

'Did she give you a reason?'

'She said I was too immature for her, but she got really upset and cried, like I was the one binning her off. So maybe it'll be fine.'

He pretended to flick through a stack of forms on his desk, so Charlie couldn't see his face reddening. He felt bad for the lad, who was clearly devastated to lose his pretty little plaything. He might've even actually liked this one.

Their relationship couldn't continue though. Not now he was involved. He couldn't risk Charlie finding out what had happened. Even someone as experienced as he was wouldn't understand.

He gave Charlie's good shoulder a squeeze.

'I wouldn't go chasing after her, mate. She's not worth it.'

17

As she turned back towards the house, Maggie wrestled with how to keep her promise to Lou. She could explain away a brief absence to the Kinnocks by saying she had an urgent errand to run, but Umpire wouldn't be impressed if he found out she'd shot off to see her sister for the sake of £20. She just had to hope he didn't find out and be as quick as she could.

Before going inside, Maggie took a moment to admire the front of Angel's Reach. She hadn't given it more than a glance in her haste to get inside yesterday and was surprised to see that, contrary to the picture she had in her mind's eye, the brickwork wasn't red but a shade lighter than butter. How could she have thought it was a completely different colour? Her anxiety at facing Umpire must've been keener than she cared to admit.

The house was split into two wings that jutted into the driveway and a tall double front door, made from a light-coloured wood, was set back between them, with opaque glass panels either side of it. On the upper floor she counted six windows overlooking the driveway. Rosie's bedroom was at the rear of the house, with a view of the garden.

There was a large conservatory attached to the right side of the house and a detached double garage on the left. Maggie decided all that was missing was a swimming pool. That's what she'd install if she lived there. Heated too. Sod the expense.

She was about to go inside when a car turned into the driveway, its tyres crunching against the gravel. When she saw who was behind the wheel she wished she'd gone inside sooner. DC Anna Renshaw was also part of the team at Mansell Force CID but Maggie wasn't a fan. Renshaw spent as much time gossiping as she did working and was both duplicitous and manipulative. Maggie particularly loathed the way she acted as though every time she broke a confidence or repeated a conversation it was somehow out of concern for those involved, when in fact the opposite was true and she just liked talking about people behind their backs. Maggie had as little to do with her as she could.

'I'm glad I bumped into you,' Renshaw said, flashing a smile that didn't quite reach her eyes as she climbed out of her car. 'How brilliant that you're back being an FLO. I won't name names, but quite a few of the others thought you wouldn't be.'

Maggie wouldn't give her the satisfaction of asking who those 'others' were and simply shrugged.

Renshaw's smile didn't falter. 'I knew it would blow over once DCI Umpire realized the Fowler case wasn't as screwed as it could've been after what you did.'

The comment stung. She didn't believe she had

seriously jeopardized the case – what she did had had no direct bearing on the arrest or subsequent conviction of Megan's killer. If Renshaw was angling for some kind of admission of guilt she'd have a long wait. Maggie had no regrets about what she'd done – her only mistake was thinking that Umpire would understand.

Renshaw smoothed a strand of shiny auburn hair behind her ear. Her character could be perceived as ugly but, annoyingly, her face couldn't. She had a cute button nose and naturally thick eyelashes that Maggie's spindly ones would need at least three coats of mascara to replicate. Today's outfit was a fitted black skirt suit that flattered her athletic frame and black court shoes with heels so high Maggie was surprised Renshaw could walk in them, let alone drive. Having not yet showered herself – she didn't feel she should avail herself of the facilities until she'd asked the Kinnocks if it was okay to – she felt even grubbier standing next to her. In the boot of her own car was a battered brown leather holdall she kept packed with a change of clothes and spare toiletries ready for FL duty, like a pregnant woman preparing for the dash to the labour ward. Hopefully she'd be able to freshen up soon.

'So where is he?' said Renshaw.

'Who?'

'The husband. Ballboy's sent me to take a statement from Mack about all the begging letters they've been sent. He wants it done properly.'

'He's upstairs in his study,' said Maggie airily, unwilling to let Renshaw see that her last remark had needled her. 'Second door from last on the left.'

Renshaw eyed her nastily. 'Be a love and stick the kettle on. I'd love a brew and I know how good you FLOs are at making tea.'

She flounced inside. Furious, Maggie was about to follow her when her phone rang again. It was Umpire.

'Mack's phone records show he made repeated calls to one particular mobile number while he was in Scotland. It's the same number he's called multiple times over the past few weeks, sometimes as often as twice a day. It's registered to an address in Scotland, in Falkirk.'

'Isn't that where his parents and brother live?'

'It's not them. The phone is registered to a woman called Suzy Breed. Mack called her three times on Saturday after he arrived at the hotel and once again on Sunday morning. There were no calls after that, which leads me to wonder if they were arranging to meet and did so once he'd checked out.'

With Belmar's rumours about the two of them ringing in her ears, Maggie squirmed as she asked if he thought Mack was having an affair.

'That's one explanation. She could also just be a business contact or a relation he's not mentioned. Until we look into her, we don't know. Interestingly, he does have an alibi for Monday daytime: he was back at St Andrews playing golf with the rest of his party. But he didn't show up again to meet them yesterday morning.'

'Why don't we just question him about her, sir?'

'Because the second the media finds out we've brought him in for a formal interview they'll peg him as a suspect when we already know he wasn't in the country when

Rosie went missing. I want to know exactly who Suzy Breed is first before I go down that road.'

'So you think she might be relevant to the case?'

'I don't know. Could Rosie have found out her dad was having an affair and staged this whole thing to get back at him? Lesley said they were close – she might have been devastated to find out he was cheating.'

'But even if she did cut herself as part of a scam to punish her dad, Matheson said he doubted she could've got over the back fence on her own.'

'She could've had help. Let's face it, she's got access to enough money to pay someone to be in on it. My gut feeling says it's tenuous but I can't afford to rule anything out. We're about to pass the twenty-four-hour mark and we're no closer to finding her.'

She could hear the frustration in his voice and knew how he felt. The clock was ticking and the pressure starting to build. They desperately needed a breakthrough, and soon.

'I want you to interview Lesley alone and raise Suzy Breed's name to see how she reacts. You also need to question her again about Rosie's skirt.' He paused. 'Forensics found traces of PDM, a lubricant commonly used to coat condoms, on the inside lining, so it looks like Rosie might have been engaged in some kind of sexual activity before going missing.'

Maggie grimaced. 'I asked both Lesley and Kathryn whether Rosie was seeing anyone and they're both adamant she's never had a boyfriend, either here or while living in Mansell, because Mack is really strict about that.'

'She could be seeing someone secretly. She wouldn't be the first teenage girl to hide a boyfriend from an overbearing father.'

'Christ, I hope she is hiding someone.'

'Why do you say that?'

'Because if it wasn't a secret boyfriend who used the condom, I hate to think who did.'

18

Lesley did not stir as Maggie re-entered the lounge and sat down beside her. Her eyes remained fixed on the television but they were glazed over, suggesting she was watching but not seeing.

Mack was upstairs in his study with Belmar and DC Renshaw. Umpire said he wanted the interview to be between only her and Lesley and had ended his call by stipulating exactly what she could and couldn't say during the course of it. While outlining what details could be imparted was standard when an SIO prepped the FLO ahead of interviews, the threat that came attached to Umpire's briefing wasn't.

'I don't want you to mention the lubricant when you talk to Lesley,' he'd said. 'I want to keep it quiet for now, in case we need it for leverage further down the line. If you get another attack of conscience, DC Neville, come straight to me and we'll deal with it. I won't tolerate a repeat of the Megan Fowler case, got that? Because this time you won't just get kicked off DI Gant's roster – I'll have you back in uniform. Am I making myself clear?'

'Yes, sir,' she said quietly, knowing he meant it.

Once off the phone, Maggie wrote down in her notebook the questions she needed to ask Lesley and how
best to word them, particularly the ones relating to the
mysterious Suzy Breed. During training it was drummed
into FLOs that if questions were not posed sensitively
they could arouse far more suspicion than intended.

'Lesley, I need to talk to you.'

There was a nod, but Lesley did not avert her gaze
from the screen. Maggie reached over, took the remote
control out of her hand and turned the television off.
Lesley looked round and glared at her.

'I'm sorry,' said Maggie, 'but it's really important we
do this now.'

She must have sounded serious enough to shake
Lesley out of her stupor.

'Has something happened?' she asked.

'Not exactly. We've got a couple of specific lines of
inquiry we're urgently following up and that's why I
need to interview you now.'

'Interview?' said Lesley worriedly.

'It's what we call a witness interview. I'll ask you some
questions and take notes, which I will then pass back to
DCI Umpire. You're not under caution or anything like
that,' she assured her. 'We just want to clarify some
details about Rosie, in particular about her skirt.'

Lesley's face mottled and she bit her bottom lip.

'Are you fine for me to start?'

'I guess.'

'You said yesterday you have two women who come in
every Friday to help, is that right?'

'Yes, Joasia and Alicja. They're sisters, from Poland.

We employ them through an agency. Why? Do they know something?'

'No. They've been interviewed by my colleagues and can account for their whereabouts yesterday morning. What are their main tasks on Fridays?'

'They clean the house and do our laundry.'

'Do you oversee that?'

'What do you mean?'

'Sorry, I meant do you decide what needs to be washed and get it ready for them?'

'Oh, I see. Yes, I take my and Mack's clothes down to the laundry room on Friday morning, but they collect all the bedding from all the rooms and also Rosie's washing because she doesn't like me going in her bedroom.' A tear escaped the corner of Lesley's eye but she wiped it swiftly away.

'That must be a lot of washing.'

'They're here all day on Friday, so they put the first load on when they arrive and either dry it outside or put it in the tumble dryer. They usually do two or three washes. But I don't always leave it to them,' Lesley added hotly. 'If something needs washing urgently, I do it myself. Or I'll do the delicates that can't be machine-washed by hand.'

The conversation was going exactly the way Maggie hoped it would.

'Is Rosie's skirt something you might wash yourself?'

Lesley's face went even redder.

'All those sequins . . . it couldn't go in the washing machine, could it?' Maggie probed. 'And I'm guessing that if it's hand-washed separately, it doesn't go on the line with the rest of the washing where Mack can see it.'

Lesley's expression – pinched and scared – betrayed her.

'When I spoke to him this morning, he was adamant it's not Rosie's skirt,' Maggie continued. 'But you said you bought it for her, didn't you?' She was careful to make it sound like a statement of fact rather than an accusation.

Eventually Lesley nodded.

'Yes, I did. She begged me to. She just wanted something like her friends would wear.'

'What occasion did she want it for?'

'A birthday party for one of the girls from school,' said Lesley, her voice barely above a whisper now. 'It was a Friday night when Mack was away golfing. I said she could go.'

'He doesn't know she went?'

'He gets het up about her going out so I thought if he didn't know, it wouldn't hurt him. She wasn't out all hours, she was home just after midnight.'

'Who was the friend?'

'Her name is Sasha. She was on the list of friends I gave to the police yesterday.'

'Is that the only occasion Rosie's worn the skirt?'

'There have been a couple of other times. A couple of weeks ago she had a sleepover at Kathryn's and took it with her. She just wants to be like her friends.'

Maggie backtracked. 'Sasha's party – was it just girls from their school or were there others there?'

'To be honest, Rosie didn't say much about it, other than she had a good time,' said Lesley. 'I know Lily went and she doesn't go to their school, so there must've been others. Oh, do you mean boys? That I don't know. Rosie never said.'

'Does she have any friends who are boys?'

'She had a couple when we lived in Mansell, but they were the sons of friends that we don't see any more. I doubt she still talks to them either.'

'Yesterday you said you were sure she's not seeing anyone.'

Lesley stared at her. 'She isn't, but you asking me again makes me think you know something I don't.'

'I honestly don't,' said Maggie, and she gave the explanation she always reached for when someone got rattled during questioning. 'My job as your family liaison – and Belmar's – is to build up a picture of Rosie's life, from the tiniest details like what she eats for breakfast to the clothes she wears and who she spends the most time with. Sometimes we have to go over the same ground and repeat certain questions to ensure we're being as accurate as possible when we report back to the rest of the team. It doesn't mean we're fixated on a particular subject, we're just being thorough.'

'Okay, I'm sorry. This is just so difficult.'

'I know, but if I don't ask the questions, I might miss something. So, on the subject of boyfriends still, is there a chance Rosie might be seeing someone but keeping it a secret because she's scared of what Mack might say?'

'I don't think she would take the risk. She knows Mack would ground her for lying to us. He says she has to wait until she's sixteen to have a boyfriend and even then it has to be someone he's met and is happy with.'

'Has he always been so strict?'

'I suppose so, but he just sees it as being protective. He has got worse since we won the money though. I think he worries she'll get taken advantage of.'

'Does she chat to her friends online a lot?'

'Yes, she's always on her iPad or she uses apps on her phone.'

'So she could be talking to a boy that way?'

'It's possible,' Lesley conceded. 'Mack wouldn't dream of checking either because he trusts her to not disobey him.'

Maggie knew the High Tech Crime Unit was already going through Rosie's iPad and social media profiles to check her online history. If she was engaged in some kind of cyber romance, they'd soon know about it.

'I don't think Rosie would break his trust either. She's not devious like some teenagers who give their parents the runaround. She can be stroppy and argumentative, but really she's quite immature for her age, which is partly my fault.'

'Why?'

Tears slid down Lesley's face. 'I babied her too much when she was little because she's an only child.'

'Did you never want more children?'

'Mack didn't. I was thirty-three when I had Rosie and it was a difficult pregnancy, so when he said one was enough I went along with it. It's not something I've deeply regretted either: I had friends with children the same age as Rosie who went on to have a second baby and when I watched them struggle with two I was glad I only had her to worry about. But now,' she gulped back a huge sob, 'I keep thinking what this would be like if Rosie had a brother or sister.'

'How do you mean?' asked Maggie gently.

'What if you never find her? What if she's dead?' Lesley's voice broke. 'Being a mum is all I'm good for. If she doesn't come back, what's the point of going on? What will I do?'

Maggie let her cry. She had no answer to salve her distress and she wasn't going to insult her with a clumsy attempt at pretending everything was going to be okay. Because right now none of them knew if it would be. At the same time, she made a mental note to call Victim Support for advice. Even if Mack and Lesley wouldn't talk to them directly just yet, they might still be able to help.

'I'm sorry,' said Lesley eventually. 'You must think I'm awful. It must sound like I want to replace Rosie, but that's not how I meant it. I just, well—'

'I didn't think that's what you meant.'

'Do you have children?'

'No, but I hope to one day. My sister has three, two boys and a girl, and I spend a lot of time with them. I can't imagine not having my own,' said Maggie, truthfully.

'Three? She's brave,' said Lesley, managing a small smile.

'I'm not sure that's how she sees it.'

Maggie glanced down at her notebook to remind herself what else she needed to ask. The name Suzy Breed leapt out from the page.

'There is one more thing I want to check,' she said,

mindful of how she posed the question. 'We're working through the list of people that Rosie comes into regular contact with, and someone's mentioned Suzy Breed as an acquaintance. Does that name mean anything to you?'

Lesley frowned. 'Where did you hear that?'

Maggie was deliberately vague. 'I'm not sure. DCI Umpire passed it on to me. Do you know her?'

'Not really, but Mack does.'

'In what way?'

'Suzy was his first girlfriend. They went out in their last year at school. They haven't spoken in years though, because she moved to New Zealand in her late twenties and they lost touch. I met her once or twice before she left but that was it. I can't think why her name would come up now.'

'So she's never met Rosie?'

'No. She emigrated a few years before Rosie was born. Suzy wouldn't have seen a picture of Rosie, let alone met her, because she and Mack aren't even Facebook friends. I've never mentioned her to Rosie and I'd be surprised if he has, so Rosie wouldn't have a clue about who she is. None at all.'

19

Satisfied she'd covered everything Umpire wanted her to, Maggie closed her notebook. But Lesley wasn't done yet. She chewed nervously on a fingernail.

'I've been thinking about what you said about Rosie cutting herself. I still don't think she does, but I am starting to wonder if there was something bothering her, something other than her exams,' she said.

'Go on,' said Maggie, flipping her notebook open again.

'She's been very moody lately, more so than usual. I guess I just put it down to her schoolwork and being a teenager, but now I think there was more to it. She hasn't been sleeping well lately, either waking really early or getting up in the night to come downstairs and watch TV. I asked her about it and she said she was fine. I guess I should've kept on until she told me.'

'Any idea what it could be?'

'That's the problem, I don't know. It could be something to do with her friends, it could be something to do with us.'

'Okay, well let's start with that. Has anything happened at home that's unsettled her?'

'Besides winning fifteen million? Sorry, I shouldn't be glib,' she said apologetically. 'I suppose there has been some tension between me and Mack that Rosie might have picked up on. You've probably noticed it too. The thing is, I'm not comfortable with having lots of money. I struggle with spending it, whereas Mack has no problem. It just seems so . . . so wasteful. There are things he buys that I think we just don't need, like clothes and jewellery and paintings I can't stand the look of. Thousands and thousands of pounds on, well, tat.'

'And Mack doesn't understand how you feel?'

'Doesn't care, more like. Actually, I'm being unfair. He just wants us to enjoy ourselves. But I can't seem to. It stresses me out, the responsibility of having all that money. I've even lost weight worrying about it.'

That would explain the photograph in the hallway of Lesley looking plumper, thought Maggie. It must've been taken before the win, when she was happier.

'Do you argue about it in front of Rosie?'

'We've always tried not to row when she's around as a rule, but I imagine she has heard us, yes.'

'This is an awkward question, I know, but if she were to take sides, whose would she take?'

Lesley flushed. 'Mack's. They've always been as thick as thieves, ever since she was little. She adores him.'

'Do you think she might have confided in him about whatever was bothering her, and for whatever reason he's chosen not to tell you?' said Maggie. 'Are they inclined to keep things from you?'

Lesley nodded. 'Take the new shoes missing from her room. He bought them for her knowing I'd said she couldn't have them. That's typical of them both. I meant it when I said I was the one who gets in their way.'

'But she definitely wouldn't discuss relationships with Mack, would she? Knowing how he feels about boyfriends.'

'No, she wouldn't.'

'So if what's bothering her is something along those lines, the chances are she wouldn't talk to either of you about it?'

'I guess not.' Lesley groaned and rubbed her face with her hands. 'I feel terrible.'

'If Rosie doesn't want to talk to you, that's not your fault—'

'No, I mean I actually feel terrible. I feel grimy.'

Maggie knew it was a good time to take a break.

'Look, I think we're done here and I've covered everything I need to, so why don't you have a shower before the press conference?'

Lesley pulled a face. 'To look nice for the cameras?'

'No, it's not about you looking your best, that's not important. I just think you'll feel a bit better if you freshen up. To be honest, I could do with a shower myself.'

'You should've said,' Lesley exclaimed, getting to her feet. 'Come with me, I'll show you to one of the guest bedrooms. You can use it tonight if, well . . .'

Maggie nipped outside to the driveway to get her overnight bag from her car. At the same time she quickly tried to call Umpire to tell him about the interview but he didn't answer. She left a message. Back indoors, Lesley led her upstairs to one of the bedrooms at the opposite end of the corridor to Rosie's bedroom, one door down from Mack's study. As they passed, she could hear the low hum of voices but couldn't make out whose.

'Here you go,' said Lesley, pushing the door open.

'Wow, this is lovely,' said Maggie, shrugging her suit jacket off as she stepped through the doorway.

The guest room was twice the size of the main bedroom in Maggie's flat. The floors were stripped pine, matching the double wardrobe along one wall and the beautiful dressing table in the corner next to the window. The room's centrepiece was a king-size bed covered in a snow-white duvet and scattered with half a dozen crimson pillows in different shapes and sizes. The walls were painted a soft cream and there were red-and-white-checked curtains hanging at the window. It was the kind of room that made Maggie wish she were more creative when it came to decorating.

'The bathroom is just through there,' said Lesley, pointing to a door along the wall between the wardrobe and the dressing table. 'You'll find everything you need, shampoo, shower gel, towels. There's also a hairdryer in the cabinet under the sink.'

'Thank you,' said Maggie. 'I won't be long.'

'Take as long as you like.'

Lesley was about to leave, but stopped by the door. Looking nervous again, she twisted her wedding ring round her finger.

'About what I said downstairs just now . . . I don't want you to think Mack and I aren't happy. We do argue about the money, but on the whole our marriage is fine. We've been together for eighteen years now and it'll take more than a few million to split us up.'

The bathroom was as luxurious as the bedroom, with a shower large enough to fit two people. Maggie lathered shampoo into her hair as water blasted down on her – it was so powerful her skin went numb where it hit. She felt her fatigue wash away with the shampoo suds and by the time she'd rinsed the second application out of her hair, her mind was buzzing again.

She couldn't wait to speak to Umpire and tell him what Lesley had said during her interview. Hopefully he'd be pleased with how she did and it would no longer feel like she was treading on eggshells around him.

Shower done, she quickly dried her hair and rooted around her holdall for the make-up bag that contained a few basic essentials: blusher, mascara, pressed powder. She never wore lipstick because she couldn't stand her lips being sticky. She got dressed in fresh clothes, repacked her bag and went to take it back downstairs to her car.

The thick carpet muffled her footsteps as she padded down the hallway. As she approached Mack's office, she realized the door was open and she could hear him talking to someone. Thinking it was Belmar she stopped to say something, then caught a glimpse of Mack through the open crack and saw he was alone and on the phone. He didn't notice her, though, because he was too busy whispering angrily at whoever was on the other end of the call.

'Stop ringing me,' she heard him say. 'I won't tell you again.'

Maggie knew it was wrong to eavesdrop on a private conversation and that she should carry on walking but she couldn't drag herself away.

'I don't want Lesley knowing about this,' Mack went on. 'Yes, of course I'm going to tell her, I told you I would, but not right now. Not with Rosie missing.' He suddenly swore. 'Don't be so fucking selfish. I told you I'd fix it and I will. Now leave me alone.'

20

A week after their win, when it still hadn't sunk in despite the champagne ceremony and an oversized cheque for the full amount being handed to them, despite their faces being all over the papers, Lesley drove to their nearest Sainsbury's, to the row of cash machines lined up outside the entrance. In a daze she printed out dozens of balance receipts and each one told her the same thing: Lesley Kinnock, you are rich beyond your wildest dreams.

Then someone recognized her and a crowd gathered. They all wanted to know the same thing: what did it feel like to have so much money and what was she spending it on? She could still remember that horrible feeling of being cornered. Nervous and tense, she'd tried to walk away but the crowd took that as a sign she was blanking them. Someone shouted, 'Fucking snob!' at her retreating back as she hurried to her car.

Someone took her photo too, presumably on a phone given the quality of the image that appeared in one of the national tabloids the day after. It showed Lesley checking one of the balance receipts, her face set in a frown, under the headline: *EURO OUT OF LUCK!* The same someone had given the paper false quotes claiming she wasn't able to get any money out of the machine and the piece was littered with puns about her being cash strapped.

Lesley wondered if the reporter who wrote the story was among the group waiting in the conference room next door. She, Mack and Maggie were holed up in a small office on the first floor of Mansell police station and she could hear the buzz of voices in the conference room next door growing louder as the minutes ticked by until the start of the press conference.

She plucked at the hem of her cardigan. It was one she hated, bought at Mack's insistence during a shopping trip to London. Pale green, cashmere, with ribbon-covered buttons, it didn't suit her colouring and made her look washed out.

Maggie had been right about the shower helping though. As she had stood beneath the jet of hot water and let it pound against her skin, for a moment she had felt revived. But the respite didn't last and panic overwhelmed her as she thought about Rosie and where she could be. She'd dropped to her knees and cried and that was where Mack found her, hunched over on the shower floor, water spraying relentlessly against the curve of her spine. Without a word he stepped into the cubicle, took her in his arms and held her as her tears washed down the plughole with the shower spray. It was only after, when he lifted her out and gently wrapped her in a towel, that Lesley realized he'd been fully dressed the entire time.

He stood by the window, watching the white-grey clouds gather speed across the darkening sky. The white shirt and navy trousers that were soaked by the shower had been swapped for an identical white shirt and a pair of grey cords. He decided at the last minute not to wear a tie because, he rationalized to Lesley, Rosie rarely saw him in one since he'd given up work and she might think it odd if, somehow, by some miracle, she watched the press conference on TV.

His face was set in a frown as he watched the clouds and she knew he was dealing with their daughter's disappearance the only way he knew how, by keeping his emotions tightly coiled inside. It was an insular coping mechanism she'd grown used to over the years they'd been together. 'That man's so stoic it'll take a hurricane to bend him,' her mother had observed the first time Lesley took him home. She had taken the comment to be a compliment but her mother confided some years later, after she and Mack were married, that she feared her son-in-law's tendency to put on a front might make Lesley unhappy in the long run. 'I don't know if he'll let his guard down enough to love you in the way you need to be loved.'

But Mack did love her, in his own way. He might struggle to pay her compliments and she could count on one hand the times he'd bought her flowers, but Lesley never felt lonely in her marriage. Even when quiet, Mack had a looming presence and she always found comfort in knowing he was close by, as did Rosie.

She had yet to tell him about Maggie mentioning Suzy Breed to her. She was perplexed as to why her name would've suddenly come up and it felt strange to suddenly be reminded of the girl, or rather woman, who had once been such a target for her jealousy. Suzy Breed was the only girl Mack had really loved before her and for a long time Lesley felt like she was stuck in her shadow. It was only when Mack proposed that she finally exorcized the ghost of their relationship. What possible reason was there for Maggie to mention her now? She wanted to speak to Maggie again about it before she told Mack.

The office they'd been asked to wait in was small and basic but Lesley found its sterility oddly comforting. With just a square table, four chairs and beige walls, it was frugal in a way she found she missed living in Angel's Reach, with its opulent wallpaper, inches-thick carpet and huge rooms. Cool air breezed into the room from a unit on the wall above the clock, making her shiver. She pulled the cardigan tighter around her. Beneath it she wore a plain white cotton shift dress.

Nearly half an hour had passed since they'd arrived and she asked Maggie, who was sitting at the table next to her, why it was taking so long.

'They're still setting up. It won't be much longer. You can blame my driving – I'm afraid I got us here a bit too early.'

Lesley cupped her face in her hands as bile rose in her throat. She was petrified of saying the wrong thing in front of the press, even though in the car on the way there Mack said he would speak about Rosie on their behalf.

She felt a hand gently touch her arm.

'Are you okay?' asked Maggie.

She looked up and nodded, not trusting herself to speak. The buzz from next door rose abruptly, as if the door had been opened and the noise suddenly escaped. Her eyes widened in panic.

'I can't do it. I can't face them.'

Mack hurried over and knelt down by her chair. His eyes were red-rimmed and he looked exhausted. Seeing him in that state made her want to cry and she fought back tears as he held her hand.

'Sweetheart, we need to do this for Rosie,' he said, his voice thick with emotion. 'She needs both of us out there telling the world what an amazing kid she is and why we want her to come home. If someone's got her, we need to show the bastard she has a mum and dad who are suffering because we don't know where she is. I can't do it by myself. I need you with me.'

Lesley nodded as he gently wiped the tears from her cheeks.

A second later there was a knock on the door and DCI Umpire entered solemnly. He looked at them and then looked at Maggie, who nodded.

'We're ready,' she said.

Umpire sat down next to Lesley. Mack remained crouched beside her.

'The press conference should be straightforward. I'll be speaking first and releasing some details I hope will help encourage witnesses to come forward,' he said. 'Then, if you feel able to, you can address the room directly. Tell them what Rosie's like as a daughter and why you think she would never go off without telling you. Tell them how much you miss her and want her home. If the press have any questions at the end, I'll deal with them. Do you want to ask me anything before we go in?'

'Yes,' said Lesley, faltering. 'Will this work? Will this help find her?'

DCI Umpire looked grim. 'I sincerely hope so.'

The room lit up as he led them in. Lesley's instinct was to shield her eyes against the camera flashes with her hand but, mindful of how that would look, she instead lurched forward with her head bowed, clinging to Mack's hand. At the front of the room, in front of a blue back-drop with the police force's logo on it, was a table covered in microphones propped up on mini tripods. Lesley and Mack sat down with DCI Umpire alongside them. Glancing to her right she saw Maggie and Belmar standing at the side of the room with their backs pressed against the wall. Their presence was comforting.

As Umpire began his introduction, Lesley stared at the surface of the table. She didn't want to watch the press watching her and waiting for her to react. She wanted to pretend they weren't there, that this wasn't happening to her and Mack, and so she willed herself to block out the sound of Umpire's voice as he thanked everyone for coming and began to recount the timeline of events that had brought her and Mack to a police conference room with a carpet the texture of a Brillo Pad and an underlying smell of stale sweat.

Her mind rolled back to the previous morning, to the last time she'd seen Rosie. Had the start of the day been different to any other? Rosie was up early by her usual standards, just after 8 a.m. Another night of not being able to sleep, which Lesley put down to exam stress. Perhaps there had been more to it. God, she wished she'd asked her.

They had eaten breakfast in silence but there was nothing odd about that, as Rosie was always monosyllabic before 9 a.m. There had been one brief interlude though, when she'd asked if her dad had rung yet.

'I doubt he's up yet,' said Lesley, finishing the last bite of her toast. 'But you can give him a try if you want.'

'What, and have him get the hump with me because he's got a hangover? No way.'

They had both laughed because it was a standing joke that Mack couldn't handle his drink – he was the antithesis of what the reputation of Scotsmen dictated. As Rosie pretended to vomit into her cereal bowl and dissolved into giggles, Lesley revelled in the brief suspension of hostilities. When they weren't arguing or ignoring each other, the atmosphere could be wonderful.

DCI Umpire's voice eventually broke through her self-imposed daze. She tried to shut the sound of him out but her ears refused to obey and eventually her mind joined them in focusing on what he was saying.

'An item of Rosie's clothing has been recovered from an area close to her house that indicates she has not gone missing of her own volition. I shan't reveal any more detail at this stage but I cannot stress enough how important it is that anyone who knows anything or saw anything comes forward. Rosie's parents are suffering greatly right now and want her home . . .'

Umpire cleared his throat and Lesley finally looked

up to see dozens of strange faces staring solemnly at her. There was one on the front row she recognized, a female reporter for the *Mansell Echo* who interviewed them after their win. As their eyes locked, Lesley realized the girl's were wet and shiny, as though she was fighting back tears. It shocked Lesley and she began to cry. She was only distantly aware of Umpire asking Mack if he wanted to say anything.

'I do,' he said, getting to his feet.

Then all hell broke loose.

21

He perched on the edge of the sofa with his hands clasped in front of him, fingers interlaced as though in prayer. As he watched the parents take their places alongside the police officer in charge, he felt surprisingly calm and imagined that anyone listening to the relaxed rhythm of his heart would think he was watching something as sedate as it was innocuous, like the *Antiques Roadshow* or *Countryfile*, and not a press conference about the girl whose disappearance could see him sent to prison for a very long time.

He'd nearly missed it, too. He was walking through the gym to collect his next client from reception when he'd caught sight of the large TV screen above the rowing machines. It was tuned to Sky News and the ticker along the bottom said a press conference about missing teenager Rosie Kinnock would take place in half an hour, at 3.30 p.m. He sacked off his client by feigning a migraine and rushed home.

He aimed the remote at the TV to turn the volume up. As the officer in charge began talking, a picture of the girl's smiling face filled the screen. How different she looked to yesterday when she'd backed away from him on all fours like a crab scuttling along sand, her face contorted in terror. When he'd raised a hand to her she'd sprawled backwards onto the grass but never cried out. It was as though she had no more screams to give.

On the television the mum had started crying. Not silent tears but great, undignified sobs.

'What kind of woman goes out and leaves her child like that?' he spat out loud, as if he was addressing her directly. 'The selfish kind, that's who. And I know just how selfish you are, because I've been on the receiving end of it. You shoved ahead of me that day as though I didn't exist. Didn't even look at me, let alone say thank you for what I did.'

The memory made him burn with anger. Lesley Kinnock did not warrant anyone's sympathy. She was a thief. She stole from him and losing her daughter in return was a just punishment as far as he was concerned. It wasn't like she even wanted the money she took from him: on the few occasions she left the house and he was able to follow her, she always looked as though she had the weight of the world bearing down on her. What the fuck did she have to worry about? People like her didn't deserve to be rich.

The dad was talking now and he turned the television up even louder. As he watched the man plead for his daughter's return, pressure began to build in his temples. Soon the pain was too intense for him to concentrate and he jumped to his feet. 'SHUT UP! SHUT UP! SHUT UP!' he screamed as he clenched his fists against the sides of his head and willed the avalanche of white noise to stop. Harder he clenched, until eventually the noise began to abate and it was replaced by shouting coming from the television. He snapped open his eyes to see that the press conference was in uproar. The dad was trying to say something directly into the camera but the police officer was talking over him and the mum was telling him to stop as she pulled at the front of his shirt.

'No, that can't be right,' he muttered aloud.

He grabbed the remote control and rewound until the moment the dad got to his feet. Pressing play, he watched open-mouthed as anger exploded inside him like a bomb going off. Didn't he warn the stupid bitch of a mother that they weren't to spend any more until he'd got his rightful share?

All he wanted was enough to stop the agonizing pain he was in. There was a doctor in the States he'd found online who was pioneering a new technique to treat his type of spinal injury but charged the price of a house to do so. If the girl's parents had just given him what he needed when he'd first asked for it, it wouldn't have gone this far. It was their fault.

His injury could've been a lot worse, so his doctors said. An act of extreme folly is how the police described what happened. Egged on by his equally inebriated and now former best friend, he had almost scaled the scaffolding veiling the three-storey building when he lost his grip and fell backwards. Wooden boards that had been fashioned into a platform halfway down broke his fall and his surgeon said he was lucky not to be paralysed. Instead, all he had to contend with was a lifetime of constant pain. Lucky him!

That's why he wanted the money, to get his back fixed properly. The steroids could only do so much and while he knew from his own training that working out was important to keep the muscles surrounding his spine as strong as possible, what was he meant to do when he got older? Wither away? Already it was becoming harder to do his job: he had to turn down clients with more complicated injuries because his back hurt too much when he had to adopt certain positions.

He burned with fury as he watched the commotion on screen.

'YOU'RE MEANT TO GIVE THE MONEY TO ME!'

22

The reporters were on their feet, bellowing questions at Mack, and the noise pinned Maggie to the wall. They all looked as stunned as she was and were all asking the same thing: 'Mr Kinnock, are you really offering a million pounds as a reward to find your daughter?' Then Umpire caught her eye and she propelled herself into action. Rushing to the front of the room, she practically tipped Lesley out of her seat and guided her out of the room and back into the office while Umpire did the same with Mack. His face claret with fury, Umpire told Maggie to leave them alone and slammed the door shut behind her. As she walked away, in no mood to contradict him, she heard Mack shouting.

Maggie went in search of Belmar and collared him further along the corridor. He, too, looked dazed. Speaking in a low voice so as not to be overheard – the corridor was filling up with journalists tapping excitedly on their mobiles and tablets, anxious to be the first to report on what had happened – she asked him if he'd known Mack was going to put up the reward.

'Not exactly,' said Belmar, beads of sweat glistening

on the skin below his trim hairline. 'Earlier on he asked if it was usual in cases like this. But it was just a passing mention.'

'That's bad enough,' said Maggie with a groan.

'I put him straight though.'

A reporter stopped beside them. He was talking into his mobile but Maggie couldn't tell if he was faking the call to listen to them, so she pulled an unresisting Belmar further along the corridor by the arm.

'How did you put him straight? I need to know exactly what you said to him.'

'I said it was probably too early to think about that and he should talk to the DCI. I also said that even if the investigation did go down that route there were strict guidelines that needed to be followed. After that he changed the subject.' Belmar sagged against the corridor wall. 'Ballboy's going to go mental, isn't he?'

'He's not going to be happy, no. A reward that size will have every chancer and nutter from Cornwall to Carlisle crawling out of the woodwork claiming they've got information about where Rosie is and the team will have to check out each one. It'll slow things down.'

'What should I say if Ballboy asks if I knew?'

Maggie had to think fast. Mack pledging a million pounds to find Rosie was an unmitigated disaster. It was the biggest reward she could recall anyone offering and now the media focus would be on that instead of finding Rosie. But right now her priority was also to ensure they weren't unfairly blamed for it and taken off the case. As the officers entrenched in the family home, people would assume they must've known about it.

'Did you record the chat in your log?' she said.

Belmar shook his head. 'Not yet. I write mine up at the end of the day.'

'Do it now. Make sure you write down exactly what you just told me – that it was a casual remark by Mack and you told him explicitly there were procedures to follow and that he should talk to Umpire.'

'You want me to doctor my log?' said Belmar, shocked.

'It's not doctoring when you're writing down what was actually said,' she hissed. 'I just want you to fill it out now instead of later.'

'But if the DCI finds out—'

'If he brings it up, I'll just say Mack raised the subject and you've recorded it in your log as a passing comment but had you suspected for a single second he was going to pull that stunt, you'd have gone straight to him about it.'

'You think he'll buy it?'

'I'll make sure he does. Go on, go and do it now.'

Bracing herself, she knocked on the office door then entered before Umpire could tell her to stay out. Suit jacket removed and shirtsleeves rolled up, he leaned over the table, hands splayed out on its surface like he was doing a press-up, the lean muscles of his forearms taut with tension. He was trying to reason with Mack, whose own arms were crossed defiantly over his chest.

'The reward you're offering is not going to help us find your daughter any quicker,' Umpire was saying. 'If you won't withdraw it we'll have to find some way to reduce it instead.'

'No way,' said Mack. 'What would Rosie think?' He

affected a voice that was high and shrill, like an old woman's. "'Oh look, love, your dad's changed his mind and decided you're not worth it after all.'" He shook his head. 'No, the reward stands.'

Umpire glared at Maggie and she met his steely gaze full on. She'd done nothing wrong and while Belmar was an idiot for not mentioning Mack's question about a reward sooner, neither had he. No one could've predicted what Mack would do faced with a room full of journalists. Then she glanced across at Lesley and her heart sank.

She looked like she'd aged twenty years. Her eyes were unfocused as they gazed at the opposite wall and her posture was slack, as though her body was being crushed by the enormity of the situation she faced. Maggie had seen it happen before. Facing the press meant families having to admit the situation was real and not a horrible, terrifying nightmare they would at some point wake up from. Ignoring Umpire, she crouched down by Lesley's side.

'How are you doing?' she whispered.

Lesley looked at her like she had no idea who Maggie was.

'She needs to go home and get some rest,' she said to Umpire. 'They both do.'

Umpire looked at Mack, who was by the window with his back to the room. The discussion was over as far as he was concerned.

'Fine. Take them home and I'll call you after the next briefing.'

'Did you hear that, Lesley?' said Maggie. 'You're going home now.'

Maggie smiled gratefully at Umpire. He could've chosen to hammer away at Mack over the reward until he cracked but instead he'd listened to her. As he said his goodbyes and left the room, she could've sworn he gave her the briefest of winks. Was it further proof of a thaw towards her? After what Belmar had said about them, she didn't want to think it meant anything else.

'Belmar is going to drive you home and I'll follow in a bit,' Maggie told the Kinnocks. 'There's something I have to do first.' Neither acknowledged they'd heard her, so she left them in the office and went to find Belmar. He was in the now-empty conference room, sitting alone on a row of chairs as he wrote out his log. Quickly she filled him in on the argument she'd interrupted between Mack and Umpire.

'Mack won't budge on the reward so the DCI said we should take them home,' she finished.

'When he came out and saw me here I thought he was going to ask me about the reward but he didn't,' said Belmar, setting down his pen. 'Thanks for backing me up. I appreciate it.'

'If you really want to thank me, you can take Mack and Lesley back by yourself while I run a quick errand.'

'But we came in your car. Mine's back in Haxton.'

'Your insurance covers you to drive other vehicles, doesn't it? So take mine.' She gave him the keys.

'How will you get back?'

'I'll cadge a lift from uniform or get a taxi if needs be. I won't be long – an hour, tops. But, listen, if Lesley's still in a state when you get back to Angel's Reach, call a doctor out to check her over.'

'Sure. So where are you going?'

She gave him a wry smile. 'To do a money drop.'

23

Lou lived in a mid-terrace house on a road on the out-skirts of the town centre. It was a fifteen-minute walk from the police station and Maggie texted ahead to say she was coming. As she approached the front door, it swung open and Lou greeted her with a scowl on her face and Mae balanced on her hip.

'Have you got my twenty quid?' she said brusquely.

Maggie sighed. She was too tired to be goaded into a row and clearly Lou was angling for one. Instead of answering she reached over and took hold of Mae, who crowed with delight to see her.

'Can I come in?' she said, cuddling her niece to her chest.

Lou stood aside to let her pass. There was no hallway leading from the door, so Maggie stepped straight from the pavement into the small lounge.

'I'm doing spag bol for tea,' said Lou.

'Sounds great but I can't stay.'

Mae wailed as Lou snatched her back from Maggie's arms.

'If you're not stopping you may as well go now. The

boys are down the road at Toby's playing Xbox, but I'll tell them you couldn't spare the time to wait for them. Let yourself out.'

Lou flounced into the kitchen. Maggie went after her.

'Hey, don't you think you're overreacting?'

Lou ignored her as she lowered Mae into her high chair and gave her a lion-shaped rattle to chew on. She opened the fridge door and took out a sealed tray of raw mince, which she lobbed onto the counter beside the oven. A foul stench suddenly filled the room.

'Christ, what's that smell?' said Maggie.

'Nothing,' said Lou, taking a couple of carrots from the crisper drawer and shutting the door quickly.

'It smells like something died in there.'

'Some chicken's gone out of date and I haven't had time to clear it out, okay?' she said testily.

As she looked around, Maggie saw the entire kitchen needed cleaning. Dirty crockery was piled precariously in the sink and every worktop was littered with the debris of a dozen meals: half-full baked bean tins and packaging for a ready meal shepherd's pie jostled for position next to a Honey Monster Puffs cereal box and an empty four-litre plastic milk bottle. On the hob was a white patch where something had spilled and dried out. The mess unnerved her – even with three kids to look after, Lou always kept the house neat. Her own flat was a tip by contrast because she was rarely there to tidy it.

'Lou, what's wrong?'

'Nothing. I haven't had a chance to tidy up because you've not been here to mind the kids while I do it.'

Lou threw a carrot into the sink, knocking a stack of

unwashed mugs over. Then she leaned back against the sink unit, clutching the edge with her hands. It was then Maggie realized that Lou looked as much of a state as the kitchen. Her bright pink top had unidentifiable stains all down the front and her denim boot-cut jeans looked like they hadn't been washed for weeks. They also emphasized how much weight she'd gained in recent months. Already on the plump side before she got pregnant with Mae, Lou had put on at least another stone since giving birth. Her stomach spilled over the waistband of her jeans and the line of her bra beneath her top revealed it was too small to fully contain her large breasts. Her auburn hair, usually a sleek, graduated bob, was now an unconditioned cloud of split ends. Maggie felt awful: she spent so much time with her sister and yet somehow she'd become immune to the obvious signs she was struggling.

'Lou, is everything okay?' she asked.

'Rob came round earlier.'

Maggie scowled at the mention of Lou's estranged husband.

'What did he want?'

'He's asked for a divorce.'

'Oh, Lou.'

She went over and gave her sister a hug. She wasn't a fan of Rob's but she knew Lou loved him and how much she wanted their relationship to work. Their marriage, though rocky at times, gave her and the boys the stability they needed and Jude and Scotty had missed him terribly since he'd moved out. Rob was the only dad either of them had known.

'He says he wants a divorce so he can marry *her*,' said Lou, her deep-set hazel eyes brimming with tears.

'Her' was Lisa, Rob's new girlfriend. They'd met when Lisa began working part-time as a receptionist at the gym Rob was a member of and it wasn't long before their flirty exchanges by the front desk had spilled over into a physical affair. Within two months Rob had walked out on Lou to move in with her.

'I'm so sorry.'

'I thought you'd be pleased.'

Maggie saw the pain etched on her sister's face and felt a wave of hatred towards Rob for the callous way in which he'd dumped her. There was no warning: he just got up one Sunday morning, packed a suitcase and left.

'Of course I'm not pleased. I hate the way he's treated you.'

'It's my fault though.'

'Don't you dare say that,' Maggie flared up. 'You didn't do anything wrong. He's the one who cheated.'

'Can you blame him looking elsewhere when he always felt like he was second best? No bloke likes to think he's not the love of your life. Rob has always felt like he's in Jerome's shadow.'

Maggie's pulse accelerated. She found it hard to talk about Lou's dead fiancé – she hated being reminded of what had happened.

'But you love Rob just as much.'

'He's never believed it though,' said Lou, emitting a long, sad sigh. 'He always went on and on about how you never forget your first love and that I must still be hung up on Jerome. In some ways he was right. You don't forget, do you?'

Maggie swallowed hard. 'No, you don't.'

'It's like you with Danny.'

Danny Burroughs was a fellow police cadet Maggie met at Hendon and the boyfriend Lou always assumed was her first love. Maggie had dated him for six months until the pressure of their new careers split them up. But while Maggie had liked him a lot, Danny wasn't her first real love. He wasn't the one who haunted her dreams, the one whose kiss she could still remember.

That honour went to Jerome as well.

She left Lou's a few minutes later with a promise to ring the boys before they went to bed to say goodnight. She also offered to talk to Rob about the money he owed.

'If he wants a divorce, you need to get him to start paying regular maintenance for Mae.'

Her sister agreed, albeit reluctantly. She wasn't in a rush for anything to be made formal because that would mean admitting her marriage really was over.

Ducking through the alleyway at the end of Lou's road, Maggie felt jittery and upset. Even now, a decade on, she still fretted when Jerome's name came up in conversation, as though Lou might suddenly guess after all this time what she'd done.

Their affair started at a friend's house party, when she was seventeen. Lou was at home in bed, felled by flu, so Maggie went alone. Halfway through the evening, having necked a quarter-bottle of Smirnoff on her own, she staggered outside for some air and bumped into Jerome smoking a joint with some lads she didn't know. She was thrilled when he introduced her to the group not as 'my girlfriend's little sister' but 'my friend Maggie'. They started chatting and one by one his friends drifted away and left them to it.

Maggie would never forget the look Jerome gave her just before he leaned over to kiss her. It made her skin blaze then and still made her shiver now when she thought about it. She knew she should've pushed him away, but the truth was she didn't want to. She'd fancied him from the second Lou brought him home; he was all she ever thought about and she wanted him for herself, regardless of the consequences. Ten minutes after that first kiss they had sex – her first time – on their friend's bathroom floor, which was everything she expected it to be with her back pressed against cold lino and someone banging on the door asking to use the loo. She didn't care though – it was still the best moment of her life up until that point. Afterwards, back downstairs, she tried to blame it on the vodka, telling Jerome it wouldn't have happened if she hadn't been hammered. But they both knew that was a lie and he just grinned and said, 'When can I see you again?'

For months they met in secret behind Lou's back, the guilt Maggie felt at betraying her overridden by the way she felt about Jerome. She loved him and to her teenage mind that took precedence over whatever her sister felt. Then Lou dropped an unexpected bombshell: she was pregnant.

Maggie hadn't expected the unplanned pregnancy to

change anything though, because she never thought Lou would go through with it. Her sister was only twenty and Jerome a year older: why would they want to be shackled with a kid? But Lou announced that not only was she keeping the baby, but she wanted to get married too. With both of their families piling on the pressure, Jerome proposed.

Lou wanted an engagement party in the function room of a local pub but it was the end of November and she feared everywhere would be booked up with Christmas office parties. So the following Friday lunchtime while she was at work – she was an accounts clerk for a skip hire firm – she sent Jerome, then unemployed, to speak to the landlord of one pub that still had some dates available. Maggie, looking for an excuse to spend time with him, offered to go as well to check the venue was okay and Lou agreed she should.

It wasn't easy listening to Jerome tell the landlord how excited he was about becoming a dad but Maggie knew he had to make it sound convincing. He'd reassured her nothing would change between them once the baby was born and, he promised, when the baby turned one, he would leave Lou and they'd be a proper couple. The teenage Maggie gave no thought to what that would do to her sister – she was too besotted to care.

After agreeing the fee, the landlord gave Jerome a pint on the house to celebrate and he and Maggie ended up spending the afternoon sitting in the pub and getting drunk. It was dark when they left around 6 p.m. and the blast of cold air that hit them when they walked out made them feel even more inebriated. Leaving the pub, they'd staggered down the road arm in arm.

What happened next remained scorched on Maggie's memory like it was branded with a hot iron. As they reached the zebra crossing, she'd tried to kiss Jerome but he ducked away. 'What if someone sees us?' he'd slurred. Too drunk to take any notice, she'd giggled and tried again, grabbing at the front of his coat to pull him towards her. By now Jerome was laughing too. Then, with no warning, he hollered, 'You can't catch me!' and jogged backwards onto the crossing – straight into the path of a car. The impact was so fast there was no time for either of them to react.

He landed on the pavement opposite, legs bent awkwardly beneath him and blood seeping from his ears and mouth. As the stricken driver of the car and other passersby tried to help, Maggie screamed at Jerome not to leave her, but he died less than a minute later as she cradled his head in her lap. Having to break the news to Lou that he'd been killed and that she'd watched it happen was the worst thing she'd ever had to do.

Afterwards, she couldn't mourn him properly, not in the way Lou was able to as his fiancée. She had to bury her grief deep inside where no one could see it and sit in anguished silence as a procession of friends and family paid their respects to her sister. Her only memento of their time together was a photo of the two of them with Lou, which she still kept in the drawer of her bedside cabinet along with a Valentine's card he'd sent her. Taken a month after the house party, the photo showed a grinning Jerome standing between the sisters with an arm around each of them.

The guilt finally kicked in six months after his death, when Jude was born. It devastated Maggie to know her nephew would grow up without his dad because of her. If Jerome hadn't run onto the crossing because she was trying to kiss him, he'd still be alive.

After that, ditching university to stay in Mansell and help Lou raise Jude seemed the least she could do. A decade of reflection had also altered her perspective on Jerome and she had come to accept what a shit he was to be sleeping with both of them at the same time. But acknowledging his duplicity didn't mean absolving herself from blame and her continuing guilt meant that whenever Lou needed something – money, babysitting, emotional support – she gave it without question.

But it was still nowhere near enough.

24

Lesley lay in a foetal position on her side of the bed. She had her back to Mack, who was stretched out on his side with his legs crossed at the ankles and his shoulders propped up on pillows. She could hear a faint *tap-tap-tap* as he pecked out messages on his phone.

She was pretending to be asleep and had been for half an hour, squeezing her eyelids shut to keep out the daylight. But her mind was too fretful to rest and the climax of the press conference played on a loop in her mind: Mack standing up . . . Umpire trying to stop him . . . the reporters going crazy with questions . . . Mack yanking his arm away as she tried to persuade him to sit down. The impact of his words didn't sink in at first. In fact, her first thought was could they afford to spare a million? Ludicrous now she thought about it. It was only when she clocked Umpire's frantic expression and the reporters' excited faces that it dawned on her Mack had just made a terrible mistake.

She squeezed her eyes tighter but it was no good. Her skin felt hot and prickly, as though her pent-up fury was trying to leach out through her pores. She rolled over on the bed to face her husband and sat up.

'You should never have said we'd pay that much.'

Mack, in the same grey cord trousers and white shirt he'd worn to the press conference, glared at her and climbed off his side of the bed. 'Don't start, I had enough earache from Umpire.'

She rolled off her side too, the bed a gulf between them. 'Well, he knows more about these things than you do. You heard what he said: we've got to withdraw the reward. It's too much.'

'No,' he said, hands balled into fists on his hips.

'Lower it then. Ask DCI Umpire what he thinks it should be.'

'I said no, and that's the end of it.'

'No, it's fucking not.'

Mack's eyes widened in shock and Lesley knew it was because she rarely swore, let alone answered him back.

'I'm warning you, Mack. Withdraw the reward or . . . or . . .'

'Or what? You're being hysterical, Lesley.'

'No, I'm putting our daughter first.'

'And I'm not? How is putting up a reward to find her me not putting her first?'

'Because this is not about Rosie: it's about you being the big man and flashing your money about.'

Mack reeled backwards as though she'd slapped him.

'How can you say that?' he rasped.

'Because it's true! All you care about is throwing money around and showing off to your mates down the golf club, who,' Lesley jabbed her index finger at him, 'wouldn't give a flying fuck if it wasn't for the fact you pay for everything.' She was shaking now and couldn't stop the words tumbling out of her mouth. Every one she aimed at him like a dart. 'We used to be happy, but now you care more about fucking Caesar beds and bathroom chandeliers than you do your own wife and child.'

She leapt forward and started yanking the duvet off the bed.

'It's crap,' she screamed. 'It's just stupid, expensive crap.'

She gathered as much of the duvet as she could in her arms and dragged the rest to the window. Flinging it open, she stuffed the duvet through the gap and watched it plummet onto the driveway below. The pillows went next. Mack stood frozen in shock on the other side of the bed.

She pushed her hair roughly off her face as she wrenched the door open to her walk-in wardrobe. Rows of never-been-worn clothes greeted her; designer outfits Mack picked out during their trips to London. She pulled as many items as she could from their hangers then raced to the window and flung them on top of the duvet and pillows down below.

'I don't want any of this!' she shrieked. 'Don't you get it? None of this will bring Rosie home. By making this about money, all you've done is make things worse.'

Mack finally lost his temper.

'Why do you hate us having money so much?' he shouted. 'Do you really want to go back to living in that shitty semi on that godawful estate? Be my guest! But don't tell me what I can and can't spend our money on.

Fuck it, I should've offered five million if that's what it takes to bring Rosie home.'

'Why, so you can impress Suzy Breed?'

Mack's face contorted.

'What are you talking about?'

'The police have been asking about your darling ex,' Lesley spat.

'Did they say why?'

Lesley stopped. She realized Mack no longer looked angry or surprised but worried.

'Does it matter? Suzy's in New Zealand still, isn't she?'

'How the fuck would I know?'

His expression made Lesley suddenly feel afraid. He was lying, she was sure of it.

'When was the last time you heard from her?'

'I don't know, years ago. Don't start all that again.'

'What?'

'You, banging on about me still wanting to be with Suzy. It was bollocks then and it's bollocks now.'

A chill ran through her.

'I wasn't thinking that. But now you mention it, don't you think it's strange the police have brought up her name?'

'I'm not having this conversation,' Mack said angrily. 'It's nonsense. We should be thinking about how to find Rosie. That's why I'm not lowering the reward, no matter what that Umpire says.'

'But it won't make a difference!' she shrieked back. 'I saw the blood on her skirt. Someone hurt our baby and whoever did it isn't going to come forward for a reward. They're not going to want to get caught.'

Mack suddenly looked stricken and let out a sob as he pitched forward onto his hands and knees.

'I just want my little girl home,' he cried. 'I just want to know where she is.'

Lesley stumbled across the room and sank to her knees on the floor next to him.

'I know you do. So do I.' She wanted to wrap her arms round him but something held her back.

'I'm going crazy not doing anything.'

'We need to let the police do their job, Mack.'

'But I'm her dad. I should do *something*.'

As he buried his face in his hands and cried, all Lesley could think about was his reaction to her bringing up Suzy Breed. Looking up, she saw that his phone, a sleek, limited edition BlackBerry Passport, was still on the bed. Carefully, she reached out and pocketed it.

'It's okay, love,' she shushed, patting his back gently.

After a moment, Mack sat up and wiped his eyes. 'I can't stand much more of this.'

'I feel the same. Look, why don't you go and talk to Belmar about the reward? If he thinks it's fine, then let's leave it as it is.' She didn't imagine Belmar would disagree with DCI Umpire but she just wanted Mack out of the bedroom.

'That's a good idea. I'm sorry I shouted at you, sweetheart,' he said, leaning over and gently kissing her. It took all her willpower not to pull away. 'I'll make you a cup of tea while I'm at it.'

She smiled thinly as he hauled himself off the carpet and left the bedroom. With one eye on the door in case he came back, she got out his phone. It was password protected but she knew the code: Mack used the same four digits for everything.

She went straight to his message inbox. The first few text exchanges were from the golf friends he'd gone to Scotland with, asking if they could do anything to help. That did not include, she noted, cutting short their trip.

The fourth message thread stopped her in her tracks. It contained three texts, all from a contact Mack had saved as Suzy B. It had to be her, Suzy Breed. The first text read:

Any news? xoxo

The message had been sent that morning but Mack had not replied. Frowning, Lesley scrolled back further. Yesterday evening there was another one, again with no reply from Mack.

Let me no if I can do anything 2 help. xoxo

Still on the floor, Lesley leaned back against the bed. The text speak irritated her irrationally. Suzy must've got in touch with Mack after hearing the news about Rosie and, she reasoned, he lied because he knew she'd be jealous and didn't want to add to her distress. She was about to put the phone down, embarrassed and annoyed with herself for not trusting him, but the urge to keep reading was too great. The third message sent by Suzy B had arrived at 9 p.m. yesterday, around the same time Mack's plane landed at Heathrow. Now she understood why he'd lied about being in touch with her.

I won't tell any1 u were wiv me. xoxo.

25

His knuckles throbbed as he pummelled the wall next to
the television, hitting it with as much force as he could
muster. He paid no attention to the smears of blood he
was leaving on the paintwork or the damage he was in-
flicting upon himself. With every punch he imagined it
was Mack Kinnock's stupid face he was hitting and
reducing to a bloody wreck. He slammed his fist into the
wall again, consumed by fury. The money that bastard
had just offered for a reward was HIS. They OWED
him.

Thoughts of what his life might be like had he
objected to Lesley Kinnock pushing ahead of him in the
queue at the petrol station that day drove him demented.
That instead of being gentlemanly and saying nothing
when she ducked between him and the man in front,
muttering something about being late for work, he'd
said no and told her to join the back of the queue like
everyone else. But that wasn't how he'd been raised. She
seemed stressed and upset and his act of selflessness
made him feel good about himself. He didn't even mind
when she held him up even longer by darting out of her

place to snatch a EuroMillions slip from the stand and fill it out for a Lucky Dip ticket, like he had already done.

It wasn't until four days later that he read in the local paper she'd scooped the £15-million jackpot. At first he tried to laugh it off, the cruel twist of fate that meant the winning numbers randomly spewed out by the computer went on her ticket and not his. He tried not to think about what he could have bought with the money, how he could have finally got his back sorted out, knowing it was an exercise in futility. But when he saw the picture of the house they'd bought in Haxton a few weeks later he snapped. The very least Lesley Kinnock could do was compensate him for his good manners.

He hit the wall again. The pain felt good.

Eventually he slumped against the wall and laid his cheek against it. His head felt swollen, as though his brain was pushing against his skull, only he knew it wasn't a symptom of his imagination. In the last month a painful ridge had developed on his forehead above his eyebrows. Concerned, he'd posted a question about it on a forum for steroid users and was told it was probably cranial swelling and almost certainly a side effect of the human growth hormone he stacked alongside twice-weekly testosterone shots to build up muscle and the Equipoise he injected daily to combat water retention. Throw in the Nolvadex he took to stop abnormal breast growth and it was a heady cocktail he ingested just to stay upright.

It took a few minutes for the white noise in his ears to stop hissing and for his heart rate to return to normal. As his thinking became clearer, he knew he needed to move forward with his plan. He had to establish a way for the parents to get his money to him, a secure drop-off point. He knew the area around their house well thanks to the hours he'd spent watching them. But with the police about, it wasn't going to be simple . . .

His thoughts were interrupted by one of the phones on his coffee table ringing. It was her, calling from Scotland. He debated for a moment whether to pick up, then rationalized that to ignore her might force her into a lone act of stupidity, like telling the police about them.

'Hey, you okay?' he said, trying to sound like he was pleased to hear from her.

'No, I'm fucked off. Have you just seen what's happened?'

'The press conference? Yeah, I'm watching it now.'

'If he can stump up a million just like that, he can give me a few more thousand. He's not returning my messages though.'

You stupid bitch, he wanted to yell at her. If she kept hassling Mack, he might crack and confess everything. That would be a disaster. He fought to maintain a passive tone, knowing he couldn't afford to rile her.

'I thought we said it wasn't a good idea to get in touch right now.'

'I don't care,' she said petulantly. 'Time's running out for me. I've only got a couple of weeks left to sort this out.'

He knew he couldn't wait that long either. She was becoming a liability and he needed to get shot of her before she did something that got them both arrested. Suddenly he had an idea.

'Look, why don't you come down here? Get the over-night sleeper to King's Cross again and I'll meet you at the station in the morning. Then we can decide the next move together.'

He'd already made one person disappear. He could do it again.

Her voice brightened. 'Are you sure? Because that would be great. I'm going nuts up here on my own.'

'Of course. I'll even pay for your ticket. Like I've said all along, we're in this together, Suzy.'

26

Maggie decided to take another quick detour before heading back to Haxton. The gym where Lou's husband Rob was a member was off Mansell High Street and on her way to the taxi rank. She knew he'd be there because he always went to the gym before his evening meal, creature of habit that he was.

The shops still in business on the high street were closing up for the day, so there was little foot traffic to slow her down. When Maggie was young, the thoroughfare had been the hub of the town centre, with an independent department store, furniture shop, chemist and upmarket jewellers doing a roaring trade alongside the generic chain stores. Every Saturday and Tuesday a market would set up along its pavements, including a record stall from which she and Lou would buy badges featuring their favourite bands to pin on their schoolbags. Now every other store was a charity shop and the only place that seemed busy was Poundland. The chains had long since migrated from the high street across town to the new shopping centre and with more shops now than any other kind of industry, the only reason to move to Mansell was the forty-seven-minute train commute into the capital. In the years she'd lived there, Maggie had witnessed its forlorn transformation from a bustling town with a proud sense of identity to an extended London suburb.

The gym was down a side road off the high street. It was council-owned but managed by a private contractor. Maggie persuaded the young girl on reception to let her through to see Rob without having to resort to flashing her warrant card.

Her brother-in-law had grown even bigger in the two months since Maggie had last seen him. Always toned and fit, his arms were now as beefy as hunks of meat hanging in a butcher's window and his chest muscles strained against the front of his old Nirvana T-shirt as he pulled weights on a machine known as the pec deck. Maggie tried not to gape at his neck, which was now roughly the same width as his shaved head.

Rob didn't stop when he saw her, not even when she stood right in front of him. The gym was half full and a few people working out watched them curiously. Maggie guessed she must've looked odd as the only fully dressed person in there. She wouldn't give Rob the satisfaction of asking him to stop and waited patiently until he finished his reps. Finally he acknowledged her presence.

'Whassup?'

He sounded like the meathead he looked and until the end of her days she would never get what Lou saw in him. Whatever redeemable qualities he had, they were invisible to her.

'Mind if we have a chat?' she said. If he wasn't going to start off with hello, neither would she.

'About what?'

She resisted the temptation to give a sarcastic answer like 'world peace' or 'the merits of wind turbines'. She was pretty certain he wouldn't get irony.

'Lou, of course.'

Rob slowly wiped his face on a hand towel bearing the gym's logo. She knew he was trying to give himself more time before answering but she was no longer in the mood to be patient.

'You can't just stop paying her the money you owe her,' she said. 'It's for Mae.'

'It's got fuck all to do with you, Maggie.'

'It does when she's upset and can't afford to pay her bills. You have a responsibility to her and Mae.'

'I know, but what can I do? I've got bills too.'

She looked down at his feet. 'New trainers?'

'Lisa paid for them.'

Maggie crossed her arms.

'You can't just bail on Lou and leave her skint.'

Rob's cheeks, already puce from his workout, turned an even darker shade of red.

'Who the fuck do you think you are, telling me what I can and can't do?'

The anger in his voice unnerved her but Maggie tried not to let it show.

'Look, I'm worried about her, that's all. I've just been round there and she's really upset. It's affecting Mae.'

He wiped his face again.

'Okay, I'll try to pay her by the end of the week.

Someone owes me a few hundred and I'm due to get it tomorrow. She can have that for now.'

'Thanks,' said Maggie, and she left it at that. She didn't care who was giving him the cash or why, just that they were.

She arrived back at Angel's Reach to find Belmar in the kitchen with a message for her from Umpire.

'He said he tried to call you but there was no answer.'

'My phone was in the bottom of my bag and I didn't hear it ring,' she lied.

She'd let the call go to voicemail for two reasons. Firstly, she didn't want him to know she wasn't back at the house with the Kinnocks yet, and secondly, she needed time to compose herself before she spoke to anyone. Lou bringing up Jerome and her confrontation with Rob had unsettled her and it took the return journey from Mansell to Haxton in a taxi to clear her head. By the time the concrete sprawl of homes, shops and industrial units gave way to green fields and wide avenues lined with trees and houses only accessed by driveways, she was focused again.

'Where did you say I was?' she said.

'Just busy.' He smiled. 'Do you want a coffee? I was about to make one.' He took a jar of Nescafé Gold Blend from the cupboard next to the fridge. 'Instant okay? I can't work out how to use their coffee maker.'

'No, I'm fine. What did Umpire want?'

'He wants to speak to Kathryn Stockton. Some new information's come to light about her that sounds pretty

197

significant. Yesterday Rosie's old friends in Mansell claimed they hadn't heard from her for months. But after the press conference aired, one of them – a girl called Cassie Perrie – rang the incident room and asked to change her statement. It turns out Rosie emailed her on Sunday.'

'Sunday just gone? Saying what?'

Belmar spooned coffee into a mug, fastidiously levelling the measure out first by tapping the teaspoon against the inside of the jar.

'Rosie wrote that she hates living in Haxton because she's being bullied by some girls she knows and, get this, she named Kathryn Stockton as being involved when one of them assaulted her after school recently.'

'You're kidding,' said Maggie.

'That's what the email said. Rosie claims she was ambushed and Kathryn just stood there and let it happen.' Steam lifted from the coffee's surface and Belmar blew on it. 'You look shocked,' he said.

'That's because I am. If it's true, Kathryn puts on a bloody good act about being her friend. She seemed genuinely upset yesterday.'

'Maybe she was upset because she was worried we'd find out about the bullying,' said Belmar. 'Ballboy wants you to arrange with Sarah a time for him to call round today.'

'Why isn't he interviewing her at the station as a significant witness? Shouldn't her statement be recorded?'

'He doesn't want to make that leap yet. I'm guessing he doesn't believe there's necessarily a link to the bullying and Rosie going missing and wants to check it out first. Hauling a sixteen-year-old in for questioning is a pretty big step to take. I mean, do you peg Kathryn as the crayon writer?'

'No, I don't, but she was the last person to see Rosie,' Maggie pointed out. 'Why does he want me to speak to Sarah and not you?'

'He didn't say but it's fine. I'm just glad he hasn't brought up the reward. I really thought he was going to ask if I knew. Even though I've filled in my log like you said, I still wouldn't know what to say to him.'

Maggie just about managed to stop herself from rolling her eyes. While she appreciated it was only Belmar's second case as an FLO and he didn't want to screw up, she also didn't want to keep having the same conversation about what Umpire might or might not say about Mack offering the reward.

'He's not mentioned it to either of us, so you need to forget about it,' she cautioned. 'Seriously, or you won't be able to do your job properly. The only thing we should be concerned with right now is supporting Lesley and Mack. We're looking at another night with no sign of Rosie.'

'I know, I know. Poor kid. What do you think has happened to her?'

'I don't think she's run off willingly, but I want to believe she's still alive for Lesley and Mack's sake.'

'Yeah, me too.' He took another sip. 'Do you fancy a biscuit? I saw some Hobnobs in the cupboard.'

'No thanks, if I have one I'll want the whole packet,' said Maggie. She never paid much attention to what the scales said because her height meant she could carry off being a size 14 and she looked good for it. But she did have a sweet tooth that required restraint and swam regularly to stay in shape. 'Is there anything else the DCI wants us to do?'

'Yeah. Rosie didn't use her current Outlook email address to send the message. She used an old AOL account instead, but didn't log on to it from either her iPhone or her iPad. He wants us to find out what other computers she has access to. They've checked the account itself and the email to Cassie is the only time she's used it in about eighteen months.'

'Fine. Is that it?'

'He just mentioned that Camelot, the lottery provider, has confirmed the Kinnocks were the sole jackpot winners for their draw, so the crayon writer has no legitimate claim to their money.'

Maggie gathered up her phone and bag as she prepared to leave. 'How was Lesley when you got back?'

'It all kicked off while you were gone. I was getting something from my car when all of a sudden a bloody giant duvet nearly lands on me.'

'An actual duvet?' said Maggie, bemused.

'Mack and Lesley were rowing upstairs. It sounded pretty nasty – I could hear them both shouting when I went outside. Then she starts chucking stuff out of their bedroom window. First the duvet, then some pillows and clothes. I brought them all in and left them in the laundry room; they'll probably need a wash now they've been on the ground outside.'

'Any idea what triggered it?'

'I heard her shout something about him only caring

about money.' Belmar shook his head in wonder. 'Can you imagine what it must be like waking up one day and finding out you're worth fifteen million quid?'

'I'm not sure I'd like to. I'd hate to have to give up my job for one thing. I think I'd get bored not working.'

Belmar scoffed. 'What, you'd prefer to carry on doing long hours and drowning in paperwork when you could be lying on a sun-drenched beach all year round? Nah, not me, I'd love my numbers to come up. I think most people would.'

'Have you spoken to them since?'

'They've shut themselves away upstairs. I did ask them again on the way back about talking to Victim Support but they're not interested.'

'We can't force them to, but let's keep suggesting it.' She picked up her bag. 'Right, I'll go next door to see Sarah Stockton. If either surfaces, ask them about any other computers Rosie has access to.'

'Why are you going round? Just call Sarah. She gave us her number.'

'No, I want to see Kathryn's reaction when she finds out Umpire wants to speak to her himself.'

'Why?'

'I want to see if she's rattled. She's doing a good job of pretending she and Rosie are as close as sisters but there's only so long a person can keep up a lie.'

27

A woman calling herself the Stocktons' housekeeper let Maggie in through the front gate. As she walked the length of the bricked driveway, cold air needled her skin and the blue sky they'd basked beneath for almost a week was now blanketed by thick, grey cloud. The down-turn suited her mood and she knew the rest of the investigative team working out of the incident room in Mansell would share her frustration that Rosie still wasn't found.

The housekeeper, who said over the intercom that her name was Janice Gifford, was waiting for Maggie at the front door. She might've looked the part in a single-breasted black coatdress with white lapels and grey-streaked brown hair pulled back into a chignon but as a welcoming committee she fell short. Her round, plump face, marked by a smattering of fine lines, was set with suspicion, and when Maggie fished her warrant card from her bag to prove she was who she said she was, Janice studied it through narrowed eyelids.

'I'm here to see Mrs Stockton,' said Maggie.

'Is she expecting you?'

'No, but she knows me. We met yesterday at the Kinnocks' house.'

Janice's face pinched with concern. 'Such an awful business. You'd better come in.'

The contrast between the Stocktons' entrance hall and the one at Angel's Reach was startling. The floor was covered in small black and white diamond-shaped tiles, the effect of which was dizzying, while the walls were starkly white and decorated only by large prints of abstract monochrome shapes. Unlike the Kinnocks' staircase, which was flush against one wall, here it rose imperiously from the middle of the room, and the steps, which looked like they were made from some kind of marble, had been left bare. Maggie suspected Janice's uniform had been chosen deliberately to blend in.

'You must know Rosie pretty well,' she ventured. 'I understand she and Kathryn are very close.'

'I wouldn't know, I'm afraid,' said Janice, clasping her hands in front of her.

'Doesn't she come round often to see Kathryn?'

'I suppose.'

'Have you been questioned by my colleagues yet?'

'I spoke to an officer last night,' said Janice. 'I told him I didn't see or hear anything.'

'Are you certain? I know these gardens are big but some noise might carry.'

'I was collecting some dry-cleaning for Mrs Stockton in the village and then did a bit of shopping. I must've been out for a couple of hours. I did explain this to the constable who came round.'

Maggie detected a trace of annoyance in Janice's reply.

'I'm not here to double-check your statement,' she placated her. 'Have you seen much of Kathryn today?'

'She's been in her room most of the day. I haven't really spoken to her about what's happened.'

'Not even to ask how she's coping?'

'Why would I do that?'

Her attitude was starting to grate on Maggie. She forced a smile.

'I just thought you might have said something, what with it being her best friend who's missing.'

'That's not how we do things in this household,' said Janice, stony-faced. 'Now, please let me escort you to the sitting room. You can wait there while I see if Mrs Stockton is available to see you.'

Maggie let Janice lead her into an imposing room where the monochrome theme continued. Along one wall was a black leather corner sofa that could seat seven and next to it was a glass-topped, metal-legged coffee table the size of a door upon which a pile of magazines was neatly stacked. The top one was a pristine copy of *The Economist*. Fixed to the wall above a white marble mantelpiece was a flat-screen TV even bigger than the Kinnocks' and several colourless prints of landscapes Maggie didn't recognize were hung on the wall around it. The only splash of colour was from a waist-high crimson glass vase in one corner. Was it Sarah's choice of decor or her husband's, thought Maggie? It certainly wouldn't have been hers. There was also the marked smell of air freshener in the room and Maggie spotted a plug-in device in a socket on the wall nearest the door.

'Is Mr Stockton at home?' she asked Janice, who told her to take a seat.

'No, he's in New York for work. He left on Monday morning and won't be back until Friday night. I told the constable that as well.'

'Right. Thank you.'

Janice nodded stiffly then left the room.

Sarah burst in two minutes later. She greeted Maggie like a long-lost friend.

'Detective Neville, how lovely to see you again,' she said, clasping Maggie's right hand between both of hers. Her skin was dry and papery to the touch. 'How can I be of help? Is it Lesley, would she like me to pop round and stay with her for a bit?'

Sarah's eyes were slightly unfocused and Maggie, who had yesterday spotted the signs that pointed to her drinking, thought she might be tanked up on something other than alcohol. She was jiggling from foot to foot in a pair of scarlet mules that were too tight for her feet – her toes were blanched white from being squashed – and a sleeveless shift dress in the same colour.

'No, but I'll tell her you offered. I'm here because DCI Umpire, the officer leading the search for Rosie, would like to interview Kathryn and he's asked me to set up a convenient time this evening to come round.'

The jiggling stopped abruptly.

'Why does he want to question Kathryn?'

'Some new information has come to light that she might be able to clarify for us. It's important he speaks with her as soon as possible.'

The frown darkening Sarah's face was replaced by a smile.

'Oh, that's fine. You let him know we can see him right away and I'll have Janice call her down. I thought you were going to say she was in trouble again. I never know with that girl.'

Maggie bit back a retort, knowing it was for Umpire to bring up Rosie's accusation of bullying, not her. But she couldn't let it go completely – she wasn't happy Kathryn might've deceived her during their chat yesterday.

'Has she been in trouble with the police before?'

'Heavens, no.' Sarah giggled. 'When I said trouble I meant the usual nonsense: unsuitable boys, staying out past her curfew, not doing her homework, answering me back. But I can't really talk, as I was exactly the same at her age. Let me get Janice to fetch her.'

Watching her skip out of the room, Maggie knew the bad behaviour Sarah had just reeled off was unexceptional and that of a typical teenager. Would her mum even know if Kathryn was bullying others? Few kids would admit that kind of thing to their parents.

A few moments later Sarah returned.

'She'll be down shortly. Can I get you anything, Detective Neville?'

'No, thank you. And call me Maggie,' she said, wanting Sarah to think they were on the same side because they were on first-name terms. It might make it easier to deal with her in the long run.

'Did you see us on the news earlier, Maggie?' Sarah chirruped. 'I wasn't sure whether we should say yes to appearing, but Kathryn's so upset about Rosie being gone that I thought it might help.'

'Let's hope so,' Maggie replied noncommittally.

'She's worried you think badly of her because of the row they had. It was just a silly argument. They really are the best of friends.'

'Do they argue a lot?'

'Certainly not. Kathryn looks out for Rosie. That girl is such a tiny scrap of a thing, there's hardly anything of her. She looks more like eleven than fifteen.'

Sarah spoke with such conviction that Maggie was convinced she was telling the truth. Or at least what she believed was the truth.

'So I can call DCI Umpire to let him know he can come round now to interview Kathryn?' she said.

'Of course. We want to do anything we can to help. I can't imagine how Lesley must be feeling,' said Sarah. Her face twisted into a scowl. 'If anyone hurt Kathryn, I'd kill them . . . Oh, the look on your face! I'm joking, of course. I wouldn't really kill someone. You know what I meant.'

Maggie wasn't sure that she did.

28

Umpire took only ten minutes to arrive because he was already in Haxton when Maggie called him, overseeing a search of the river that wound around its perimeter. So far the divers had nothing to report.

He insisted that Sarah stay with Kathryn while he spoke to her. Given how hyper she was, Maggie wasn't sure Sarah fitted the bill of an appropriate adult and took Umpire to one side when he arrived to explain why.

'She might be under the influence of something, sir.'

'But you don't know that for sure?' he whispered back.

He stood so close to her that Maggie could see a tiny pinprick in his right earlobe that suggested at some point it had been pierced. She edged backwards, un-nerved by his proximity.

'Well, no,' she said.

'Then it's fine. It's not her I'm interviewing.'

'Are you sure? She tends to go on a bit as it is. If she's lubricated, we'll never shut her up.'

'Good. If she prattles on for long enough, she might let something useful slip.'

Umpire didn't waste time with preamble as the interview began.

'We've uncovered an email Rosie sent to a friend on Sunday evening, two days before she went missing. In the email she claims a group of girls, of which apparently you're one, have been bullying her and she makes an allegation of assault. Not against you specifically, but someone who was with you that day.'

Kathryn's eyes widened. 'Which friend?'

'She didn't say.'

'No, not who hit her. I meant who was the email sent to?'

'Darling, I don't think it matters who Rosie emailed, just that she did,' said Sarah, showing a better grasp of the situation than Maggie presumed she would. Kathryn frowned at her mum.

'You don't actually think I've been bullying her?'

'Of course not, darling,' said Sarah, reaching for her daughter's hand and squeezing it.

'I haven't done anything to Rosie.'

Maggie eyed Kathryn suspiciously. Her outfit was virtually the same as yesterday's – jodhpurs, another T-shirt but blue this time, the same silver Superga trainers – but her demeanour was markedly dissimilar. Dry-eyed, sitting bolt upright, she didn't appear rattled by the accusation she'd bullied Rosie, just annoyed.

'She's lying,' said Kathryn, shrugging her slim shoulders to convey her apparent bewilderment. 'It's just not true. Are you sure the person who says they got the email isn't just making it up? Is it someone she used to know in Mansell?' she asked astutely. 'Because it won't be anyone from around here.' When neither Maggie nor DCI Umpire answered her, Kathryn pulled a face.

'They're lying to stir up trouble. Rosie told me they're jealous because she's rich now and she won't have anything to do with them.'

'Officers, I have also heard Rosie speak disparagingly of the girls she used to go to school with in Mansell,' said Sarah. 'They sound like a horrible bunch, always swearing and smoking and bunking off school. They'd be far more likely to bully her than someone from round here.'

'Rosie didn't name the person who hit her,' said Umpire, 'but she said, and I quote, "They were all there waiting after my last lesson, even Kathryn. When I tried to get away, I was smacked across the nose with a book."'

A strange look crossed Kathryn's face, like she knew what he was talking about but was also scared. Had Umpire seen it too? Maggie glanced over at him but his expression gave nothing away.

'I never stay behind after school – I always go to the stables to ride my horse. The staff there can vouch for me. I don't know anything about Rosie being attacked.'

'And you've never assaulted her yourself?'

Kathryn looked horrified. 'No way. God, how many more times do I have to tell you? Rosie's my best friend.'

'You've only known her a year,' said Maggie.

'So? We see each other every day. She's the person I'm closest to in the whole world.' Kathryn turned to her mum, her long ponytail swinging across her back. 'I don't understand how this is helping find her, Mum.'

'My daughter's right. She's told you she hasn't bullied Rosie. Are we done?'

'Not quite. Tell me about the row you and Rosie had yesterday morning.'

Kathryn glowered at Maggie, which this time didn't go unnoticed by Umpire.

'I know you went through it with DC Neville, but I would be grateful if you could tell me again.'

The teenager repeated the same account she'd given Maggie but this time there were no tears, no wailing, no hand-wringing. Her voice was a monotone as she listed the names she'd called Rosie for refusing to go with her to the stables. If Maggie hadn't heard her tell the same story the day before she'd have thought it was rehearsed.

'What about Rosie self-harming?' he asked.

Sarah looked appalled. 'Whatever do you mean?'

'Kathryn told DC Neville that Rosie cuts herself.'

'It's the truth,' said Kathryn indignantly. She shot Maggie a dirty look.

'If she says it's true then it is,' said her mum.

'Where does Rosie cut herself?' Maggie interjected.

Kathryn hesitated. She pulled her hand out of Sarah's grip and folded her arms across her body. 'I'm not sure.'

'You're certain she does, though?' said Umpire.

'Lily told me she does.'

'You mean you've never spoken to Rosie about it yourself, or actually seen her do it yourself or seen any cuts on her person?'

'I never said that I had.'

Maggie tried to interrupt again but Umpire held his hand up to silence her. Annoyed, she sank into her seat. She could've sworn Kathryn had said she'd seen Rosie cut herself. Why was she backtracking now?

'How was Rosie when you left her?' said Umpire.

'Upset because we'd rowed and stressed about our exam tomorrow because she hates science. That's why I thought she should come riding, to take her mind off it.'

Umpire changed tack again.

'Does Rosie ever confide in you about boys she likes?'

'I guess,' said Kathryn, glancing at Sarah again, who nodded at her daughter to continue. 'But she talks about pop stars she likes, like Liam from 1D, not real boys. Rosie doesn't really know any boys who live round here, as her dad is really weird about her going out.' The teenager suddenly turned on Maggie. 'I told you all this yesterday. Why do I have to say it again?'

'Because DCI Umpire wants you to,' said Maggie simply.

'Does Rosie ever talk about boys she knew when she lived in Mansell?' he asked.

'No.'

'So,' he began carefully, 'as far as you know, Rosie isn't sexually experienced.' When Kathryn and Sarah both reacted with shock, he held up his hands. 'I know, it's a very personal question, but it's an important one. Is she?'

'No way. Rosie hasn't even kissed anyone properly yet,' said Kathryn.

'Properly?' queried Umpire.

She stared at him. 'With tongues.'

The DCI was lost for words and Maggie would have found his embarrassment amusing were it not for the feeling of unease creeping over her as she watched Kathryn bat his questions away. Where was the girl she met yesterday, the one who cried so hard trails of phlegm ran from her nose and she never noticed to wipe them away? Even allowing for people's emotions seesawing in cases like this, she couldn't recall seeing anyone so effectively turn theirs off.

'Can I ask *you* something?' said Kathryn.

Umpire nodded. 'By all means.'

'All these questions you're asking me about being a bully – do you think I've got something to do with Rosie going missing?'

Umpire didn't miss a beat before answering.

'We have to explore every avenue that presents itself while we search for her,' he said. 'It looks like you were the last person to see her yesterday, you've since admitted to rowing with her and then this email turns up. My job is to ask difficult questions.'

Clever, thought Maggie. He'd made it sound like he'd answered the question when in fact he hadn't at all. Sarah seemed to buy it, but Kathryn stared at him blank-faced for a moment then burst into tears.

'I do understand why you're asking. I want her home too. I can't bear the idea that someone's hurt her.'

Maggie couldn't hold back any longer.

'You think someone's hurt her now?' she blurted out. 'Yesterday you thought the blood was caused by Rosie cutting herself. Have you changed your mind?'

'That's not what I said. You're twisting my words.'

Maggie knew she hadn't twisted anything and wanted to make sure Umpire knew it too. She didn't want him thinking she'd got Kathryn's statement confused. But when she tried to speak again, he shot her a warning look.

'That's enough, DC Neville.'

Across the table, Kathryn smirked.

Umpire had parked his car on the drive at Angel's Reach and he and Maggie walked back there in silence. She was desperate to discuss the interview with him but reluctant to speak first. It wasn't a fear of leaping in and saying the wrong thing that made her hesitate, more that he might not actually care what she thought. But by the time they arrived at the gates of Angel's Reach, her desire to know what he was thinking got the better of her.

'What was your impression of Kathryn, sir?'

Umpire looked at her with something approaching surprise, as though her question was unexpected. Maggie realized his mind was elsewhere and not on the interview at all.

'I don't think Rosie accusing Kathryn of bullying has anything to do with her going missing,' he said distractedly.

They came to a halt by his car.

'Kathryn was behaving oddly though,' said Maggie. 'Yesterday she was in pieces, but today she's calmer than pond water.'

'So because she pulled herself together before being questioned we should be suspicious?'

'Sir, she didn't know you were coming until ten minutes before you turned up. And did you see her face when you read the email out?'

Umpire scratched his scalp roughly with his fingertips. The folds of skin beneath his eyes were dark and puffy, a sure sign of fatigue. Maggie knew from working with him previously that he wouldn't rest until Rosie was found, even if that meant not going home and sleeping in the office.

'What if she was lying? I still don't think it's relevant. You heard Matheson: the amount of blood found on Rosie's skirt suggests a serious injury and there's the condom lubricant trace to consider too. You really think Kathryn had anything to do with that?' His voice grew firmer as he warmed to his theme. 'You think she somehow spirited an injured Rosie away, leaving barely a trace of her behind? Has she got magical powers we can't see?'

He was mocking her, but Maggie wouldn't rise to it.

'I'm not saying she's responsible, sir. I just think she might know more than she's letting on.'

'I disagree. I think the key to this lies with what's left of the fifteen million in Mack and Lesley's bank account. The crayon writer's already made that clear enough. That's what we need to stay focused on.' He fumbled in his trouser pocket for his car keys, unlocked the vehicle and folded his lanky frame into the driver's seat, but left the door open for a moment.

'So that's it with Kathryn?' asked Maggie.

'Until something more concrete turns up, yes.'

But Maggie couldn't let it drop.

'Can we at least check she did go to the stables after leaving Rosie yesterday? You said yourself that we had to rule everything out.'

'I'd put fifteen million on her alibi panning out.' He gave her a weary look. 'Okay, I'll have someone verify it.'

'Thank you, sir.'

'Now, tell me again about your interview with Lesley. You said she was surprised Suzy Breed's name came up?'

Apart from a snatched conversation when she'd arrived at the station for the press conference with Mack and Lesley, this was the first opportunity she'd had to brief him because the reward had distracted them all. He listened intently as she repeated her conversation with Lesley about Suzy Breed and mentioned Belmar over-hearing the Kinnocks rowing about money.

'Well, Lesley's wrong about Suzy Breed being in New Zealand. She arrived back in Britain mid-April and is staying at her mother's address in Falkirk.'

'Shit. So Mack could've been with her instead of stay-ing at the hotel.'

'Officers from Forth Valley have been round there but there was no sign of her. They're going back later.'

'Are you going to interview him about it now?'

'And ask him what exactly?' Umpire snapped.

'About him and Suzy.'

'Frankly, I don't care if he's having an affair with half of bloody Scotland. All I care about is what's relevant to the investigation and I don't think him sneaking off to meet an ex-girlfriend is. We've had a threatening letter from someone who's made it very clear they know about the blood on Rosie's skirt and phone records put both Mack and Suzy four hundred miles from Haxton at the time Rosie went missing. Suzy Breed isn't going to help us find Rosie, but the crayon writer will. So let's worry about that, shall we?'

Maggie recoiled from his outburst and, as she floun-dered for something to say, a black Mercedes-Benz minivan slowed to a halt outside the gate. Driving was a young man with streaked blond hair and an overbite that diluted his good looks. He waved at them before pulling away.

'I wonder who that was,' said Maggie.

'Security patrol,' said Umpire. 'He's been helping to man the main gate with our officers. The firm's called Umbra, which is Latin for "shadow" and it's a good fit. It doesn't like to advertise itself, hence the unmarked vehicle.'

'Everyone working for the firm has been questioned, haven't they?'

He shot her a disparaging look and she quailed again.

'Your friend DC Berry took the statements. None of them reported anything out of the ordinary.' He stuck his key in the ignition then paused. 'Should the Kinnocks stay somewhere else tonight with everything that's going on? I want the back garden and Rosie's room to stay sealed off for the time being.'

'I'll suggest it, sir, but I think Lesley will want to stay put just in case Rosie turns up.'

'Much as I'd love that to happen, DC Neville, I don't think she's going to stroll back in asking what's for tea,' he said grimly. 'But we will find her, wherever she is and whatever state she's in.'

His eyes locked on hers and she hated that she knew what he meant. Cases involving children were always the worst.

'But seriously, let's think about moving the parents. They must have friends they can stay with.'

'I don't think anyone around here other than the

Stocktons would take them in and I'm guessing that's not a good idea now.'

'No, it's not.'

'Lesley's got one close friend back in Mansell but she's away until the weekend. But I'm not sure that's a good idea anyway – the friend lives on the Corley estate and the press could get to them too easily there.'

'A hotel then. There's that place the other side of Mansell, what's it called? Reuben House. Very expensive, very popular with pop stars and footballers, so I'm told. EuroMillions winners should fit right in.'

'Is it really necessary to move them, sir? Lesley's pretty fragile right now and I think it would unsettle her even more.'

Umpire started the engine.

'If that's what you think as their FLO, then fine, they can stay put for now. But make sure you log I suggested it, Neville. I wouldn't want another conversation to be forgotten.'

She smarted. 'Of course, sir.'

'In the meantime, tell Lesley about Rosie's email to Cassie. I want to know if it changes her view about her and Kathryn's friendship.'

He was about to pull the driver's door shut when his phone rang. Maggie stepped back while he took the call, so it didn't seem like she was eavesdropping. His side of the conversation was brief – *yes, no, yes, no* – and when he ended the call she was surprised to see him grip the steering wheel so tightly his knuckles went white.

'That was the High Tech Crime Unit. They've recovered an explicit picture downloaded to Rosie's iPad a month ago. It had been deleted but was still on the hard drive.'

'Of what?'

'Of her.' He turned off the engine and got out of the car. 'They're sending it to me now.'

The picture arrived almost instantly by email and it was as explicit as Maggie feared. It showed Rosie lying topless on a bed. She wore a pair of lime-green strappy sandals with vertiginous heels and even though she had knickers on, her legs were splayed open, leaving nothing to the imagination.

'It's definitely her,' said Maggie despondently. Then she took a closer look at Rosie's face, which was plastered in thick make-up. Her eyes were shut. 'Sir, she looks out of it to me.'

Looking at the photograph more closely, the lines around his eyes becoming more pronounced as he squinted, Umpire agreed.

'I think you're right. If she was drunk or even drugged, she might not have been aware the picture was taken until she got hold of it. HTCU are trying to see where it originated from, but they're saying she hasn't mentioned its existence in any email or text she's received in the past six months, or on any of her social media accounts. They're having to start from scratch to find the source.' He looked at the picture again and glowered. 'My daughter's ten and has just got her first mobile and already she's had other kids texting her asking her to send them pictures of herself like this. Technology and the Internet are turning our kids into amateur porn stars.'

'My nephew Jude is the same age as your daughter and I know he's seen stuff no child should ever be exposed to,' said Maggie. 'My sister has parental controls on their home computer and he doesn't have Internet access on his phone but other kids in his class do, so he sees it anyway.'

'It makes me want to lock my daughter up until she's at least eighteen,' said Umpire, looking troubled.

'Maybe that's why Mack's strict with Rosie, because he knows what teenagers get up to these days and it worries him. Sexting's so widespread that kids think it's normal behaviour.'

'This picture proves he's right to be fearful. It's going to be difficult to work out where it was taken and who by. There's not much to go on in the background.'

'Hang on, what's that?' said Maggie, pointing to the right-hand edge of the photo.

'I can't see anything.'

'Just there, see? It looks like a shadow but it's actually fabric, dark blue or even black. Maybe it's clothing, sir.'

Umpire squinted at the photograph again. 'You're right. I can see it now. I'll have HTCU magnify the picture, see if they can work out exactly what it is. Well spotted, Neville.'

His praise fell on deaf ears though, as Maggie was more concerned with what happened next.

'Do we tell the Kinnocks about it? God knows how they'll react.'

'No, let's keep it from them until we've got more to go on. But see the shoes she's wearing? Find out from Lesley if they're Rosie's.'

'I doubt it very much. A short skirt is one thing, but I think Lesley would baulk at buying shoes like that for Rosie to wear behind Mack's back.'

'Exactly. So if they're not Rosie's, whose are they?'

29

As she went in search of Lesley, it dawned on Maggie
that it wasn't the size of Angel's Reach that was so unsettling, but its stillness. It was so quiet she could hear her
every breath as she walked back through the house. It
was hardly surprising, she decided, that Lesley was so
out of kilter with her surroundings. How discomfiting
Angel's Reach must be after living on the Corley estate,
where the streets and houses were so tightly knitted
together that you could practically hear someone sneeze
three doors away.

When Maggie lived on the estate as a child, it throbbed
with the noise of kids playing outside, neighbours shouting to one another over garden fences, all-night parties
and cars shrieking up and down the roads with boy racers
behind the wheel. It was vibrant, exciting and probably
the reason why the trains running below her town-
centre flat never bothered her. She liked background
noise and craved it. She could never live somewhere like
Angel's Reach, or Haxton for that matter. The village
was too rural for her, surrounded as it was by acres of
protected green space and not much else. Until this case,

she'd only ever ventured there on two other occasions, the first being when she was six and her parents took her and Lou to the toy museum in the village centre. Her abiding memory of the trip was not being able to understand why all the toys were trapped behind glass and not free to be played with.

She found Lesley perched on the top step of the terrace. The lawn was still taped off. Maggie was surprised to see she was smoking.

'Are you okay?' she said.

Lesley was mid-way through taking a drag and motioned with her free hand for Maggie to sit down. After a second she exhaled loudly, sending a thin wisp of smoke across the lawn.

'I haven't smoked a cigarette for twenty years but suddenly I was desperate for one. One of your lot outside gave me this.' Lesley took one last drag then ground the butt into the flagstone step. 'That was disgusting,' she sighed. With an unsteady hand, she pushed her hair off her face. It hung in rat's tails where she hadn't combed it properly after her earlier shower. She'd also changed out of the dress and cardigan and back into the denim skirt and navy T-shirt. Maggie asked her why.

'I want everything to be like it was when Rosie went,' Lesley said, keeping her gaze trained on the firs at the bottom of the garden.

'It's so quiet round here,' Maggie commented, after they'd sat in silence for a while. 'It must take some getting used to after the Corley.' When Lesley gave her a quizzical look, Maggie explained she'd once lived on the estate too. 'We were on Sherwood Street.'

'I know it – it's on the other side from where we were. Yes, it's very different. Sometimes when Rosie and Mack are out I stand out here and everything's so silent I imagine myself the only living, breathing creature for miles. I've always said this house is far too big for the three of us.' She gave Maggie another sideways glance. 'You still haven't found her, have you? You would've said if you had.'

'No, we haven't. I know it's frustrating and it must feel like it's going at a snail's pace but really it's not. Everyone's working round the clock and dozens of leads are being investigated. We won't stop until we find her.'

Lesley nodded. 'I know. I just can't get my head around the fact she's not back yet. I keep expecting her to bowl through the front door like nothing's happened and ask what all the fuss is about. I'm scared because the longer it goes on, the more numbed I feel. I keep thinking I should be crying and screaming and tearing down walls or something, but I just feel flat and empty.'

Maggie listened to Lesley's outpouring but made no reply, conscious she wasn't supposed to counsel her. The air began to fill with drizzle and the dark clouds hanging low overhead suggested it would soon turn to rain.

'Shall we go inside?' asked Maggie.

'I'm fine out here,' said Lesley, even though her arms were dappled with goosebumps. Maggie, in a short-sleeved, white cotton shirt, had no choice but to stay put too. She hugged her arms tightly to her sides.

'There's something else I need to discuss with you,' she said, trying not to shiver.

'Is it about Kathryn? Belmar said you'd gone round to

talk to her. He and Mack are upstairs in the study with a man from your press office, talking about the reward. Apparently it will be difficult to retract it, but if Mack makes up some sob story about saying the wrong amount because of the stress he's under we might be able to get away with reducing it.' She shook her head.

'Isn't that what you want?'

'Part of me is starting to think Mack's right. Why shouldn't we offer what we want to get Rosie back?' Lesley sighed again. 'I wish we hadn't won a single penny. I wish that instead of buying that bloody ticket I'd done what I was going to do and spent the money on a KitKat. But I was on a diet.'

Maggie tried not to smile but couldn't help it.

'I know, it's mad, isn't it? Right now I'd rather be fat than rich. Oh, I know what you must be thinking: You're wealthy, how hard can it be? But money divides people,' said Lesley bitterly. 'What I've learned in this past year is that people who have money like to think they're better than those who don't, and those who aren't wealthy think people who are always flaunt it. It's impossible trying to please everyone.'

'So why bother? Why not ignore what other people think and just enjoy the money?'

'That's easier said than done. People can be vicious.'

'Like the people round here?' said Maggie, curious to know what living in a place like Haxton meant for a lower-middle-class family like the Kinnocks.

Lesley nodded. 'It's difficult. People look down their noses at us because of where we're from. There's this unspoken snobbery that we're not good enough for

Haxton. If it wasn't for Rosie's exams, I'd move again.' She paused. 'Sorry, you wanted to ask me something, didn't you? Instead I've been going on about KitKats and moaning about money.'

'It's fine, I was happy to listen. But you're right, I do want to talk about Kathryn. Although, before we do,' she began tentatively, 'can I just ask if Rosie owns any high-heeled sandals? Lime-coloured?'

Lesley raised an eyebrow. 'No, and frankly they sound hideous.'

'Okay, I thought as much.'

'Why are you asking?'

'I can't tell you at this stage, I'm sorry.'

Lesley shrugged resignedly. Maggie knew it wasn't because she didn't care, but because she understood and trusted there was a very good reason not to tell her yet. It made Maggie's job much easier: the hardest cases were when relatives were so suspicious they refused to let any-thing lie.

'So, about Kathryn. Have you ever had concerns about her and Rosie's friendship?'

'None at all. She's lovely.'

'How often do they see each other out of school?'

'I'd say pretty much every day, usually when they're riding. Rosie's a bit scared of horses but she still goes. All the girls she knows ride.'

'Has Rosie mentioned anything about falling out with Kathryn recently?'

Lesley gave her a searching look. 'What's this really about?'

Maggie told her about the email Rosie had sent to Cassie.

'Oh my God,' said Lesley, stunned. 'Rosie's being bullied and Kathryn's involved?'

'That's what the email says, but Kathryn has categorically denied it. She was very upset when we brought it up.'

'Rosie wouldn't lie about something like that,' said Lesley, rubbing her brow roughly with her fingers. 'Kathryn's meant to be her best friend. Why is she ganging up on her?'

'Rosie doesn't give a reason in the email.'

'You know, now I come to think of it, I do remember her coming home with a cut on her nose, right across the bridge, about a month ago. She said someone knocked into her during netball practice but that must've been when she was hit.'

'Rosie didn't send the email from her usual account. She used an old AOL address and Cassie told my colleagues it was the one she had before your win.'

'She's right. Rosie stopped using it when people she didn't know kept emailing her asking for money. She also locked her Instagram and Twitter accounts so she'd be left alone. The things people used to write to her were just awful. If they weren't asking for money, it was grown men hassling her to go out with them because they'd seen her picture in the papers.'

'Did you report any of the men?'

'I wanted to but Mack said he'd deal with it. I think he replied to them threatening to tell the police if they didn't leave her alone and that did the trick.'

'I would've thought that for someone as protective of their child as Mack is, calling the police would have been his automatic response to her being threatened.'

'He wanted to sort it out himself,' Lesley said hotly. 'He likes to think of himself as our protector.'

Maggie let it slide for the time being.

'What's odd,' she went on, 'is that Rosie didn't log on to the AOL account using her phone or her iPad. We've accessed the account and there are no other recent emails from her, so we need to know what device she used instead. We can trace the IP address but that takes time. It's quicker to just ask you what other computers she has access to.'

'Well, none at home. Mack doesn't like her using his laptop and I don't have my own. Perhaps she wrote it at school?'

'The message was sent on Sunday. Maybe she went to an Internet cafe?'

'Impossible. She was here all day with me on Sunday, and Mack had his laptop with him in Scotland, so I have no idea . . . Oh!' Lesley suddenly jumped up from the step. 'I think I know where she might've sent it from.'

'Really?' said Maggie, clambering to her feet.

'Come with me.'

Lesley shot through the kitchen, across the entrance hall and up the stairs as Maggie struggled to keep pace. On the landing they turned left, away from Rosie's bedroom with the crime scene tape snaking back and forth across the doorway. Lesley came to a halt outside a door opposite the one leading to the guest room where Maggie had showered earlier. As she went to open it, Lesley paused, the knob half turned in her hand.

'You can't tell Mack about this. We can make up something else about where it came from, but I don't want him to know. It's meant to be a surprise.'

'Lesley, I—'

She released the knob. 'Then we don't go in.'

'I'm family liaison to both of you,' said Maggie. 'It would be unprofessional to lie to him on your behalf.'

'I'm not asking you to lie – I'm just asking you not to say anything. There's a difference.'

'I really can't.'

'Fine. Let's go back downstairs.'

Burying the thought of what Umpire would say if he found out, Maggie gave in.

'Okay, I won't say anything, but neither can you. If DCI Umpire finds out I agreed to this I'll be in a lot of trouble.'

'Deal.'

Lesley opened the door and they stepped inside a bedroom that was marginally smaller than the guest room Maggie had used. An antique fitted wardrobe covered one wall and the only other furniture was a day bed. The window was bare of curtains.

'This is the smallest bedroom and we never use it,' Lesley explained. 'Or rather Mack doesn't. I use the wardrobe to store some things he doesn't know about.'

Lesley retrieved a key from a little glass pot on the windowsill and unlocked the doors to reveal more than a dozen boxes stacked neatly in two columns. They were fairly big – Maggie estimated around four times the size of a shoebox – and each one had a number written on the side in thick black marker, from one to fourteen.

'What are these?' she asked.

'Every year to mark Rosie's birthday I make her a birthday box. I put in things like books, school projects and holiday souvenirs: anything that's a nice reminder of what she did in the year leading up to her birthday.'

'What a lovely idea,' Maggie exclaimed.

'I know exactly what's in each box too,' said Lesley proudly. 'Her first Barbie doll is in number six. The first Valentine's card she received, from a boy in her class, is in ten. Box number twelve contains Justin Bieber posters but One Direction have since replaced him in her affections and box fourteen is pretty much filled with stuff relating to them. Box number one is my favourite though. It's got her first baby-gro, first dummy, first shoes, first teddy bear, the first lock of hair we had cut.'

'This is incredible, Lesley,' said Maggie in awe. 'Does Rosie know about them?'

Lesley's voice cracked. 'No, and nor does Mack. He hates hoarding things and I didn't want him to chuck them out. At our old house I used to keep the boxes hidden in the loft and managed to sneak them out during the move. I don't think either of them come in here and even if they do, I keep the wardrobe locked. My plan is to give the boxes to Rosie on her eighteenth birthday.' She dropped to the carpet and wailed. 'What if I never get to give them to her?'

Maggie knelt down beside her and hugged her as she cried, close to tears herself. Even though she knew it wasn't wise to get emotional around the family, she defied anyone not to be moved by the sight of all those boxes.

When Lesley finished crying she looked wrung out and Maggie had to help her to her feet.

'Why did you bring me up here to show me these?'

'Rosie's old laptop is in box fourteen,' said Lesley, wiping her eyes with a grubby, balled-up tissue she pulled from her skirt pocket. 'She had it for a couple of years before she got her iPad for her birthday last year. It's the only computer I can think of that she might've used to send that email on Sunday.'

'I thought you said she didn't know about the boxes?'

'I honestly didn't think she did.'

Maggie reached for box fourteen, which was on the top of the second stack. She pulled it towards her and laid it on the carpet. The tape sealing the box had been torn off. Opening it up, she saw a pink Sony Vaio laptop inside.

'She must've come in, wondered why the wardrobe was locked and gone looking for the key,' said Lesley. 'I can't believe she's never said anything.'

'Perhaps she realized you were keeping the boxes as a surprise and didn't want to spoil it for you.'

'Or she didn't care,' said Lesley sorrowfully.

Maggie fetched a pair of protective latex gloves from her bag before removing the laptop from the box and booting it up. The browsing history confirmed Rosie had indeed used it on Sunday to log on to her AOL account: the email she wrote to Cassie was in the account's Sent box. As confirmed by the High Tech Crime Unit, it was the only email Rosie had sent in almost eighteen months and Cassie hadn't replied.

Maggie closed the browser and checked the desktop. There was only one folder on it, untitled. Clicking it open, she saw it contained a dozen or so Word documents.

'What are those?' said Lesley.

Maggie opened the first one, named 'Nov8', which she assumed was the date it was written. A quick glance at the first line told her Lesley couldn't be privy to its contents just yet and she lowered the laptop's lid.

'I'm sorry, Lesley, but I can't let you read this.'

'Why not? If Rosie wrote that, I want to read it.'

'I need to see what it says first, in case it ends up being evidence. We can't risk prejudicing a future court case. Please understand.'

'Let me see it,' Lesley demanded, her fingers furling and unfurling like she wanted to snatch the laptop out of Maggie's hands.

'I'm sorry, but no,' said Maggie firmly.

Lesley stared at her defiantly for a moment, then her shoulders sagged like the fight had gone out of her.

'Fine,' she said wearily.

She slammed the door behind her as she left. The noise must've echoed around the house.

Maggie opened the laptop again. By the time she'd read through the fifth Word document she could see there was a theme to them. Rosie – she was certain it was her – was using her old laptop like a diary, typing out her misery and fears in each document then stashing them away in the belief no one but her would ever read them.

Rosie had laid out the details of her bullying in graphic detail. She was being targeted for still being a virgin. It sounded like some girls she knew – she didn't name any names this time – wore their promiscuity like a badge of honour and were putting pressure on her to dish out sexual favours to the boys they hung around with, just as they did. To them it was no big deal but clearly to Rosie it was and she wrote of her extreme distress at being told she was pathetic and a loser for not wanting to take part.

Maggie sat back on her haunches. She wasn't easily shocked – she'd been a police officer far too long for that. But this . . . this was something else. She scrolled through the documents again to see if there were any clues as to who the boys might be. Nationally there had been a number of high-profile court cases involving groups of Asian men grooming vulnerable young girls for sex, but there was no mention of ethnicity here. The only specific reference she found was someone who went by the initials GS.

GS won't leave me alone . . .

GS was hassling me again when Mum was out. I hid upstairs and pretended I wasn't in. Kathryn thought it was funny . . .

GS is trying to force me to have sex. I know everyone says I'm too old to still be a virgin but I'm not ready. I don't want to do it . . .

Maggie closed down that entry and opened the last Word document Rosie had saved. It was dated Monday, the day after she'd emailed Cassie and the day before she went missing. It was the shortest entry of all, only three sentences long, but the few words made Maggie's blood run cold.

Every time I think about it I want to cry. I was so out of it I don't remember what happened but GS said I have to do it again and if I don't Mum and Dad will find out. I'm so scared.

Maggie scrabbled for her mobile and rang Umpire. When he didn't pick up, she tried the incident room. One of the admin support staff answered and she asked to be put through to him.

'Tell him it's DC Neville and I need to speak to him urgently.'

After a few moments, the same person came back on the line.

'I'm sorry, DCI Umpire can't talk to you right now. I've been told to put you through to DC Berry instead.'

Maggie swallowed her disappointment as Steve came on the line. Part of her wanted to hear Umpire's reaction when she told him what she'd found. Instead, she found herself recounting it to a distracted Steve. At one point she had to stop and check he was still on the line because he was so quiet.

'Sorry, Maggie, I am listening. I'm just knackered. Bobby had us up half the night with colic.'

'But can you make sure you tell Umpire exactly what I've just told you? We need to identify this GS character, so tell him I think we should speak to Kathryn Stockton again, and it's probably worth trying Lily Flynn too.' She wondered if they were among the girls Rosie referred to who slept around.

'Sure.'

'Steve, this is serious. Rosie wrote on Monday that she

was scared about GS hassling her. Tuesday she vanishes. That can't be a coincidence.'

'Okay, okay, I'll tell him,' he said irritably.

'Can you send someone over to collect the laptop? It needs to go to HTCU as soon as possible.'

'Yep, I'll do that too.'

She softened a little. 'Listen, when this is over, I'd love to come round and meet Bobby.'

'Isla would love that,' said Steve, sounding perkier. 'We could both do with some cheering up. She's not best pleased with me at the moment.'

'It's Umpire she should be cross with.'

'Try telling her that,' he said as he hung up.

It would take at least half an hour before someone arrived to collect the laptop. Resting her notebook on her knee, Maggie scrolled down the screen with the cursor until she reached the first message Rosie wrote, back in November. Opening it up, she began to read again.

30

Thursday

The normality made her want to scream. How could they just *sit* there? Lesley watched with growing resentment as Mack slowly spread butter onto a slice of toast. Across the table, Maggie gingerly sipped a coffee as she checked her phone for messages. It was nearly eight a.m. and Belmar hadn't arrived yet.

They were sitting at the table in what Mack liked to call the kitchen annexe but to her was just a conservatory. Lesley looked down at her place setting. Both her bowl and cup were empty, as she could stomach neither food nor drink. The only thing she could keep down was water. She craved another cigarette.

The emptiness of the fourth seat goaded her. It was where Rosie sat on the rare occasions the three of them dined at the table. More often than not they ate in front of the TV with their plates balanced on their knees. So much space and still they crammed onto one sofa, jostling for elbow space.

Lesley tried not to dwell on what it would be like if Rosie never came home, if that space at the table was never filled. No, she mustn't think that way. What was it her dad always said? 'Until there's no hope there's always hope.' She had a sudden yearning to speak to him. A former army lieutenant, he was a complex man, an oil-and-water mix of authority and optimism. She never remembered him being around much when she was a child – his tours would take him away from home for months on end – but as adults they were close. He'd know how to deal with all this and say the right things. She'd spoken to him half a dozen times since Tuesday and he'd offered to come up from Cornwall, but she told him to stay put. It would be too confusing for her mum to stay at the house with the police there.

She caught Maggie's eye as she glanced up from her phone. She'd said little after Rosie's old laptop was collected yesterday and Lesley hadn't pushed it, deciding she was probably better off not knowing. Instead, the two of them had watched a film in the lounge to pass the time while Mack stayed upstairs in his study. Lesley couldn't remember what the film was called or what it was about, only that Jack Nicolson was in it, being shouty.

She was relieved Mack had kept himself out of the way. Every time she looked at him her brain screamed that he was a liar and a cheat and it was exhausting trying to be normal around him. She still hadn't decided what to do about the text messages she had found from Suzy. Before sneaking his phone back onto the bed where he'd dropped it, she'd copied Suzy's number onto a piece of paper and slipped it into the pocket of her denim skirt, where it remained. She couldn't imagine calling it, not right now, but at some point she might.

Maybe after Rosie was home. Maybe then she'd confront Mack about his deception.

She'd gone to bed before him and surprised herself by drifting off quickly. But she hadn't stayed asleep for long. The fear that was now her constant companion fashioned itself into a fist and punched her awake. *Don't go to sleep*, it cruelly reminded her as her eyes flew open in fright. *Your child is missing, Lesley Kinnock, don't you dare forget she's gone.* The rest of the night was an exhausting merry-go-round of drifting off and jumping awake and her fractious mood that morning reflected her lack of rest.

'How did you sleep?' she asked Maggie.

'Pretty well, thanks.' The officer set her phone down on the tablecloth.

'It doesn't sound like it.'

'Another coffee and I'll be fine. Are you sure you don't want one?'

'I don't think there's any milk left,' said Mack. 'We'll need to get some more.'

Lesley gaped at him. Did he honestly think she was going to pop to the shops for a couple of pints? Don't mind me, my daughter's missing but I'll just be off to Tesco?

'Shall I pick up a loaf while I'm at it?' she spat.

'Love, I didn't mean it like that.'

'I can pick up some things as I have to go back to Mansell this morning for a briefing,' Maggie offered.

'What do you suggest we do in the meantime?'

'Lesley—' Mack chastised.

'I don't mean about the milk,' she snapped. 'I mean,

do we just sit around again, waiting? I don't think I can do that for another day. Can you?' she asked her husband.

'It's hard, I know,' said Maggie. 'I guess you could go for a walk if you wanted to get out of the house.'

'What, through the gate at the top of the road? The reporters would love that. Or maybe we could stroll around the meadow where our daughter's bloodstained skirt was found. How scenic.'

'Lesley, stop it. She's just trying to help.'

'If she wants to help, she should be out there looking for Rosie with the others.' Lesley scraped her chair away from the table and it tipped backwards onto the floor with a crash. She left it where it was and stormed out of the kitchen. Crossing the entrance hall, she heard footsteps behind her but didn't slow down.

'Lesley, wait,' said Maggie.

'I'm going to see the Stocktons. I want to talk to Kathryn.'

'I'm sorry, but you can't.'

Lesley turned on her.

'Don't tell me what I can and can't do.'

'I'm sorry, but in this instance I need to. It's better for the time being if contact between you and the Stocktons is limited.'

'Is this because of what you found on Rosie's laptop?'

'You know I can't answer that.'

Their stand-off was interrupted by Belmar's arrival.

'Is everything okay?' he asked Maggie.

She shook her head as her phone rang. 'Umpire,' she mouthed.

Lesley shook with anger. They had no right to dictate who she spoke to.

As Maggie turned away from her to talk on the phone, Belmar hovered at his colleague's shoulder, eavesdropping. Neither noticed Lesley as she began to back away from them, towards the front door. Five seconds later she was gone.

31

It was going to be more difficult than he'd anticipated. The size of the crowd waiting outside, and the number of officers standing guard, surprised him. How stupid to think he'd be able to just drive through without being stopped, but it was too late to turn round now. They'd come after him if he did and start asking questions and he wasn't prepared for that.

As he drove slowly towards the security gate at the mouth of Burr Way, adrenaline surged through his veins and slammed into the base of his skull and he felt light-headed and shaky. An inner voice told him to hold it together, stay calm. Don't lose it at the first hurdle. Then he spotted a familiar face by the gate and broke into a broad grin. Oh, of all the people. Perfect.

He brought the car to a halt inches from the gate and a police officer walked slowly round to his window, motioning for him to lower it.

'Can I ask why you're here, sir?' said the officer in a not particularly friendly tone.

Before he could say a word, another voice interrupted. 'It's all right, I know him.'

He smirked.

The young man who had spoken came over and stood next to the officer. He looked anxious and like he wanted to be anywhere in the world but there.

'Hey,' he said with a nod.

The young man, whose name he knew to be Eddie, ignored him. Prick.

'I have an appointment with one of the residents,' he explained to the officer. 'Eddie can vouch for me. I come at the same time every week.'

He did too. Landing a client living in the same street as the Kinnocks was a masterstroke; it allowed him to keep tabs on them and what they were spending his money on. At first he'd contented himself with just driving past the house, then one day he'd seen Mack leaving and impulsively followed him. After that, he'd spent as much time as he could monitoring the family's movements as he waited for them to reply to his earlier letters, the ones he'd signed. After months of frustration it felt like he'd been gifted the opportunity of a lifetime when he'd come across the daughter in the garden on Tuesday.

'Yeah, he does,' said Eddie.

'Name and address?' the officer asked.

He gave his real name, knowing they could all too easily ask his client to corroborate it. But the home address the officer diligently wrote down was false. His client only had his office address at the gym and he was banking on the belief that by the time the police checked out the one he'd just given them, if they bothered at all, he'd have his money and would be long gone.

'I'm a registered sports injury osteopath and my client lives at Verma Lodge.' He made a show of looking at his watch. 'Will this take much longer? I'm already five minutes late.'

Eddie's mouth opened and closed like a fish floundering on the deck of a boat after it has been caught. He knew why. Eddie thought his name was Simon, because he'd told him his name was Simon. That Eddie had never questioned it or doubted it was hardly his fault and, given the circumstances during which he told him, he could've said his name was Mickey Mouse and Eddie would've accepted it. It was hard to hear anything over all that screaming.

Eddie, in his security company uniform, appeared to be on the verge of questioning the discrepancy when he silenced him with a look. *Don't even think about it.*

'Did you have an appointment on Tuesday, sir?'

'No. The only day I'm here is Thursday.'

Now that *was* a lie and Eddie's eyes widened as it tripped smoothly off his tongue.

'It's just routine, sir. We need to check out everyone who comes into Burr Way on a regular basis.'

'Of course. I hope you find the poor girl soon.'

The officer gave him a stern look. 'Do you know the Kinnock family?'

'No, not at all. I'd never seen the girl until her picture was on the news. When I visit my client I just drive straight in and out. You don't usually see anyone around at this time.'

From the corner of his eye he saw Eddie give the briefest shake of his head. His stomach clenched with

243

anger. If the little fucker carried on like that, he'd get them both into trouble.

'Thank you for your cooperation, sir. I'll let you through now. Eddie, get the gate.'

As he steered the car through the gap, reporters penned in behind police tape on the grass verge watched with interest, then quickly turned their attention back to each other.

Eddie moved to the side of the road just inside the gate and motioned frantically at him to pull over. He was tempted to floor the accelerator and keep going, but he knew it would be reckless given the police presence. His window was still lowered and Eddie bent down so their faces were only inches apart. The security guard's breath was sour and he wrinkled his nose in distaste.

'What the fuck are you doing back here?' Eddie hissed.

'I'm seeing my client,' he said with an ambivalence he knew would wind Eddie up.

'I told you to stay away. Didn't I make myself clear?'

'Oh, you actually meant that?' he deadpanned. 'But if I don't keep my appointment, my client will wonder where I am.'

'I told you I'd sort it.'

'But you haven't, have you?'

'I'm warning you—' Eddie spluttered.

'Or what? What exactly will you do? Tell the police?'

Eddie looked like he was about to combust. Laughing to himself, he revved the engine and put the car in first gear to pull away.

'Step aside, you little prick. You know you can't stop me from being here. But don't worry, I'll tell her you said hi.'

32

Lesley hammered on the Stocktons' front gate with her fists. She was out of breath from sprinting down the road but still managed to scream loudly at the same time.

'Come out here, Kathryn! I know what you've been doing to Rosie!'

She pummelled the thick wooden gate until her knuckles were red raw but it stayed closed. Stumbling over to the post where the intercom speaker was mounted, she pressed the button repeatedly until finally a voice that sounded like Sarah's crackled through it.

'Lesley, you need to go home.'

'Where is she?' Lesley shrieked. 'Where's that daughter of yours?'

'We have nothing to say to you, Lesley. Please leave us alone.'

'You fucking get her out here now! I want to know why she's been bullying Rosie.'

The intercom fell silent. Lesley pushed hard against the gate to force it open but it wouldn't budge. She then tried to scale it but couldn't get any purchase on the smooth wood. Eventually she accepted her attempts to

gain access were futile and decided instead to get as far
away from Burr Way as she could. Darting across the
road, she was so distracted she didn't see the car until it
was almost too late.

It swerved in an arc to avoid her and Lesley dragged
herself back onto the pavement knowing she should be
grateful it hadn't hit her but almost wishing it had.
Knocked out cold, not having to think or feel, no more
worry, fear, no anything. It was an inviting prospect.

The car, which was small and silver, stopped on the
other side of the road and the driver got out. Lesley took
another step back.

'Are you all right?' the man called out.

He didn't appear to be angry, although he had every
right to be. She hadn't been looking where she was
going, had run into the road without thinking, and it was
only his deft reaction that stopped him hitting her.

'I'm fine,' she said, nodding.

The driver walked towards her then stopped. Shock
rippled across his face.

'Oh – it's you.'

His comment surprised her. It implied they knew each
other but he was younger than her and wore trendy
trainers with orange neon flashes up the sides and a
T-shirt with tracksuit bottoms. Not scruffy bottoms, like
the grey marl ones Mack used to change into when he
got home from work to lounge around in, but ones made
from lightweight fabric designed to soak up sweat. She
looked him up and down again, lingering briefly on his
handsome face, and concluded he definitely didn't look
like someone she would know – and yet at the same time

she could've sworn she had seen him somewhere before.

'Do I know you?' she asked.

He shook his head quickly and started backing away, car key in hand, ready to make a getaway.

'No. I'm sorry, I didn't mean—' He took a deep breath. 'I'm sorry about your daughter.'

'Do I know you?' she repeated.

He looked panicked now and shook his head even more vehemently.

'God, no. I – I saw you on the telly yesterday.'

The look of horror that stamped itself on Lesley's face sent him scurrying back to his car.

'I'm sorry,' he called over his shoulder. 'I really am.'

As he drove away, bile burned in her throat. It was bad enough being recognized for winning the lottery, but not for that.

She debated whether to return to the house to tell Mack but thought better of it. She couldn't face the inevitable discussion that would ensue with Maggie and Belmar, of having to listen to them carp on about how it was good people knew who she was because it meant people were paying attention and that would help them find Rosie quicker. Like that was any kind of comfort.

She walked down Burr Way in the same direction the car had gone. She hadn't noticed which driveway it turned into but guessed it must be parked up in one of them because the road dead-ended by the meadow where Rosie's skirt was found and the vehicle was nowhere to be seen. The people who lived down that end were a mystery to her: they hid themselves behind locked gates and walls even higher than those at her end of the road and if she ever saw any of them driving past they averted their eyes. She wasn't sure how many people even lived down there.

The meadow stretched between Burr Way and the fringes of the village centre. Walking straight across was the quickest route into Haxton but she couldn't bring herself to go that way. She didn't know exactly where the bush was that Rosie's skirt had been stuffed into, but just knowing it was one of them was enough. So she took the long way into the village, turning left at the bottom of the meadow and continuing on until she reached another residential road that would take her where she wanted to go. There was no purpose to her journey, other than to get away. She didn't have her purse with her, or her phone, and she was wearing lace-up canvas plimsolls that were giving her blisters because she wasn't wearing any socks. The wind had picked up since yesterday, the temperature dropping with it, and she was chilly in just her navy T-shirt and denim skirt. But she kept going and by the time she reached the centre of Haxton her mind had gone blank – she could think of nothing but walking.

When she finally came to, she was in the chilled food aisle in M&S Simply Food, right in front of the yoghurts, and wondering how the hell she'd got there. She didn't even like yoghurt.

'Excuse me, do you need any help?'

She looked up to see a store assistant next to her, a young girl with long, blonde highlighted hair, who was chewing gum that swirled around her mouth like a lone sock in a washing machine.

'Do you need any help?' the girl repeated. The chewing did not relent for speech, it turned out.

'No, thank you,' Lesley managed.

'Are you sure? You've been standing there for ages.'

'Have I?' she said wonderingly.

The shop assistant nodded, her lips smacking loudly as her lower teeth ground the gum into her upper ones. The noise made Lesley uptight.

'Yes, for about fifteen minutes. Are you sure you don't need any help?'

'For crying out loud, leave her alone!' a voice burst in between them. 'Can't you see she's upset?'

A young black woman pushing her toddler son in a buggy rounded on the shop assistant.

'That's the missing girl's mum,' she hissed.

The shop assistant's mouth fell open to such an extent that Lesley was surprised the chewing gum didn't drop out.

'Oh God, I'm so sorry,' she spluttered.

The mum took Lesley's hand, even though she hadn't offered it to be held.

'What are you doing here?' she asked her.

The gentle lilt of her voice and the warm pressure of her hand were too much and Lesley burst into tears.

'We've run out of milk,' she sobbed. 'But I haven't got any money.'

The next few minutes passed in a blur as the mum corralled the shop assistant into getting Lesley four pints of semi-skimmed, which she then insisted on paying for. She was vaguely aware of people watching, of hushed words and nudged elbows, of sympathetic looks and heads being shaken. As she struggled to hold it together, it felt like she was drowning in pity.

Outside, her rescuer offered to drive her back to Angel's Reach but she refused. She'd stopped crying now and felt more in possession of her body, even though her mind was still somewhat disconnected.

'Let me call someone to come and get you then. You can't walk back on your own,' the woman fretted.

'I'm fine. You've been really very kind but I'm okay, honestly.'

She could see the woman was weighing up what to do, chewing her bottom lip anxiously as she did. Lesley touched her arm lightly.

'Please, I'd much rather walk. I need a bit of time . . . well, you know.'

The woman didn't know, couldn't possibly know, but she nodded knowingly all the same. With a last thank you, Lesley walked away in the direction she'd come from, avoiding the meadow again.

Across the street a small silver car eased away from the kerb.

33

A distraught Mack begged Maggie and Belmar to look for his wife. 'I'll stay here in case she comes back,' he said. 'Please hurry, I can't cope with her disappearing too.'

'She won't have gone far,' Maggie tried to reassure him, 'and she could only have gone one of two ways. I'll head up to the meadow and Belmar will check with the officer stationed down by the gate to see if he's seen her.'

They left him hunched on the sofa, head in his hands, his muffled crying soundtracking their exit.

The only people she spotted in the meadow were two scene of crime officers from Matheson's unit milling along the hedgerow border furthest from where it met Burr Way; she presumed that was where Rosie's skirt had been found. As she headed towards them, she noticed the meadow floor had been flattened in places and guessed it was the result of the inch-by-inch search carried out by her colleagues and volunteers earlier that morning, just as the sun came up. As far as she was aware, they hadn't found anything.

'Hey, where are you going?'

Maggie jumped in fright and swung round to find Kathryn and Lily walking behind her.

'Bloody hell, where did you two creep up from?'

'Did we scare you? Sorry,' said Kathryn, looking anything but. 'Why are you out here? Aren't you meant to be with Rosie's parents?'

'Are you looking for her mum?' Lily interrupted. 'She went past about ten minutes ago.'

'After banging on our gate for ages first,' Kathryn sniped. 'It was like she'd gone mad.'

Maggie ignored Kathryn and directed her question at Lily. 'Did she say where she was going?'

'I didn't talk to her, I just saw her.'

Kathryn sniggered as she fiddled with a button on her fitted denim jacket. Lily looked cosy swaddled in a bottle-green Barbour.

'Is something funny?' said Maggie coldly.

Kathryn shrugged.

'What are they doing here still?' asked Lily, pointing to Matheson's officers. Her hand trembled.

'They need to make sure they've checked the whole area thoroughly.'

Lily looked downcast. Rosie's disappearance wasn't just taking its toll on Lesley and Mack, it seemed.

'Can I ask you both something?' said Maggie.

'If you want,' said Kathryn, answering for them both as she twirled a loose strand of her long, dark hair in her fingers.

'Do you know anyone with the initials GS? I think it might be a male.'

Lily shook her head but Kathryn kept her focus on the ground as she dug the toes of her trainers into the meadow floor.

'Kathryn?' Maggie prompted.

'GS? No, I don't,' she said, not looking up.

'Has Rosie ever mentioned knowing someone with those initials?'

'Not to me.' She glanced sideways at Lily. 'You?'

Lily shook her head again. She was ghostly pale.

'Is that it?' said Kathryn.

'Actually, there is one more thing I'd like to check. Are you certain Rosie told you she self-harmed?'

'Not this again,' Kathryn huffed.

'Rosie told me she did,' said Lily. 'I believed her. Why would anyone lie about something like that?'

Maggie wasn't sure what to believe. Rosie wrote in her online diary about how isolated she felt because of the bullying and how scared she was of GS, whoever he was, yet had made no mention of self-harming. If she had been cutting herself, surely something that serious would warrant a mention or two as she poured out her heart on her laptop?

'Lily, you said to me the other day that Rosie didn't deserve what was happening to her. What did you mean by that?'

'I don't know,' Lily mumbled. 'I was upset.'

'Do you still think the blood in the garden was caused by her cutting herself?'

'Yes,' she said, her voice the firmest it had been during the entire conversation.

'Can we go now?' asked Kathryn.

'Sure. Mind how you go.'

Haxton was far prettier than Maggie remembered. The focal point was the village green and the sizeable buildings circling its edge were made from either flint or brick. One had been converted into a general store, but most were cottages and houses with front gardens overflowing with foliage. Her mum, Jeanette, was a keen gardener and the knowledge she'd passed down to Maggie meant she could tell apart the geraniums from the roses and clematis that clung to any patch of brickwork they could reach. There were hanging baskets decorating some of the cottages that mirrored larger ones suspended outside the sole pub, the Copper Kettle. Maggie could tell Haxton was a village that cared greatly about appearance.

One of the roads leading off the village green led to a bigger parade of shops. Maggie was about to turn up it when Belmar called to say Lesley had been spotted coming back up Burr Way. She told him she'd head straight back herself.

Walking briskly, on the way she called Lou and was pleased to hear her sound more upbeat than she had yesterday.

'Rob rang late last night to say he's got some money to give me.'

'About sodding time.'

'Was it your doing?'

'I had a quiet word, yes.'

'I guessed as much. It would've been nice if he'd decided to give me the money because he realized he should and not because you told him to, but I'm not going to complain. It was nice to talk to him.'

'When's he paying you?' said Maggie, ignoring her last comment. 'Nice' was not a word she'd ever use in the context of Rob and she wouldn't believe he was paying what he owed until the money was in her sister's hand.

'That's the thing. He's saying he can't for a couple of days because he's too busy but if I want I can go and get it myself. Except obviously I can't go round to his and collect it if *she's* there.'

'Busy with what?'

'Job interviews apparently. Anyhow, I know it's a lot to ask as you've got this case going on, but is there any way you could get it for me at some point today? I wouldn't ask unless I was desperate.'

'I guess I could try to pick it up later,' said Maggie, clueless as to how she'd manage to sneak off again. She'd just have to find a way.

'How's the search going?'

'It's tough. There's still no news.'

Maggie reached the mouth of the meadow and picked up her pace.

'Her poor mum and dad. What do you reckon has happened to her?'

Maggie didn't want to speculate with Lou. She trusted her sister, but at the same time didn't want to blur the lines between her work and home life.

'I don't know, sis. Look, I've got to go now. When did Rob say he'll have the money ready?'

'He said later this afternoon, but send a text first to say you're on your way. Oh, and if you see that bitch Lisa, don't be nice. Don't even look at her, let alone smile.'

Maggie grinned. She didn't blame Lou for hating the woman who'd contributed to ripping her family apart. Their paths had crossed only once since Rob walked out, when he stupidly brought Lisa with him to see Mae one weekend. The expletives that spewed from Lou's mouth that day had made Maggie grateful her niece was too young to understand words yet.

'What if she's nice to me?' Maggie teased.

'Ignore her. From what I've heard, she's so bloody needy that if you act like she doesn't exist it'll drive her mad.'

'Did Rob mention wanting a divorce again?'

'No, he didn't say a word. He was pretty grumpy, actually. Maybe they've had a row.'

It was the happiest Lou had sounded in months.

34

He cancelled his appointment right there on the doorstep, telling his client he'd been overcome by dizziness on the drive over and needed to go home. It wasn't even a lie. Seeing the girl's mother like that and talking to her face to face had sent him into a tailspin. A crushing pain now filled his head and he could barely lift his chin off his chest to address his client, who was furious that he wanted to reschedule.

'Are you sure you can't help me today?' Mrs Roberts queried, clearly not buying his explanation. 'I'm still too weak to go upstairs and I've had to have my bedroom moved down here. It's hard to manage on my own.'

You're not an invalid, you stupid old bag, he inwardly screamed at her. *You've just hurt your bloody arm.*

Her injury was in fact an overextension of the joint in her left wrist, sustained when she had reached forward to grip the banister while climbing her stairs. An inexplicable, freak accident exacerbated by the arthritis already making her elderly joints crumble like a coastline battered by the sea.

'I am sorry, Mrs Roberts,' he said through gritted

teeth, the pain behind his eyes pounding in time with his speech. 'But I must go.'

She proffered him her arm like a puppy might its paw.

'But it's not getting any better. What am I paying you for if it's not getting better?'

What she paid him was a lot less than others in his profession charged and a drop in the ocean compared to what she had stashed in the bank. He'd done some digging around on her after Charlie, his rugby-playing client, had introduced them and he'd found out her husband had left her well provided for when he widowed her. The fact she could maintain a house this size on her own, with an outdoor pool in the grounds, was proof of that.

'Why don't I come back at the same time tomorrow?' he suggested.

He had to come back. It wasn't just about missing the appointment and forfeiting his fee. He needed to make sure everything was as he'd left it on Tuesday and, more importantly, he needed to be there to work out his next move. Seeing the girl's mother like that had rattled him. He could no longer afford to wait.

'How do I know you'll be fine by then?'

'It's a migraine, Mrs Roberts,' he said, even though it was far worse than any migraine he'd had before. It was like his skull was splitting open. 'I just need to sleep it off. It's not like I make a habit of cancelling.'

She pursed her lips in annoyance as she smoothed a loose strand of white-blonde hair off her forehead. She was still attractive for a woman of seventy-eight and, despite how her injury supposedly impeded her, was immaculately dressed in a red linen skirt and cream blouse. Attractive, yes – but even he had limits.

'Fine. But I want you back here tomorrow at nine a.m.'

It would take some juggling of his appointments but he would do it. He had to.

He hadn't been lying when he said his plan was to go straight home and sleep off the pain either. But as he drove out of Burr Way and turned right towards the centre of Haxton, he saw the girl's mother again, walking along the approach to the high street. Curious to find out where she was going, he forgot all about his headache and followed her.

She loitered outside M&S for ages, while he parked across the road in a pay-and-display bay outside Barclays Bank. She didn't seem to have much awareness of her surroundings – he probably could've walked right up to her and waved a hand in her face and she wouldn't have noticed.

After she went inside the store he waited in his car for precisely two minutes, counting it down on his watch, before crossing the road and following her inside. The store was crowded and he had to go up and down the aisles a few times before he found her. He was hovering a few feet away when the shop assistant approached. The voice in his head, the same one that had screamed at Mrs Roberts to shut up about her arm, cautioned him to leave before he was spotted, before suspicions were aroused and someone made a note of his description. But he couldn't tear himself away. The mother fascinated him. Her complexion was fairer than the girl's but her frame was exactly the same now she'd lost weight. Small and slight, like all it would take was a gust of wind to blow her over. Would she be as easy to lift as her daughter, he wondered? She couldn't weigh much more.

A woman with a buggy was getting involved now. He inched forward on the pretext of browsing the yoghurts like she had done. Then he heard her distinctly say she didn't have any money and instantly the pain returned behind his eyes and the ridge on his forehead swelled in protest. No money? Was she fucking joking? What about HIS money?

He slipped away unnoticed. Outside, as he waited for the traffic to part so he could cross the road back to his car, he knew it was time for decisive action. The Kinnocks clearly hadn't taken his last note seriously. He had to show them and the police that his intentions were serious.

Using the Google app on his phone, he looked up the number for the police incident room in Mansell and dialled it. Then he pulled the hem of his T-shirt over his mouth to muffle his voice and lowered it by two octaves.

'I have something to report about the Kinnock girl.'

The officer who answered sounded fed up, like it wasn't the first crank-sounding call of the day.

'What's that, sir?' the officer said with a sigh.

'I want the million-pound reward though.'

'Ah, well, I don't think that stands presently.'

'Tell the fucking parents to reinstate it then.'

The officer sounded pissed off now. 'I don't think that's going to happen. It was an incorrect amount.'

'You'd better fucking make it happen. It's my money.'

'That's what they all say, sir.'

'Oh yeah? I can prove the Kinnocks stole it from me. Or rather that bitch of a mother did. They should've taken more notice of the letters I sent.'

The officer's interest was suddenly roused.

'What letter would that be?'

'Are you going to give me the reward or not?'

'Sir, why don't you tell me what you know first?'

There was a loud whooshing noise in his ears as anger thundered around his head and he was overwhelmed by the urge to punch his fist clean through the windscreen. As he snarled into the phone, he let go of the cotton fabric covering his mouth and his voice rose to its normal pitch. He was too angry to notice.

'Tell the parents they've got twenty-four hours to reinstate the reward or I'll send their daughter back piece by fucking piece – starting with her toes and that pretty blue nail varnish she's wearing on them.'

35

When she arrived home to find Mack waiting for her on the doorstep, Lesley braced herself for another row. But something in her husband's expression stopped her in her tracks. He looked scared, not angry. She started to shake.

'Have they found her?' she rasped.

He nodded over his shoulder to Belmar, who was in the entrance hall talking on the phone. She could tell it wasn't good news. Terrified, she gripped Mack's arm.

'Oh God, please don't say she's dead,' she moaned. 'Please don't say she's dead.'

Belmar gestured for them to come closer.

'We haven't found Rosie but there's been a development and DCI Umpire wants to talk to you. I'll put you on speakerphone.'

Umpire's voice crackled into the entrance hall.

'I'm sorry to have to do this over the phone but I need to ask you this as a matter of urgency: does Rosie wear nail varnish?'

The question surprised Lesley. Mack too, judging by the way he raised his eyebrows at her.

'Yes, sometimes,' she answered.

Her husband rolled his eyes disapprovingly.

'Really, Mack? You're going to start that now?' she snapped.

He looked stung but kept quiet.

'Mrs Kinnock, was Rosie wearing nail varnish on Tuesday?' Umpire pressed.

'I, um, I'm not sure . . .'

'It's really important we know if she was,' he urged.

She closed her eyes and tried to picture her daughter the last time she saw her at the breakfast table.

'She might have been wearing blue nail varnish on her toenails. She knows she's not allowed to wear it on her fingernails. It's a very bright shade, like kingfisher blue. It's her favourite colour. Why are you . . . ?' She tailed off, too terrified to finish her own sentence.

'Someone we believe could be the crayon writer called the incident room five minutes ago. He specifically mentioned the fact Rosie was wearing blue varnish on her toenails when she went missing.'

Lesley swayed violently on the spot, just as Maggie bowled through the front door. She saw what was going on and raced over to Lesley, who clawed at her like a drowning woman trying to reach shore.

'No, no, no . . .' she moaned.

The room spun around her. Maggie gripped her tighter as Belmar gave a quick rundown of what had happened.

'We should move you to a safe house,' Umpire's disembodied voice announced. He spoke with an urgency that accelerated Lesley's own panic.

'Why?' croaked Mack, by now ashen.

'The caller made a specific threat against Rosie. He's asking for money and is obsessed with the idea that Mrs Kinnock somehow stole from him. I want to move you for your safety.'

'You think he might come after us here?' asked Lesley.

'I'm not prepared to risk finding out. I'm going to arrange for you to stay at one of our safe houses; we have a number in and around the area we can use. I know you don't want to be too far from home in case there's any news about Rosie, but hopefully it won't be for long. DC Neville and DC Small will go with you.'

'No,' said Mack. 'We're not going anywhere.'

'Mr Kinnock—' Umpire began.

'No, you listen to me. We live in a gated road, the house is completely secure now and if you do the job you're meant to, the bastard won't be able to get us. I am not running away.'

'He's right,' said Lesley. 'What if Rosie comes home and finds the place empty? What will she think?'

'We'd have officers stationed here all the time,' said Umpire. 'They would bring her to where you are.'

Lesley looked at Mack. His mouth was set in a firm line.

'They can't make us go, love.'

For the first time since she'd read the texts from Suzy Breed, Lesley felt a rush of love for her husband. Nothing would bend him, not even this.

Umpire decided the Kinnocks should hear the recording themselves, in case they recognized the crayon writer's voice. He told Belmar he'd be at the house in fifteen minutes then hung up.

Maggie asked Mack and Lesley to excuse them and motioned for Belmar to step outside onto the driveway so they could talk privately.

'When did Lesley get back?' she asked.

'About five minutes before you did.'

'Did she say where she went?'

'She didn't have the chance. After I rang you to say she was on her way back, I was straight on the phone to Umpire and then he wanted to speak to her about the nail varnish.'

The previous evening Maggie had called Belmar at home to brief him about the diary Rosie had typed out on her old laptop and about GS.

'I just bumped into Kathryn and Lily. I asked them if they knew who GS was and both said they'd never heard Rosie refer to anyone like that, but I'm convinced they weren't telling the truth. I'm pretty sure Lily would've admitted it if Kathryn hadn't been there to interrupt her every word. They still seem convinced the blood found in the garden was caused by her self-harming though.'

'What did Ballboy say about the laptop?'

'I don't know,' she said. 'He wasn't around yesterday so I had to brief Steve Berry. You know what it's like – once we pass the info on, it can be ages before we find out what's going on.'

'Always the last to know,' said Belmar resignedly.

The DCI looked uncomfortable perched on the sofa next to Mack and Lesley. The seat was quite low down and his long legs were bent at an awkward angle. He was exasperated by Mack's refusal to leave Angel's Reach.

'We're certain the person who called the incident room is the crayon writer because he's made another specific reference to Rosie and talked about sending you letters after your EuroMillions win. He seems particularly angry at you, Lesley, presumably because you bought the winning ticket.'

'We're safe here,' said Mack firmly. 'So unless you have some kind of court order to move us, forget it. This is our home and we're staying put.'

'Fine,' Umpire snapped. 'But you're staying against my wishes.'

'Duly noted,' Mack replied sarcastically. 'Now, can we listen to the call or not?'

Umpire had the recording downloaded on his phone. Maggie saw Lesley shudder as the room was filled with two voices, one of the caller and the other of the police officer who spoke to him. Mack wrapped his arm round her shoulders as the crayon writer finished by issuing his threat to return Rosie home to them in pieces.

'Why the fuck is he tormenting us?' said Mack as Umpire shut the recording off. 'Look, just give him what he wants. Tell him he can have the money.'

'I know that seems like the easiest solution but what we have to bear in mind is that giving him the money is no guarantee of Rosie's safe return,' said Umpire, shifting awkwardly in his seat again. 'He hasn't issued any instructions about being paid, either, so I think he hasn't properly thought it out. It sounds like the call was a knee-jerk response because he's panicking.'

Mack was furious. 'For fuck's sake. So we just wait until he panics a bit more then starts chopping our daughter up?'

'Don't,' wailed Lesley, 'don't say that.'

'No, Mr Kinnock, we find him first,' said Umpire emphatically. 'Now, is there anything about his voice that rings a bell? Anything at all?'

'What's the point? It sounded like he was trying to disguise it,' said Mack. He flopped back down on the sofa like a sullen teenager.

'Not at the very end he's not. Listen again.' Umpire replayed the recording. 'See? Whatever was covering his mouth must've slipped. Does he sound familiar?'

Lesley and Mack both shook their heads.

'I'm having the tape analysed for background noise, to see if there are any clues as to where the call was made. Once we've done that, I might consider releasing part of the tape to the press in the hope a member of the public recognizes his voice.'

'Can't you just trace the number?' said Lesley.

'It was a pay-as-you-go phone with an unregistered SIM card. It's impossible to trace.'

'It doesn't feel like we're getting anywhere,' she fretted. 'Just give him the money so we can get our little girl back.' She turned to Mack, who had tears in his eyes. 'I'm so sorry, this is all my fault. I wish I'd never bought that bloody ticket.'

Maggie had a sudden blinding flash of inspiration.

'Actually, do you remember when you bought it?' she asked excitedly.

'It was a year ago,' said Lesley.

'I know that, but is there anything you can remember about actually buying the ticket?'

'Only that I was in a rush. It was a Friday morning and I was late for work. But I needed petrol so I stopped at the first petrol station on my route, the Texaco garage on Middle Lane. I filled up, and then I went inside to pay. Like I told you yesterday, I wasn't planning to buy a EuroMillions ticket but I saw a couple of other people holding the slips you have to fill in so I changed my mind at the last minute.'

'There was a queue in the garage?' said Umpire.

Maggie beamed at him. He'd worked out where she was going with her questions.

'I guess there must have been four or five people ahead of me. I remember thinking it was going to make me even later, but one man let me go ahead of him.'

'Do you remember anything about him?' said Belmar, who'd also cottoned on.

Lesley shook her head. 'I wasn't paying attention.'

Maggie could barely contain herself. 'Sir, do you think we should check the CCTV footage from that day?'

The tiredness had vanished from Umpire's face.

'Yes, we should. Well done, DC Neville.'

'I don't understand,' said Lesley helplessly. 'Why do you need to see me buying the ticket?'

'The crayon writer seems to think you stole the money from under his nose,' said Umpire. 'What DC Neville is suggesting is that he might have actually *been* there when you bought it. We need the CCTV from that moment to see who else was in the queue with you.'

Lesley gasped. 'Oh my God. You mean . . .'

Mack jumped up. He, too, looked more invigorated than he'd done in days.

'Hang on, there's no need to get the CCTV. The *Mansell Echo* already published a picture of Lesley in the queue. The garage gave it to them.'

He whipped out his BlackBerry Passport and called up a story on the newspaper's website headlined, *LUCKY MUM'S £15-MILLION MOMENT!* Accompanying the report was a grainy image of Lesley waiting to pay inside the garage. The image was taken from above and Lesley was partially side on to the camera, as was everyone else in the queue, including three men behind her. Maggie shivered. Was one of them the crayon writer?

'Fantastic,' said Umpire, giving the phone back to Mack. 'We can start trying to trace everyone who was in the garage that day.'

'Let me have a look at that,' said Lesley, taking the handset from her husband. She lifted it up to her face so the screen was almost touching her nose. She peered at the screen closely for a few moments then lowered the BlackBerry into her lap. Then she raised the handset to study the screen again, her face flushed.

'What is it?' asked Maggie.

'This man, the one standing right behind me in the tracksuit bottoms, I'm sure I've seen him before.'

Maggie held her breath and she imagined Umpire, Belmar and Mack were doing the same. Then, to her dismay, Lesley burst into tears.

'I know I've seen him, I just can't remember where.'

36

Mack demanded that he and Lesley be left alone for a while. Despite the potential breakthrough with the CCTV image, he was still shell-shocked after listening to the incident room recording, as was his wife.

Maggie and Belmar trailed Umpire into the entrance hall. To her astonishment, once the lounge door was shut to cut them off from the Kinnocks, he turned round and gave her arm a quick squeeze.

'That was inspired, Maggie, well done.'

She was lost for words. Then Belmar caught her eye and winked, embarrassing her even more. She glared back at him. The rumours that she and the DCI had had an affair would never peter out if Belmar spread it around that Umpire was being affectionate towards her.

'If Lesley can remember where she's seen the man behind her in the queue, even better,' Umpire added, seemingly oblivious to the looks Maggie and Belmar were shooting each other.

'I just hope it's not her mind playing tricks on her,' said Maggie, recovering her composure. 'She could be convincing herself there's something familiar about him because she's desperate to do something constructive.'

'Even if that proves to be the case, tracking down those customers might still give us a breakthrough. If none of them are the crayon writer it could be someone they know, a partner or a brother, who's angry on their behalf that they missed out.'

'What would be amazing was if one of them has the initials GS and turns out to be the person Rosie wrote about on her laptop.'

'GS?' Umpire looked puzzled. Maggie got a horrible sinking feeling.

'Didn't DC Berry pass on my message last night?'

'He said you'd found some kind of diary in which Rosie mentioned being bullied and that the laptop had gone to HTCU but he didn't give me specifics,' said Umpire tightly.

'You're kidding me?' she shot back furiously. 'Steve didn't fully brief you last night? But I made it clear to him that it could be really important. What if GS is the crayon writer and we've just been sitting on the lead for a whole day while poor Rosie's still bloody missing?' Maggie flushed red, upset that Steve's sloppiness reflected badly on her just as she and Umpire were getting on. 'I am so sorry you're only hearing about this now, sir.'

'So am I, and I'll be dealing with DC Berry later,' said Umpire, looking as furious as she felt. 'Tell me everything.'

'I found the laptop Rosie emailed Cassie from and she's also been using it as a diary. She wrote in a series of Word documents about being bullied and about being pestered by someone with the initials GS.' She gave him a quick outline of what Rosie had said about girls she knew being promiscuous and pressuring her to be the same. 'On Monday, the day before she went missing, the last thing Rosie wrote was that GS would tell her parents if she didn't do it – presumably have sex – again.'

'For fuck's sake, why didn't I know any of this last night?' Umpire snapped at her. 'Right, come with me.'

'Where to, sir?'

'To see Kathryn Stockton again. DC Small, you stay here in case the Kinnocks need anything.'

He stormed out of the front door and Maggie had to walk fast to keep up. The look on his face told her Steve was going to be in a lot of trouble for not passing on her message and even though he was her friend, deservedly so. She couldn't believe he hadn't taken her seriously when she said GS could be an important lead. Why hadn't he passed it on? The delay could make all the difference to them finding Rosie alive.

'Sir, I've done some digging of my own about GS. I've already asked Kathryn if she knows anyone with those initials and she said no. But I'm not convinced she was being straight with me.'

'So we ask her again,' said Umpire abruptly. She couldn't tell if he was angry with her as well as Steve and mentally she kicked herself for not thinking to call him again last night.

'She might have seen GS hanging around the house on Tuesday, sir,' Maggie suggested, almost breaking into a jog to keep up with him.

'Kathryn wasn't in the area when Rosie disappeared,

though. She was seen leaving the house at ten fifteen a.m. and then we have a witness who saw her on the other side of Haxton fifteen minutes after that.' He gave her a sideways glance. 'Yes, I double-checked her alibi.'

Maggie was disappointed to be proved wrong and scolded herself for letting her personal feelings about Kathryn cloud her judgement. She didn't like the girl but she knew better than to let it sway her.

If Sarah Stockton was surprised to find them back on her doorstep she hid it well. As did Kathryn, who'd skipped her GCSE science exam because she was so upset about her friend being missing. Maggie thought about Rosie's diary entries and bit her lip.

'Will this take long?' Kathryn asked Umpire.

'That depends on whether you're going to tell the truth or not.'

Kathryn blanched and sat down next to her mum on the leather corner sofa in the sitting room.

'Who is GS?'

Kathryn immediately became flustered.

'I've already said, I don't know.'

'Don't bullshit me, Kathryn, I'm not in the mood,' said Umpire, unsmiling. 'I think you know who it is because Rosie told you about him.'

'I have no idea who you're talking about.'

As Kathryn leaned against her mother for support, Maggie was struck by how young and scared she looked now she'd dropped the bravado.

'We have evidence in our possession which suggests

Rosie was being harassed by someone she knows as GS and we think you are an acquaintance of his. If GS turns out to be the person responsible for her going missing and you refuse to tell us who it is, you could be in serious trouble for obstructing the investigation.'

Kathryn burst into tears. 'I don't know anyone whose name begins with GS. You can check my phone, my computer, everything. I'm not lying and I haven't done anything wrong. Mum, tell him!' She fell into her mother's arms and sobbed. Sarah turned on Umpire furiously.

'How dare you threaten my daughter like that? She's just a child.'

'So is Rosie, and she's been missing for two days. I need to find out who GS is,' he shot back.

'If I knew, I would tell you,' wailed Kathryn. 'But I honestly don't.'

Umpire was about to reply but Maggie lightly touched his arm to stop him. 'Can I ask something?' she whispered. He nodded.

'Kathryn, have you introduced Rosie to any boys recently who have taken a shine to her? Maybe they told you afterwards that they fancied her?'

Maggie posed her question in the gentlest voice she could manage, which seemed to calm Kathryn down. The teenager wiped her eyes roughly with the tips of her fingers.

'She met a couple of my friends at Sasha's birthday party, but neither liked her in that way, if you know what I mean. I don't mean to sound horrible, but they both preferred Lily.'

'So you haven't given Rosie's mobile number to boys you know?'

'Are you for real?' Kathryn almost laughed. 'If her dad found out she was texting or chatting to a boy he'd go mad. I wouldn't want to get her into any more trouble. Her dad's strict enough as it is.'

Was she lying again? Before Maggie could decide, Umpire suddenly announced he had no further questions and that he and Maggie were leaving.

'I'm sorry if I upset you,' he said to Kathryn.

She tried to look nonchalant as she shrugged but her tear-streaked face showed how upset she was.

'If you suddenly remember who GS is, you must tell us,' he added.

'I promise you I don't know who that is,' said Kathryn with such conviction that Maggie finally believed her.

They were almost at the door when he turned back.

'Actually, I do have one more question, Kathryn. Do you own a pair of bright green, high-heeled sandals, with an ankle strap? Sort of summery?'

Kathryn looked like she'd just swallowed something unpleasant.

'No way. I can't stand green.'

'I think she's telling the truth,' said Umpire as they walked back to Angel's Reach. 'She doesn't know who GS is.'

'But it can't be a coincidence Rosie wrote about someone harassing her and then she goes missing. Maybe GS aren't his real initials.'

'Did Rosie make any mention of GS asking her for money anywhere in her diary? No? Yet we know the crayon writer is obsessed with the Kinnocks' win. This GS character, on the other hand, is obsessed with her,' said Umpire as they reached the Kinnocks' front gate. 'I'm not convinced they're the same person. GS will turn out to be some poor kid who's got an unrequited crush on Rosie. If it sounds dramatic from the way she writes it, it's probably because she doesn't know how to handle the situation.'

'But what about the condom trace on the skirt in the bush? What if GS had something to do with that getting there?'

'There's been an update on that. Matheson doesn't think Rosie was wearing the skirt when the blood loss occurred. Apparently, the tests he ran show that the blood soaked into the tulle overlay first and then onto the skirt fabric beneath it, rather than the other way round. He thinks it's more likely the skirt was used to staunch whatever wound the blood was coming from and that the condom trace was most likely left there another time.'

'I don't know whether that's good news or bad,' said Maggie darkly. 'It doesn't change the fact a condom was used at some point.'

'I hate to break it to you, DC Neville, but fifteen-year-old girls do have sex sometimes, underage or not. You seem really intent on holding up Rosie as some kind of paragon of virtue.'

Maggie stared at him, shocked. 'Do I?'

'Yes. I didn't realize you were so conservative. It's the

same every time Suzy Breed's name crops up,' he said, looking amused.

'I'm not a prude, sir,' she blustered.

'I'll have to take your word for that.'

Maggie felt herself blush. Keen to steer the conversation away from sex, she suggested GS might be someone Rosie knew from living in Mansell.

'The diary entry implied Kathryn knows him, but what if Rosie introduced him to Kathryn and not the other way round?' she said.

Umpire pondered her theory for a second. 'Okay, call Cassie Perrie, the friend Rosie sent the email to, and see if she knows anyone called GS.'

'Me?'

'Yes, you. I can't spare anyone else. It's just a phone call; I'm not asking you to interrogate her. Admin support will give you the number for her mum. Cassie's only fifteen so you'll need to go through her first.'

Maggie was delighted to be trusted with a task that went beyond her remit, however small. It felt like another big step forward in repairing their working relationship.

'I'll get on to it straight away,' she said.

'Good.' He stopped by his car. 'Right, I need to get back to the station to chase up Suzy Breed's phone records. Hopefully they'll tell us what's going on between her and Mack and whether it has any bearing on Rosie going missing. I seriously doubt it has, especially now we know about the crayon writer, but we can at least put that line of inquiry to bed, so to speak.'

Maggie caught the humour in his voice and blushed

again. She stared down at the gravel driveway, wishing it would swallow her up.

'Keep on at Lesley until she remembers where she's seen the suspect before and call me the minute she does,' Umpire went on. Then he stopped abruptly and stared at her. 'You look tired, Neville. I don't want DI Gant on my back telling me you're overloaded, so DC Small should stay with the Kinnocks tonight if they want him to and you can have a break.'

'Sir, I'm fine, really,' she said, appalled to think she looked otherwise.

'It wasn't a request, Neville. I'm well aware how draining FL duty can be because DI Gant tells me often enough. But he's right to worry and I need you rested and ready to deal with what's ahead.'

'What do you mean, sir?'

The smile fell from his face and he looked pained. 'We're almost at the end of day three and it feels like we're no closer to finding her. I think we're in for the long haul.'

37

He sang all the way home listening to Absolute Radio. It didn't matter whether he knew each song as it came on, he still belted out the words at the top of his voice, substituting 'la-la-la' for those he didn't know.

His headache had finally dissipated and he felt invincible. He swept back along the M40 to Mansell as though he owned it and ignored the motorists who sounded their horns at him for cutting them up. Let them beep. Soon he'd own a car they'd all wish they could drive, rather than this crappy, second-hand Peugeot that wasn't even his.

His conversation with the police officer in the incident room played on a loop in his head. Every time he reached the end he burst into gales of laughter. Surely now they'd sit up and take notice: there was no question in his mind that they wouldn't bow to his demands.

The previous evening he had spent hours on the Internet trying to establish the best means for them to send him his money. Dropping it off in a bag like they did in films was quickly dismissed; banknotes could be too easily traced through their serial numbers and the police were bound to stake out the handover. Then he toyed with the idea of getting the Kinnocks to deposit it into an untraceable Austrian bank account called a 'Sparbuch', but further digging revealed he would have to involve a third party to set it up and that was out of the question. Other offshore accounts he researched required him to present his passport to set them up – too easily traceable – so the only other feasible option was a prepaid credit card. The Kinnocks would have to get their bank to issue one in a false name provided by him, then arrange a collection or delivery point. It wasn't ideal – there was a risk they could trace him through his purchases if he wasn't careful – but he should be able to sell the card on and pocket the balance. There were a couple of websites he found that explained exactly how to do that. And although most pre-paid cards had a load limit of only £5,000, he expected customers as wealthy as the Kinnocks could demand more. He'd come across a Visa card called a T24 Black that could take $50,000.

Back indoors he ran straight upstairs, the soles of his trainers slapping hard against the stripped floorboards. He reached the door to the spare room, which he'd commandeered as an office, and threw it wide open. The painted green walls were hidden beneath piles of newspaper cuttings, photographs and pages of A4 paper filled in his neat handwriting. Above his desk, in the centre of the wall, was a snapshot of the girl's family that was originally published in the *Mansell Echo*. He wanted to scream every time he looked at it. The parents were smiling as they raised their glasses of champagne at the camera, while the girl clutched a matching flute filled with what looked like orange juice. Propped up in front of them was an oversized cheque made out for the sum of £15 million from Camelot, the distinctive crossed-fingers logo of the National Lottery in one corner and the EuroMillions logo in the other. He clenched his fists as he studied the cheque. It wasn't even like he was asking for the whole lot. He just wanted something as a thank you.

Next to the photograph was a torn-out page from the *Echo* with his picture on it. Or rather his side view, taken inside the garage moments after he'd let the mother shove in front of him. He'd kept it to remind himself why he was doing all this.

'You will pay up,' he spoke aloud to the parents' smiling faces. 'You have no choice.'

The alarm on his watch beeped to remind him it was time for his testosterone injection. As he retrieved his syringe kit from his sports bag, he saw there was hardly any liquid left in the vial. Rooting around the bottom of his bag he realized it was his last one and immediately he broke out in a sweat. He had just enough now, but if he didn't get some more before his next injection was due in a couple of days, his body would go into withdrawal. The last time he tried to come off it he'd become depressed, could barely eat or sleep, and the pain in his back was agonizingly worse than it had been before. He couldn't face that again.

He reached for his phone.

'It's me,' he said. 'I need some pumpers.'

The person he'd called knew exactly what he meant.

'Already? I only got you that last batch a fortnight ago. It was a month's supply.'

'Don't fucking lecture me. Can you get me some or not?'

The line went silent for a moment and he kicked himself for being rude to the one person he needed to keep on side.

'Sorry, I didn't mean to snap. Can you sort me out?'

'Yeah. When do you want it?'

'Today. I can meet you at the gym.'

'It's a bit short notice. I don't know if I can . . .'

'Please, I need it,' he said, hating himself for begging but knowing he had little choice.

'Okay. I'll text you when it's ready. I'm at home now. Just think about how much you're taking though, mate. This stuff can fuck you up big time.'

He rubbed the ridge on his forehead, the incontrovertible proof that it already had. But he couldn't cut back, not now. He had to stay strong.

'I know it does, I just lost track of my dosage. I'll be more careful with the next lot. Thanks, Rob, you're a mate.'

38

No matter how deep into the recesses of her memory she trawled, Lesley couldn't place the man behind her in the queue. The police said they were going to enhance the CCTV image so she could see it more clearly but, until that happened, she was left with only the grainy shot to ponder.

There was a kernel of recognition, but from where? Biting her nails as she perched on the edge of the sofa, she thought about everyone she knew. Was it someone's son or brother? What about a customer at the optician's on the high street where she used to work part-time, or maybe a teacher from Rosie's old school? But still she drew a blank and Mack grew more and more frustrated with her until Belmar, hearing him shout, came back into the lounge and persuaded him to leave her alone to give her space to think.

Mack left his phone with her so she could use the picture on the *Echo*'s website to jog her memory. Straight away she checked his text messages to see if there were any more from Suzy Breed but there were no new ones, and the ones she'd previously read had been deleted.

Had he cut off contact because the police were asking about her, or was he using another means to stay in touch? Lesley debated bringing it up but decided to bury her anger for the time being. She didn't have the emotional capacity to deal with it on top of everything else.

Instead she thought about the man who'd called the incident room and made the vile threat towards Rosie. She fantasized about hurting him, of digging her nails into his face as hard as she could and dragging them through his skin. Her desire for violence was overwhelming, a primal urge she'd experienced only once before when a much older child had deliberately pushed Rosie over at school and the fall fractured her wrist. Back then, she'd tempered the urge with the knowledge that to act upon her rage would not only be wrong but would probably get her arrested too. With the crayon writer she wouldn't suppress it. If she got her hands on him she'd let herself kill the bastard.

She wondered how long he'd been waiting to make his move. Had he been watching them, biding his time for when Mack wasn't there and she'd gone out and Rosie was home alone? Was it days, weeks, even months? She shook her head. No, he must've acted on the spur of the moment because she would've *known* if someone was spying on them. The house might be veiled behind its boundaries but its very isolation meant she reacted to the tiniest of disturbances. She might not have seen or heard anyone lingering outside, but she was adamant she would have sensed it.

'Lesley?'

'In here.'

Maggie came in. She had an energy about her that made Lesley feel a bit better. If Maggie thought tracking down the people in the queue was something to be excited about, then she would be, too. Christ knows she was tired of feeling tired.

'Any luck remembering?' Maggie asked.

Lesley felt weighed down by pressure. So much was riding on her recalling where she'd seen him but her mind just wouldn't cooperate.

'I'm sorry, I just can't think,' she said balefully.

'Hey, it's okay, don't be upset. It was a while ago. Just keep looking at the pictures and hopefully it will come back to you.'

'I wish I shared your confidence. I know I've seen him somewhere before but every time I try to think my mind goes blank,' she said. 'Look, I'm really sorry for the way I spoke to you at breakfast about doing more to help find Rosie. I shouldn't have been rude and I want you to know that I do appreciate everything you're doing for us. I'd think I'd be in a far worse state if you weren't here.'

'No need to apologize. It's already forgotten,' said Maggie airily.

'Well, still, I'm truly sorry.' Lesley rubbed her eyes and yawned. 'I think I might go and lie down. I didn't get much sleep last night. Come and get me if there's any news.' She took Mack's BlackBerry upstairs with her and napped with it next to her on the pillow, her last thought before drifting off about the man in the queue and where she'd seen him before. She was soon fast asleep and she didn't stir when her husband's phone beeped to signal the arrival of a new text message.

Mack, I'm waiting . . . xoxo

39

Miriam Perrie was shopping when Maggie got through to her just before 3 p.m. and she sounded harassed. Twice Maggie said her name, but Miriam couldn't hear her over the clamour of background noise.

'Hang on a minute, let me go outside so I can hear you better. I'm in John Lewis.'

Maggie heard muffled sounds as Cassie's mum left the store in Mansell.

'Sorry about that. Who did you say you were?'

'Detective Constable Maggie Neville. I'm part of the team investigating Rosie Kinnock's disappearance.'

'Oh! Have you found her?'

'No, not yet I'm afraid. I would like to speak to your daughter Cassie though. There's a line of inquiry that's emerged that I'm hoping she might be able to help us with.'

'What line of inquiry?'

'Well, I think it's best if I talk to Cassie about it in person. Can I come round later? It won't take long.'

'She does taekwondo after school on a Thursday. The class takes a couple of hours.'

'Could I speak to her on the phone beforehand? It's rather urgent. You could give her my number and have her call me.'

'I suppose I could – if I knew what it was about.'

Miriam Perrie was clearly no pushover and if Maggie wanted to get to Cassie, she'd have to appease her first.

'I want to ask Cassie if she's ever heard Rosie talk about someone with the initials GS. We think it's a male,' she said.

'GS? That's all you've got to go on?'

'Yes, but it's someone Rosie came into contact with quite often by the sound of things.'

Miriam fell silent for a moment. Rosie could hear traffic in the background and assumed she was either in the store's car park or nearby.

'I'll bet you anything the initials don't stand for the person's real name. It'll be a nickname Rosie came up with to keep who they are a secret,' said Miriam. 'It's what Cassie used to do so I wouldn't have a clue what she and her friends were talking about. Everything was in code or abbreviated, like BFN, bbz and YOLO.'

'Sorry?'

'That's what I used to say too,' said Miriam. 'BFN means bye for now, bbz is short for babes and YOLO is you only live once. So don't assume GS stands for the person's real name – I know full well Cassie used to call me BN for Bloody Nag. Look, I guess she might know. Let me call her now and I'll ask her to ring you. She'll just be finishing school.'

'Thanks. I'll text you my number to forward to her.'

Cassie rang shortly afterwards but their conversation

left Maggie deflated. She had no idea who GS was and swore the email Rosie sent her on Sunday was the only one she'd received in the past six months. She hadn't sent a reply because she no longer considered Rosie a friend, and she didn't tell the police about it because she'd only given the email a cursory glance when it arrived in her inbox. It was after she saw Lesley crying on television that she realized she should say something. She also confirmed, as Miriam suspected, that Rosie was probably using false initials to disguise GS's real identity.

'We did it all the time for the boys at school so they wouldn't know we were talking about them,' Cassie told Maggie. 'There was this one lad in the sixth form we both fancied who always wore a red jumper to school. So he was RJ. Another we nicknamed BB, for bad breath. It was just silly kids' stuff.'

'You really don't remember Rosie mentioning GS?'

'No, it must be someone in Haxton. It's not anyone from around here as far as I know.'

'Are there any other friends in Mansell who might know?'

'I guess Emma might. She and Rosie were close too.'

'What's Emma's surname?'

'Mitchell.'

'Do you have a number or address for her?'

'She lives in the same road as me, number forty-four.'

'What street is that?'

'Dartmoor Road. Rosie lived around the corner until she moved.'

Maggie did a quick mental calculation. Dartmoor Road was also on the Corley and only a five-minute drive from Rob's flat. She could see Emma first, drop round to collect Lou's money on her way back to her flat, then call to update Umpire on what Emma said.

She sent Rob a text to warn him she was coming.

40

He couldn't relax as he waited for Rob to text him. He roamed aimlessly from room to room in search of something to fill the time and occupy his mind. His thoughts were all over the place, one minute brooding on the girl, the next jumping to how soon he could have his operation done. In the kitchen he made himself a ham sandwich but tossed it in the bin after the first dry mouthful caught in his throat and made him gag. He tried watching television, but his limbs were too twitchy and he couldn't sit still. Was that another side effect of the steroids creeping up on him or simply his anxiety? Turning the television off, he went upstairs to the back bedroom, which used to be his parents' room. He'd cleared it out after their funeral, throwing away all their clothes and belongings as well as the furniture, and now its only occupant was a solitary exercise bike. He climbed on and began pedalling furiously.

He rarely thought about his parents these days. They'd been dead for almost half his life now. He was nineteen and at university when they were killed in an accident on the M40, crushed into the central reservation by a lorry whose driver didn't see their car in his blind spot. The sole heir, he'd kept the house that was his childhood home but none of the furnishings. Everything went. Then he returned to his student digs in Loughborough to finish his degree, coming back only during the holidays. On graduating, he went travelling on the money his parents had left in their will, staying in Australia for eighteen months on his way round the world. By the time he moved back to Mansell three years later, memories of his parents had dimmed and his bank account was empty.

Settling back into suburban life was hard and that's when the heavy drinking began. Seven nights a week down the pub, all day at weekends. It took the fall off the scaffolding to sober him up and he hadn't touched a drop of alcohol since. He no longer needed that form of self-medication when painkillers did just as effective a job. It was only when his doctor wanted to cut down his dosage to protect his liver function that he was forced to find an alternative and was introduced to Rob by one of the trainers at the gym.

As he cycled, his phone lay on the floor next to the bike. Every minute or so he glanced at it, willing a text from Rob to appear. He hated being this needy, this dependent. But a lifetime of pain was something he simply couldn't contemplate.

He had just reached 6 km according to the bike's LCD console when the doorbell rang downstairs. The muscles in his thighs clenched in protest as he stopped the pedals dead and climbed off. He wasn't expecting any visitors, nor was he due to have anything delivered.

But there was no way to check who was at the front door as the porch roof obscured his view from the upstairs window that overlooked it. He waited for a moment at the top of the stairs, panting from exertion but also from fear. Was it the police? Had they worked out who he was?

The doorbell rang again, for longer this time. Then he heard a female voice call his name and his stomach somersaulted in shock. He flew down the stairs and wrenched the door open.

'What the fuck are you doing here?'

She looked as bemused as he was. 'Surprised to see me?'

'How did you know I was here?' he said. 'I told you I'd be in London.'

'This is where you live, isn't it?' She crossed her arms defiantly. 'I think we have things to talk about, don't you?'

Fury engulfed him. He wanted to kill her. With his bare hands, a blunt instrument, he didn't care how. She'd shown up on his doorstep in broad daylight, risking everything, and now he had to get rid of her.

'Well, aren't you going to ask me in?' she snapped.

'Do I have a choice?'

'What do you think?'

He stepped aside and let her through. She started to say something about his house, but he couldn't concentrate on her words. The sound of her voice drove him mad. It drilled into his skull and burrowed into his brain and made him want to rip his ears off.

'Shut the fuck up,' he howled. 'You had no right to come here.'

'Don't talk to me like that—'

Her eyes widened with fear as he raised his right fist. She tried to move away but he grabbed hold of her arm with his left hand. The first blow knocked her sideways. The second knocked her out cold.

Silence, at last.

41

The Corley was to the east of the town centre. As ugly as it was sprawling, the estate was built on a steep hill-side that had a high percentage of chalk in its soil and many of the houses had gaping cracks in the walls due to subsidence. Maggie's parents had to knock almost ten thousand pounds off the asking price because of the problem when they sold up and moved to the other side of town, to a brand-new development.

The estate still felt like home to Maggie, even though she hadn't lived there since she was twelve. The tangle of streets with their tight corners, dead ends and sharp inclines were as familiar to her as the back of her hand and as she drove towards Dartmoor Road she felt a prick of belonging she had never experienced anywhere else. Her and Lou's devastation at being forced to leave the Corley was only tempered by their parents driving them back to see their friends as often as they could.

Emma Mitchell's mum answered the door clutching a grimy yellow duster in one hand and a can of Pledge in the other. She squinted at Maggie's warrant card then shook her head.

'Emma told everything to the other police lady who came round yesterday. She's very upset right now.'

'The last thing I want is to upset her further, but it's important that I speak to her. I wouldn't ask if it wasn't.'

Mrs Mitchell hugged the polish and duster to her chest like a toddler might a soft toy. She was solidly built and wore a voluminous dark green blouse over baggy black trousers that made her appear even larger.

'I'm not trying to be difficult,' she said, 'but Emma's not stopped crying since she heard about Rosie going missing.'

'But this might help find her, Mrs Mitchell. Please, I'll be quick, I promise. Ten minutes, that's all I need.'

She looked Maggie up and down.

'You've got five. Wait here.'

Emma showed herself to be just as suspicious as her mum. Poking her head around the front door, she barked, 'What do you want?'

If it wasn't for the school uniform she wore, Emma would have passed for a girl much older than sixteen. Her skin was covered in a thick layer of foundation and her eyes heavily ringed with black kohl. Both ears were pierced multiple times and her hair, dyed almost black, was twisted into a side ponytail. She was the kind of scary-looking girl Maggie had gone out of her way to avoid when she was at school. But Emma's made-up eyes were also red and puffy from crying and when Maggie explained why she was there, she blinked back fresh tears.

'What do you want to know?'

'Can I come inside?'

Emma's guard stayed up. 'Here's fine.'

'If that's what you'd prefer. I just wanted to check when you last spoke to Rosie?'

'Ages ago.'

'I think you're lying, Emma. I think, like Cassie, you were in touch with Rosie as recently as last week,' she said. It was a gamble, based on nothing but a hunch that Rosie might have reached out to more than one old friend because she was so upset at being bullied. Maggie's legs were like jelly as she waited for Emma to answer.

The girl's eyes widened. 'Who told you that?'

'Well, did you speak to her last week?'

'Fuck off and leave me alone.'

'This isn't a game, Emma,' said Maggie, her voice hardening. 'Do you want to help find Rosie or not?'

Emma scowled as though readying herself to argue back. Then her face fell.

'I'm sorry. I did talk to her.'

Maggie wanted to punch the air but managed to keep her face straight. 'When, exactly?'

'Last Wednesday. She called me when I was on my way to school.'

'From a mobile?'

'Yes.'

'You're sure it wasn't a landline?'

'It came up as her number.'

'My colleagues have traced all her last known calls and I'm pretty certain your name and number didn't crop up.'

Emma shrugged. 'I don't know why it didn't. She called me, not the other way round.'

'Why did she ring?'

'She wanted advice.'

Emma's guard was rising again. She kept glancing over her shoulder and Maggie suspected her mum was hovering behind the door, listening to their conversation.

'And?' she prompted.

'I can't say.'

'Come on, Emma, that's not going to wash. Either you tell me what she said or we go down the station and continue the questions there.'

The threat worked.

'She was being hassled by some bloke and wanted me to tell her how to deal with it. She didn't say who.'

'Is that all she said?'

'No. She said she didn't like the guy but he kept on pestering her, going on and on about how much he wants to sleep with her and do other stuff.'

Maggie didn't want to think about what 'other stuff' involved.

'She definitely didn't mention his name?'

'No. It was only a quick call because I had to go to registration.'

'Do the initials GS mean anything to you?'

'No, why?'

Maggie explained what Cassie had said about her and Rosie making up names for people. Emma was scathing when Maggie asked if she'd done the same.

'Yeah, maybe when I was ten,' she said, pulling a face.

299

'Okay, tell me what else Rosie said about this guy.'

'Only that she met him at a party before Christmas.'

'Where was that?'

'She didn't say. Like I said, it wasn't a long call.'

'Did she talk about her friends in Haxton?'

Emma hesitated. 'She did say some of them were giving her a hard time for being a virgin and were trying to get her to sleep with this guy as a favour. I told Rosie to tell them to fuck off. It's a shitty thing to expect her to sleep with some bloke just because some friend owed him one.'

'Has Rosie had much sexual experience as far as you know?'

'Not really. She's kissed a couple of guys but I don't think she's gone any further. That's why I told her she should tell these friends to fuck off. She shouldn't do anything she doesn't want to.'

'Did she name who's been pressuring her?'

'No, she didn't.'

'When was the last time you saw each other?'

'On her birthday last August. Her mum and dad paid for a meal at Prezzo and me and Cassie went. But we fell out with her after that.'

'How come?'

'She didn't want us there. I think it was her mum who said she had to invite us. There were all these girls she goes to school with and goes riding with and they were being total bitches. They talked to me and Cass like we were crap and Rosie never said anything. She just sat there while they were being horrible, like she was too scared to say anything in case they started on her. It was pathetic.'

'Can you remember any of them?'

'There was one with dark hair who lived next door to Rosie, she was the worst. She kept asking if our road was like the one on that programme, *Benefits Street*. I should've lamped her, thinking about it. A couple were okay though. Lily seemed all right, although I did over-hear her being nasty about Cassie's dress when I went to the loo. Anyway, after that we didn't bother with Rosie. There was no point,' said Emma sadly.

'You'd say Rosie's easily influenced by others then? She'll just go along with something to fit in?'

'I s'pose.'

Was that how Rosie ended up being photographed sprawled on a bed in next to nothing? Peer pressure? Maggie thought about asking Emma if she was aware of the image but decided against it. That was Umpire's call.

'Is that it?' said Emma, getting fidgety.

'Not quite. In all the time you've known Rosie, have you ever known her to cut herself?'

Emma looked shocked. 'What, you mean like self-harm? No, I haven't and I would be amazed if she had. That's not like Rosie. She's too straight to do anything like that.'

'You should've mentioned the phone call from her to the officer who interviewed you yesterday,' Maggie said sharply.

Emma flushed beneath her thick foundation.

'Look, me and Rosie hadn't spoken since August. When she called I thought it was just an excuse to tell me some rich boy fancied her. If I'd thought for one minute she was really upset by him bothering her, I'd have gone round there and sorted him out myself.'

42

Lesley's eyelids fluttered open as Mack woke her with a soft kiss on the lips.

'Wake up, sweetheart,' he whispered. 'If you nap any longer you won't be able to sleep later.'

She lay still, not wanting to talk or move, as Mack traced his index finger down her cheek. Exhaustion had scored deep lines on both sides of his mouth, his eyes were bloodshot and his hair had aged overnight with the arrival of more grey flecks. The deterioration in his appearance alarmed her. Mack was meant to be the strong one, the one who held it together while she let the smallest worries swamp her. She couldn't cope if he crumbled too.

'I had Belmar get the papers for us. I thought you might want to see them,' he said.

The plush mattress impeded her effort to sit up but with one last push on her elbows she heaved herself upright and rested her shoulders against the headboard. Her gaze fell upon the newspapers fanned out across the foot of their bed.

'I don't want to read them. Just tell me what they say.'

Her throat was scratchy, like she was coming down with something.

'Most of them have led on the fact we've reduced the reward. It doesn't look good,' he admitted. 'I'm sorry, love. I wish I'd never said it.'

She took his hand and squeezed it.

'Stop torturing yourself. It doesn't matter what the press thinks. Let them write what they want.'

'Oh, they already are,' he said grimly. 'A couple of the tabloids are insinuating we must be hiding something for going back on the reward.'

She thought about Suzy Breed but said nothing.

'We needed them on our side and I blew it,' said Mack.

'Let's talk to Maggie about it. She might have an idea what to do.'

'She's already gone home for the evening. She didn't want to wake you before she left.'

'Okay, we'll talk to Belmar then.'

'Fine.'

Lesley looked around on the bed but couldn't see his phone anywhere.

'Where's your BlackBerry? I want another look at that picture from the garage. If I can remember where I've seen that man before, we can tell the papers and give them something else to write about.'

The phone was on his bedside table and Mack moved off the bed to retrieve it. The loss of warmth as he withdrew his hand from hers made Lesley shiver as though gripped by a sudden chill and she tucked the duvet tightly round her.

'Did you go through my messages?' he suddenly asked.

'Sorry?'

'My text messages. Have you looked at them?'

Lesley tried to keep her voice even.

'Now why would I do that, Mack?'

'I'm not saying you did, I'm just asking.'

'It's the same thing. Either you think I did or you don't.'

He looked at her sternly.

'I don't want you going through my phone.'

Lesley sat back, eyes wide with surprise.

'I beg your pardon?'

'You heard me. You'll just get the wrong end of the stick.'

The way he spoke to her made her furious. 'How is me reading a text from your ex saying you stayed with her in Scotland when you should've been in a hotel getting the wrong end of the stick exactly?' she shot back.

'See, you did read them!'

'That's beside the point!' she shouted. 'Why is Suzy Breed texting to say she won't tell anyone you were with her?'

'It's not what you think. The woman's stalking me.'

His answer stunned her.

'She's *what*?'

'Stalking me. She has been ever since we won the lottery. I didn't want to tell you because I know how you feel about her and how upset you get when people ask us for money. But that's why she's texting me and trying to make it sound like I was with her.'

'Why didn't you say anything?'

'I thought I could make it go away.'

'How exactly?'

As Mack floundered for an answer, Lesley tried to marshal her confused thoughts into some kind of order.

'Right, start at the beginning,' she said. 'What exactly has been going on?'

'About a month after we won, she emailed me out of the blue saying she was really pleased for us and how great it was we never had to worry about money again. I stupidly replied saying thanks and the next thing I know she's saying that if I don't give her some money she'll tell you we've been having an affair.'

'Well, have you?'

'Had an affair? Oh, come on, sweetheart, I wouldn't do that to you.'

'No, I meant have you sent her any money.'

He paused. 'Yes.'

'Oh, Mack—'

'I know, I know. It was completely fucking stupid of me. I just thought that if I gave her something, she'd leave me alone. But she came back asking for more and more.'

'How much have you given her?'

He shook his head. 'It doesn't matter.'

'Yes it does. How much?'

He dropped his head into his hands. 'I've been such an idiot.'

'I shan't argue with that,' said Lesley, pulling back the covers and crawling over the mattress to reach him. She took his hand again. 'How much, Mack?'

'About fifty grand.'

'How much! Are you mad?'

'It wasn't all at once. First it was just five thousand but she kept asking for more.'

Lesley wasn't convinced. 'If she's got nothing on you, why pay her?'

'I knew how you felt about her and I was scared you'd believe her.'

'Oh, so it's all my fault, is it?'

'I just wanted her to leave us alone. But now Rosie's missing she's making all sorts of threats.'

'Like what?'

He took a deep breath. 'I did something stupid in Scotland.'

Lesley went still. 'Did you sleep with her?'

'No, I went to see her on Sunday and I gave her another grand. Then I stayed in Falkirk.'

'With *her*?' Lesley hissed.

'No, I checked into a hotel nearby. I didn't want to go all the way back to St Andrews late at night.'

'Mack, did you have sex with that woman in Scotland?'

'No, I bloody well didn't. I spent the whole time trying to reason with her. I was trying to get her to leave us alone.'

'By screwing her?' Lesley shook her head. 'You must think I was born yesterday.'

'It's the truth. I haven't laid a finger on her, not even a kiss on the cheek. But she won't give up. She's been sending me messages saying she'll tell the police I hit

Rosie and made her run away unless I give her more money. She wants half a million.'

'That's sick!'

'The woman's a nutcase.' Mack looked so stricken and desperate that Lesley found herself believing him.

'We should tell the police ourselves. They can arrest her—'

'No!' he shouted. 'Let me handle this, love. I don't want anyone else knowing. It's our business.'

'I can't believe she could stoop so low,' said Lesley, slumping back on the bed. She felt like the stuffing had been knocked out of her. 'What if the police mention her to me again? What should I say?'

'Don't say anything.'

'But if Suzy goes to them first . . .'

'She won't.'

'How can you be so sure? She's taken no notice of what you've said so far.'

'She will when I'm done with her. That bitch has had her last penny out of me, don't you worry.'

43

Maggie almost gave up waiting for Rob to answer the door. Twice she buzzed up to his flat and twice there was no response. After the third attempt she was about to walk back to her car when his voice echoed through the intercom and told her to come up. There was a click as the communal front door unlocked.

She was surprised to be invited upstairs, having expected him to come down to her, and guessed it was because Lisa was not at home. No way would she, Lou's sister, be allowed over the threshold otherwise.

The flat was on the top floor of a block that used to be council-owned. The landlord had bought up a swathe of them around Mansell and Maggie knew of him because he'd been arrested on four occasions for threatening tenants. None of the cases ever made it to court, as the witnesses always proved too unreliable for the Crown Prosecution Service to risk proceeding. Intimidation was almost certainly a factor but could never be proved.

Maggie waited on the landing outside Rob's front door. When he didn't appear, she knocked loudly.

'Come in,' he yelled from somewhere inside.

Now she knew for certain Lisa wasn't at home. Feeling curious, she stepped into a dingy, narrow hallway with grubby magnolia walls and a beige carpeted floor. So far, so average. The hall led to an open-plan lounge-diner, where she found Rob sitting at a small stripped-pine table counting out ten-pound notes into a neat pile. A quick glance around suggested he and Lisa had yet to make the flat a home – there were no pictures on the walls, no cushions on the dark blue futon sofa. A small table lamp sat forlornly on the floor, which was carpeted in the same beige as the hallway.

'Hey,' he said.

Manners forced her to be polite. 'Hi. How are you?'

'Yeah, fine. I didn't get the job I went for, but, well, you know.'

Articulation had never been Rob's strong point.

'I'm sure you'll find something else,' she said. 'Is that Lou's money?'

'Yeah. It's all here. You can count it if you want.'

'No, it's fine.' She glanced around. 'No Lisa?'

He shifted in his seat. 'She's gone to stay with a friend in Manchester.'

'Nice for her. When's she back?'

'Tonight I think.'

His reaction suggested he didn't know for sure, and it occurred to Maggie that Lisa might be giving him the runaround already. It was no less than he deserved.

'Right, I'd best get off,' she said, taking the envelope of cash he held out to her and making for the door.

'How are the boys?' he suddenly asked.

Maggie turned round. Rob shrugged sheepishly.

'I know I don't have the right to ask, not being their dad and all that. But, well, you know.'

He looked so downbeat that Maggie found herself – against her better judgement – feeling sorry for him.

'You're their stepdad; it's okay for you to miss them. And –' she crossed her fingers behind her back, knowing Lou would hate her for saying it – 'the boys miss you too.'

He brightened. 'Do they?'

'Yes, a lot. It'd be good if you could make more time to see them.'

'Lou won't let me. Says I'm not their proper dad so I don't get access.'

Maggie was annoyed with her sister. However angry she was with Rob, not letting the boys see him wasn't on. It wasn't fair to punish them for his leaving her.

'I'll talk to her about it,' she said.

'Really? Ah, cheers. She'll listen to you.'

Maggie wasn't sure she shared his optimism but said she'd try her best for the boys' sake.

'One more thing . . .' he began.

Here we go, she thought uncharitably. There was always something else with Rob. 'Go on.'

He squirmed in his chair and Maggie realized he was nervous, which surprised her. Loud, blunt, rude? Rob was all those things. Skittish? Hardly.

'You got anything to do with that missing girl case in Haxton?'

'Yes,' she said suspiciously. 'I'm the FLO to her family, in fact.'

His Adam's apple bobbed up and down as he swallowed hard. 'What if someone older goes missing? Do you lot do the same then?'

'You mean do the police investigate in the same way? No. With an adult you have to wait twenty-four hours to file a missing person's report, unless they're particularly vulnerable, like they're elderly or ill. Why do you ask?'

He shrugged again. 'No reason.'

There clearly was one, so she waited for a few moments, hoping the elapsing silence might prompt him to elaborate. When he didn't, she decided it wasn't worth worrying about.

'Thanks for the money,' she said, as Rob waved her out. 'Try not to leave it so late next time.'

44

He drummed his fingers impatiently on the steering wheel. Rob hadn't said anything about someone else going round to see him first and he didn't like being made to wait.

He had been halfway up the path when he saw the woman press the button for Rob's flat on the entry intercom and doubled back before she noticed him. He wondered who she was. She looked too classy for Rob's usual type, the trouser suit at odds with the miniskirts and halter-necks that girlfriend of his usually wore. She must be someone official. In any case, she was too tall for his personal taste – he liked his women short and slight, so he could tower over them. If she wore heels, she'd be the same height. He'd hate that.

She didn't see him sitting in his car because he was parked not outside the flats but around the corner in the next street. He didn't want Rob to know he was driving this crappy little car. After fifteen minutes he saw the woman drive past in a cherry red Toyota and knew it was safe for him to go up.

Rob wasn't in the best of moods when he arrived at

the flat. He assumed it had something to do with the woman.

'Who was that who just came round?' he asked. 'The woman I saw leave?'

'My sister-in-law.'

'Bit smartly dressed, wasn't she?'

'She's a copper. CID.'

He froze. 'A detective?'

'Yeah.'

'What was she doing here?'

'Picking up some cash I owe her sister, my ex.'

'Shouldn't she be at work?'

'I suppose. She's on that missing girl case. She does family handling or whatever it's called.'

His heart beat wildly as it dawned on him how close he'd come to meeting the officer whose job it was to look after the parents. What he'd have given to ask her about their reaction to his phone call! Were they ready to pay him his money? A plan began to form in his mind. He needed to draw up the instructions for the parents to sort out the pre-paid credit card and get it to him. Rob's sister-in-law might just be the glue that held his plan together.

'There was something on the radio about that just now. What does she think has happened to the girl?'

'Didn't ask. Wait here, I'll get your gear.'

Rob went into the kitchen. He heard the sound of a fridge door being opened and closed then Rob came back holding a Tupperware box. He opened it up and took out two vials from the dozen or so inside it. Both contained clear liquid and as Rob held them up to the light he saw the language printed on the side was again one he didn't understand.

'It's the same stuff as last time,' said Rob. 'Same price.'

He reached into the pocket of his tracksuit bottoms, pulled out a roll of money and peeled off six fifty-pound notes. 'Here you go.'

'This is two months' supply. Try to make it last this time. It's fucking nasty stuff if you don't use it right.'

He bristled. Who the hell did Rob think he was talking to? These business transactions did not make them friends – Rob should consider himself lucky he gave him the time of day.

'You're hardly one to talk,' he said, nodding at Rob's hulking arms.

'Yeah, but I'm not stupid.' Rob grinned.

That's debatable, he thought wryly. He pocketed the vials.

'What have you done to your hand?' said Rob. 'Looks nasty.'

He flexed the sore, bruised knuckles on his right hand, from where he'd hit the wall. 'Oh, it's nothing. I just caught it on a door,' he lied.

'You been at the gym today?' Rob asked.

'No, I've been seeing private clients. Why?'

'Just wondered if you saw Lisa there.'

'Your girlfriend Lisa? The one you live with? Mate, wouldn't she tell you if she'd gone to the gym?'

Rob went red. 'It's nothing. Forget I mentioned it.'

'No, come on, you can tell me.' It was written all over Rob's face that something was up.

'Lisa went to stay with a friend at the weekend. She

was meant to be back by now but hasn't come home yet. I've tried calling but her phone's off. I thought she might have gone straight to work.'

'Oh yeah, I forgot she sometimes covers the reception when Kelli's off. Sorry, like I said, I haven't been in today.'

Rob shrugged. 'I bet she's pissed off about something. I'll talk to her later.'

He pretended to be interested but he was bored talking about Lisa now. She wasn't what he'd ever consider girlfriend material, with her slutty clothes, straw-like black hair and her habit of being over-familiar with customers. Fine for a fuck, if you were prepared to lower your standards, but nothing more than that. Even Rob could do better than her.

'Maybe she found out about your little visit from your hot sister-in-law?' he joked.

Rob pulled a face. 'Maggie, hot? I don't think so. Her tits aren't even that big.'

So she was Maggie. Nice name.

'I suppose Lisa's a bit funny about you seeing your ex-wife still. You've got a kid, haven't you?'

'Yeah,' said Rob, breaking into a smile. 'Girl called Mae.'

'Do you get to see much of her?' he fished.

Rob pulled out a picture to show him from his wallet of a baby with fluffy blonde hair. It could've been a boy or a girl for all he could tell.

'She's lovely,' he lied. 'Do they live close by?'

'Yeah.' Rob rattled off the name of the road where his

ex-wife lived. He had a rough idea where it was but would look it up on his phone to be sure.

'Was her sister going round to give her the money?'

'Probably.'

'But she doesn't know where you get your cash from?'

'Fuck no,' said Rob, laughing. 'If she knew I was dealing 'roids she'd fucking arrest me.'

'I can't believe you're related to a police officer.'

He feigned panic while beneath the surface he fizzed with excitement. If he followed the sister-in-law, this Maggie, she could be his ticket to ensuring he got what he wanted out of the Kinnocks.

'If anyone finds out I'm stacking, I'm done for. I'd lose my job.'

In truth, he didn't care in the slightest. Once he got his money, he'd go to the States for his operation and stay there, try his hand at something else.

'Who's gunna find out?' said Rob. 'I've been dealing for years and Maggie's never suspected a thing. Believe me, I'd have known if she had.'

He made a show of pretending Rob had calmed him down, then said he needed to get going.

'I've got an early client tomorrow and I need to get a good night's sleep.'

'Sure,' said Rob. 'Listen, if you do see Lisa—'

'Don't worry, I'll let you know straight away. Mates look out for each other, don't they?'

He must've sounded more convincing than he realized because he thought Rob was going to hug him when he showed him out. He managed to sidestep the embrace and slapped him on the back instead. By the time he reached his car he'd called up a map on his phone showing the street where Rob's ex lived. It would take him less than ten minutes to get there. A slow smile spread across his face.

Coming to get you.

45

Maggie's flat was on the top floor of a converted Victorian townhouse overlooking the train station. The unrelenting rumble of commuter and freight trains passing beneath her front windows had thwarted the previous owner's attempt to sell it at the same price other two-bedroom flats in Mansell went for, and Maggie was happy to put up with the noise in return for having a spare room.

Having not been home for two days, the flat was musty and airless. She yanked up the sash windows even though it was drizzling outside and sighed as she surveyed the clothes scattered over the lounge floor and sofa, the washing-up that had been in the kitchen sink for a week and the pizza box with one slice left uneaten still open on the coffee table.

For the past four months she'd lived there alone, ever since her lodger, Susan, had moved out; Maggie never referred to her as a flatmate because that term implied they spent actual time in each other's company. Susan, who was a veterinary assistant, moved in after answering Maggie's ad on Gumtree. Maggie had told her to treat the place as her own and looked forward to cooking meals together, sharing bottles of wine in the evenings and having someone to talk to who wasn't Lou or anyone to do with work. But whenever they were in the flat at the same time, Susan slunk off to her bedroom to watch TV and after six months announced she was moving out. Maggie wasn't bothered when she left but she did need to find a new lodger at some point. She needed half the mortgage covered so she could afford to help Lou out with her bills.

Maggie had thought about going straight round to her sister's with Rob's money but decided to go home first and grab something to eat. She needed an hour to herself to process the past couple of days. When she checked, however, there was nothing in the fridge save a half-drunk bottle of white wine, a chunk of mature Cheddar cheese, an iceberg lettuce that was browning around the edges and a couple of bottles of Budweiser. Maggie rummaged through the takeaway menus she kept in a drawer next to the cutlery. Disregarding the ones for pizza and curry, her taste buds steered her towards Thai and she went to ring through her order. But as she waited for the restaurant to pick up, her phone beeped to signal another call waiting and when she saw who was on the other line she knew dinner would have to wait.

'Where are you?' barked Umpire, typically brusque.

'At home, sir. You said it was fine for Belmar to stay with the Kinnocks tonight,' she added defensively.

'Yes, I know. You live above the station, don't you?'

Maggie was thrown. 'Um, yes. Marshall Street.'

'What number?'

'Twelve.'

'I'll be round in five minutes.'

She almost dropped her phone in shock. He was coming here, to her flat? What the—?

Before she could say anything, he'd rung off.

She stood stock-still, her mind churning with all the reasons why on earth Umpire would want to come to her home. Then it occurred to her what a state the flat was in and she panicked. Getting a black bin bag from under the kitchen sink, Maggie raced around the lounge throwing the pizza box and piles of old newspapers into it. Then she grabbed her clothes an armful at a time and rushed them into her bedroom, chucking them down on the carpet. Back in the kitchen she knew she wouldn't have time to wash up so she took the bowl full of dirty dishes out of the sink and shoved it into the cupboard below. Thirty seconds later her doorbell rang.

She buzzed Umpire into the house and opened the front door to her flat, listening with growing trepidation as his footsteps got louder coming up the stairs. Suddenly there he was in front of her, his face set in its usual frown. The landing outside her front door was small anyway but now it seemed tiny with his tall, lanky frame taking up most of it. He had already taken his suit jacket off and draped it over the crook of his arm, and his tie and top shirt button were undone to reveal a tangle of downy, reddish-blond hair creeping up towards the base of his throat. Maggie quickly averted her gaze.

He spoke first. To her surprise, he sounded a bit nervous.

'So, Neville, well, I just thought that with you not being able to come to all the briefings I should make sure you're up to date on everything. Save you coming into the station. I was driving past anyway,' he added hastily.

'Um, thanks,' she said, even more baffled. He was the SIO – if he wanted her to be at a briefing, all he had to do was order her to be there. 'Come in.'

He followed her into the lounge. 'Nice room. I like the high ceilings,' he said, glancing up.

Maggie had no idea how to answer him. It was like she'd lost the power of speech.

'Have you lived here long?' he said, cocking his head to one side to appraise the spines of the paperbacks stuffed onto shelves in an alcove near the window. She was thankful there were a few classics among the holiday reads she'd collected at airports over the years.

'Erm, not really. About three years.' She wanted to kick herself for how stupid she sounded.

'On your own?'

'I had a lodger, but she moved out.'

Neither of them spoke as he moved slowly round the room, taking in his surroundings. All Maggie could think was what people would say if they knew he was there. Belmar and his gossips would have a field day. She shook her head to dislodge the thought. Get a grip, she ordered herself.

'Please, sit down. Can I get you a tea or coffee?'

'Have you got anything stronger?'

It was earlier in the day than she'd normally have a drink but she was hardly going to refuse him.

'Is red wine okay?'

She had a bottle of Chilean Cabernet Sauvignon stashed away that was meant to be half decent.

'I'd prefer beer if you've got one,' he said, flopping down onto the sofa. He stretched out his long legs and she had to hop over them on her way to the kitchen.

Her hands shook as she poured herself a glass of white wine from the bottle already opened in the fridge. She stopped short of giving herself too large a measure but did sneak a quick gulp before grabbing one of the bottles of Budweiser, cracking the lid off with an opener and returning with both drinks to the lounge.

'Sorry, do you want a glass with that?' she said, as Umpire reached up and took the beer bottle from her.

'No, this is fine.'

Maggie perched on the edge of the sofa, pressed up against the arm, as far from him as possible. Worried she reeked because she hadn't had a chance to change her clothes, she clamped her arms to her sides.

'Have you seen the papers today?' Umpire asked, taking a swig of beer.

'I scanned the headlines but that's it.'

'The Chief Constable's on my case. She thinks the Kinnocks should follow up the press conference with an interview. She's worried a backlash is building because of their win and it's harming the investigation.'

'A backlash based on what?'

'Some papers have laid into them about reducing the reward and are insinuating they must somehow be involved in Rosie's disappearance. They've also republished some of the rumours being written on Twitter and Face-book.'

'Written by trolls, I bet,' said Maggie, unimpressed. 'Why do we even care what idiots like that think?'

'Because people believe what they read and we need everyone on Mack and Lesley's side. We don't want a situation where witnesses won't come forward with information because they're jealous of their wealth or think that with all the money they have they should've taken better care of their daughter. Yes, I know, it's ridicu-lous, but that's what people are saying. So we need the public to see that they're still normal despite the money.'

'You're saying people think they deserve what's hap-pened because they're rich?' Maggie retorted. 'That's crazy.'

'Yes it is, but that's what we're up against. I think we should get them to sit down with the *Mansell Echo* first, get the locals on side.' Umpire relaxed back onto the sofa cushions. 'Do you think they'll be up for it? I know we can't force them to do an interview, but we could do with some more breaks on the case.'

'Actually, sir, I may have one.'

'From Cassie Perrie?'

'Not exactly. I talked to her but she has no idea who GS is. She then suggested I speak to another of Rosie's old friends, a girl called Emma Mitchell, so I've just been round to see her on my way back here. Basically, I got Emma to admit that Rosie phoned her last week, saying some bloke has been harassing her for sex. Rosie didn't call him GS when she was talking to Emma, but it sounds like the same person. She was also scathing about the suggestion Rosie self-harmed.'

'You went to a witness's house without telling me?' said Umpire, in a tone that sounded unnaturally dispassionate to her ears.

'Yes,' she faltered. 'It's not far from here—'

'But you didn't think to clear it with me first? You are the FLO first and foremost on this case.'

Frustrated, Maggie set her glass of wine down on the coffee table. 'I was driving past the door, sir.'

'That's not the point, DC Neville, and you know it.'

She held her nerve. 'Look, I know I appear to be in a minority of one but I think what Rosie wrote on her laptop is significant. She rang Emma because she was upset about being harassed and she wrote about someone called GS who wouldn't take no for an answer. What if GS is the crayon writer?'

'I've told you I don't think they're the same person,' he challenged her. 'GS is obsessed with sex, the crayon writer is obsessed with money.'

'Oh, come on, you can't just dismiss the possibility there might be a link between them,' Maggie exclaimed.

Umpire raised an eyebrow. 'Remember who you're talking to, Neville. I don't think I need to remind you what happened last time you overstepped the mark.'

'If you're not prepared to listen to me, why did you want me on the case?' she snapped, her frustration getting the better of her.

'Because you were right all along about telling Megan Fowler's parents.'

For a second she thought she'd misheard him.

'Excuse me?'

'You were right. I should've trusted her parents with the truth and let them see her body. I made a mistake.'

Maggie slumped backwards on the sofa alongside him. She turned her head to look at him.

'Why now? Why have you suddenly changed your mind?'

His gaze didn't waver from hers.

'The Fowlers were not happy you were removed as their FLO. They wrote to me a month ago, after the trial, and said you didn't deserve to be punished for putting their feelings first. I thought about it and decided they had a point, so I asked DI Gant to lift your suspension. What their letter made me realize is that you have an almost unique empathy for victims and their families. That's why I asked you back. I suppose you could say I need you as my conscience.'

She was stunned and it took her a moment to recover her voice.

'Well, good,' she said, sounding haughtier than she intended.

Then, just when she thought he couldn't shock her any further, Umpire smiled at her. Not his usual, pinched, half-smile, but a wide, beaming grin that lifted the corners of his mouth and crinkled the skin around his eyes. It transformed his face and the force of it made her insides capsize. Thrown, Maggie leaned forward to grab her wine glass and knocked back another large mouthful.

'I'm glad we've sorted that out then,' he said, his voice laced with amusement.

'Hardly,' she spluttered. 'What about the complaint you made against me? That will still be on my record.'

'I can't do anything about that now. You did disobey a direct order, don't forget.'

'You know what,' said Maggie, emboldened by the effect of the alcohol hitting her empty stomach, 'I think the bollocking you gave me was worse than being suspended. It was brutal.'

Umpire's blue eyes glittered as he took another swig of beer. 'I shouldn't have shouted at you like that, but I was so bloody angry. Probably the angriest I've ever been on the job. I felt completely let down.'

'But you understand now why I told Mrs Fowler?'

'Yes, but my reaction wasn't even about that really. I was angry because I thought so highly of you and what you did felt like a slap in the face.'

'You thought highly of me?'

He smiled again, another stomach-flipper. Maggie hastily necked another mouthful of wine.

'I still do. You're the best FLO I've ever had on a case, Maggie. The way you are with people is a gift. You make them feel comforted and supported during the worst time of their lives but you never lose sight of the job you're there to do for our side, because you're a great detective too.' He hesitated. 'I like ... I like working with you, Maggie.'

There was something in his voice that rattled her. She tried to appear calmer than she felt.

'I'm sorry I disobeyed your order, sir. I stand by my reasons for doing so, but I guess, talking about it now, I finally understand how upset you were.'

'Let's put it behind us.'

Umpire proffered his beer bottle and Maggie clinked her wine glass against it. As she did, her eyes strayed to his left hand. His ring finger was bare, confirming what Belmar had said about him splitting from his wife. Umpire followed her gaze and shrugged.

'It's been four months now, but it was on the cards for a while. Kim, my wife, is a city girl and she didn't want me to leave the Met or for us to leave London. She's never settled into the sticks, as she calls it. She and the kids are back in Finchley now.'

'It's okay, you don't have to tell me,' said Maggie, embarrassed to be discussing something so personal with him.

'It's fine. I think most people are aware of it now. You know how they talk.'

Oh God, she thought. Did that mean he knew what people had been saying about them? She tried to drag the conversation back onto safer ground.

'So, I'll speak to the Kinnocks about the interview with the *Echo*. I agree, I think it's in their best interests.'

Umpire said nothing. He just sat there and watched her. Maggie's face grew hot, but she ploughed on.

'And there must be someone who knows who GS is. Maybe I'll ask Lesley again.'

'See, this is what I mean about you, Maggie. You're a great family liaison officer but you love investigating too. You really should be a detective sergeant by now.'

'If I do that, sir, I'll have to quit being an FLO. DI Gant says it's impossible to do both with a DS's work-load.'

'So give it up. You've specialized for a few years, try something else.'

The idea horrified her. 'I can't imagine not doing this. It's really important to me.'

'But you're denying yourself the chance of promotion. Look, if you were a DS, I'd offer you a position on my team in a heartbeat.'

Maggie shook her head. 'I'm not ready.'

There was a long pause as they stared at each other.

Umpire took a slug of drink first.

46

Friday

The sensation of her cheek being jabbed by a fingertip dragged Maggie from the depths of a sound sleep. She lashed out in surprise and almost sent her nephew Scotty flying across the room.

'Auntie Maggie!' he yelped. 'It's me!'

She sat bolt upright on the sofa and the cushion she'd been using as a pillow tumbled onto the floor. Scotty picked it up and handed it back, his little face a picture of hurt.

'I'm sorry, Scotty, but you made me jump poking me like that. I was fast asleep.'

'I know – you were snoring.'

'Me, snore? Never!'

Maggie reached forward and pulled him onto her makeshift bed. Scotty squealed with mock indignation as she rained kisses on his cheek.

'Get off me! I'm not a baby!'

After a few seconds, she let him ago. He scrambled off the sofa and stood near the door, beyond arm's reach. He was still in his pyjamas – navy blue with footballs dotted all over them – and his thick brown hair stuck up at odd angles from where he'd rolled about and fidgeted in his sleep. It was a family joke that Scotty couldn't stay still even when he wasn't awake and Lou said she'd never got a moment's rest when she was pregnant with him.

'What time is it?' asked Maggie.

'Breakfast time. Do you want anything to eat?'

'Not yet, but a cup of tea would be nice.'

He pretended to write down her order on a notepad like a waiter then, with a grin, dashed from the room.

Maggie fell back on the cushions with a groan. She should've stayed at home last night, gone to sleep in her own bed, but after Umpire left she was too jittery to eat anything so instead she went straight round to Lou's with Rob's money. After putting the kids to bed, her sister poured them both a glass of wine, cracked open a tube of sour cream Pringles and insisted she went over every detail of what Umpire had said.

'At least he's apologized for being a cock,' said Lou after she'd finished.

'Yeah, it's nice to be vindicated,' said Maggie, taking a sip of wine.

'So, do you fancy him?'

'Lou!'

'Don't give me that look. I'm not asking if you want to marry him, just if you want to have sex with him,' she said, laughing.

Maggie squirmed. 'I don't think about him like that. He's married.'

'I thought you just said him and his wife are separated?'

'Well, yes, but that's still technically married.'

Lou rolled her eyes at her sister. 'Why are you always so weird about fancying someone who's in a relationship? There's no law against looking.'

Maggie knocked back the rest of her wine. 'It just feels wrong, that's all. If someone's taken, you shouldn't think about them like that.'

'But you don't think about single ones either!'

'I do,' Maggie protested. 'You're forgetting I dated that firefighter Craig last year.'

'For three weeks, and that was the first relationship – if you can even call it that – you'd had in five years. I think Jude's probably kissed more girls than you have blokes and he's only ten.' Lou laughed. 'I don't know why you won't give the blokes who ask you out a chance. You're twenty-eight now and if you carry on like this you'll be single forever.'

Maggie had changed the conversation at that point, fearing Lou might bring up Jerome. Instead she distracted her sister by suggesting they open another bottle of wine and resigning herself to a night crashed out on her sofa. Now, waking up with a sore head and backache, she wished she hadn't. She checked the time and saw it was 7.40 a.m. Shit, she needed to get going. Umpire expected her back at Angel's Reach by 8.30 a.m.

There was a rap on the living-room door and Jude walked in. He was already dressed for school in grey trousers and a bottle-green jumper over a white polo shirt, and was clutching an exercise book. It was always to her immense relief that he barely resembled his dad, as she couldn't have coped with a constant living, breathing reminder of Jerome. Jude's features instead reflected

Lou's hazel eyes, her aquiline nose and wide, open face, similar to Maggie's. The only nod to Jerome was his darker skin and tight, unruly curls.

'Hiya, Auntie Mags. Mum said can you check my homework, then Mae's nappy will need changing.'

Maggie smiled to hide her irritation at Lou dishing out orders again.

'Of course. But if it's long division, you're stuffed. I was rubbish at maths at school.'

'It's French,' he said, handing her the book. 'I had to put some English words into French. Can you see if I've done it right?'

She didn't want to admit her knowledge of French was probably on a par with his but when she checked over the homework, the phrases were basic enough that she could see he'd pretty much got most of it right. A couple of mistakes she didn't correct, reasoning he would never learn if she did all the work for him.

'Looks good to me, sweetheart,' she said, handing the book back. 'Now scoot while I get dressed.'

Jude was almost at the door when he turned and looked at her shyly.

'You will find her, won't you, Auntie Mags? The girl whose mum and dad you're helping.'

Lou must've said something to him about Rosie, because Maggie had pointedly made no mention of the case when she'd turned up the previous evening. Mindful of the boys being in earshot, she'd kept the conversation to schoolwork and football and when they were going to reschedule their visit to Pizza Hut.

She gave her nephew a reassuring smile. 'I'm doing

my best, Jude, we all are. Hopefully we'll have some good news soon.'

'Was it her dad?'

Maggie was shocked. 'What makes you say that?'

'A boy in my class is on Twitter and he said people are tweeting the dad did it. He showed us at lunchtime.'

Ten-year-olds on Twitter, Maggie despaired, and at school too. She rarely used social media herself: the accounts she'd set up were purely for when she needed to look up something relating to a case. She had no interest in sharing her private life with the world, especially when she knew just how far an electronic trail could spread. If people understood how vulnerable it made them posting pictures and personal information online, the indelible fingerprint it left, they'd never surf the Internet again.

'Firstly, if your mum found out you were looking at Twitter, she wouldn't be happy. There are some not very nice people on it, trust me.'

'Mum's on it.'

'Right. Well, it's for grown-ups, not kids, okay?'

Jude nodded.

'As for her dad, we already know he was in Scotland when she went missing, so whoever's saying otherwise has got it wrong.'

Jude seemed satisfied with her answer, even rushing over to her for a quick hug before running out of the room. Her smile fell, however, when he yelled from the hallway, 'Don't forget Mae's nappy!'

She found Lou in the kitchen.

'Oh good, you're up,' said Lou. 'Can you take the boys to school?'

'Sorry, I have to go,' said Maggie, accepting the mug of tea Lou handed her.

'Please, it'd be doing me a massive favour.'

'I'm sorry, I've got to leave in a minute. Why can't you take them?'

'I want to take Mae to the doctor's. Her cold's gone to her chest.'

'I'd love to help but I'm needed back in Haxton. Isn't there anyone else you can ask?'

'I could ask Toby's mum but the boys would much rather go with you,' said Lou as she mixed some white-coloured mush that might or might not have been porridge into a plastic Winnie the Pooh bowl for Mae.

'I know they would, but not today. I'm sorry.'

'Bloody hell, can't you just do this one thing?' Lou snapped. 'It's only five minutes out of your way.'

Crabby from her hangover and a poor night's sleep, Maggie wasn't in the mood to be nagged.

'Stop being so bloody bossy. Get my money, change Mae's nappy, take the boys to school,' she mimicked.

Lou looked wounded. 'I didn't realize it was such a big deal to help your family.'

'Now you're being ridiculous. I do enough for you already so don't you dare give me a hard time about this. Why not ask Rob to do it? He'd love to see them.'

Lou's face darkened. 'What, are you on his side now?'

'Of course not. But the boys want to see him and he could help you out. I can't run around after you all the time.'

Instead of retaliating, Lou turned her back and began folding the pile of clothes on the ironing board set up in the middle of the kitchen. Being ignored only made Maggie angrier.

'What about me, Lou? When do I get a life? Between you and the kids and work, I have no time to myself.'

Lou laughed bitterly.

'You chose that job, sis. You're the one who wanted to be the bloody saviour of families, running around like a cross between Supercop and Supernanny. Don't complain to me if it's too much for you.'

Maggie exploded.

'No, *you're* too much. You and these sodding kids of yours. I'll tell you what, you find some other mug to take them to Pizza Hut because it bloody well won't be me.'

Maggie stormed out of the kitchen – and barged straight into Jude. One look at his face told her he'd heard every word. Immediately she felt awful and sank to her knees in front of him.

'Oh, sweetheart, I'm sorry, I shouldn't have said that about taking you to Pizza Hut. I'm just a bit tired,' she said, reaching out for him. 'Please, come here.'

He backed away and the look he gave her was like a kick to the stomach.

'Please, Jude. I didn't mean it.'

'Go away. I hate you!'

He ran upstairs and seconds later his bedroom door slammed shut. She thought about following him upstairs to talk him round but knew that if she didn't leave now she'd never get to Haxton by 8.30. She'd have to make it up to him later. Again.

47

The atmosphere in the kitchen was thick with tension. For the first time since Tuesday, Lesley resented the police presence. She wanted to be left alone with Mack and to not feel like their every move was being scrutinized. The situation was starting to feel forced, like she was having to act her role, and it exhausted her to the point of making her bones ache. And she was worried about Mack. After his revelation about Suzy Breed blackmailing him, he had become withdrawn and last night refused to sleep in the same bed as her, saying he preferred to sleep downstairs. When she'd crept down to the kitchen in the early hours for a glass of water she'd found him sitting in the lounge in the dark, crying his eyes out.

He was sitting opposite her now, head bowed, reading a report in the *Independent* about Rosie's disappearance. Belmar had tried to talk them out of reading the papers again and Lesley had laughed at the absurdity of his concern.

'Our daughter's been missing for three days and you think we're worried about headlines?' she told him. 'I lie awake wondering if she's dead in a ditch somewhere and you think what some bloody reporter writes will upset me?'

'We also know what people are writing about us, or rather me, on the Internet,' Mack chimed in, waggling his BlackBerry in the air.

'You shouldn't read that stuff,' said Belmar. 'It's written by idiots who don't know any better.'

'People believe what they read though.'

'We know you were in Scotland, Mack. End of story.'

Eventually Belmar relented and sent someone to get the papers, which they were now reading at the breakfast table. Lesley couldn't face eating and left the toast Belmar had made to go cold while she sipped a cup of tea.

Rosie's disappearance was still front-page news. Lesley had the *Daily Mirror* in front of her and on the front page was the blurred CCTV image from the garage with a plea to the public to help identify who was in the queue. DCI Umpire was quoted as saying none of them was a suspect at this stage – they just needed tracking down so they could be ruled out of the inquiry.

Anger shook her as she gazed down at the paper. That someone might hate her so much for winning that they'd abducted Rosie was incomprehensible. What kind of sick person did that? Why did money matter so much to some people? It made her want to give every penny away and live on handouts.

She turned the page and let out a cry as she was confronted by multiple images of her daughter. There was Rosie as an apple-cheeked toddler, giggling as she tried to pull an ornament off a Christmas tree; gap-toothed and hair tied in bunches for her first school photo; at a bowling alley celebrating her thirteenth birthday with friends; and, finally, Lesley's favourite picture of her at Disney World, taken down from the corkboard in the kitchen. Snapshots of Rosie shared with every newspaper, website and broadcaster in the hope they would prick the conscience of whoever had her or knew where she was. Lesley traced her finger over the most recent picture, the one she'd given to the police on Tuesday after reporting her missing. A tear rolled down her cheek and splashed onto the page.

'Hey, it's okay, love,' said Mack as he reached over and put his hand on hers. It felt warm and reassuring. She met his stare and shook her head.

'I know,' he said, 'I know.'

They sat for a few moments with their hands clasped. Then Maggie walked in, looking so solemn Lesley could only assume the worst. Mack must've thought the same, because he immediately got to his feet. Lesley, however, couldn't find the strength to stand.

'There's no news. I'm sorry,' said Maggie.

Lesley burst into tears as Mack erupted.

'I don't know how much more of this I can take,' he said. 'Why the fuck haven't you found her yet?'

To Lesley's horror, he began thumping his fists down on the table, sending plates and cups crashing to the floor. She tried to stop him but he shrugged her off.

'Mack, please—'

'Leave me alone,' he howled. 'Just leave me the fuck alone.'

As Belmar tried to placate him, Maggie ushered Lesley into the hall.

'Let's give him some space,' she said. 'Why don't we go for a walk?'

'We can't leave him like that,' Lesley cried. 'I've never seen him in such a state.'

'Belmar will look after him.'

'No, I should stay with him.'

'I really think Mack could do with being alone. Belmar knows to call if he needs us.'

They walked down Burr Way towards the meadow. Before they left, Lesley had belted a cream-coloured rain-coat over her denim skirt and navy T-shirt but Maggie only wore a suit jacket over her thin cotton shirt and she pulled it tighter around her as the wind nipped at her exposed skin. The temperature had cooled again and it felt like the heavens might open at any point.

'Which way shall we go?' she said, fervently wishing she had a jumper on under her jacket.

'If we cut along there we could go to the riding school,' said Lesley, pointing to a pathway on the right. 'The people who run it are lovely.'

'Does Rosie have her own horse?'

'No, but she tries to ride the same one every time she goes. I think it's called Hoff.'

They walked in silence, with Lesley leading the way. Brambles and stinging nettles reached out to claw her bare legs and Maggie was grateful to be wearing trousers.

The path led to a narrower one, until eventually they

stumbled out by the side of a wide, uneven road covered in shingle. Up ahead, Maggie could see what looked like a cluster of farm buildings.

'That's the riding school,' said Lesley. She started to walk up the track but Maggie stopped her. She'd bided enough time.

'Before we go in, I need to ask if Rosie's in the habit of using initials to abbreviate people's names, like when she's sending texts or emails?'

Lesley looked baffled.

'Do the initials GS mean anything to you? We think she used them to describe someone she met recently. Someone male,' said Maggie, deciding to be honest.

'I have no idea. Have you asked her friends?'

'A couple, but they had no idea either. Talking of which, do you know if any of the girls Rosie hangs out with have boyfriends?'

'I think Lily might. I once overheard Kathryn tell Rosie that Lily couldn't go riding one weekend because she was going to the cinema with some boy from a school in Mansell.' Lesley's face clouded. 'I suppose I should say sorry to Kathryn's mum for banging on their gate yesterday.'

'I think it's best if you stay away from the Stockton family for now.'

'Why? In case I lose my temper again? I'm sorry, but I can't just sit back and pretend none of this is happening. I mean, Kathryn's at our house all the time. Why would Rosie ask her round if they weren't getting on?'

'I don't know.'

'No, you don't and neither do I. I can't make sense of any of this.'

Maggie kept quiet. She could see Lesley was getting agitated.

'But you know what I *really* don't understand?' she went on, her voice getting louder, 'is why you haven't found my daughter yet. I don't understand how she could just disappear from our garden, covered in blood, and you find no trace of her.'

'We're doing our best,' said Maggie lamely.

She could almost feel Lesley's frustration burning off her. She wanted to say she felt the same, that she was just as desperate for Rosie to be found, but she didn't think it would be well received. Or believed.

'It should be easy with all the technology you police have got – DNA, tracing phone calls, CCTV images. Why is none of it working?'

Maggie suddenly held up her hand. 'Wait – did you say tracing phone calls?'

'Well, yes,' Lesley blustered, 'but that's not—'

'I'm such an idiot! Why didn't I think of it before?' Maggie exclaimed. 'Emma Mitchell told me last night that Rosie called her on her mobile last week. She said Rosie's number came up on her phone, but the call never showed up on the records for the iPhone that Rosie left in the garden. I thought it must be a mistake but it couldn't have been. Lesley, how long has Rosie had her iPhone?'

Lesley quivered with frustration. 'Oh, for God's sake, what are you going on about now?'

342

'Please, I need you to think. This is important. How long has Rosie had her iPhone?'

'She upgraded in February.'

'So she's had it less than four months?'

'Yes.'

'Is it the same number as her old one?'

'Actually, it's not. She had a BlackBerry before she switched and Mack thought it would be a good idea if she got a new number at the same time as getting the iPhone, because she needed a different SIM card for it anyway. She'd had her old number for a while and he thought it would stop people we used to know calling her and asking her for money. I remember she was pretty annoyed she had to change it, but she went along with it.'

'Do you know what happened to the BlackBerry?'

'She probably threw it out or recycled it.'

'Is there a chance she didn't do either and has still been using it like she has her old laptop?'

Lesley frowned. 'To do what?'

'To message or call old friends like Emma?'

'But she would've cancelled the contract on it when she switched to the iPhone.'

'Maybe she didn't. Do you pay the monthly charge yourselves?'

'No, she pays it out of her allowance.'

'Could she afford to have two phones on the go?'

Lesley exhaled. 'Yes, she could.'

'I bet you anything the number that came up on Emma's phone is for Rosie's BlackBerry. We have to find it. It might help us identify who this GS is.'

'Is he something to do with her going missing?'

'Possibly, but I'm afraid that's all I can say for now.'

Lesley nodded. 'If you honestly think Rosie didn't throw her old phone away, it must be back at the house somewhere.'

'Let's go.'

They returned to find a scribbled note from Belmar on the island counter saying he and Mack had gone out for a drive to get a change of scenery.

'It'll do him good,' said Maggie as Lesley fretted over the note. 'Belmar will look after him.'

'I should be with him. He's not coping.'

Maggie noticed how troubled she looked.

'Is something else the matter?' she asked.

'No, no,' said Lesley hurriedly. 'It's nothing.'

'If there is, I might be able to help.'

Lesley wouldn't meet her eyes and made a show of reading the note again. 'I wonder how long they'll be?'

Maggie had to respect the fact that Lesley didn't want to share whatever was bothering her, even though she was intrigued and wondered if it related to the case. She'd ask Belmar when he got back if Mack was acting the same. If he was she'd tackle Lesley again.

'Shall we look for the BlackBerry in the meantime?' she said.

'Sure,' said Lesley, pocketing the note.

Maggie's phone rang and her pulse misfired when she saw it was Umpire. She tried to collect herself as she answered but any fear she had that their first conversation

344

since his visit to her flat would be awkward proved unfounded. Umpire was business as usual.

'Are you at Angel's Reach, Neville?'

'Yes, sir, I'm here with Lesley now.'

'Kathryn Stockton was mugged last night. She's in hospital.'

Maggie's face must've registered her shock because Lesley asked in a panic what was wrong.

'It's Kathryn. She's in hospital,' Maggie relayed. 'Is she okay?' she asked Umpire.

'Her face is badly beaten but she managed to fight her attacker off, although he took her phone. It happened on the other side of the village, by the river. We're looking into it but at this stage there's nothing to connect the incident to Rosie's disappearance.'

Lesley tugged at Maggie's sleeve, so she broke off briefly to explain what Umpire had said. Lesley was not convinced by his theory.

'It must be the same person who hurt Rosie, it must be!' She lowered herself into one of the chairs around the kitchen table and began to cry softly. She looked exhausted.

'I couldn't interview Kathryn last night because she was too out of it to talk,' said Umpire. 'I'm on my way to the hospital now.'

'The attacker must've been standing in front of her to hit her in the face, so she might have got a look at them first,' said Maggie.

'I bloody well hope so.'

As he hung up, Maggie turned her attention back to

Lesley. She had stopped crying and was staring down at one of the newspapers on the table in horror.

'I can't believe some bastard took my picture yesterday.'

Maggie went over to see what Lesley was looking at and was startled to see it was a photograph of her in a shop, crying her eyes out, as two women comforted her. The headline above the picture was *A MOTHER'S ANGUISH* but as Maggie read the copy she saw there was no mention of the anguish the paper was piling on by publishing the picture.

'How are they allowed to get away with this kind of thing?' Lesley asked her. Then she suddenly gasped.

Maggie, who was still reading the copy, gave her a sharp look. 'What is it?'

'It's him. It's him,' said Lesley, jabbing the page excitedly.

'Who?'

'The one I couldn't remember. From the queue!'

She pointed to a young, good-looking man just in frame on the left-hand side of the photograph. Wearing gym clothes, he stood side on and was looking intently at Lesley as she cried. Maggie saw his hands were clenched into fists.

'I swear to God he's the one who was behind me in the queue when I bought our lottery ticket.'

'Are you sure?'

'I'm certain, because I also spoke to him yesterday.'

'You did what?' said Maggie, stunned.

'Yesterday, when I went out. I spoke to this man after he almost ran me down. It was him.' Lesley pointed again to the picture. 'It was definitely the same man. That's where I'd seen him before, when he got out of his car.'

Maggie struggled to take it all in. 'You think the man in this picture is the same man who let you push ahead of him in the garage queue over a year ago and now you're saying you spoke to him just yesterday? Where?'

'Here. He was right outside the house.'

48

Mrs Roberts was not going to make it easy for him. He had arrived at one minute to nine and still she pointedly tapped the face of her wristwatch like he was late. Then she insisted he treat her in one of the rooms at the front of the house rather than the conservatory, which was his preference because he could gain access to the garden from it. It was a complication he could do without.

'You must try to pull your hand back as far as it can go,' he said as her bony fingers clutched the weight he'd brought along for her exercises. He was trying to get her to strengthen the flexor muscles in her wrist but there was a distinct lack of effort on her part. 'Here, like this.' He demonstrated the movement with his own hand, flexing it back until it was at a ninety-degree angle with his forearm.

'I can't possibly do that, it's far too painful,' she said, and she dropped the weight onto the floor, where it rolled beneath the chair opposite. She arched her eyebrows. 'Pick it up then.'

If he didn't have a reason to stay, he'd tell her to fuck off and walk out. But he needed to get into the garden before he left. Keep your cool, he told himself, because soon you won't need the stupid bitch's money.

'Don't just sit there,' Mrs Roberts sniped. 'Let's get on with the next exercise. I haven't got all day.'

'Are you going out?'

If she was, he could do what he did last time and let himself into the garden.

'Good God, no, not with this injury,' she said, as though she'd lost a limb rather than just strained it. 'I have someone coming round at ten thirty regarding the installation of a stairlift and I want you gone by then.'

'You don't need a stairlift, Mrs Roberts,' he said exasperatedly. 'It's your wrist you've hurt, not your legs.'

'If it's my wrist now, it'll be something else tomorrow. My arthritis is getting worse and I need to be prepared. Not that it's any of your business what I do in my own home.'

He flexed his own wrist again as he looked her up and down. She was frail enough that he could probably kill her with one hand. Quick grab of the throat, squeeze the life out of her and shut her up for good. It was that easy. He found the idea thrilled him so much that he had to pick up the other weight he had in his bag and squeeze it to release the tension.

As he did, he checked the time. It was already 10.07 a.m., which meant he didn't have long before she expected him to leave. His stomach churned with anxiety. He had to go outside before he left. Everything depended on it.

'This one doesn't seem to be making a difference either,' Mrs Roberts sighed. 'The pain is too much. I thought you knew what you were doing but clearly you have no idea. I should've known not to trust that idiot boy's recommendation.'

She sat back in her chair. As he watched her close her eyes and feign exhaustion, the urge to hit her consumed him. It was addictive, the sensation of punching his knuckles into flesh and feeling bone crack from the force of it.

'You can go now,' said Mrs Roberts, keeping her eyes closed.

'Now? But we haven't finished.'

'I've had enough for today. Your money's on the table in the hall.'

'Are you sure?' He knew he sounded desperate but after last night's failure he was starting to feel it. Rob's detective sister-in-law had eventually showed up at her sister's house as he waited outside, but instead of leading him back to where she lived, as he'd hoped she would, she stayed the night. With that part of his plan unravelling he had to gain access to Mrs Roberts's garden now to make sure the rest of it was still in place. Unsettled, he felt a shooting pain in his head. Not a migraine now, he thought despairingly. Not fucking now.

'Why don't you have a glass of water or tea or something, then we can start again?' he suggested, teeth gritted against the pain as it mushroomed.

'Good God, man, don't you ever listen? Just go. Go on, leave now,' said Mrs Roberts, flapping her hand at him like she was trying to shoo a pigeon.

The migraine blurring his vision, he left the room without saying goodbye and went into the hall. How the fuck was he going to handle this? It was now 10.14 a.m. He was running out of time.

His fee was where she'd said it was, on the table near the door, on top of a bundle of leaflets and envelopes. As he picked it up, he noticed one of the leaflets was for a company that installed stairlifts. Turning it over, he saw someone had written a mobile number on the back in a spidery scrawl. He pulled out his phone and called the number.

'Good morning, I'm calling on behalf of Mrs Roberts, from Verma Lodge in Burr Way,' he said, careful to keep his voice at a level she wouldn't hear from the room she was in.

'I'm almost there,' said the man who answered. It sounded like he was driving.

'I'm terribly sorry, but I'm afraid Mrs Roberts has been taken ill and needs to reschedule her appointment.'

'But I'm just around the corner,' said the man, sounding pissed off. 'Are you sure I can't pop by? It won't take that long.'

'She's really not up to it now. Could you come at the same time next week instead?'

'I suppose so,' said the man grumpily. 'If she feels better by then.'

'I'm sure she will.'

His mood jumped from anxious to triumphant and he felt his headache ease a little. As quietly as he could, he tiptoed back along the hallway and into the conservatory. To his relief, the doors leading to the garden were un-locked. He slipped outside then broke into a run across the lawn, which squelched underfoot from overnight rain. He knew exactly which way to go and in no time had reached the large, Scandinavian-style pool house next to the swimming pool, hidden behind a tall hedge-row on the right side of the garden. Pulling open the door, he was at once struck by the scent of flowers and sneezed violently as it triggered his allergy. Looking round, he saw some idiot had left a bunch of daffodils stuffed into a jar by the day bed. Annoyed, he kicked it to one side as he checked everything else was in order. Satisfied it was, he went to pull the door closed as he left.

'What the hell are you doing?'

Jolted, he spun round to see Mrs Roberts standing right behind him, her face twisted with fury. She was out of breath but otherwise fine. So much for her legs being the next to go.

'How dare you go traipsing around my property without my permission! Are you trying to steal from me? I should've guessed as much. I knew I should've got better references before letting you in. Right, you've got ten seconds to leave before I call the police . . .'

She stopped and her hand flew up to her mouth. He tried to move but it was too late. She was looking past him at the day bed and had seen everything.

'Oh . . .' she croaked. 'You did this in my house?'

'It wasn't me,' he said as calmly as he could, advancing towards her.

'I'm not stupid,' she screeched, pointing at the open doorway. 'Oh my God, here, all this time.' She started backing away. 'I'm calling the police and don't you dare try to stop me.'

The pain in his head exploded like someone had

pulled a trigger and it took every bit of strength he had not to drop to his knees and howl.

'I can't let you do that,' he managed.

'Stay back, stay away from me,' she screamed.

The pain blurred his vision again and he clutched his left hand to his forehead in a futile attempt to salve the agony. He could barely see Mrs Roberts now, but he knew she was right in front of him. He reached out with his right hand and it smacked against her collarbone. She tried to scream but it came out more like a cough and as he inched his fingers up and closed them round her throat, her veins were like gristle beneath his grip. Her bony fingers clawed at his arm to let go but he didn't.

With just one hand he squeezed.

49

Hearing that Lesley had recognized the man in the queue as the same one she'd encountered outside Angel's Reach had a similar effect on Umpire to a shot of adrenaline. Crowing with excitement after Maggie rang to tell him, he ordered HTCU to enhance the image of the man taken in M&S as much as they could before the press office circulated it to the media.

'It will take a couple of hours but someone's bound to recognize him when it's made public,' Maggie told Lesley afterwards as they headed upstairs to search for Rosie's old phone.

'How can you be so sure?'

'He's someone's son and grandson. He may also have siblings, cousins, uncles and aunts, a wife, girlfriend or boyfriend, colleagues, neighbours. It's almost impossible for a person to go through life having no connection whatso—'

'Hey, Maggie, can I have a word?' said a male voice.

Almost at the top of the stairs, Maggie turned to see Steve Berry at the foot of them. His appearance shocked her. His skin was pasty and his eyes hooded beneath folds of puffy skin. He looked like he hadn't shaved for days.

'Why don't you start looking and I'll join you in a minute?' she said to Lesley. 'I just need to talk to DC Berry.'

Lesley nodded and continued her ascent. Reaching the bottom step, Maggie detected a rank smell emanating from Steve, like his clothes were musty and needed washing.

'No offence, Steve, but you look bloody awful.'

He dropped his voice to a whisper, even though they were alone in the entrance hall.

'I'm in fucking serious shit.'

'Is this because of you not telling Umpire about the laptop? I'm sorry, Steve, I didn't want to drop you in it but you should've told—'

'It's not that,' he gulped.

'What is it?' she said, her concern spiralling.

'I've just heard about the mum recognizing the bloke who spoke to her yesterday, the one from the queue. The thing is, I've also seen him.'

Maggie swallowed hard. 'When?'

'On the CCTV tapes. When I went through the ones from the area on Tuesday morning, I found footage of him talking to one of the security guards by the main gate. He pulled up, they exchanged words, then he drove off. I didn't think anything of it because he didn't come inside Burr Way.'

'Are you sure it was him?'

'Absolutely. You know me – I never forget a face. He

was driving a silver Peugeot 205. I meant to forward the registration to be checked but I was knackered from being up all night with Bobby and I forgot.'

'Oh, Steve,' she said, appalled.

'I didn't think there was anything suspicious about them just talking. I shouldn't even be on this case,' he lamented, 'I should still be on paternity leave. I did interview the security guard later on, but I didn't ask him about it, it just slipped my mind. I haven't slept in a week. Bobby's up half the night with colic and Umpire's got us working eighteen-hour days.'

'Yes, because a young girl is missing,' said Maggie reproachfully. 'If you're so tired you can't do your job properly you should've told him.'

'I didn't think he'd listen. Look, the guard is a good bloke. He's only young, twenty-one or so. I did a background PNC check on him with all the others and he was clear.'

'Did you get the feeling they knew each other?'

'I can't say for sure. I need to look at the tape again, but if I do that Umpire's going to know I've ballsed up. Maggie, what am I going to do? When he finds out I saw the suspect and did nothing he's going to slay me.' He went even paler and grabbed the top of her arm. Even through her cotton shirt she could tell his palm was sweaty. 'You were up to your neck in it on your last case with him and he let you off the hook. How did you manage that? I need to know how to play this.'

'Play this?' said Maggie furiously, wrenching her arm out of his grip. 'You don't *play* anything, Steve – you tell him you screwed up and then you talk to the security guard, find out what he knows.'

'MAGGIE!'

A panicked-looking Lesley flew down the stairs towards them holding her phone aloft.

Maggie ran to the foot of the staircase. 'What is it?'

'It's Mack.'

She took the phone. 'Mack?'

'No, it's me,' said Belmar. She could hear traffic rumbling past in the background and the sound of people shouting and laughing. 'I need you to come quick. Mack's lost it.'

'What do you mean, "lost it"?'

Lesley choked back a sob. Steve looked like he wanted to throw up.

'He's withdrawing money from cashpoints and giving it away to whoever walks by. I can't make him stop.'

'Where are you?'

'Mansell High Street.'

'Shit,' said Maggie. 'It's lunchtime, there must be loads of people about.'

'You don't say,' said Belmar, sounding stressed.

'Is he manic?'

'No, he's deadly calm, which is scarier. It's like he's in a trance. You need to bring Lesley down here to see if she can get through to him. There's a bloody great crowd gathering and someone's bound to tip off the press.'

'We'll leave now.'

She hung up and passed the phone back to Lesley.

Then she turned to Steve. 'You need to tell Umpire. I can't cover for you.'

'I know,' said Steve miserably. 'Don't worry, I'll make it right.'

50

The paramedics tucked a red blanket around Mack as they strapped him into a wheelchair. His face was waxy and partially shielded by an oxygen mask, and his eyes were closed so he was oblivious to the crowd of rubber-neckers craning to watch as he was loaded into the back of the ambulance. Some were holding their mobiles aloft and Maggie wondered how many pictures of him in a state of collapse were already circulating on the Internet. The thought made her angry and she glared at two women standing nearest to her. They had the decency to look embarrassed and move away, but they were the only ones. The rest stayed put, gawping as the paramedics, one male, one female, got Mack ready for the short journey from the high street to Mansell General.

The crowd had already gathered when Maggie and Lesley arrived and people were laughing in astonishment as Mack shoved fistfuls of banknotes at them. Belmar said most had declined to take the money at first, fearing it was some kind of ruse or hidden-camera stunt. But once a couple gladly accepted, others held out their hands too and some even encouraged him to keep going back to the cashpoint to withdraw more when that ran out. On the drive to Mansell, Lesley admitted to Maggie their daily cashpoint limit had been raised to £1,000 after their win and Mack had at least six debit and credit cards he could take money out on. By the time they got there, Belmar estimated he'd made up to twenty withdrawals from four different banks and a building society, taking out various amounts each time.

As Maggie waited by the ambulance, a couple of police community support officers began to disperse the crowd. Two young men in paint-splattered overalls walked past her, each holding a bundle of cash.

'How much did you get?' one was saying.

'Must be at least four hundred here. Fancy one down the pub after we knock off?'

'Too fucking right. Let's call Tommo. He's not gunna believe this.'

Lesley, who was standing beside her, let out a sob.

'How can people be so horrible? They're exploiting a sick man.'

An elderly woman in a purple coat, orange felt hat and sheepskin ankle boots approached them. She handed Maggie two fifty-pound notes and said sorry to Lesley.

'I heard what you just said, love, and I shouldn't have taken it. He wasn't ranting like a madman though; it looked like he knew what he was doing.' She muttered 'Sorry' again as she shuffled away.

'Will he be okay?' Lesley asked the paramedics as they finished securing Mack's wheelchair into the back of the ambulance.

'He looks as though he's suffering from nervous

exhaustion and we want to admit him to hospital to get him checked over,' said the male one. 'You can come in the ambulance with him.'

'I can't believe this is happening to my family,' she said to Maggie, choking back tears. 'It's like watching a horror film of someone else's life.'

'The doctors at the hospital will look after him,' Maggie reassured her. 'Now, are you ready? Belmar and I will follow behind in my car.'

'This is all Suzy Breed's fault,' Lesley sobbed.

Maggie was surprised. 'Suzy Breed? Mack's told you?'

'Only after I forced it out of him. She's been blackmailing him and he's given her tens of thousands of pounds already but she's still demanding more, even knowing what we're going through right now. It's no wonder he's like this, all the pressure he's been under. I could kill her for what she's done.'

'Blackmail?' said Maggie incredulously.

'Yes. She's been threatening to tell me they've been having an affair. She's even sent him texts to make it look like they are.'

'You've seen texts from her demanding money?'

Lesley hesitated. 'Well, not exactly. Just of her saying other stuff about meeting up. But Mack said she's definitely been blackmailing him.'

Maggie remained impassive. Why hadn't Mack told them about Suzy's demands? He knew they needed to investigate everyone who had demanded money with menaces from the family. His silence made her think he'd spun Lesley a line to cover up his affair with his ex.

'I need to tell DCI Umpire about this,' said Maggie.

'You do that. I want the bitch arrested.'

'Come on, love, we're ready for you,' the female para-medic called out cheerily from the ambulance's rear door. She held out her hand to help Lesley up the step.

'I'm coming,' said Lesley, wiping her eyes. 'Oh – wait.' She reached into the pocket of her raincoat and pulled out a BlackBerry handset studded with baby-pink crys-tals. She passed it to Maggie.

'It's Rosie's old phone. I found it at the bottom of birthday box fourteen – she must have hidden it in there when she used the laptop. Do what you need to with it.'

Belmar, who had been helping to disperse the crowd, came over as Maggie slipped the phone into her jacket pocket and the two of them buffered Lesley from the crowd's stares as she climbed into the back of the ambu-lance. The paramedic adjusted the mask over Mack's face and said her name was Tracie.

'I bet he'll be fine once he's had some rest. You can sit here and hold his hand if you want.' She moved aside to let Lesley perch on a bench fastened to the interior wall next to Mack's chair. She took his hand in hers and held it up to her lips.

'We'll be right behind you,' Maggie told her.

As the ambulance pulled away – blue lights flashing but its siren silent – someone shouted Maggie's name. She looked round to see a young woman with a mop of curly auburn hair bearing down on them.

'Hi, I'm Jennifer Jones from the *Mansell Echo*,' said the young woman hurriedly. She proffered a hand to shake, which Maggie ignored.

'Have you got time to answer a couple of questions?' said Jennifer.

'No, I haven't.' Maggie frowned. 'All requests need to go through the press office, you know that.'

'Well, yes, but no one's getting back to me,' said Jennifer breezily. 'Your DCI is apparently keen for us to interview the Kinnocks and I thought you might have an idea when we can do it? My editor's on my case about it.'

'Nothing to do with me,' snapped Maggie, irritated by the reporter's apparent lack of sensitivity. 'But I don't think Mr Kinnock will be talking to anyone anytime soon, do you?' Then she caught herself, mindful that anything she said might end up in the *Echo*. 'What I mean is you need to keep trying the press office. I can't help.'

Belmar, who had joined them, raised his hands and shrugged. 'Me neither,' he said.

'How about I interview you two instead? I'm quite interested in what a family liaison officer does and I'm sure I can persuade my editor it'll make a good background feature until the interview with the Kinnocks is sorted.'

'We make tea,' Maggie deadpanned. From the corner of her eye she saw Belmar smirk.

The reporter laughed nervously. 'I'm sure there's more to your role than that.'

'Sometimes we make coffee too. Now if you'll excuse us, we have to go.'

Maggie stalked off. Belmar was still laughing as he caught up with her. He was wearing a soft grey light-weight raincoat over his suit and the tails billowed behind him as he walked. He looked like he'd just stepped out of a menswear advert.

'That told her,' he said with a chuckle.

'She was getting on my nerves.'

'I'll keep trying the press office then, see what they can set up,' Jennifer yelled to their retreating backs.

'You do that,' Maggie hollered back, not turning round. 'Let's take my car,' she said to Belmar. 'It's parked at the other end of the high street. You can collect yours later.'

'An interview's not a bad idea,' Belmar mused as they headed up the high street. The crowd had melted away now the ambulance had gone. 'You could dispel some of the myths about FLOs, like the way newspapers always mention we've been assigned to help relatives but never explain why or what we do. It's just a throwaway line in the final paragraph. I think the only time we get a proper mention is when we read statements out on the families' behalf at the end of a trial.'

'Except Gant doesn't even like us doing that now.'

'I didn't know that. Since when?'

'Do you remember that case about eighteen months ago when the student murdered his girlfriend for going off with another man on a night out and the victim's parents complained to the press that the police seemed to think she'd asked for it? After the trial her family asked their FLO to read a statement on their behalf but he didn't check it first and ended up standing on the steps of the court slagging off everyone from the PC who answered the 999 call to the Chief Constable. Ask

DI Gant about it – I think the officer eventually asked for a transfer to another force.'

'Blimey, that's harsh,' said Belmar. 'I still think you should do the interview though.' A drop of rain fell on his forehead and he wiped it away.

'Sorry, I don't fancy being splashed across the pages of a newspaper.'

'It's only a local one.'

'If it's such a good idea, you do it,' she snapped.

'I was just saying,' Belmar replied with an edge to his voice. 'You're being really prickly today.'

She knew he was right and apologized.

'I didn't get much sleep last night.'

'Fine. I'd just rather you told me than take it out on me.'

'Point taken. Listen, Lesley said something weird just now.' She told him about Suzy Breed blackmailing Mack.

'I don't get it.' Belmar looked puzzled. 'His ex is trying to get money out of him and now his daughter's missing – you'd think he'd want us to look into it. When he gave his statement to DC Renshaw about the begging letters, he was adamant he'd never pay a penny to anyone who resorted to threats.'

'He wouldn't be the first person to lie to cover up the fact he's a victim of extortion,' Maggie reasoned. 'He could be ashamed – she's someone he had a relationship with after all. It's a huge betrayal.'

'Nah, I'm not buying it. I think he would've said something.'

'You think he's lied to Lesley?' she said.

'He holds back on things, that's for sure.'

'Lying or not, it's up to the DCI how to deal with it.'

Her car was up ahead and she fished inside her hand-bag for her keys. It was starting to rain quite heavily now and her Toyota's lights blinked back welcomingly as she aimed the key fob at the car and unlocked it.

'Do you think there was anything we could've done to stop him flipping out like that?' Belmar asked.

'I don't think so. He's been under a huge amount of strain these past few days but there was no obvious sign he was cracking up. Lesley maybe, but not him.'

Mack lay in a cubicle in the A&E department as he waited to be seen by the consultant.

'You don't both have to be here,' Lesley told Maggie. 'You'll stay, won't you?' she directed at Belmar, who nodded.

Maggie was baffled by the brush-off. 'No, we should both stay for the time being.'

'Aren't there other things you need to get on with?' said Lesley pointedly and she nudged her hand against Maggie's pocket.

In all the drama, Maggie had forgotten about Rosie's old phone.

'Are you sure?'

'Yes,' said Lesley even more forcefully. 'Belmar can call if we need you.'

'I'll drop by the station to see if there are any new leads we need to know about. I'll ring as soon as I know anything,' she told him.

He ducked out of the cubicle behind her.

'What the hell's going on?' he said in a hushed voice. 'What are you not telling me?'

'There's nothing to tell.'

'Do I look stupid?'

'Of course not,' Maggie replied.

'I don't believe you. Just remember that we're meant to be a team and if you fuck up I'm in trouble too.'

'I know that.'

He rubbed his chin. 'Well?'

'Okay, I'll tell you,' she said, and she filled him in about Rosie's old phone. 'I am going to give it to Umpire. Once I've taken a look at it.'

He paused for a moment, as though weighing up the consequences, then nodded. 'Sounds like a good plan. Christ knows we need some new leads on this case. All right, I'll cover for you here. Let me know how it goes.'

There was a sign on the wall opposite indicating the way out and moments later Maggie found herself outside in the fresh air. She slipped Rosie's phone into her bag and was about to head back to the car park when she saw the sign for the main hospital building next door. All thoughts of going to the station evaporated and she walked straight through the sliding doors.

In the middle of the foyer, on a stand drilled into the floor, was a floor plan of the building. Different colours denoted the various departments and Maggie scanned it until her gaze fell upon blocks of blue indicating the general wards. They were split between the second and third floors. She headed towards the lifts.

It took her three wards before she found what she was

looking for. Reaching the fourth, she slipped through the double doors behind a patient in pyjamas who stank of cigarette smoke and had most likely just come from outside. The nurses' station was unmanned, so she poked her head round the first doorway she came across. Inside was a ward with four metal-framed beds separated by curtains and surrounded by a few hard plastic chairs. Two elderly women occupied the two beds closest to the door and in the one in the far right corner lay Kathryn Stockton.

Maggie barely had time to react before Kathryn's mum Sarah saw her. Her chair scraped noisily against the floor as she pushed it away from her daughter's bed-side to stand up, causing one of the elderly women to tut. Oblivious, Sarah rushed to greet Maggie, engulfing her in a cloud of syrupy perfume.

'How nice you've come to visit. First Lily, now you!'

'I wanted to see how Kathryn is.'

Sarah took her by the hand and led her to Kathryn's bedside. The girl was awake. Maggie flinched at the extent of her injuries: the teenager's right eye socket was swollen to the size of a plum and her eyelid, clamped shut, was almost black, as was the skin beneath her left eye. There were vivid grazes on both of her cheeks and her lips were split and swollen. Whoever attacked her had done so with some force to inflict such appalling injuries to her face.

'I'm so sorry, Kathryn,' Maggie said softly. 'We'll do everything we can to find whoever did this to you.' She meant it sincerely too. Whatever concerns she had about the girl and her behaviour towards Rosie, seeing her in such a state made her sick to her stomach.

'Sit down,' said Sarah, noisily pulling another chair up to the bed. 'I'm afraid these aren't very comfortable though. I did think about having her moved somewhere nicer –' Maggie assumed she meant to a private ward – 'but it's only for one more night. She should be able to go home in the morning.'

Maggie lowered herself into the chair. She wanted to talk to Kathryn alone but couldn't just ask her mum to leave. Thankfully, Sarah provided the solution herself by announcing she had to use the bathroom.

'Would you mind watching her? I shouldn't be too long.'

As Sarah reached for her bag, Maggie glimpsed the neck of a glass bottle with a red screw cap that looked suspiciously like a well-known brand of vodka.

'Sure. Take your time,' she said.

As Sarah hurried out of the ward, shoes squeaking against the linoleum floor, Maggie asked Kathryn if she was up for chatting. She nodded.

'Have you been interviewed yet?'

'Yes, the tall one came. He was nice this time,' Kathryn mumbled, her swollen lips compromising her ability to talk.

Maggie assumed from the description that she meant Umpire.

'You must've been terrified when the attack happened.'

'I was. I begged him to stop but he wouldn't.'

'It was a he? You got a good look at who did it then?'

'Not really. He came up from behind.'

'But you know it was a he because he hit you from the front?'

'Yes.' A tear slid out of the corner of the girl's left eye. Her right eye was too swollen for any to escape. 'He really hurt me.'

'Can you remember anything about him at all?'

'He had on a dark blue top and a hat that might've been the same colour or it was black. I think his hair was light.'

'Light brown?'

'No, lighter than that.'

'It sounds like you got a pretty good look.'

'I guess.'

'Kathryn, did you recognize him? Is it someone you know?'

'Stop it!' she moaned, turning her head from side to side as she dodged the question. An extreme reaction and Maggie couldn't tell whether it was put on or not.

'Kathryn, if you know who did this to you, you have to tell us.'

'Even if it was someone I knew, I wouldn't say! They might come back and do it again.' She tossed around on the bed and burst into tears. As sobs wracked her body, Maggie grew concerned.

'Kathryn, I can see you're scared but you can't let the person who did this get away with it.'

There was a long drawn-out pause punctuated by Kathryn hiccupping as she fought to get her tears under control. Maggie sat patiently by the bed and hoped Sarah wouldn't come back yet. Then, after what felt like an age, Kathryn's swollen lips parted again and she whispered, 'I think GS was behind it.'

Maggie's eyes widened with surprise. 'So you do know who GS is?'

'Yes, but I can't tell you. I don't want to get hurt again. I think they did this to shut me up.'

'Kathryn, you must tell us.'

'No,' she sobbed. 'You can't make me. It's my own stupid fault. I should never have left Rosie alone in the garden.'

'Rosie? Are you saying GS definitely has something to do with her going missing?'

'Please stop. I don't want to talk to you any more.'

'Why are you covering up for him? Is he threatening you like he did Rosie? Is it because you introduced them in the first place? Has he taken photographs of you too?'

Kathryn recoiled with horror. 'How . . . ?'

'How do we know? We found the picture of Rosie in the green shoes I asked you about. Did you set her up so GS could take it, Kathryn?'

'No! I didn't do anything, it wasn't me. Please leave me alone.'

Maggie glanced over her shoulder and saw the two elderly women in the other beds watching them intently. She dropped her voice to a whisper.

'Not until you tell me who GS is. Maybe I should talk to Rosie's parents about it. Oh, but I can't, because her dad is next door in A&E hooked up to a drip because the stress of losing his daughter has made him collapse, while her mum's at his bedside crying her eyes out. Shall I tell them you won't tell me who GS is?'

'Why are you being so horrible?'

'I'm not,' said Maggie, aware she was perilously close to crossing a line by questioning her so aggressively. 'I'm worried about you. I know you're scared but I can help you if you just tell me who it is. I won't let anything happen to you.'

'Leave me alone!' Kathryn was shouting now.

'I'm not going until you tell me his name. I know he's somehow involved in Rosie's disappearance.'

'Why won't you listen to me?' Kathryn sobbed. 'I can't tell you. I'll be in so much trouble if I do.'

'No you won't, we'll protect you.'

Kathryn began to scream at the top of her voice and kept on until a nurse came running into the ward. Maggie jumped to her feet.

'What's going on?' the nurse demanded.

'Please make her leave, she's upsetting me,' Kathryn wailed, pointing at Maggie.

The nurse turned on her. 'Who are you?'

She flashed her warrant card. 'I'm working on the Rosie Kinnock case.'

'You should've cleared this with us first,' said the nurse angrily. 'Now please leave. Miss Stockton needs to rest.'

Maggie wouldn't budge. 'No, I need her to answer me. Kathryn, who is GS?'

The girl screamed again. The nurse, apoplectic now, ordered Maggie to leave. 'I'll call security if you don't go now.'

Maggie knew she'd pushed it as far as she could.

'Fine, I'll go.' As she reached the doorway, she fired a parting shot. 'I will find out who GS is, Kathryn, and why you're covering for him. This doesn't end here.'

51

Shaking with frustration, Maggie stalked out of the ward, into the lift and back down into the hospital's foyer. She stamped her feet, but the thin soles of her loafers barely made a sound. Thick-soled boots she could stomp in would have been far better, or spiky heels that gave a satisfying clack as their metal tips hit concrete – she wanted shoes that could scream for her.

She knew she should go straight to the station to brief Umpire but she needed to get her thoughts in order first. The spectre of the Megan Fowler case still loomed large, despite their conversation at her flat, and she knew he would be furious that she'd questioned Kathryn without his say-so. A defence lawyer might even question the validity of the girl's statement if it was found she gave it under duress. Maggie didn't want to disappoint Umpire again, not when they were back on such a good footing.

She decided to leave her car at the hospital and walk to the station to clear her head. On her way, close to the centre of town, was a park. Stretched across sixteen acres, it had a children's play area, tennis courts, bandstand and a small lake that at some point in its history was nicknamed the Puddle by locals and the tag stuck. On the shore of the Puddle was a small cafe her parents used to take her and Lou to as children, where they would badger them to buy fishing nets on bamboo sticks so they could hunt for minnows in the shallows. Their dad always cracked and reached for his wallet first.

It had stopped raining but was still overcast. Maggie bought a bottle of water from the cafe then walked along the paved path lining the water's edge. She was sweaty enough from her walk for the water to look inviting, although she didn't imagine the swans that called it home would take kindly to her plunging in, nor the park wardens whose job it was to ensure the lake was free of humans unless they were in boats that cost £15 to hire for twenty minutes.

The setting made her think of Lou. She tried her number and it went to voicemail, so she sent another text, asking her to call. They'd had worse rows than the one that morning and she knew they'd get over it. She'd go round in person later, say sorry and tell Jude and Scotty that of course she'd take them to Pizza Hut. It would blow over. It had to. The thought of not seeing the children terrified her.

As she put her phone back in her bag, she caught sight of something glinting prettily at the bottom of it. She was confused for a second then it hit her: Rosie's BlackBerry.

She scrabbled to pull it out and switch it on. Her heart leapt when she saw it was still fully charged, with an activated SIM. When she went straight to the call history, her suspicions were confirmed: the BlackBerry *was* the phone Rosie had used to call Emma Mitchell.

Maggie opened the text message folder and gasped. There, in black and white, were dozens of texts Rosie had received from a caller she'd saved in her contacts simply as GS. Some of the texts bordered on nice, but the contents of the majority were so vile that she wanted to throw the phone down in disgust. Despite a fondness for largely indecipherable text speak, GS made it very clear what kind of sexual favours were expected from Rosie. Maggie could see Rosie had not replied to any of them and the last message GS had sent was three months ago, which must've been just before she switched to her iPhone.

As tempted as she was to call the number herself and find out who it was, Maggie knew she couldn't. Instead, as she hurried towards the park exit closest to the police station, she used her own phone to call Steve. He answered on the second ring and sounded upbeat for someone who had just confessed to his boss that he'd cocked up.

'It's me. Have you spoken to Umpire yet?'

Steve's voice hardened. 'I'm just about to. He's been tied up with something.'

Maggie didn't believe him. 'If you don't tell him, I will.'

'I thought we were friends,' he said huffily.

'We are. But this is serious, Steve. You have to tell Umpire about the sighting.'

'Is this why you've called? To have a go at me?'

'No, I need a mobile number checked.' She read GS's number from Rosie's phone then repeated it. 'Can you run it through the system?'

'Give me five minutes.'

Next she rang Pearl, a CID admin support assistant she was friendly with, and begged her for a favour too.

'Is that birdsong I can hear?' Pearl asked, after Maggie had told her what she needed.

'I'm in the park,' Maggie explained.

'Bit wet for that, isn't it?'

'Pearl, can you help me or not?' said Maggie, trying not to snap.

'Not if it gets me into trouble, young lady.'

Maggie didn't blame her for being wary. FLOs didn't usually call up during an investigation wanting to check alibis.

'Anything happens, it's back on me,' she told her. 'But if I'm right about this, it'll be fine.'

Pearl didn't sound convinced, but said she'd do as Maggie asked.

'Do you want me to email it as an attachment?'

'That would be great.'

'Give me a few minutes to dig it out.'

Maggie was at the park exit by the time Steve rang back in a panic.

'Tell me where you got this number from,' he said.

'Remember those diary entries on Rosie's old laptop I asked you to tell Umpire about?' she said pointedly. 'About someone called GS harassing Rosie? The number is stored in her old phone under those initials. I want to know who it is before I speak to the DCI.'

'Shit, Maggie, this is really, really bad,' said Steve dolefully.

Her skin prickled with alarm. 'Why? Whose number is it?'

'It's registered to an Edward Sinclair, one of the security guards who patrol Burr Way.'

Maggie's insides lurched like she was on a fairground ride that had just tipped upside down.

'Steve, he's not the guard you saw on the CCTV with the suspect?'

'Yes, it's him.'

52

The small metal plaque screwed into the wall said the lift could take up to twelve people. Maggie was grateful to be its only occupant as it ascended steadily from the bowels of the building. The claustrophobia that had dogged her since she was little, from the time Lou locked her in a wardrobe for a joke, added to the nerves she already felt at the prospect of seeing Umpire in person for the first time since he was at her flat yesterday. Only when the lift had jolted to a halt on the station's third floor and the doors opened to spew her out did her breathing begin to steady.

Her arrival in the incident room caused heads to swivel in surprise. News of Mack's hospitalization would be common knowledge by now and as she weaved through the banks of desks towards the front of the room, Maggie guessed the team was wondering why she wasn't with him and Lesley while he was being treated. One officer she knew, a DC named Nathan, said hello with a raised eyebrow, but Renshaw was less circumspect and declared loudly from her desk, 'Should you be here?'

Ignoring her question and the curious stares, Maggie

didn't stop until she reached Umpire, who was deep in conversation with his deputy SIO, a detective inspector called Sol James she knew only by reputation. Umpire faltered when he saw her approaching then smiled. His reaction pleased her.

'What are you doing here?' he said. 'How's Mack?'

'Still waiting to be seen by the consultant but it doesn't look serious, thankfully. I've found out something though, something I think is important, and I thought it was better to tell you in person,' she said nervously.

'Go on,' said Umpire.

'Here?' She could feel her colleagues' stares boring into her back and didn't savour having an audience.

'Yes, here's fine,' he replied, crossing his arms. As he listened intently, Maggie launched into how she'd come to find out GS's identity. She didn't pause for breath, anxious to get to the end of her account before he could interrupt or explode, whichever came first.

'. . . DC Berry checked the number for me just now,' she finished, hoping that by mentioning Steve in a good light, Umpire might go easier on him later, 'and it's registered to Edward Sinclair, a security guard who works for the firm that patrols Burr Way. So it looks like Sinclair's the one who's been harassing Rosie, and Kathryn indicated to me that GS might be behind the attack on her last night. It's just a guess, but Rosie might have nicknamed him GS because it's the reverse of SG, for Security Guard.'

The room went very still. Maggie's face was inflamed and she couldn't read Umpire's expression at all; he just stared at her, unblinking. In the end, it was DI James who gave him a nudge in the side with his elbow and snapped him out of his stupor.

'You're sure about this?' said Umpire.

She handed him Rosie's BlackBerry.

'The messages were sent from a number registered to him.'

Umpire's brow furrowed as he and DI James huddled together to read them. When he looked up, Maggie saw his eyes were flinty and filled with anger. But, to her relief, it wasn't directed at her.

'It's eleven thirty now so let's assume he's at work. Renshaw, Thomas, I want you to come with me and DI James to bring Sinclair in.' There was a scuffle of noise as Renshaw and Nathan jumped out of their seats and began pulling on their jackets. 'Akinyemi,' he barked at an officer Maggie didn't know, sitting at the desk next to Nathan, 'find out where Sinclair lives, get a warrant organized and let Matheson know. I want his place turned upside down for any sign of Rosie.' He snatched up his suit jacket, which was hanging on the back of a chair, and said to DI James, 'I'll let the Chief Constable know what's going on while we're on the road.'

As she watched her colleagues race into action, Maggie felt like the invisible eye of the storm. Had this been a Force CID case, she would most likely have been one of the officers dispatched to arrest Sinclair. Here, as FLO, her job was to stand back and let others follow up her lead.

'Did Kathryn say anything else that makes you think Sinclair is GS?' Umpire asked her.

Still waiting for a rebuke, she was momentarily taken aback. 'Only that whoever attacked her was wearing a dark blue top, which is the same as Sinclair . . .'

Their eyes locked and she knew immediately what he was thinking. Without a word, his eyes never leaving hers, he picked up the telephone on the desk nearest him and dialled an extension.

'Tom, it's me, DCI Umpire. Have you got anything back on that photograph of Rosie Kinnock yet?' He paused for a moment to listen. Maggie's heart was in her mouth as she waited. 'You're sure about that?' A few more seconds dragged by. 'Great, thanks.' He hung up. 'HTCU have enhanced the image and you were right about it being some kind of clothing. They can't say exactly what it is, but it looks like woollen material . . .'

'Like a dark blue jumper the guards employed by Umbra security wear,' she finished for him.

Her heartbeat accelerated as the implication that Sinclair was the one who took the near-naked picture of Rosie hit home. It was all starting to add up: he had unfettered access to Burr Way, which allowed him to stalk Rosie, and an insider knowledge of the security system at Angel's Reach, which meant he could've easily disabled the CCTV cameras on Tuesday morning before she vanished.

'If it is Sinclair's jumper in the photograph and we can prove he took the photo, we can get him for taking indecent images of a child and engaging a child in sexual activity just for starters. You've done really well with this,' said Umpire, shrugging on his jacket. DI James already had his on and was waiting by the door to leave, 'and because of that I'm prepared to overlook the fact you interviewed Kathryn without my knowledge.'

Maggie had a comeback already prepared.

'Sir, Lesley asked me to check on her while we were at the hospital. I only popped my head round the door and then she got upset.'

The look he shot her suggested he was no more convinced by her excuse than she was herself. But he seemed prepared to let it go.

'Can I tell Lesley an arrest is imminent?' she asked.

'Yes. Tell her it's Edward Sinclair, but that's it—'

A sonorous voice broke through their discussion.

'Did someone mention an Edward Sinclair?'

It was Pearl, the admin support assistant Maggie had called earlier. Almost as wide as she was tall, she waddled up the office towards them, her girth draped in a voluminous navy cotton dress patterned with huge red poppies that demanded attention and matched the shade of her lipstick.

'I thought I recognized you from across the room,' she said to Maggie, and handed her a sheet of A4 paper. 'Here, this is what you wanted. It sounds like that Sinclair's been a very busy boy indeed.' She was out of breath, even though she'd barely walked twenty paces.

Maggie read what was printed on the paper and groaned. 'I don't believe it.'

'What is it?' Umpire demanded.

'I was curious to know who gave Kathryn her alibi for the time Rosie went missing.' She thrust the paper at him. 'According to this, it was Sinclair. This says he left the Umbra office in Haxton on Tuesday morning around the same time Kathryn said she left Rosie to go to the stables and he saw her on his way.'

'Shit,' said Umpire. 'If he wasn't near Burr Way, he can't be the one who took her.' He pored over the document. 'Ah, it says that he saw Kathryn on the approach to Burr Way, not long after ten, so the timing still fits.'

'But we already know he's not the person who was behind Lesley in the lottery queue,' Maggie pointed out.

'That doesn't mean he's not involved. Or he might have seen something but not reported it because he didn't want us to find out about his photography hobby. Right, I'll speak to you when you're back at the hospital.'

'Oh, just one more thing before you go,' said Maggie hastily, suddenly remembering her conversation with Lesley in the high street. 'Lesley told me Suzy Breed has been blackmailing Mack for money and that's why they've been texting.'

Umpire looked across the office. 'Renshaw!' he bellowed. She trotted confidently towards them, unruffled by the loud summons.

'Have we got Suzy Breed's phone records yet?' In an aside to Maggie, he added, 'Bloody phone company was meant to get them to us yesterday but didn't.'

'Yes, and they prove Mack did go to the house where she was staying when he was in Scotland because there are messages between them arranging when,' said Renshaw. 'Police up there have been round again but she seems to have vanished.'

'Is there anything in the messages to suggest she was extorting money from him?'

Renshaw smirked. 'That's his cover story? How

unoriginal. No, there isn't, sir. The messages are affectionate, not aggressive. Reading between the lines, it does sound like there's something going on.'

Maggie felt sick. 'Lesley will be so upset when she finds out he's lied.'

'So don't tell her,' said Umpire. 'Wait until Mack's in a position to talk, tell him we know and let's see how he's prepared to deal with it. If he decides to stick to his story, that's his business.'

'What, so we just let Lesley carry on thinking he's telling the truth?' said Maggie, aghast.

'It has nothing to do with our investigation,' said Umpire. 'It's their marriage, let them sort it out.'

53

By the time he'd finished, his entire back throbbed with pain. Mrs Roberts hadn't been as easy to manoeuvre as he imagined she might be after death. It had taken him almost an hour to wrap her body up in the square of blue tarpaulin he'd found next to the pool house and lug her all the way to the rear of the garden where he deposited her onto the compost heap. It wasn't the ideal place to leave a body – it wasn't exactly concealed – but it would do until he could find a better solution for its disposal.

Returning to the pool, he lay down at its edge and scooped up a handful of water to splash on his face as heavy raindrops beat a tattoo on the crystal blue surface.

Then he started to cry.

This was not how he'd planned any of this. When he'd found out his client Charlie knew someone who not only lived in the same road as Mack and Lesley Kinnock but happened to be looking for someone like him to treat an injury, he was full of hope, seeing it as the perfect opportunity to get to know the Kinnock family and perhaps show them he wasn't just another chancer begging for a handout. He had been confident that once he'd explained who he was and the role he'd played in their winning the EuroMillions jackpot, they'd gladly help him out.

He shouldn't have been so impatient. He should've waited until he could engineer a proper introduction, instead of getting sucked into a situation from which he had no idea how to extricate himself. He should've listened to reason, but it was drowned out by all the deafening white noise in his head.

'You've just fucking strangled an old woman,' he berated himself as he cried. 'You've just killed someone.'

He wasn't a bad man, but he'd just done a very bad thing and he had no idea how to undo it. The ridge on his forehead throbbed as he cried tears of self-pity.

'What are you doing here? You're not meant to be here now. If anyone sees you hanging around they'll call the police.'

The voice startled him. He sat up and wiped the tears and chlorinated water from his face, bristling with anger as he saw the figure coming towards him. This was their fault, not his. They were the ones who'd fucked everything up with those stupid photographs. He stood up and reached in his back pocket for the Stanley knife he'd found in Mrs Roberts's shed and used to cut up the tarpaulin. Slowly he slid the catch back so the blade was exposed. For days now he had put up with their stupidity making matters worse. Not any more. Now he was running the show on his own.

'I thought you were going to the hospital?' he said.

A shrug followed, but no explanation. They asked again what he was doing.

'I came out for some air after the treatment session and I thought I saw some movement inside the pool house,' he lied.

'Really? Oh God. That's all we need.'

But before the figure could reach the glass door at the front of the pool house, he sprang forward and pressed the blade to their neck.

'Don't move or I'll cut you . . . just like you cut Rosie.'

54

Lesley raised her head and yawned. She'd dozed off with her cheek resting against the blanket covering Mack's bed and as she rubbed her skin she could feel the creases it had left. Mack was sleeping too, his face whiter than the cotton pillow his head rested against. But his breathing was regular now and the oxygen mask he'd needed in the ambulance had been removed.

Lesley watched the gentle rise and fall of his chest as he slept. A tube inserted into the back of his hand silently pumped fluids into his weakened body from an IV drip positioned next to the bed. Mack wasn't just exhausted, his doctors said; he was severely dehydrated too. Had he drunk much water in the last few days, they'd asked? She didn't know, was her honest answer. Drinking water, remembering to eat, trying to sleep – those things had all been irrelevant to her since Tuesday and to Mack too, or he wouldn't have ended up in a side room off a packed ward at their local hospital.

Rosie would be so upset to see her dad like this, she thought as she gently traced her fingertips over the back of his hand. When this was all over, she vowed, when

Rosie was home and Mack was better, they'd go away, just the three of them. Instead of resenting the money, she'd bloody well make herself enjoy it. They'd go to Australia and go diving on the Great Barrier Reef. Or maybe to the Far East: Mack had always said he wanted to go to Tokyo to see if it was as crazy as it looked on TV and in films. As she rhythmically stroked his hand, Lesley added more destinations to their itinerary: a stop-off in Los Angeles to see the Hollywood sign; sightseeing in New York; a cruise around the Caribbean. Then back to Europe, to Rome, a city she'd always wanted to visit; Milan, to take Rosie shopping; followed by Moscow, because someone from Mack's old office went once and said it was a beautiful city. Last would be a long holiday somewhere hot, like the Maldives, where they'd lie in hammocks, sip cocktails and pretend none of this had happened.

She grew more excited as she ticked the destinations off one by one, until the sound of people talking outside the door dragged her back into the present. She rested her head back on Mack's bed in despair. She wanted to rewind to the weekend when her only worry had been whether to have chicken or fish for dinner. Her grief at Rosie going missing manifested as a physical ache, like her body was being stamped on repeatedly. Tomorrow was Saturday and Rosie would have been gone for four days. It felt like a lifetime already.

There was a gentle knock on the door and it opened to reveal Belmar.

'Have you got a minute?' he said.

Lesley leapt to her feet and flew around the end of the bed to the door.

'What is it? You've got that look on your face. It's bad news, isn't it?'

Glancing at Mack asleep on the bed, Belmar shut the door quietly behind him.

'Maggie just called. We're making an arrest in connection with Rosie's disappearance.'

'Who?'

'Edward Sinclair, one of the security guards who works for Umbra.'

Lesley gasped. 'Really? Does . . . does that mean you know where Rosie is?'

'Not yet, but hopefully we'll have some news when he's questioned.'

'But he must've said something! Haven't you asked him?'

Belmar spoke stiffly, as though he'd been coached in what to say.

'As soon as there's a development you'll be the first to know. I'm going to wait outside for an update from the station as I can't use my phone in here. Will you be okay on your own for a bit longer, until Maggie's back?'

'I don't have a bloody choice, do I?' she snapped, then immediately regretted it. 'I'm sorry, I know I shouldn't take it out on you. It's just that I thought you'd find my daughter before you caught who did it.'

'We need to question him to determine his involvement.'

Belmar's police handbook babble was starting to annoy her.

'Fine, just go,' she sighed. 'I'll wait here.'

He gave a half-smile then ducked out of the room. Lesley turned to her husband's inert form on the bed.

'Did you hear that, Mack? They've arrested someone. That's got to be good news, hasn't it?'

As she waited for Belmar to return, she couldn't keep still. Flitting between the chair, window and door, she tried to remember which of the guards Edward Sinclair was. She couldn't remember talking to him or seeing him at the house, but then Mack dealt with all the security issues.

She checked the time again, but the hands on her watch had barely moved since the last time she'd looked.

'I'll go crazy if I wait in here,' she told her sleeping husband. 'I'm going to get some fresh air.' She leaned over him. The nurses had removed his glasses and there was a small red indent either side of his nose where the frames pressed into his flesh. She gently kissed each mark, then the tip of his nose, and then his lips. He didn't stir.

It was only when she was outside the front entrance that she remembered Kathryn was being treated at the hospital too. She debated what to do for a moment then went back inside. Even though Maggie said she wasn't to talk to Kathryn or the rest of her family, her injuries had sounded bad and, despite the bullying allegation, she still wanted to see how she was.

She made a beeline for the information desk.

'I need to find out about a patient who's being treated

here,' Lesley told the smartly dressed, middle-aged man sitting behind the desk. He smiled but told her in a rich, mellifluous West Indian accent that he couldn't give out confidential patient information unless she was a relative.

'I'm a friend of the family,' she implored. 'I just want to know that she's okay. She came in last night.'

He gave her a sympathetic smile. 'I wish I could tell you, but they'd have my hide.'

'Can't you make an exception? She's my daughter's best friend and, well, my daughter . . .' she faltered. 'The thing is, my daughter's gone missing. My husband is in the hospital too, because he collapsed. He's on ward 3A. You can check if you want. His name is Mack . . . Mack Kinnock.'

She hadn't meant to divulge so much but the man's face emanated kindness in such a way that she couldn't help herself.

He leaned over the desk and dropped his voice.

'Are you the lady with the young girl that's gone astray in Haxton?'

She flinched. 'Yes, I'm her mother.'

'Oh, ma'am, I am so sorry,' he said. 'I hope you get her home soon.'

'So do I,' she said, trying not to cry.

He tilted his head to one side. 'What did you say her friend's name was?'

'I didn't—'

'Tell me what it is.' He winked and nodded down at the desk, where his other hand already hovered over his keyboard.

'Thank you,' she said, overwhelmed with gratitude. 'It's Kathryn Stockton. Kathryn with a K and a Y.'

His fingers flew over the keys. 'She's on the second floor. Ward 2F. Don't tell them I sent you.'

'I won't, I promise. You've been so kind.'

'If my little girl was missing, I hope someone would do the same for me. You take care now, ma'am.'

As she said goodbye and turned away from the desk, Lesley frowned. A vaguely familiar-looking woman with cropped dark hair was walking towards her, her face taut with apprehension. She suddenly realized who it was. The last person she expected to see.

'What the hell are you doing here? Haven't you done enough?' she burst out.

Suzy Breed gathered herself and took a deep breath.

'I know this is the worst time to do this, but you need to know the truth about me and Mack. Right now.'

55

The incident room had fallen silent again now Umpire and the others had departed. The few officers who stayed behind were hunched over at their desks, eyes trained on their computer screens. Maggie didn't know any of them to talk to, but that was often the case when an SIO was brought in from another part of the county to run a Major Crime Inquiry, as Umpire was, and had their own team to work alongside local Force CID officers like Maggie, Steve, Renshaw and Nathan.

She decided it was time to head back to the hospital and gathered her coat and bag. On her way to the lift she paused to get a drink of water from the dispenser and shivered as the ice-cold liquid it supplied set her teeth on edge. She was gulping down her third cupful when she saw Steve barrelling down the office towards her, beaming widely.

'That's not the face of a man who's just told his boss he screwed up,' she said shrewdly.

'I need to talk to you. Come on,' he said.

She followed him to the lift.

'Steve, what's going on? Have you told Umpire yet about seeing the suspect on Tuesday?'

'I might not have to. I'll tell you everything once we're outside.' He pushed the button on the panel to take the lift to the ground floor.

'I've got to get back to the hospital.'

'Just hear me out.'

He led her into the car park at the rear of the station. As they stepped outside onto the tarmac, it was drizzling again. Maggie briefly raised her face to meet it, enjoying the coolness against her flushed cheeks. Then she turned to her friend.

'What's with all this cloak-and-dagger stuff?'

'I managed to get another look at the CCTV from Tuesday morning while you were talking to Ballboy,' he confided. 'I still can't tell whether Sinclair and the suspect were arguing, but I did get the licence plate for the Peugeot he was driving. I ran it through the system and the registered owner is a woman living in Mansell and – get this – the electoral register says there's a man living at the same address. It must be him.'

'Steve, that's brilliant. Umpire's on his way to arrest Sinclair now at the Umbra office in Haxton. Ring him and tell him.'

'Not yet. I want to do some more digging first. I need to sort this out without telling Ballboy I missed the suspect first time round.'

'Steve, you can't do that, Rosie's life's at stake. Umpire needs to know now. You know that.'

He tried to argue but Maggie wouldn't back down.

'Look, you made a mistake with the CCTV but you'll

make things a million times worse for yourself if you go off on some reckless chase on your own. Umpire needs to know who the suspect is right now.'

He sighed. 'You're always right, aren't you?'

Maggie grinned. 'Of course. I can't believe it's taken you this long to realize.'

Steve tugged his phone out of his suit pocket with one hand and flipped open his notebook with the other. As he scrolled for Umpire's number, Maggie caught sight of the name written on the page and gasped. She reached out to still his arm.

'That's not the woman whose car it is?'

'Yes. Lisa Charleston,' Steve read from his notes. 'Lives at 4 Shelby House, Hawthorn Close, Mansell.'

'Oh, fuck.' Maggie groaned.

Steve looked at her, alarmed.

'Christ, you don't know her, do you?'

'In a manner of speaking. She's the woman Rob left Lou for.'

56

'What happened to telling the DCI everything and not going off on a reckless chase on your own?' Steve grumbled as he shifted in the driver's seat, the light grey fabric of his suit trousers, shiny from over-wear, pulling tightly across his thighs as he tried to get comfortable. He kept the engine ticking over as they parked outside the gym.

'I have to talk to Rob first,' she beseeched. 'He's still technically married to Lou and he's Mae's dad and the boys' stepdad. He's family.'

'Umpire's not going to be happy if he finds out.'

'But we already know Rob isn't our suspect. He's six foot two, which is at least four inches taller than the bloke pictured in the garage queue and in the paper today.'

'That doesn't mean he's not involved, Maggie.'

'No, it doesn't. But I know Rob and, while he's an idiot, I know he wouldn't hurt anyone, least of all a fifteen-year-old girl. I'd stake my job on it.'

That was enough to convince Steve.

'Okay. You speak to him first. Show him the pictures of the suspect and find out if he knows who was driving Lisa's car on Tuesday.'

'You don't want to come in with me?'

'Like you said, it's family. It's probably better if you speak to him alone. I'll wait here.'

As Maggie climbed out of the car, she received a text from Belmar.

'He's asking when I'm getting back to the hospital,' she told Steve.

'Tell him you'll be half an hour. This shouldn't take that long.'

She found Rob on a rowing machine, grunting loudly as the seat slid back and forth. She put her foot on the frame to stop his momentum.

'I need to talk to you about Lisa,' she said.

'What about her?'

'Not in here.'

Maggie led him to a quiet corner in reception where they couldn't be overheard.

'What's going on, Maggie?' he said worriedly.

She told him about Lisa's car being spotted in Burr Way on the day Rosie Kinnock went missing.

'That's bollocks. It must be a mistake. Why would she be in Haxton?'

'Where is she, Rob? We need to talk to her.'

'I told you, she's visiting a friend in Manchester.'

'Still? When did you last speak to her?'

'I dunno,' he said sulkily.

She began to lose patience.

'Rob, this is serious. Lisa's car has been seen near the

scene of a serious crime. Is there anyone else she allows to drive it?'

'Only me, and I've not been anywhere near Haxton.'

She decided to show him the photograph of the suspect in M&S with Lesley. Using the Google app on her phone, she found it on the website of the newspaper it had been published in.

'Do you know the man on the left?'

'Yeah, that's Adrian Farley, Ade.'

'How do you know him?'

'He works here. He's a sports massager or whatever it's called, for injuries. An osteo-summat.'

Maggie was seized by an overwhelming sense of apprehension.

'Is he here now?'

'I haven't seen him since yesterday.' Rob frowned. 'Why are you asking about Ade? Where's that picture from?'

'I can't say right now.'

His reaction to seeing Farley's photograph convinced her Rob knew nothing about his involvement in Rosie's disappearance. He wasn't clever enough to lie with conviction. But there was still something in his expression to suggest he knew more than he was letting on.

'How well do you know him?'

'I don't, really.'

There was that look again.

'You're not in trouble, Rob, I just need to know.'

He shrugged. 'Can't help you.'

'If he works here, does he have an office or a treatment room?'

'Yeah.'

'Show me.'

The door was locked.

'I need the key,' she told Rob. 'We've got to get this open now.'

As she double backed to reception, she tried calling Steve outside. To her annoyance it went to voicemail and she hoped it was because he was already on a call to Umpire. The girl on reception handed over a Chubb key after Maggie flashed her warrant card and explained it was an emergency.

Farley's room was small but accommodated a treatment table pushed against one wall, a desk, two chairs and a filing cabinet. The walls were covered with posters featuring anatomical diagrams of bodies stripped of skin and their muscles exposed, red and raw. She began searching through the papers stacked neatly on the desk.

'Don't you need a warrant to do that?' Rob remarked.

'Not if there's a potential threat to life. If Farley's got Rosie or knows where she is, I'd say that qualifies.'

'I know where he lives,' Rob suddenly blurted out. 'Cedar Crescent. Number sixty-two.'

'The road by the top end of the park?'

'Yeah, that's the one. It was his mum and dad's place and he got it when they died.'

So not only did Rob know where Farley lived but he also knew the house's provenance.

'I thought you didn't know him that well.'

Rob flushed red as Maggie crossed the room. Even though she was tall, she was no match for Rob's height.

Yet it was him and not her who cowered as they stood toe to toe.

'Don't fucking play games with me, Rob,' she said in a quiet but firm voice. 'I'm not in the mood. There's a young girl missing and if you're covering for Farley I'll nick you for obstruction. Just have a think about what it would be like for Mae and the boys seeing you once a month at prison visiting time.'

Rob's eyes widened. 'I'm not covering for him,' he blustered. 'I don't know nothing about that girl.'

'But you are keeping something back, I can tell. It's written all over that ugly mug of yours.'

Rob squirmed. 'I've been sorting him out with some gear, that's all, I swear.'

'You're supplying drugs?' said Maggie, shocked.

'No, well, not really. Just steroids. Stuff you usually need a prescription for . . .' He tailed off.

Maggie wanted to shake her brother-in-law for being so stupid.

'*Just* steroids? Like that's somehow okay? So what is Farley taking?'

'You name it. It's what's known as stacking. It's, like, mixing them up to make them work better, but he takes way too much. I've told him that.'

Maggie took a step back. 'I can't say I know much about steroids but I know enough that if he's abusing them, he may well be experiencing violent mood swings, sexual urges he can't control, even psychotic hallucinations. They could be making him very dangerous and unstable. We need to find him before it's too late, Rob.'

Her brother-in-law stared at her for a moment, his

face creased in a deep frown. Maggie could almost hear the wheels turning.

'You asking me about Lisa's car . . . are you saying he was driving it?'

Maggie nodded. 'How well does she know him?'

'Only to say hi to when she's on the front desk.' Rob paled. 'He must've stolen it and that's why she's not come home yet. If that fucking bastard's hurt her, I'll kill him.'

'Hang on, you said she's at a friend's in Manchester.'

'She should've been back days ago,' said Rob miserably.

'Shit, is that why you were asking me about missing persons the other day? Is Lisa missing?'

'I don't know. She didn't come home when she said she would and she's not picking up her phone. I thought she was narked off with me about something. She's like that.'

'When did you last speak to her?'

'Monday night. She was due home on Tuesday.'

Now she wanted to throttle him for his idiocy.

'You should've told me the truth. Right, I need to speak to my boss so he can get a team round to Farley's house.'

Adrenaline surging through her, she dashed out of Farley's office and headed outside to let Steve know what was going on. Rob followed her.

'How long will it take to get your lot round there? What if he's hurt Lisa?' He was almost crying now. 'I know you hate me for what I did to Lou, but I love Lisa. You've got to help her.'

Maggie ignored him. As she passed reception the girl behind the desk called out to her.

'DC Neville, I've got a message from your colleague DC Berry. He's had to go home for a family emergency. His baby boy's sick.'

Maggie groaned. 'Please tell me you're joking.'

The receptionist smiled prettily. 'Sorry, that's what he said.'

Maggie pushed through the revolving door into the street and, just as the receptionist said, Steve and his car had gone.

'Shit, shit, shit.'

She called Umpire but he didn't pick up. She left a breathless message: 'Sir, I think I know who the crayon writer is. Please call me urgently.'

Rob hovered beside her.

'That's it? You're just gunna wait for him to ring back?'

'I can't go round there on my own,' she said. 'I need back-up.'

'I'll come with you. We can go in my car. He won't touch you if I'm there. Please, we're five minutes away. I love her, Maggie. I'll go mental if anything's happened to her.'

Maggie felt a sudden pang of sorrow for Lou. Her sister would be devastated if she could hear the way Rob was talking about Lisa right now. But she also knew Lou would want her, would expect her, to do the right thing.

'Okay, let's go.'

57

Cedar Crescent was one of the more salubrious addresses in Mansell. A long cul-de-sac, there was no uniformity to the houses that lined it: some were made from flint, others the standard red brick, while a few were painted varying shades of white and cream. Most of the driveways were empty of vehicles but Maggie imagined that whatever cars were usually parked there were probably top of the range.

As they cruised slowly along the road in Rob's old Ford Focus, Maggie scoured the front of the properties for house numbers. Frustratingly, most didn't appear to have one. Was Farley's home the bungalow half screened by bushes or the impressive detached house that reminded her of a child's drawing, its front door slap-bang in the centre and four windows equally spaced around it? Or perhaps it was the ivy-clad semi on the corner?

'This is it,' said Rob as he pulled up outside a whitewashed detached house with a tarmac driveway that was empty. The front garden was neat and ordered. It looked like a house whose owner took pride in it.

'You stay here,' she ordered Rob.

'No fucking way. I'm coming too.'

She didn't argue. Umpire still hadn't called back, despite her also leaving a message at the incident room for him to call her, and Steve wasn't picking up either. In desperation, she'd called Belmar at the hospital and told him what she was doing. She'd expected him to talk her out of it but to her surprise his reaction was calm and considered.

'There's no harm in going to check out the address, but if for a second you think there could be a problem, you step down and call for back-up.'

'What about Mack and Lesley? I should be there with you.'

'It doesn't take the two of us to sit around until Mack wakes up. Lesley's fine for now. Go and make yourself useful.'

'Thanks, Belmar, I appreciate you saying that.'

'Well, it's like you're always reminding me – we're still detectives when it comes down to it.'

Belmar's encouragement didn't change the fact Umpire would have a fit if he knew what she was up to. When she looked up, Rob was already at the front door and she had no choice but to follow him up the garden path, which was wet and slippery from the rainfall.

Rob went to hammer on the door but she stopped him.

'Let's try ringing the bell first. If we go storming in, he might run.'

The bell was loud and Maggie pressed it twice.

'Did you hear that?' said Rob.

'No, what?'

'I can hear banging inside.'

He was right. As Maggie strained to listen, she could hear thumping coming from somewhere downstairs. She went to peer in the front window but the curtains were drawn. She rapped on the glass and was answered by more thumps.

'Let's go round the back,' she whispered.

She and Rob raced down the side of the house. There was a high wooden gate separating the narrow pathway from the back garden but mercifully it was unlocked. However, the back door to the kitchen and the patio doors, also obscured by drawn curtains, were all firmly shut.

'I'll kick the back door in,' said Rob, raising his foot to take aim.

'No! If you do that, you're breaking and entering. I'll have to do it. It's legal forced entry then.'

Rob stood back. 'Be my guest.'

But Maggie wasn't going to kick the door in. She pulled her baton off her belt and crouched down by the patio doors. Remembering the advice given to her by Craig, the firefighter she'd dated last year, she hit the corner of the glass – the weakest part – until it shattered. Then she held her breath, convinced an alarm would start screeching at top volume and Farley would suddenly appear. When neither of those things happened, she grabbed one of the metal garden chairs and continued to smash through glass until there was a hole big enough for her to climb through.

The room she entered was long and open plan. Baton still raised, she eased round the dining-room table and crept towards the living area where the sofa and television were. She suddenly stopped. Face down on the floor, hands tied behind her back, was a girl dressed in a T-shirt that was at least three sizes too big for her. She didn't appear to be wearing any underwear. Small and slight, her dark hair fanning across her back, she was using her feet to bang on the floorboards.

Maggie's heart skipped a beat.

'Rosie?'

She raced forward and gently lifted the girl up off the sofa. But when she turned her round to sit her up, she was stunned.

'Lisa!'

Her face was battered, swollen and tear-stained but there was no mistaking Rob's girlfriend. Maggie removed the gag from her mouth.

'Get me out of here before he comes back! He's a fucking psycho. Please, get me out of here!'

'Lisa? What the fuck?'

Rob had followed Maggie inside.

'I'm so sorry, I'm so sorry,' she sobbed over and over as Maggie quickly untied her wrists and ankles with trembling fingers. 'Don't hate me, please don't hate me.'

Rob dropped to the carpet next to his girlfriend and held her in his huge arms.

'Sssh, it's okay, you're safe now.'

As touching though the reunion was, Maggie needed answers.

'Lisa, is Rosie Kinnock here?'

'No, she's not, but he knows where she is. He's

keeping her somewhere until the parents give him some money.'

'She's alive?'

'I think so.'

'But you don't know where she is?'

'It's somewhere close to where she lives. He thinks it's funny that she's right under your noses. He's a fucking nutter.'

'She could still be anywhere. We need to narrow it down, Lisa.'

'It's somewhere to do with a client of his.'

'Are you sure?'

Lisa started crying again. 'He's got a client he treats in Haxton every Thursday. I've met him a couple of times at the Swan Hotel after the appointment.'

Rob looked crushed. 'You've been seeing Ade behind my back?'

'Not now,' Maggie urged him. 'We don't have much time. How did you end up here?' she asked Lisa.

'I really did go to Manchester to see my friend but I stayed a couple of extra days.' She shot Rob a look. 'After that row we had about you wanting Mae to come on holiday with us. I don't want to look after the baby for that long,' she explained to Maggie, who said nothing but shot Rob a look of her own. 'Yesterday I got back and came straight round here because Ade had borrowed my car again,' Lisa continued. 'Anyhow, he got really angry when I turned up because he told me I was never allowed to come to his house.'

'You've never been here before?' asked Maggie.

'No, he said he didn't like visitors messing the place

up. He lets me in but then he starts laying into me, like hitting me and I blacked out for a bit. When I woke up he started on me again and I couldn't get to the front door so I ran upstairs thinking I could lock myself in the bathroom and call the police. But I ended up in a bedroom by mistake and that's when I saw it.'

'Saw what?'

'The missing girl's picture on the wall, with her mum and dad. Ade found me and lost the plot. He started screaming that it wasn't his fault the girl got injured and he'd been the one who'd saved her and taken her to safety because he thought he could get some money from her parents by looking after her.' Lisa shivered violently. 'When I told him I'd tell the police, he tied me up.'

'Did he harm you in any other way?' asked Maggie gently.

Lisa squeezed her eyes tightly shut as she nodded.

'But he said it didn't count because we were already sleeping together. Oh God, if he's done the same to her . . .' She broke down again and Rob held her tighter.

'We need to get you out of here,' said Maggie. 'I'll call for an ambulance. You need to go to hospital.'

'You've got to find her,' Lisa sobbed.

'We will. Is there anything else you can think of that might help?'

Lisa shook her head miserably.

After Maggie placed the call for the ambulance, she tried Umpire. Again there was no answer.

Baton still drawn, she went upstairs as quietly as she could, even though she was certain Farley wasn't there.

What she was hoping to find were client records that would tell her who he treated in Haxton.

A chill ran through her when she opened the door to the smallest bedroom and saw the photograph of Mack, Lesley and Rosie on the wall, surrounded by newspaper cuttings about their win. Obsessed didn't come close. Going through the desk, however, she hit her own jackpot. In the bottom drawer, separated by dividers, were Farley's client records, filed alphabetically. She tore through them, taking out the cover sheets that listed Haxton addresses. Eventually she reached 'R'.

Mrs Vivienne Roberts. Verma Lodge, Burr Way, Haxton.

'Yes!' she exclaimed.

It all made sense. Matheson said Rosie was most likely carried from the pathway behind Angel's Reach because there was no trace of her beyond that point. All Farley had to do was take her round the corner, across the bottom of the meadow and into Verma Lodge. He could've carried her easily, but how did he manage to get her past Mrs Roberts?

She ran back downstairs with the cover sheet in her hand.

'Lisa, has Farley ever mentioned a woman called Mrs Roberts or a house called Verma Lodge?'

Lisa thought for a moment.

'We were out for a drink once and he told me about a party he'd come across when he was working at a lodge one day in Haxton. I guess that could be the same place?'

'Did he say anything else about it?'

'I think he said it was organized by a girl he knew through another client. She'd been throwing these secret parties for her friends so they could all get drunk and take drugs and get up to God knows what, but it wasn't her house, it belonged to her nan. I remember Ade saying the nan had found out what was going on, but he covered for the girl and stopped her getting into trouble. He said she owed him a favour after that.'

'Did he say what the girl's name was?'

'No, sorry, he didn't. He only mentioned the party in passing.'

Maggie's first thought was the girl had to be Kathryn. Sarah said she was always getting into trouble for missing her curfew and dating unsuitable boys – the parties sounded right up her street. But if Mrs Roberts was related to the Stocktons, surely they'd have found out before now? Maggie shook her head, folded up the cover sheet and put it in her pocket.

'You know what, right now it doesn't matter who the girl is,' she said to Lisa and Rob. 'All that counts is getting to Rosie before it's too late – if it's not already.'

58

Suzy suggested they find a quiet corner near Mack's room to talk but Lesley refused point-blank. She wasn't letting her anywhere near him.

'There's a cafe over there,' she said, pointing across the foyer. It wouldn't hurt to have witnesses to their conversation, not just to overhear what was said, but to stop her doing something she might later regret.

As they crossed the foyer in silence, Lesley stole a surreptitious look at Suzy. Her hair was short and boyish – the last time she'd seen her it was past her shoulders – but the style suited her delicate features and emphasized her big brown eyes. There were lines on her face that hadn't been there before, but her figure, not dissimilar to Lesley's in build, was exactly the same and flattered by her slim-fit indigo jeans and fitted fuchsia blouse. Suzy also wore a thick, intricately designed silver necklace and sand-coloured wedge sandals with peep-toes. Lesley felt a stab of jealousy at realizing how good she looked.

'Do you want a drink?' Suzy asked as they reached the concession.

'This isn't a social occasion,' sniped Lesley, even though

the strong aroma of coffee wafting out from behind the counter made her long for one. She sat down at one of the two tables that were free.

'Suit yourself. I'm going to have one.'

Her jealousy grew as Suzy strolled confidently to the counter and ordered a latte. How dare she turn up now, acting like she had every right to be here? She thought about just walking out but curiosity pinned her to the seat. However furious she was with Suzy for turning up, she still wanted to hear what she had to say.

Suzy sat down across the table from her. As she took a sip of her drink, Lesley saw she was wearing a wedding ring. Did her husband know what she'd done?

'What is it you want, Suzy?' she snapped. 'Isn't fifty grand enough for you?'

Suzy didn't even flinch. 'No, it's not.'

Speechless at her audacity, Lesley could only stare at her open-mouthed.

'Yes, I want more money, but not for the reason you think. I'm not blackmailing Mack, nor are we having an affair. He told me you'd seen the texts I sent him and the explanation he's given you and I'm bloody furious with him.' Her accent was an odd, lilting hybrid of Scots and Kiwi. 'He should've been honest. But,' she hesitated, looking nervous for the first time, 'with Rosie missing, I guess he didn't want to upset you. I'm really sorry, Lesley, I can only imagine what you must be going through. If it was my daughter, I don't know how I'd cope.'

'You have a child? That makes you coming here even worse. I don't need this right now.'

'I had no choice. The police have been round to

where I'm staying and I don't want any trouble. If Mack won't tell the truth, I will.'

'So go on,' Lesley challenged her. 'Explain to me why you've been blackmailing my husband for money.'

'I haven't. Mack paid me because he wanted to.'

'I know my husband and there is no way he would just give someone money, even you, without a very good reason.'

'Oh, there's a very good reason,' said Suzy abruptly. 'And that reason is why I'm here now. I know this is the worst time possible to do this and I am very sorry for adding to your distress, but I will not have Mack distort the truth just to save his skin.'

Lesley's insides turned to liquid. 'So you are having an affair,' she croaked.

'No, we're not. There has been nothing between me and Mack for years, since before I emigrated.'

'But I saw the text saying you wouldn't tell anyone he was with you in Scotland when he told me he was in a hotel.'

'Yes, he did visit me in Falkirk at the weekend.'

Lesley hugged her arms tightly round herself. 'I don't think I want to hear this.'

'You need to. You need to know that Mack is a good guy, one of the best, who loves you very much. I don't care what you think about me, but you need to know what's really going on before the police dig any further and the press find out. I need to protect my family too.'

'What the hell are you talking about?'

'I'll tell you, but please let me finish before you say anything.'

Lesley nodded reluctantly.

'Me and Mack are not having an affair. But eighteen years ago, right before I emigrated to New Zealand, we had a one-night stand. You two had just got engaged.'

Oh, Mack. Lesley squeezed her eyes shut to stop tears escaping. She would not let this woman see her cry.

'It was completely my doing. We were both stupidly drunk and I came on to him so strongly he'd have needed a cattle prod to get me off. The next day he was in pieces. He loved you so much and he hated himself for letting it happen. By the time I left Scotland, we weren't talking. He refused to have anything to do with me and that's probably how things would've stayed between us if it hadn't been for Faye.'

Lesley slowly opened her eyes. 'Who?'

'Our daughter.'

The cafe seemed to tilt violently, like the world had suddenly shifted on its axis. Lesley clutched the table to steady herself.

'Your daughter?' she rasped.

'Yes, Mack is the father of my child. I'm sorry, I never wanted you to find out like this.'

'I don't understand. Why hasn't he told me?' said Lesley desperately.

'He only found out about her a year ago. When I landed in New Zealand, I thought it was jet lag making me sick. I didn't realize I was pregnant until I was almost five months and it was too late to do anything about it. Don't get me wrong, I love Faye more than anything, but at the time having a baby wasn't high on my list of priorities. When I found out I was expecting, I was seeing someone, Eric, who's now my husband. I told him how I'd left things with Mack and he said he'd be there to help me with the baby. Since the minute Faye was born Eric has been an amazing dad to her.'

Lesley frowned. 'So you only told Mack when you found out we'd won the money?'

'Yes,' said Suzy simply. 'Money's tight back home since Eric got laid off and I used up all our savings flying back to see my mum before she passed away last month. I told Mack about Faye because I wanted him to help us out financially. Initially he refused, but I met this accountant by chance in London who said I had a cast-iron case and he was helping me draw up a financial agreement for Mack to sign before I go home to New Zealand. It was actually his idea to get Mack to meet me in Scotland last weekend to discuss getting a one-off lump sum payment, but then Mack had to fly home because of Rosie. My accountant, Simon, suggested I come down so we could sort it out. He should be here too but for whatever reason he didn't meet me off the train in London and now I can't get hold of him.'

'You think now is the time to sort this out?' Lesley thundered.

'I'm going home in a fortnight, so yes. Look, I could've gone after Mack for maintenance before now but I didn't,' said Suzy defensively. 'I'm only wanting what's owed.'

'How can you be sure Faye's really his? Why should we take your word for it?'

Suzy set her coffee down on the table and pulled her handbag onto her lap. From its front pocket she took out a photograph and handed it silently to Lesley, who gasped. It was like looking at a picture of Rosie, but a few years older. Faye's face was the same round shape and she had Rosie's dark hair and almond-shaped green eyes. Mack's eyes.

'That's how I know,' said Suzy. 'I told Mack we could take a paternity test to make sure, but he didn't need convincing. All the dates add up.'

Lesley could barely think straight as she handed the picture back.

'Does Faye know about Mack?'

'Yes. We told her when she was young that Eric wasn't her real father. She's never shown any interest in wanting to meet Mack though. As far as she's concerned, Eric's her dad and always will be.'

'Even though Mack's rich now?' said Lesley sceptically.

'She doesn't care. In fact, she's pretty angry with me for asking him for money. She didn't think it was fair on you or Rosie.'

Lesley groaned. 'What will I tell Rosie? This is going to devastate her.' Then she faltered.

Suzy reached over and squeezed her shoulder.

'She'll come home. And when she does, nothing will have changed. Mack's still her dad.'

'He's got another family,' Lesley hissed, shrugging Suzy's hand off.

'No, he hasn't. He fathered another child, that's all. Faye is not his daughter in any way except biologically and she's not going to suddenly turn up and whisk him away from Rosie.'

Lesley's voice broke. 'But what if Rosie doesn't come home? He'll want to be a dad to Faye then, won't he?'

Suzy sat back. 'Rosie will turn up, I'm sure of it.'

'How can you be so sure?' Lesley snarled. 'You don't know anything about it.'

'No, I don't. But you mustn't give up hope.'

Lesley rubbed her eyes with her palms. 'I can't take this in. It's – it's . . .'

'I am sorry, Lesley. I can see how upset you are and I do feel terrible. But Mack should never have told you I was blackmailing him.'

Lesley was struck by a thought. 'If Rosie hadn't gone missing and the police hadn't checked up on Mack in Scotland, I might never have found out about Mack and you sleeping together behind my back.'

'That's something you need to talk to Mack about. I said he should've told you about Faye last year, when he first found out about her. But he was terrified you'd leave him if you knew we'd had sex. He didn't want to lose you, or Rosie. He said you were jealous of me, which is ironic because it was always the other way round.'

'You were jealous of *me*?'

'Hell, yeah,' Suzy exclaimed. 'I always adored Mack and thought we might get back together one day. But when he met you I knew I'd lost my chance. I couldn't compete: you were this beautiful, intelligent blonde he met at uni while I was the boring girl-next-door who'd never left her hometown. That's why I threw myself at him that night – I wanted to prove he still fancied me.'

'If you'd told him you were pregnant, he might have left me. You'd have got your wish.'

Suzy shook her head sagely. 'It would have been for the wrong reasons. He'd have done it to be with the baby, not me. That's no basis for a relationship.'

Lesley was so conflicted she didn't know what to think. She sat for a few moments, trying to make sense of it all, while Suzy sipped her coffee.

'Was it really just the once you slept together?'

Suzy met Lesley's gaze. 'Yes.'

'Does Mack know you're here?'

'Yes, he does. I texted him this morning to tell him I was coming.'

'That's why he's collapsed,' she said accusingly.

'Look, I know I'm being incredibly selfish when Rosie's missing and you are both worried sick, but I cannot risk Faye being dragged into this by the police and being exposed by the press. It could ruin her life and she doesn't deserve it. The way Mack has been carrying on, people were going to find out about her and I had to put a stop to it. I'm sorry I've hurt you, but I'm just protecting my daughter.'

Lesley slowly nodded. 'I don't like the way you've gone about it, but I think I understand.'

Suzy was visibly relieved. 'That's why I wanted to talk to you myself. Mum to mum, if you like.' She stood up. 'I should go now. Tell Mack I'm sorry too.' Lesley could see her eyes were shining with tears. 'I really hope you find Rosie soon.'

Lesley couldn't quite believe the words as they came out of her mouth, but as she got to her feet too she found herself saying, 'Maybe, when this is all over, we should sit down and talk again and try to work out something.

For Faye, I mean. To see her right.' She paused for a moment. 'Rosie's always said she wanted a sister.'

Suzy flashed a grateful smile. 'Faye's the same. Who knows, maybe they'd get on if they met.'

'Yes, maybe they would.'

59

Umpire called Maggie just as the patrol officer waved her through the security gate at the mouth of Burr Way. He was back in Mansell, preparing to interview Eddie Sinclair, but for once she managed to get the first word in and told him everything, from Steve seeing the suspect on the CCTV to her finding Lisa, who was now on her way to hospital with Rob at her side.

Umpire was staggered.

'Lisa is certain Rosie's still in Haxton?'

'Yes, and I think I know where.' She told him about Farley's client records and Mrs Roberts. 'I'm right outside Verma Lodge now.'

'You're *what*?'

'I didn't know what else to do, sir. You weren't returning my calls and I left you a message at the incident room. I couldn't sit around the hospital knowing there was a chance Rosie's here. I don't know how Farley got her past Mrs Roberts but if Rosie's inside I should get to her now,' she said. The delay was making her jittery.

'No, you don't move a muscle. You wait until I get

there with back-up. You hear me, Neville? That's an order. You wait.'

She said yes but had no intention of obeying it. If Rosie was being held against her will inside Verma Lodge, she couldn't just sit outside waiting. After seeing the state Farley had left Lisa in, she couldn't face Lesley and Mack knowing she'd waited. Finding their daughter was more important than whatever Umpire might do to her later.

'Did you hear me, Neville? You stay where you are.'

'Of course, sir.'

White stucco brick, with bright orange roof tiles and a veranda that ran along the front of the house, Verma Lodge seemed more suited to sunnier climes, like Greece or Spain or even Florida, than it did a Home Counties village presently deluged by showers.

The front door was locked. Maggie went round the back and tried the door to the conservatory. The handle gave easily and she was inside in seconds. The conservatory led into a formal lounge with salmon pink walls. Maggie skirted round the sofa and sped into the hallway. Instinct told her to head upstairs and as soon as she was on the landing she started throwing open doors and shouting Rosie's name. If Farley was there, she wanted him to hear her and fool him into thinking she wasn't acting alone.

Yet the bedrooms were all empty and the bathrooms too. She felt a twinge of uncertainty. What if she was wrong about this? She ran back into the first bedroom, the master suite, where there was an antique double wardrobe. Maggie yanked open the doors but it was empty save for a woman's clothes and shoes. She went through all the other rooms, checking wardrobes and under beds in the same way. By the time she reached the far end of the corridor from the stairs, her concern had dissolved into fear that she'd made a terrible mistake.

She retraced her steps until she found herself back where she'd started, in the conservatory. She gazed out across the garden, which was flush to the terrace with no steps down to negotiate. It was a lot more overgrown than the one at Angel's Reach, with enormous ferns and bamboo plants bending over a stone path that wound across the grass. Without a second thought, she took off along the path, following its direction until, on her right, she came across a towering hedgerow. Maggie inhaled deeply. The air was laced with the bitter scent of chlorine. She continued walking the length of the hedgerow until she came across a wrought-iron gate set within it. Through its rails she could see shimmering blue water and on the other side was a chalet-style pool house with a floor-to-ceiling glass frontage. Despite being a distance away, Maggie still recognized the person lying on the day bed inside, a rose-patterned duvet tucked around their chin.

Rosie.

60

Maggie sprinted round the swimming pool, almost losing her footing as she slid in a puddle of water spread across the tiled surround. The door to the pool house was unlocked and she burst through it to get to Rosie. Kneeling down by the day bed, she quickly checked the teenager's pulse – she was alive, but only just. Her breathing was shallow and her skin so pale it was tinged blue, like she'd been exposed to the cold. Maggie gently peeled the duvet back and saw someone had removed Rosie's clothing and dressed her in a nightgown. It was old-fashioned, with a high, frilled collar, and Maggie guessed it belonged to Mrs Roberts.

The left-hand side of the nightgown was stained with spots of blood and further investigation revealed that a bandage had been applied to the side of Rosie's ribcage. Maggie peeled back the bandage to check the severity of the wound and was assailed by the putrid smell of pus. If blood loss hadn't taken Rosie to the brink of death, blood poisoning almost certainly had.

Next to the day bed was a bottle of water, four packets of Nurofen Plus, more bandage dressings, antiseptic lotion and cotton wool. It looked as though Farley had, in the most rudimentary way, tried to keep Rosie alive in the pool house, which was bitingly cold inside and stank of chlorine. Then Maggie noticed a bunch of battered-looking daffodils stuffed into a jar set down on the floor by the foot of the bed. He brought her flowers? The sick bastard.

Maggie gently stroked Rosie's forehead.

'Rosie, you're safe now. My name is Maggie and I'm a police officer. I'm going to get you out of here.'

'No you're not.'

Maggie twisted round in surprise. The man she now knew to be Adrian Farley was in the doorway – but he wasn't alone.

Next to him was Lily.

'Lily? What are you doing—'

Maggie faltered as she caught sight of the Stanley knife in Farley's right hand. He lifted it to Lily's throat and the fully extended silver blade seemed to glow in the dull light.

'Step back from the bed,' he ordered.

'I need to get Rosie to hospital,' said Maggie. Staying on her knees, she pulled her mobile out of her pocket. 'She's in a bad way.'

'No, she's not, I've been taking care of her.'

'With over-the-counter painkillers? She needs help from a doctor, not a branch of Boots.'

'She's not going anywhere until I get my money.'

'Don't be stupid. If she dies you won't get a penny. Send her back alive and I'll help you get the reward,' she lied.

'Like you have any sway over it,' he scoffed. 'I know who you are, you're just the family liaison officer. You're bottom of the heap. *You don't count.*'

Maggie knew she had to stay calm to get Rosie out of there. She ignored him and turned to Rosie's friend.

'Lily, are you okay? Has he hurt you?'

'I'm okay,' she whispered, trying to tilt her neck and head away from the blade.

'You don't fucking deserve to be,' Farley snarled at her. 'It's all your fault everything's gone wrong.'

'No it's not, it's yours. If you'd just kept out of it . . .' Lily tailed off.

'Do you two know each other?' said Maggie in amazement. Then it hit her. 'Lily, is this your grandmother's house? Is Mrs Roberts your nan?'

The teenager nodded balefully.

So the parties were Lily's doing. The quiet little redhead none of them had given any thought to.

'She's just asleep, you know,' said Farley, nodding at Rosie. 'I gave her sleeping tablets.'

'How many? She's out cold.'

'Enough to keep her dozing like Sleeping Beauty. I haven't hurt her, if that's what you think.'

'Really? Because I've just seen Lisa and she told me exactly what you did to her.'

'We were already fucking so I don't know what her problem is,' he huffed. 'Do you actually think I'd have sex with a fifteen-year-old child? What do you take me for? I was the one who stopped that moron security guard Eddie taking advantage of her. It's down to him she's in this state, not me. You should be *thanking* me for saving her!'

'I will if you let me get Rosie to hospital.'

'Nice try, but that's not going to happen. Not until I get my money.'

Maggie turned to Lily. 'Did you know Rosie was here all this time?'

Farley's laugh came out more like a bark. 'Know about it? She's been helping me keep her here. Who do you think brought her the flowers?'

As Maggie sat back, shocked, Lily implored her to listen.

'It's not what you think. Ouch!' she shrieked.

The knife blade had nicked her throat.

'Whoops, sorry, my bad,' said Farley with a grin. 'But really, Lily, don't think you can put this all on me. Shall we tell the nice police lady what really happened?'

When Lily refused to speak, Farley took over.

'Lily has been a very, very naughty girl. She's been inviting her friends to granny's pool house for parties and they've been getting up to all sorts of naughtiness. Not just drink and drugs, if you know what I mean. So late one afternoon I'm here treating Mrs Roberts and we hear glass breaking. She asks me to take a look and I find Lily and her friends out here with Eddie Sinclair, all high as kites. You should see the pictures he took . . . not bad for an amateur.' Farley gestured at Rosie. 'In her defence though, she looked like she was out of it and didn't know what was going on.'

Maggie felt sick as she thought about the image of Rosie in the green shoes but she kept quiet, not wanting to interrupt Farley's flow. He was talking in a singsong voice like he was performing on stage and seemed alarmingly manic. She looked around to see if there was any way out other than the doorway he and Lily were blocking, but she couldn't see any.

'Now Lily here knew she was in a lot of trouble but I covered up for her with her granny, on the understanding she owed me a favour.'

'I didn't have a choice,' Lily said, breaking down. 'But I really didn't mean to hurt Rosie.'

Farley rolled his eyes. 'Jabbing her in the side with a knife hardly helped, did it?'

Maggie finally spoke. 'You helped him abduct her?'

'No, it wasn't like that. He –' Lily jerked her head towards Farley – 'bribed Eddie to give him the picture of Rosie because he wanted to use it to force her to get money out of her parents. It was his idea to get Rosie to come over here on Tuesday morning when no one was around so he could tell her how much he wanted. But when I went round to her house, she went mad at me for letting Eddie take her picture when she was drunk and told me to go away. I panicked because I knew he –' she jerked her head at Farley again – 'was waiting, so I threatened her with a knife to get her to come. I didn't think she'd try to fight me. It was by accident she was stabbed.'

'Where did you get the knife from?'

'A drawer in her kitchen.'

'Where is it now?'

'I washed it and put it back.'

'So it was you who turned off the alarm system?'

'No, he made Eddie come with me,' Lily said, glancing again at Farley. 'He said if Eddie didn't help he'd tell the police about the photographs.' She looked imploringly at Maggie. 'They're not a big deal though. We all did a couple of topless poses in return for Eddie getting us some weed and Molly.'

'Molly is a drug, in case you didn't know,' said Farley with a grin. 'Kids today, eh?'

'We're not kids,' Lily snapped. 'It was just like doing a fashion shoot. It was a laugh.'

'Rosie didn't look like she was having fun in the photograph I saw,' said Maggie reproachfully. 'You're meant to be her friend. How could you exploit her like that? I'm assuming they were your green shoes she's wearing in the picture?'

Lily suddenly looked petrified, as though the implication of what she'd done had finally hit home. Her words spilled out as she tried to explain herself.

'It's just a bit of fun. Everyone takes topless pictures to send to guys they like. The only difference is Eddie uses a proper camera, not a phone.'

Maggie shook her head despairingly. Then a thought struck her. 'What about Rosie's skirt, the one we found in the meadow?'

'Eddie put it there, not me.'

'But you used it to try to stop the bleeding first?' said Maggie.

'Yes, it was the only thing to hand. Rosie let me borrow it last week to wear to a party and I asked if I could borrow it again. That was my excuse for going round to her house on Tuesday,' said Lily, shamefaced and shaking.

'We haven't found the shorts she was wearing yet.'

'You'll have to ask Eddie, he hid those too. He . . . he took the rest of her clothes after we brought her here,' she said, glancing nervously at Farley, who shrugged.

'They're long gone,' he said.

'We found a trace of condom on the inside lining of Rosie's skirt. I'm pretty certain she's not had sex with anyone, so if you've borrowed the skirt last week, was that something to do with you too?'

Maggie took the way Lily's face flushed deep red as confirmation it was, while Farley laughed.

'She's no innocent, is our Lily. Just ask her ex-boyfriend Charlie.'

'I still can't believe you set Rosie up so Sinclair could take pictures of her. He's a grown man, you're still kids.'

'He's only twenty-one. He's not that much older than us,' Lily shot back.

'And how could you let him keep her here all this time, knowing how worried her parents are?'

'He said it would only be for a couple of days. He said he'd tell the police it was all down to me if I didn't go along with it. I was scared.'

'Ladies, ladies,' Farley interrupted. 'Can we please get back to what's important – my money?'

'You won't get a penny out of the Kinnocks unless you let Rosie go,' said Maggie firmly.

'That bitch pushed in front of me!' he shouted. 'Do you have any idea what it's like, knowing I came so close to winning and knowing it was almost certainly my only chance because no one's ever that lucky twice – and it was just taken from me?' For a second he brandished the knife at Maggie. 'You think I'm stupid for trying to get my money back, I can see it on your face. But if you knew the pain I had to live with every day, you'd understand.'

'Pain? What pain?' Maggie scoffed.

Farley spun round and pulled his T-shirt up. She winced at the livid scar running the length of his spine.

'Nine operations I've had, and still it's no better.' He choked on his words. 'I just want it put right but they wouldn't help me, wouldn't give me a penny. I never meant for the girl to get hurt. All I was going to do was tell her I'd send Eddie's picture to her mum and dad unless she paid me.' His face clouded over. 'Then this stupid cow and Sinclair fucked it up. Once she was injured there was no way they could leave her at her house so Eddie called me and I carried her round here.'

'You've been caught together on CCTV, by the security gate.'

Farley smirked. 'Took you a while to put two and two together, did it? Yes, I drove here but I parked in the next street. I went along the back pathway on foot to get to Verma Lodge and the Kinnocks' garden.'

'How did you get Rosie past Mrs Roberts?'

'I told Nana I wanted to go shopping and she drove me into Mansell,' said Lily morosely.

'But you must've had blood on you from Rosie?'

'I didn't, Eddie did. He was the one who used the skirt to stop it.'

'Where is your grandmother now?'

'I don't know. She wasn't in when I arrived earlier.'

'Actually,' said Farley, 'she's in the compost heap. I'm afraid we had a disagreement.'

Lily burst into tears. 'No, not Nana!'

Maggie's heart hammered wildly against her ribcage. She needed to get Rosie and Lily out of there.

'Look, this is your chance to put it all right,' she told Farley. 'Let me get Rosie to hospital and I know her parents will be grateful.'

He shook his head. 'I'm not fucking stupid.'

'Listen to her,' Lily begged him. 'Let us go.'

Farley turned to address Lily, giving Maggie the split second she needed to act. But as she dived across the floor to kick his legs out from under him, he spun round and swooped his hand down and she cried out as the knife blade sliced into her forearm. As blood bubbled from the wound, she dropped her mobile in shock.

Lily screamed and ran for the door but Farley was too quick for her. The knife went into the back of her shoulder up to the hilt and the teenager jerked horribly as blood gushed through the hole it made in her T-shirt.

'Leave her alone!' Maggie yelled.

As she tried to crawl across to Lily, who'd pitched forward onto the floor, Farley grabbed her hair and pulled her off. From the corner of her eye she saw Rosie stir and she panicked. She had to stop Farley before he noticed too. Ignoring the searing white-hot pain from the wound in her arm, Maggie groped her hand across the floorboards until her fingers made contact with the jar holding the daffodils. Clenching her hand around it, she swung her arm as hard as she could and smashed the glass into the side of Farley's head. Bits of glass, petals and water went flying across the room as he keeled over, blood pouring from his temple. He lost his grip on the knife and Maggie kicked it out of his reach before managing to cuff him. Then, almost crying with relief, she staggered across the pool house to the day bed, where Rosie had slipped back into unconsciousness.

'It's okay,' whispered Maggie, squeezing her hand. 'You're safe now, Rosie. You're safe.'

61

Mack was awake when Lesley returned to his room. He smiled wanly as she entered and his lips felt dry and cracked against hers as she kissed him hello. He was wearing his glasses again.

'You gave me such a scare,' she chided him. 'Don't ever do that again.'

'I'm sorry, love. Is there any news?'

She shook her head, desperate to block out the image that popped into her mind of their daughter's cold, lifeless body on a metal gurney in a bleak, sterile mortuary. She had tried so hard in the past few days not to think about Rosie being found dead, her body battered and destroyed as it lay in a ditch or shallow grave or some other desolate and lonely final resting place, and had clung to the belief that, as her mum, she would know if Rosie had been killed because she'd feel it. But with Sinclair's arrest seemingly bringing them no closer to finding her, she was suddenly tortured by images of them cradling Rosie's body and being at her funeral surrounded by teenagers sobbing as her favourite pop songs were piped through tinny speakers.

'They'll find her soon,' said Mack. 'They have to.'

Lesley stared down at her husband. She loved him so much that sometimes the feeling overwhelmed her.

'Mack, I know about Faye.'

He was visibly stunned. 'How?' he croaked.

'Suzy came to the hospital. She told me everything.'

'I'm so sorry, love,' he said as tears spilled down his cheeks. 'I should never have said she was blackmailing me. I thought you'd go mad if you knew I'd slept with her again.'

'Maybe if I'd found out at the time I would've done, but that's in the past now. What's important is that you do the right thing by Faye.'

'You mean you don't mind me giving her money?'

'No, I don't. She's your child – of course you must support her. Suzy showed me a picture.' Her eyes brimmed with tears. 'She looks like Rosie.'

Mack leaned back against his pillow and exhaled deeply. 'You are an incredible woman, Lesley Kinnock. I don't deserve you.'

She smiled. 'I'll remind you of that—'

The door suddenly opened and in walked Maggie, face solemn, clothes dishevelled, her right forearm bandaged. Terrified, Lesley clutched Mack's hand, ready to hear the worst. Then Maggie surprised them both by breaking into a wide smile.

'We've found her. She's alive.'

Lesley stared at her in disbelief. Then she staggered forward and fell into Mack's arms.

'Oh God, oh God, our baby, I thought, I thought . . .'

She clung to her husband for a moment then turned to Maggie. 'Where is she? We want to see her.'

'She's here at the hospital, down on the first floor. We can take you there now.' Maggie held the door open to let a nurse and a porter pushing a wheelchair into the room. Both of them looked emotional as they said hello to Mack and Lesley.

'We're so pleased your daughter is safe,' the nurse told them.

Lesley fidgeted impatiently as the porter eased Mack out of bed and into the wheelchair. The nurse wheeled his IV drip alongside him as the group headed to the lifts, where Belmar waited. Smiling, he gave Mack and Lesley each a hug and told them how happy he was.

'How is she?' Mack asked him.

'She's got a stab wound to her abdomen that's become infected and she needs surgery to clean it up because she's at risk from blood poisoning. She's very poorly right now, but she should be okay,' he said.

'Where did you find her?' asked Lesley. 'What happened to her?'

'Let's get you to Rosie, then we'll talk,' said Maggie.

Lesley's insides turned to ice. 'Was she, well . . . hurt?'

'We don't think so but I'm afraid we won't know for sure until she's been fully examined,' Maggie replied.

Tears sluiced down Lesley's cheeks. 'My poor baby. I should've been there to protect her.'

Mack held her hand as they both cried.

Maggie spoke gently to them. 'I know this is hard, but try not to let Rosie see you so upset. She's been through a terrible ordeal and is a long way from the end of it.

She's going to need a lot of love and support to deal with everything that's happened to her. So you need to stay as strong as you've been all this week and let Rosie know she can count on you both, okay?'

They nodded fervently and Lesley wiped her eyes. The hurricane had hit – now was not the time to let it break them.

When the lift reached the first floor, Maggie led the group through a set of doors marked PRE-OPERATIVE SUITE. 'The nurses are just getting her ready through there.' She let go of Lesley's hand and pushed the door ajar so the porter could wheel Mack through. As the nurse positioned the drip, the porter pushed Mack up to the side of the bed.

'We'll wait out here,' said Maggie, letting the door swing shut behind them.

As Lesley approached the bed she gave a strangled cry. It was just as she had imagined in her nightmare. There was Rosie, lying on a gurney, her dark hair fanned across the pillow. Except that while her eyelids were closed, she could see a tiny flicker of movement beneath them. It was the most beautiful sight Lesley had ever seen. Across the bed, Mack wept.

'What did they do to our little girl?' he cried.

Lesley kissed Rosie's cheek. Her heart soared as she felt the warmth of her skin against her lips.

'Baby, it's me, Mum. You're in the hospital. Dad's here too.'

Despite his frailty, Mack managed to raise himself out of the wheelchair and lean against the bed just as Rosie's eyes fluttered open. Her gaze locked first on him, then on Lesley. Despite Maggie's warning, Lesley couldn't hold back her tears and they splashed onto the pillow, wetting her daughter's hair.

'Oh, Rosie, I thought we'd lost you,' she cried.

Tears trickled from the corners of Rosie's eyes.

'Mum . . .' she whispered.

'Sssh, don't talk, save your energy.'

She gently wiped Rosie's damp cheeks with her fingertips.

'I love you, sweetheart. I love you so much.'

'So do I, honey,' said Mack. 'We both do.'

Rosie's mouth lifted at the corners as she finally managed a smile.

62

Saturday

The operation went well. Afterwards Rosie was moved to the intensive care unit where antibiotics were administered intravenously to fight the infection. If she had a good night, the consultant told Lesley, she'd be moved to a general ward in the morning and the police could then begin the long, delicate process of interviewing her to find out exactly what had happened while she was kept captive by Adrian Farley.

Lesley yawned as she stretched her legs out in front of her. Mack was back in his room on the third floor and the nurses had drawn a recliner chair up to Rosie's bedside so she could sleep alongside her. Yet even though she was shattered, Lesley knew she wouldn't be able to sleep. She daren't close her eyes for a second, scared that if she did she might wake up and it would all be a dream and Rosie would be gone again. She doubted she would ever sleep properly again.

As the hours ticked past midnight, her emotions lurched back and forth on a sliding scale with joy at one end and sadness at the other. As overwhelmed with happiness as she was at her daughter's return, she also knew that the Rosie lying in the bed next to her was not the same Rosie she had waved goodbye to four days ago. How could she be? The trauma of her experience would see to that. Lesley had no idea if she and Mack had it in them to help Rosie come to terms with what she'd gone through. How did any parent prepare for something like that? There was no manual for it on the bookshelves alongside the ones dealing with weaning, potty training and puberty. But she resolved they'd get through it, one way or another.

She yawned again before deciding a cup of tea might help keep her awake. Her footsteps echoed up the corridor but the only other sound was the steady beeping of machines as they monitored and aided the hospital's most gravely ill patients through another night. The noise acted as a salutary reminder that she should be thankful Rosie wasn't more seriously hurt.

After the vending machine swallowed four pound coins in a row, Lesley managed to extract a cup of the most insipid tea she'd ever tasted. She sipped the scalding, mud-coloured liquid as she walked slowly to the relatives' room, where she was surprised to find Maggie watching the BBC's twenty-four-hour news channel on a wall-mounted TV screen with the sound down and subtitles on. Rosie being found topped the bulletin.

'I didn't realize you were still here,' she said, taking the seat next to Maggie, who was sitting cross-legged in her chair, her shoes kicked off on the floor in front of her.

'I thought I'd stick around for a while, just in case you needed me.'

'You should go home. How's your arm?'

'Sore, but it's fine.'

'Will it scar?'

'I didn't ask. Probably. It doesn't matter though.'

Lesley set the cup of tea down on the low table in front of them, next to a pile of leaflets on how to quit smoking. She couldn't face another sip.

'I know I've said it already, but thank you for what you did today.'

Maggie smiled. 'I'm just glad she's safe.'

'I spoke to Belmar earlier, before he went home, and he seemed to think you might be in trouble for going into the house on your own.'

Maggie shrugged. 'DCI Umpire wanted me to stay outside until he and the back-up team arrived. He was pretty angry with me when he got there, but I think it'll be okay. There's a debriefing in the morning and we'll talk about it then.'

'If he gives you any grief, let me know and I'll have something to say about it. You did a very brave thing today, Maggie, and Mack and I will never forget it. We owe you our daughter's life.'

Maggie looked choked for a moment as she nodded.

'You'll keep in touch, won't you?' Lesley added.

'Belmar and I will both be around for a while yet. We'll continue to be your family liaison throughout the criminal proceedings.'

'You mean if there's a trial?'

'Yes. There's still a long road ahead, I'm afraid.'

Lesley exhaled. She felt tired now, ready for sleep.

'I still can't believe Lily knew where she was all this time. How bad did you say her injury was?'

'She was lucky. The blade missed the artery in her shoulder and she should be fine.'

'I'm glad she's being treated at another hospital. I don't know if I could trust myself not to do something if she was here. Out of all of Rosie's friends, I'd have said she was the least likely to get into trouble. But what she did, the way she exploited her . . .' Lesley burned with anger.

'I thought Kathryn was the one we should be wary of. I got that wrong.'

'The nurses let her pop in earlier to see Rosie. It turns out she had been giving Rosie a hard time, but only because she thought Rosie was being too easily influenced by Lily and her crowd. They were the ones bullying her, not Kathryn. Kathryn never went to any of Lily's parties at her grandmother's house.'

'I don't understand why she kept quiet about Lily and her friends if she was worried, though.'

'Kathryn said Lily swore blind she had nothing to do with Rosie going missing and she believed her. She now thinks Lily kept going on about Rosie self-harming to make everyone think that's how the blood came to be on the lawn, to cover up what happened, and she suspects Lily might've got Eddie Sinclair to mug her as a warning not to say anything. She also said that it's Lily who Rosie nicknamed GS, not Sinclair. GS stands for Grammar School, because that's where Lily goes.'

'I *knew* Kathryn knew who GS was.' Maggie frowned.

'We still need to find out why Lily was using a phone registered to Sinclair though.'

'I guess that's something you'll have to ask them about,' said Lesley.

'Has Rosie said anything about what happened?'

'We talked for a bit when she came round from the operation. She told us about the photograph Sinclair took, although she didn't know at the time he'd taken it. She was paralytic by the sounds of it. She also said the excuse Lily gave for coming round on Tuesday was to borrow her skirt. When Rosie was hurt, Sinclair apparently used it to try to stop the bleeding.'

'That backs up what Lily told me. It's really good Rosie's opening up to you about what she's been through. It should help her in the long run.'

'That's what Jo from Victim Support said when she came by earlier. She seems really nice,' said Lesley.

'You called them? Good. They're a great resource.'

'It was Mack's idea actually. After the situation with Suzy, I think he's realized it's better to have things out in the open.'

Maggie's eyes widened with surprise.

'He's told you everything?'

'Oh yes, the whole lot.'

Lesley relayed her and Suzy's conversation in the cafe at the hospital.

'She's sure Faye is Mack's daughter?' Maggie said sceptically.

'Yes, and I am too. She's the spitting image of Rosie and Mack.'

'Wow,' said Maggie, puffing out her cheeks. 'That's a lot to take in.'

'It is, but I can cope with it now I know. Imagining Mack having an affair was actually far worse.'

'Have you mentioned Faye to Rosie yet?'

'I think we'll wait until she's out of hospital and back home. Hopefully she'll be okay when we do tell her, if we make it clear it doesn't change how Mack feels about her. But if she's not okay, we'll deal with it together – as a family.'

63

Dawn was breaking as Maggie left the hospital and the gradually lightening sky was streaked with the softest pink and orange. Her arm was too sore and stiff to drive but she didn't mind. The walk home would give her the chance to start emptying her mind of the horror of what had happened in the pool house. She wasn't even bothered by the cold breeze that whipped round her as she set off.

The town centre was quieter than usual to reflect the start of the weekend. She thought about going round to Lou's and having breakfast with her and the kids but her aching body demanded that she go home and crawl beneath her duvet for a few hours. She'd spoken to Lou late last night to reassure her she was okay and had only needed a few stitches. The news reports on TV were making it sound a lot worse.

Telling Lou about Rob's involvement in the case had been difficult. As much as she wanted to for her sister and the children's sake, she couldn't cover up the fact he had been supplying illegal steroids to Farley – and, it transpired, quite a few other gym patrons – and Rob was now facing serious charges. All Maggie could hope was that he might receive a lighter sentence, maybe even a suspended one, for identifying Farley and helping her to rescue Lisa. She promised Lou she would do everything she could to help him.

She'd spoken briefly to Steve too. She was still angry he'd left her at the gym, especially when Bobby turned out to be fine. The rash his wife Isla had assumed in a panic was meningitis turned out to be an allergic reaction.

'I've probably screwed my career,' he sighed down the phone. 'Ballboy wants to see me first thing. He knows about the CCTV footage I overlooked.'

Maggie didn't say she was the one who told him.

'I'll put in a good word for you, for what it's worth.'

'If you can, terrific. He might actually listen to you.'

Maggie reached the end of the road the hospital was on. Laid out before her at the junction was a series of mini-roundabouts and she paused as her tired brain tried to work out the best way to get across them. She didn't see the car slowing down alongside her. It was only when the driver beeped, causing her to jump out of her skin, that she noticed it.

Umpire lowered the driver's window.

'Can I give you a lift?'

It surprised her how pleased she was to see him. She didn't hesitate and got into the car.

'How are you feeling?' he asked as he pulled away from the kerb and headed in the direction of the high street.

'My arm's sore from all the stitches and the doctor has

advised me to rest it for a couple of days, but otherwise I'm fine. So what happened when you questioned Farley, sir?'

'He broke down and confessed not long after the interview started. He's admitted to kidnap, attempted extortion and perverting the course of justice. We've also charged him for the assault and rape of Lisa Charleston and for the murder of Vivienne Roberts. We found her body where he said it was, on the compost heap. He'll go before a special magistrates' hearing first thing, as will Sinclair. We're throwing the book at him too.'

'What about Lily?'

'It's not as clear cut with her. She's saying Sinclair coerced her into letting him take the photographs and she was too scared to say no. She says he would've hurt her had she tried to stop him.'

'That's not what she said in the pool house. I think she knew exactly what she was doing.'

'She's sticking to her statement though. She's saying Sinclair stabbed Rosie, not her, but it's her word against his and any prints that might have established who did it have been washed off the knife. The CPS doesn't think we can charge her yet because the allegation of grooming is a contentious one, so she's been bailed while inquiries continue. At the same time, Sinclair's confirmed the phone registered to him was stolen just before Christmas and those texts to Rosie are nothing to do with him.'

'Kathryn Stockton told Lesley that GS is Lily. It stands for Grammar School, because Lily goes to a different school to them.'

Umpire shook his head. 'Once Rosie is in a fit state to be questioned, we'll have a clearer idea of what went on in that garden on Tuesday.'

'That poor kid has got so much to deal with when she does wake up. You heard about the half-sister?'

'Yes. Quite the turn-up.'

'Lesley's handling it really well. I'm not sure I'd be as magnanimous.'

'Do you think Suzy is telling the truth about them not having an ongoing affair?'

'I do, actually. I think she just wants what's fair for her daughter,' said Maggie as she leaned back against the headrest and yawned.

'I think Suzy Breed might have a bit more explaining to do though. The pay-as-you-go mobile Farley used to call the incident room, the one that we couldn't trace? The number has turned up on the records we pulled for Suzy's phone.'

'What!' Maggie gasped. 'Are you sure? You're saying Farley and Suzy know each other?'

'That's what the records tell us. We'll know more when Forth Valley Police pick Suzy up in about an hour. She's on the sleeper train back to Edinburgh from King's Cross.'

'Bloody hell,' said Maggie. 'What game has Suzy really been playing?'

'We'll know soon enough.' He glanced across at her. 'You must be exhausted. I heard you waited outside Rosie's room all night.'

'I just wanted to make sure she was okay, sir.'

'We're not on duty now. You can call me Will.'

449

It was the first time Umpire had ever said that to her and she was so taken aback she couldn't speak.

Perhaps sensing her surprise, he quickly asked, 'Are you hungry?'

'Actually, yes, I'm starving. I can't remember when I last ate.'

'Me neither. There's a cafe on Lincoln Street that should be open by now. It does the best bacon roll you'll ever taste. My treat.'

'You want to buy me breakfast?' she asked, her pulse quickening.

He gave her an odd look. 'The rest of the team are meeting us there.'

Mortified, Maggie wanted to kick herself for not realizing he hadn't meant just her and him.

'Of course, sir, sorry – I mean Will,' she said, blushing furiously. 'That's what I thought you meant.'

'You sure about that?'

She looked across at him.

He smiled.

Acknowledgements

These words might be mine but you wouldn't be reading them without the efforts of all these people. My brilliant editor Catherine Richards, thank you for showing such enthusiasm and passion for *Gone Astray* from day one. The same goes for everyone at Pan Macmillan, in particular Sam Eades and Laura Carr. My agent Jane Gregory, for making me the happiest wannabe author ever when you took me on. It's great to have you in my corner! Likewise everyone at Gregory & Co, but especially Stephanie Glencross for always giving such terrific guidance. Erin Kelly, Tasmina Perry and Jo Carnegie, for encouraging me to follow in your footsteps and for all the advice, support and great friendship during my long journey to publication. Detective Chief Inspector Phil Murphy of Thames Valley Police, for taking the time to explain what a family liaison officer does and why the role is so vital – any errors in procedure are mine alone and I apologize for them! Kerry Needham, for sharing yours and Ben's story with me, which gave me the idea for making an FLO my central character; I hope one day soon you find the answers you seek. Hari Patience and

Austin Buckeridge, for reading *Gone Astray* in its early stages and encouraging me to keep going, and especially Hari for being the best writing buddy ever. Mum and Dad, for telling the twelve-year-old me that *of course* I could become a writer when I grew up if that's what I wanted to do, and for helping me achieve my dream. I owe you so much. My darling daughter Sophie, for being born! Your arrival was my trigger to start writing *Gone Astray*; once I understood what it was to be a mum, Lesley found her voice. And Rory, for giving me the time and space to write, pushing me to keep going all those times I hit a brick wall and for giving such great plot advice! Falling in love with you still remains the smartest thing I've ever done.